THE FIND

ALSO BY RAINER REY

Replicator Run

Day of the Dove

Cosmosis

THE FIND

A Novel

Rainer Rey

TURNER

Turner Publishing Company
424 Church Street • Suite 2240 • Nashville, Tennessee 37219
445 Park Avenue • 9th Floor • New York, New York 10022

www.turnerpublishing.com

The Find, A Novel

Cover design: Nellys Liang
Book design: Kym Whitley

Library of Congress Cataloging-in-Publication Data

Rey, Rainer.
The find : a novel / by Rainer Rey.
pages ; cm
ISBN 978-1-62045-993-5 (softcover : acid-free paper)
1. Missing persons--Investigation--Fiction. 2. Psychic ability--Fiction. 3. Shamans--Fiction.
I. Title.
PS3568.E86F56 2015
813'.54--dc23
2014040758

ISBN: 978-1-62045-993-5 (paperback), 978-1-63026-914-2 (hardcover),
978-1-62045-997-3 (eBook)

Printed in the United States of America
15 16 17 18 19 0 9 8 7 6 5 4 3 2 1

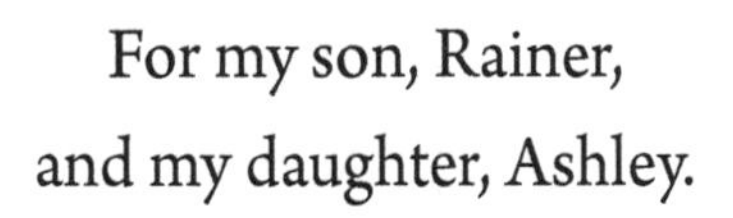

For my son, Rainer,
and my daughter, Ashley.

Acknowledgments

With gratitude to my agent, Diane Gedymin;
to Ed Stackler, whose early editing helped mold this story;
to Christina Roth for her final touches;
and to Orcas Island, its people, its wildlife, and its magic,
which inspired this tale.

THE FIND

INTRODUCTION

AS THE COLD WAR ENDED in the early 1990s, both Russia and the United States publicly admitted to the existence of various tactical self-defense projects that might have otherwise remained undisclosed.

The most extraordinary of these projects was reported in a 1995 *New York Times* article, in which the Central Intelligence Agency revealed its now defunct sixteen-year psychic research program.

If that sixteen-year effort had truly been a futile experiment, it begs the question as to why it took so long to declare it a failure. Yet the result of that experimentation and the extent of its development remain unclear even to the present day.

1

March 31, Present Day
Somewhere in South Dakota

THE MAN IN THE RAINCOAT stepped from a white van and hobbled down the wet sidewalk, carrying an object Irinia Malenchek couldn't identify.

"I see him." Irinia kept fighting to hold the image.

The white flickering had become terribly intense, and she struggled against the fragmentation. "Tell the others it's Baltimore. He's somewhere near a park."

"Is it Abbas?" Like black oil oozing through the vision, Dr. Epstein's smooth voice had seeped back into her consciousness.

"It is. I'm with him now. He's limping, just as you said. He waits for a cab to pass. Crosses the street. He approaches a brick apartment building."

Irinia felt weightless in the darkened room as she floated naked in the saline solution. Her sole contact with the sides of the tank was a perforated cushion at the nape of her neck, which contained EEG and bundled eidetic electrodes that pumped Formula 15 to her hypothalamus.

"He's holding something." Irinia focused on the hands. "A briefcase. No, something fat."

"You mean bulky?"

"Yes."

"What is it?"

"I'm sorry. I don't recognize—"

"A suitcase?"

"No. With big handles. Round."

A man's hoarse voice cut through the intercom from one of the surrounding glass-enclosed chambers. "I see it too. It's a bowling bag."

"Yes. Thank you." Irinia felt relieved. Her transference was being read successfully by the support group. She let the close-up image of the bag go and was again with Abbas, ambling along the wrought-iron railing that lined the sidewalk. "He passes a young boy now. The child begs for money. Abbas brushes past. He's nearly to the stairs."

"Can you see any house numbers?"

"Gray metal on brick. One, five, two . . ." She paused.

"Fifteen twenty-six," a woman's voice interjected over the speaker.

"Yes. You have it . . . oh, no." Irinia winced as the vision shook, shattered, and came together again. "The image is . . . splitting."

Epstein's soothing voice. "Simply a bit of synaptic dissonance, Irinia. Hold on. I'm going to give you another cc."

"My head hurts."

"Readings are up a bit, Doctor. Along with the heart rate." Though only inches away, Nurse Haupt's voice seemed to travel from some great distance, as if she were speaking over a strand of fine wire.

"You're okay, Irinia," Epstein said. "Just focus on your subject. Describe him."

"Low hairline. A mustache. Very dark. The eyes are like holes in his face."

"Lock that for me. I'm going to capture it."

Irinia's brow furrowed as she concentrated on the man's features. For a few seconds she heard the hum of the tachistoscopic scanner in the corner. Once the image had been reproduced, she relaxed and released her concentration on the likeness.

Swept away from the close-up, she again traveled back to live action. "He's inside now. Going up the stairs. It's a dirty place. He's on the second floor." Irinia's point of view hovered just behind the tufts of curly black hair that furled over the back of Abbas's gray collar, a common vantage point to the trancer when visuals were picked up through the occipital lobe. As Abbas dropped his gaze, Irinia's perspective shifted. "He has a key to a room. Now he enters. A lightbulb without a shade. No furniture. He reaches out and shakes hands."

"There's someone there?"

"Yes. A middle-aged man, wearing glasses."

"Long hair?" Epstein asked.

"Yes. Gray, I think," Irinia said.

"My God, that could be Rahid. Can you view him?"

"It's too dim. He's taken the bag. And he's turning away."

"Anyone? Anyone seeing him?"

The sound of Epstein's voice drifted off. Irinia could tell that the doctor had turned to address the six adults and one child seated in the booths beyond the glass. "Nothing yet? Anyone?"

"A dark shape. That's all I've got," the hoarse man said over the speakers.

Epstein's lilting tone became uncharacteristically frantic. "Irinia, work on this. He's their leader."

"I don't have a good view. They're talking by the window. The older man is a silhouette. I'm tired. My forehead aches. No more, please. It's too much."

"Try. Just try." Epstein moved closer to the equipment.

Irinia felt the change. Somehow, deep in the recesses of her mind, she knew. Without warning her, Epstein had flipped the tab on the IV bag and upped her dosage.

"No," she said as her mind began to sizzle.

It was her last conscious word.

Suddenly, what she had seen through telepathic remote viewing began to blend haphazardly with recollections of her own past into a series of mental movie clips. The man named Abbas was still there, but now he was talking with Irinia's mother, standing in the parlor of their old farmhouse in mid-twentieth-century Estonia.

Irinia heard Nurse Haupt say "We've got an overload," but in her mind the phrase emanated from Mara Vold, Irinia's choral director whom she'd come to know thirty years ago at the People's Middle School in Irinia's hometown of Pärnu.

Nothing made sense, nor would it ever again.

Irinia's thoughtography stuttered like a malfunctioning film projector, zoomed through an image kaleidoscope, and then tumbled across the amphitheater of her cerebral cortex.

"For God's sake, Irinia, where are you?" Dr. Epstein gripped her shoulders.

Irinia smiled. She was twelve years old again. Her father's voice called from the back porch.

"I'm here in the barn, Papa," she said happily. "Milking the cows."

2

Two Months Later
Off the West Coast of Orcas Island
San Juan Islands, Washington State

KELLEN RAND WAS NOT IN the mood to chase phantoms. He'd had plenty of excitement in his life—enough for several lives. Yet here he was, a man who no longer found fantasy fashionable, awaiting a miracle.

He brushed a hand through his short blond hair and leaned against the stern rail of the Boston Whaler *Tide Runner* as it chugged north up the President's Channel.

The moon, which had been flirting with black clouds, finally disappeared behind a cumulus mound to the east. The sea was cloaked in darkness.

Bathed in the glow of the tiny wheelhouse, Paddy cut the throttle. Gasoline fumes billowed over the stern of the twenty-four-foot fiberglass hull as his boat settled into the swells.

Kellen rubbed his unshaven chin and looked forward.

Paddy leaned out the cabin door, coughing. "He'll be up there," he said with an Irish accent, pointing at the gloom of Point Doughty's cliffs. "He thrashes about and screams. You can't miss him."

A stiff spring breeze smacked Kellen's face. He squinted up at the bluff. "I can't see anything."

"You will. He perches on the edge of that ridge. We'll lay offshore until he shows up."

Kellen buttoned the collar of his coat, staring into the darkness. Paddy had convinced him to leave the comfort of his cedar cabin.

Two hours ago, Kellen had closed the damper in his river-rock fireplace and left Long John—his ragged, rescued one-eyed tabby—lying on the sheepskin rug near the hearth.

Paddy had driven Kellen to the marina in his old VW van, promising that *this* would be the night Kellen would see something extraordinary that Paddy had witnessed a month ago . . . something that had made his hair stand on end. The gray-haired Irishman referred to the incident as a "summoning" that, according to rumor, might occur again at the waning of the moon.

Reluctantly, Kellen played along. Paddy was a good friend, and Kellen felt indebted to him. Last winter, when Kellen almost drowned and also suffered the loss of his sailing partner, Paddy had drawn him out of bereavement. He'd arrived at dawn, banging on Kellen's front door, coffee mug in hand, inviting Kellen to go fishing. "Christ knew that fishing was good for the soul," Paddy had said. "There's not a more healing thing on earth."

Kellen complied, and as the late October mornings passed with the sun rising over the Cascade Mountains, Kellen worked at Paddy's side on the waters. In the mundane chores of cutting bait, watching the fishing rods bend in the wind, and hauling the daily catch home, Kellen's grief and guilt softened. His affection for Paddy grew with each passing day, and he couldn't help smiling at his curmudgeon-like companion now as Paddy emerged from the *Tide Runner*'s cabin cradling a battered flask.

Paddy offered it to Kellen, who waved it off. Paddy took a dribbling swig, wiped his beard, and leaned toward Kellen as if to share a secret. "Are you ready for this?"

"No need to sell me, you old rascal."

Paddy squinted off toward the stern. "Just keep watching the ocean to the north."

"The ocean?" Kellen tugged at his jacket collar, fighting the breeze.

In the glow of the boat's navigation light, a mischievous smile played across Paddy's face. "It doesn't *all* happen up on the cliffs, you know. The whole place comes alive. Wait until you see the power he has over animals." He tucked the flask under his arm and rubbed his callused hands together, a sign he was about to launch into one of his stories. "Molly Creed was hiking on the back side of Mount Constitution when she saw January, standing bare chested on the rocks with a two-hundred-foot drop at his feet. She hid in the trees and watched as a bald eagle flew by. She says January stared the bird down, gave a screech of his own, and the eagle hovered over his head and landed on his arm."

"No wild eagle does that," replied Kellen incredulously.

"Molly swears January put his other hand on the eagle's chest. The bird spread its wings and wrapped January's head like a cocoon. They stood like that for five minutes." Paddy took the flask and thrust it dramatically toward the clouds. "Then the eagle flew away."

"Paddy," Kellen shook his head, "you're pickling your mind with that shit."

"Molly swears it happened."

"And she's smoking enough weed to believe it."

The tale made Kellen question why he was out here. Not that he didn't appreciate the lore of Orcas Island—he'd grown up with it, attending Camp Orkila on the opposite end of Orcas, where he'd heard tales of forest spirits and Indian legends around moonlit campfires. Kellen's father, a widower and an officer on the Seattle police force, had sent his youngest city-bred son to the island for summers while Kellen's older brother, Kyle, attended the Police Academy.

And for Kellen, Orcas Island's unique tranquility finally took hold. When Kellen's FBI career unraveled two years ago, he sought peace on Orcas. If Kyle's heroic death in the line of duty seven years before had been difficult for his dad, Kellen's subsequent dismissal had been devastating. It had been grueling for Kellen to visit his childhood home ever since. The aura of shame hovered in the Seattle house like his father's cigar smoke.

Eventually, Kellen began to avoid the city completely. He plowed his life savings into a small salmon hatchery and learned to appreciate the historic importance of salmon to the local Indian tribes, the Lummis, and their now-scarce predecessors, the Salish. He appreciated pantheistic Indian lore, but the stories surrounding the youthful Native American shaman who called himself January were absurd. As "John Harmon," January had distinguished himself academically at Orcas Island High School and moved beyond his local roots to attend Stanford University. Only after his return to the islands two years ago had he supposedly been indoctrinated into shamanism, changing his name to help hide his identity and become a hermit. The young man's alleged schizophrenia had produced outlandish rumors—January was possessed, some people said, by forces no one else could understand.

Kellen watched Paddy take another pull off the flask. Instead of fighting the night chill, Kellen should have been home under a quilt, listening to Long John purr at the foot of the bed.

"Look, I know this is important to you," Kellen said, "but maybe January's a no-show. Let's give it twenty minutes and then head back."

"You'd doubt me?" The fisherman's hands trembled as he checked his watch. "Like Thomas, who believed only after he placed his hand in the savior's side?" Paddy sidled over and, wiping the mouth of the bottle with his sleeve, pushed the flask under Kellen's nose. "Don't be a frump. It'll warm your gullet."

Kellen sighed and put the tin to his lips. As the whiskey heated the back of his throat, Paddy escaped into the cabin. "The tide's cresting," he called to Kellen. "That's when things should happen."

Paddy put the engine back into gear, spun the helm to port, and the *Tide Runner* surged against the current.

Feeling the dullness of the booze behind his eyes, Kellen hung on to the rail. Beyond the bobbing transom, Point Doughty's water-pitted cliffs rose against the sky.

Paddy tied off the wheel, letting the vessel idle in gear as he stepped back on deck, flapping his arms to stay warm. "This heading should do it."

The lapping water along the *Tide Runner*'s portside hull had grown louder, an indication that waves were building.

Paddy cocked his head. "It's coming. Can you feel it?"

"What?"

"The summoning."

Kellen *did* feel something. The wind had picked up, whistling across the bow. The smell of the sea seemed stronger. Suddenly, forked lightning reflected on the expanse of the Georgia Strait, illuminating the white slopes of Mount Baker forty-five miles away to the east. Kellen donned his stocking cap and pulled the blue knitting over his ears, preparing for rougher weather.

Across the channel, Sucia Island's trees bristled in silhouette on the dark horizon. An atoll-like satellite of Orcas Island, it looked incredibly beautiful by day, but it now seemed strangely ominous.

The *Tide Runner* pitched more violently as a wall of wind pushed in from the west. Over the Cascade Mountains lightning flashed again, revealing a spreading panorama of whitecaps.

With the rougher seas, Kellen wasn't surprised at his growing anxiety. He remembered being submerged in turbulent surf off Westport—fighting for air under Dietrich's overturned schooner, helplessly watching his partner's body being swept out of sight.

"Was it like this before?" Kellen asked, challenging his apprehension.

"Yeah. Wind. Some chop. Lightning too."

Kellen fussed with the ivory buttons on his coat. He considered going inside the cabin for his thermos—anything to ease the tension.

He rose and moved toward the door. He hesitated.

A loud splashing echoed in the night. Paddy whirled. "There they are."

Kellen squinted. Off to the northwest, something caused phosphorescent foam to fly across the darkened sea.

"Look," Paddy shouted, pointing off the port side.

As lighting flashed overhead, Kellen saw shapes under a rainsquall, advancing toward the Boston Whaler. Resembling an invasion of submarines, the small armada approached, periscopes flexing with the pulse of bodies beneath.

"They're coming." Paddy clasped his hands. "Like last time."

He was right. They *were* coming. The periscopes were dorsal fins, some bent, some straight, standing out of the water as high as seven feet. Killer whales. Orca whales, as they were also called, oddly bore no relation to the name Orcas Island, which had been named by Spanish explorers two centuries ago. The sheer number of bodies made the ocean come alive with their spray.

"Holy shit." Kellen clutched the rail in disbelief.

"I told you."

Above the flotilla, chased by a cold front, sheets of rain marched across the water. A downpour smacked the *Tide Runner,* spattering the decks. The hiss of the gale was broken by the whales' high-pitched calls.

Kellen tried to count them. At least two pods. No, more than that. He spotted another group off the bow, toward Sucia. More whales were coming from all directions, too many to count, swimming toward the cliffs and the *Tide Runner*.

When the first orca arrived, it circled the boat. The others joined, their pale bellies flashing as they slapped the water with their flukes.

The whales alternately breached and dove, causing the ocean to boil. They swam in a clockwise motion, enough of them that the boat began to rotate in their wakes. The *Tide Runner*'s keel sounded a *thump,* with more thumps following as the whales made contact with the hull.

"Did they do this before?" Kellen clutched a rail cleat.

"Hardly." Paddy grasped the cabin door, his bearded face blanched by a bolt of lightning that struck even closer.

The whales glistened under a second flash, their teeth white against the brine.

Kellen had seen orcas in the wild, but not like these. These showed no playfulness, thrashing the ocean as if to punish it with their tails. Heavy sea mist filled the air as the orcas repeatedly submerged and surfaced, puffing through their blowholes.

Thunder exploded overhead.

Paddy stepped across the deck and thrust an orange life jacket into Kellen's chest. "Put this on. This is not what I expected."

Kellen threw the bright canvas over his head, tugging at the straps. In the glow of sheet lighting, birds circled overhead. Gulls, a flock of crows, and several eagles flew in concentric ellipses.

As another thunderclap faded into the night, Kellen heard a voice, a shriek like that of a caged cat. It rose from the cliffs above.

The next lightning flash revealed the silhouette of a man with shoulder-length black hair, kneeling on the edge, his arms raised to the sky. The twisted contortions of his body made it appear as if he were a conduit between heaven and earth.

"It's January!" Paddy shouted. "Look at that. He's raising hell."

"What do you mean? He couldn't be doing all of this."

Kellen wiped the rain from his eyes to make sure he wasn't seeing things. It appeared as if January's naked upper body was flushed with a ghostly radiance. Now, against a lightning-streaked sky, several bald eagles engaged in acrobatics. They began to swoop and flutter, clashing in midair and then soaring apart.

The display seemed to affect January. His screams were now replaced by a maniacal laughter, a bitter cackle that signified an irony of having to simultaneously endure something grand yet horrific.

As if in response, the eagles plummeted from the sky one by one.

They fell past January's perch on the cliffs, appearing to brush his outstretched hands, which themselves now seemed to glow, strangely luminescent like the whitecaps below.

Above the wind and January's laughter, Kellen heard a distant vibration.

3

Augostino's Restaurant
Downtown Chicago

LORNA NOVAK WAS ANGRY AND fed up. Skip Van Hollenbeck's proposed game plan had offended her. Perspiration beaded her hairline; her appetite had vanished.

"What's the matter? Not hungry?" Skip took another bite of veal picatta.

"Actually, no." She pushed her shrimp scampi away and gazed across the restaurant, avoiding Skip's eyes. The night owls who remained at this late hour were probably here to avoid the rest of the world. Lorna wished she could avoid Skip. His heavy drinking had impaired his judgment. She'd always known Skip was a hustler, but this was intolerable.

Unfortunately, Chad Hennings, Skip's original partner and co-owner of United Radio Services, had been crippled by a triple bypass and was reluctant to engage in daily business. Chad had abdicated, and now Skip ran the company by default.

Tonight Skip's flawed leadership had surfaced. He squinted across the table. "Don't tell me you're surprised."

"Very." She straightened the cuffs of her pinstriped suit.

Skip gulped some of his third martini. "Why, for Christ's sake?"

She'd suspected trouble when Skip suggested they meet for a late supper after his arrival from out of town. A midnight snack with Chad would have yielded something constructive—Chad was the nurturer, Skip the schemer.

Contemplating an answer, Lorna twisted the stem of her wineglass. A nearby candle threw oddly festive prisms through the crystal. She wondered how many other caring, sensitive women who took pride in their work still endured similar treatment.

"Well?" Skip prompted. "What's so unexpected?"

She fixed her eyes on him. "The fact that you agreed to have me do this shows me how much nothing really changes."

Skip nodded his head, rotating his plate to skewer the veal. "Of course it does. Opportunities change—and this is a big one. Your chance to be a hero."

She suppressed a bitter laugh.

"Don't act naive with me, Lorna. Your good looks haven't been wasted on anybody. You're a trooper. You can hammer this deal."

"Hammer? With what?"

"Feminine finesse." He chewed as he unbuttoned his maroon suit jacket and leaned forward. "Look. This is a personality business." Skip's own personality had run roughshod through United's halls, ruffling employees. He would laugh loudly at his own bigoted jokes. "I know Waterman has his little quirks. He made me look at his antique gun collection, for shit sake. But I can't help that he chose to attend the American Broadcasters convention. He likes Vegas and wants to have fun. What he proposed was that you and he finalize the agreement in Nevada. It's as simple as that. He considers it a sociable occasion."

"And you agreed."

"It's a suggestion, that's all."

"But you didn't object."

"I wanted to discuss it."

"Without consulting me, you took it upon yourself to change my room reservation from Caesars Palace to the Mandalay, where Ken Waterman happens to be staying."

"You need to have meetings, don't you? Make it convenient."

"With the convention six blocks away? I have meetings at the convention too. Not to mention being a featured speaker." As station manager at WTOK five years earlier, Lorna had turned a sleeper into New York's most powerful talk station. Her success vaulted her into United's upper management, giving her national publicity.

"Understood. But this—"

"Right. *This* is downright cozy." Lorna felt heat climb the back of her neck. "Why not book me into an adjoining suite?"

Skip's eyes hardened. "You're pushing."

"I'm being pushed."

"You can decline. But remember, you played this guy like a piano before. And now, what Chad and I expect," he said softly, "is that you ease your way through this without blowing the deal."

"Ah. 'Ease my way.' Delicately put. Why don't you *ease* your way toward another solution?"

With eyes lowered, Skip pushed his plate away. "Waterman wants to deal with you exclusively. You were an effective front man and it stuck. He finds you attractive."

"Attractive? I flew to Dallas twice to redesign his communications system. If I hadn't pleaded with you and Chad to buy NuBand Networks, you wouldn't be in a position to negotiate with Waterman. *Those* are the grounds for my promotion, not my taste in lingerie."

Skip's hands rose simultaneously in mock surrender. "You're distorting. You're overreacting."

"Am I? Aren't you implying that my election to our board of directors is contingent on my performance in a Vegas bedroom?"

A flush spread over Skip's high forehead. "Don't put words in my mouth. The successful merger with Waterman is grounds for your vice presidency. How you accomplish that—" He hesitated.

A maître d' with slick black hair had approached the table and leaned over politely. "Ms. Novak?" He gestured toward the lobby. "You have a call from your secretary." Mavis was working late, prepping for Lorna's speech. "She apologizes, but you seem to have your cell phone turned off."

Skip waved dismissively. "Call her later."

"Mavis knows I'm with you. She'd never interrupt unless it was important."

Lorna rose from the table. As she walked away, Skip called, "I'll order you some brandy. You'll feel better."

Grateful for the reprieve, Lorna already felt better as she followed the maître d' toward the lobby. Lorna knew she would need to figure out an escape before she returned to Skip. She couldn't risk losing all she'd accomplished. Skip's ridiculous arrangement with Waterman posed the last obstacle to her becoming executive vice president of the nation's third largest radio conglomerate. If she flatly refused, she might get fired. Given Skip's ambiguity, a harassment suit would prove futile. And where would she go? Some station out west? Back to that mayhem? No thanks. The radio business ate station managers alive. Bobby

Raymond, a friend who managed WQRM in Miami, had lost everything—his job, his wife, and his sobriety—in the span of a few months.

She'd been fortunate. Her meteoric rise in making WTOK United's biggest moneymaker had been perfectly timed. She'd come on the scene when talk formats were hot. Then came her promotion to United's pressure-filled head office, where enormous money changed hands. She'd been involved in decisions on which stations to sell, which to buy. The blistering pace of merger mania had created an unprecedented cannibalism, and tonight she felt like the main course.

Her high heels clicked on the granite floor as the maître d' ushered her to the phone on a coffee table by a leather chair. She sat and punched the blinking button. "Mavis?"

"Sorry to break in." Her middle-aged assistant was her usual protective self. "Is Skip behaving himself?"

Her concerned tone disturbed Lorna. "Did you phone me just to check on him?"

"Of course not. You had a call from some policeman—a deputy named McMillan."

"Chicago cop?"

"Out west. Needs you to call back." She paused. "I didn't know you had a sister."

"Stepsister. What's this about?"

"Spilner? Is that her last name?"

"Yes. Tracy Spilner." Visions came of Tracy's freckled face beside Lorna's father's coffin in the shade of an Indiana churchyard. In his retirement, her alcoholic father had attended that church in Evansville. Tracy and Lorna hadn't spoken since that funeral eleven years ago, though they exchanged Christmas cards containing an occasional photo. Tracy had been withdrawn and evasive at the funeral service, perhaps because she had attended without her husband. Lorna still recalled the scent of marijuana on her clothes. Tracy was Lorna's antithesis: a spacey environmentalist who left Colorado three years ago to get away from an abusive marriage. "Why would a deputy call me at this time of night?"

Mavis's voice fell. "He wanted to tell you she's been hurt."

"What?"

"There's been an accident. Don't worry, she's being cared for. But it's her daughter—"

"Shelby?"

"I'm sorry, Lorna. She's missing."

"God." Years of minimal communication suddenly seemed unimportant. Lorna remembered the last time she and her stepniece were together. Shelby had been just a bundle in Tracy's arms in that Evansville courtyard. Big blue eyes and golden hair. Shelby had been a year old. "What sort of accident? Car?"

"I don't know. McMillan said that when they found her, Tracy asked for you. Apparently you're her only relative."

Lorna felt the desire to help but also the stab of apprehension. With the conference tomorrow and Skip's stifling intervention, what could she do? "Where's this McMillan guy calling from? And where's Tracy?"

"They brought her to a medical center at . . . um, do you know a place called Orcas Island?"

4

Off Point Doughty

HARD RAIN PELTED THE BACK of Kellen's neck as he clung to the *Tide Runner*'s gunwale, watching the spectacle.

Above January's head, under illuminated clouds, silhouettes of circling seabirds were etched in black against sheet lightning. Below, orca whales surged through the waves.

Kellen felt the effects of the display. The skin on his arms tingled as if stimulated by a mild electric current. Everything on the boat had taken on a pale green aura from the ocean's phosphorous, including Paddy's bristled face. The whites of the Irishman's bloodshot eyes appeared incandescent, reflecting the lightning as he stared at the bluff.

And just as Kellen had had enough—just when he began to feel overwhelmed by the confusion—everything about January changed. As if nature had thrown a switch, the jade hue around the bare-chested Native American disappeared. January's anguished shouts faded from the cliffs. He slumped to his haunches, arms falling to his sides, and remained motionless with his head hung in exhaustion.

Nature seemed to respond. The orcas stopped their thrashing and swam leisurely through the waves. With a final gasp from their blowholes, they dove into the depths. The eagles and seabirds rose higher into the dark mist and vanished. The lightning and thunder rolled off toward the horizon in the east, settling into the folds of the Cascade Mountains. A calm but steady downpour replaced the tempestuous winds and slashing rain.

A relative quiet had settled over land and sea, except for a distant hum that Kellen had noticed before.

"It's over." Rain dripped from Paddy's gray lashes.

Kellen struggled to apply logic to what he'd seen. "Did all this happen before? The whales and January?"

"Not quite. Last time, January ran into the woods. The whales headed north toward Sucia Island. But this time, it seems like—" Paddy raised a hand. "What the hell is that?"

The mysterious sound, like the humming of bees, had grown louder, resonating in the hills beyond Point Doughty.

Kellen cocked his head. "Heard it a minute ago. Sounds like chainsaws."

"Don't think so. Higher pitch. Something's wrong."

On the bluff, January had become aware of the disturbance. Still on his knees, he craned his neck, gazing back toward the forest and the strange drone.

Paddy snapped his fingers. "Off-road bikes."

Beyond the cliffs, dense underbrush snapped. A sizable crowd appeared to be moving through the woods.

January looked around wildly.

A large beam of light captured him, highlighting his muscular upper body as he sprang to his feet and began to run. After a few gangly strides, he hooked inland and disappeared.

"They can't do that." Kellen was amazed at his own reaction. He felt irrationally bothered by someone disrupting January's ritual.

"Who's 'they'?" Paddy asked. "You think they're cops?"

Kellen heard a shout, a man's voice somewhere to the rear, and dogs barking—bloodhounds being let off their leashes. At least two off-road motorcycles trailed the hunting party. The group appeared to be moving through a thick grove of trees that flanked the point.

Kellen imagined an outnumbered January on the run through the woods, dodging trees, taking a wrong turn, being confronted with the dogs. The pitch of their yelping intensified. The party of men and machines had again turned toward the northwest.

"They've got him cornered." Kellen knew there were only four sheriff's deputies on Orcas, not a force of this size. "There must be a dozen or more."

"There's been loose talk on the island—school teachers, politicians." Paddy slapped the cabin door in disgust. "They're afraid of him. They want him committed."

Kellen found himself wishing he could get up to the bluff. Since he'd come to the islands, he'd never flaunted his former FBI credentials, but now he felt compelled to do just that. Whatever strange phenomenon January had created, it seemed oddly personal, between himself and nature. "We've got to do something."

"What do you have in mind?"

"Let's cruise into town. Get there before they bring him in. Maybe we can help."

Paddy clutched the rail with both hands. "They're coming back."

From the frantic pitch of the dogs and the echo of several men's voices, the search was still on. On the bluff to the south, the panning beams again knifed through the trees. The off-road bikes headed into the forest as the men on foot moved steadily toward the ocean.

Suddenly off to the right, outlined in the light, January reappeared, bolting along the edge of the cliff like a hunted animal. He hurdled downed trees, weaving through rocks in a panicked dash.

"Jesus." Paddy took an impulsive step toward the helm as some hundred and twenty feet above, January hurriedly passed their position from right to left.

Fifty yards behind, the small group of men appeared, dressed in dark battle fatigues, carrying rifles. Their lights bobbed as they ran.

"Stay with him," Kellen shouted.

Paddy eased the throttle forward and the *Tide Runner* headed north, keeping pace along the rocky shore. Kellen clung to the stern rail, his eyes riveted on the pursuit. Three yelping dogs had outdistanced the pack of men, only twenty yards behind January. Off to the left from the inland side of Point Doughty, the lights of the off-road bikes appeared, blocking what had been January's escape.

The shaman had run out of real estate.

Without a second's hesitation, January made his choice. He glanced over his shoulder and, with a final burst of speed, raced toward the cliff's most prominent outcropping, his hands raised over his head like antlers.

Reaching the edge, he touched off with both moccasined feet, spreading his arms like an eagle.

Kellen and Paddy watched in amazement as January arched his back in a graceful swan dive. He dropped like a spent arrow, plunging ten stories through the darkness. Narrowly missing the rocky shoreline, January splashed into the churning waves and disappeared.

5

United Radio Services
The Sears Tower
Chicago

THROUGH THE LARGE PLATE-GLASS windows, the lights of the city twinkled along the shores of Lake Michigan. Under the fluorescent desk lamp, the brass timepiece read 12:46—not that it really mattered.

From the day Lorna had earned her corner office, she'd never punched a clock. There were no "hours" and, consequently, no overtime. Since radio never rested, neither had she.

United Radio Services occupied an entire floor of the building. With sixteen radio stations and a staff of one hundred sixty-four people, URS was usually a beehive of activity. But tonight, all forty-three of the employees dependent on Lorna's decisions had gone home . . . save one.

Mavis Winslow had married her job. Frizzy haired and delicately built, she leaned through the office doorway in her white blouse, her soft, dark eyes wide with concern. "This thing with Tracy . . . are you terribly upset?"

"I'm . . . yes. More than I thought." Lorna looked up from the computer keyboard. "This island must be terribly small. The sheriff's department has some night operator named Claire, who sounds like she's getting out of bed to answer the switchboard. She's trying to find McMillan. He's out somewhere in his car."

"And the medical center?"

"Just a recording." Lorna nervously punched at her computer keys. She was still working on a forceful ending for her thirty-minute talk. "I left this number at both places." She had also left Skip at the restaurant, using the family emergency as an excuse.

Mavis looked pale. "I'll keep calling if you like."

"You've done enough. Please go home."

"As soon as I finish your flowchart." She firmly clutched several sheets of paper. "You want to be accurate about these cumes, don't you?"

"How far did you get?"

"2012."

"That's plenty." Lorna beckoned. "Give me what you've got."

"All right." Mavis edged into the room and laid the computer printout on the desk. "I can wait with you."

"I'm fine."

Mavis hovered. "Oh, there's *one* thing from Atlanta. I checked your e-mail." With Lorna receiving more than eighty messages a day, Mavis screened communications. "WJZZ just went on the market."

"Really?" Lorna squinted at the screen. "Says who?"

"Cordelle Jacobs heard it over cocktails in Charleston this afternoon. He cc'd Chad, and Chad responded." Cordelle was a headhunter—someone Lorna had dated a few times until he got too serious. He was someone she could call if she ever needed work.

"What time was that?"

"Around eleven. Jacobs mentioned that the Turner people seem interested. Chad wants you to fly down and make a bid when you finish in Vegas. He also says 'good luck with Waterman.'"

Good luck? How much did Chad know about Skip's scheme? Chad would be asleep by now. Lorna would call him in the morning prior to her flight. Perhaps she could reason with him, where she couldn't with Skip. Twenty minutes ago, Skip had nearly spilled his Napoleon brandy trying to coerce her to rejoin him at the table, but she had pulled away and left.

Mavis still lingered.

Lorna heaved a sigh and looked up. "All right. Go ahead and book the flight."

"I have. Next Thursday, leaving McCarran Airport at 11:15 A.M. First class, nonstop."

"Good. Now leave."

"I have a couple—"

"No. It's almost one in the morning. Please."

Mavis blinked nervously. "Call me when you hear, will you?"

Lorna patted her hand. "Of course. Thanks. Now scoot. Promise?"

Mavis nodded and left.

Lorna went back to the speech. Her Caesars Palace audience of radio reps and the media press would scrutinize every word. She had received high praise at local media events in Chicago. But this was the big one . . . this one was national. Her speech topic: "Successful Advertising in a Volatile Radio Environment."

She stared at the computer screen.

Her gaze drifted to the telephone.

Waiting for a phone call from a stranger—about a stepsister who'd become a stranger. The family had been decimated. First the divorce. Then her mother's premature death from Parkinson's, followed by her alcoholic father's death from liver cancer. And then the unexpected suicide of Sheila, her father's second wife, after returning to her native Montreal.

Difficult to concentrate. She had to. Tonight—not tomorrow on the plane with its distractions. She began to doze off but quickly shook herself awake.

A few last paragraphs.

She had trained herself to produce on demand. It was part of the addiction, like the coffee she drank, the lunches she skipped, and the sleep she lost. And the men she didn't want in her life. She'd proved herself, garnering a salary of two hundred fifty thousand a year. In less than thirty-six hours, the president of the American Radio Broadcasters Association would introduce her.

Lorna heard several footsteps in the stone hallway. Mavis had broken her pledge.

"Now what?" Lorna peered over her reading glasses, surprised to find Skip leering from the doorjamb.

"That's what I'd like to know." He seemed off-balance, apparently having indulged in more after-dinner drinks.

"Skip, I told you—"

"I can't believe you walked out on me."

Lorna gestured to the telephone. "I'm expecting a very—"

"I'm expecting assurances. Tell me things are handled." His forehead glistened.

"Okay. As a professional, I'll do my—"

"Professional? Bullshit." His words slurred. "Just give me a fat fucking yes."

Lorna stared into his watery eyes, realizing that under no circumstances would she date, let alone sleep with Waterman to close a deal. Yes. Just say yes, she told herself—then deal with it. Lie to Skip, and finesse the agreement your way. She was about to utter that response when the phone on the desk began to pulse. Her glance fell to the blinking light.

Skip pointed a stubby finger. "Don't answer that until you tell me."

"I . . ." She lunged for the receiver as if awaiting a pardon from the governor. Skip cursed as she answered, "Lorna Novak."

"Ms. Novak, this is Deputy Frank McMillan, Orcas Island Sheriff's Office. I apologize for not getting back to you sooner."

"What's this about an accident? And Shelby?"

"This isn't good news. Brace yourself. Someone broke into the Spilner home."

"Oh no." Lorna switched off the computer. She suddenly flashed on Tracy's ex-husband, Bruce, whom she'd never met. Tracy had described him as a violent, insolent bastard.

"They abducted the girl. Clubbed your sister when she tried to interfere."

They? Lorna suddenly pictured the ugliness of sexual molestation. By now Shelby would be twelve years old, with attractive features like her mother and her grandmother before her. "Was it . . . rape?"

"We don't know. Obviously we can't judge the girl's condition. But the doctors see no sign of abuse on Ms. Spilner."

"Is she badly hurt?" The computer screen had faded to a dead gray.

"Took a nasty blow to the back of the head. She was knocked out. But not before she dialed 911. I was the first on the scene, probably forced the suspects to scatter. I took a quick look around, but your sister was in pretty bad shape, so I stayed with her. We do have an APB out on the island, and the ferries are being searched prior to departure. At this stage, there's no sign of Shelby."

"And where's Tracy?"

"At the medical center. They haven't moved her, afraid of aggravating the injury. No need, I guess. We have a good surgeon right here."

Skip still hovered at the doorjamb, breathing noisily.

Lorna swiveled in her chair, gazing out over the city. "You don't mean she's paralyzed?"

"Dr. Winston isn't sure. She regained consciousness for a few seconds after I found her. Murmured Shelby's name and asked for you."

Tears welled in Lorna's eyes. "We hadn't spoken."

"You're her only living relative, is that right?"

"Yes."

"Well, when you get here, you'll want to check in with me. I need your signature on my report. If surgery's necessary, you may be the only one legally entitled to sign the forms. Will you arrive tomorrow?"

"You're out in . . ."

"Orcas Island, about a hundred miles north of Seattle. You can fly into Sea-Tac Airport, catch a small plane that leaves periodically during the day."

Lorna turned in her chair. Skip folded his arms in disgust. "Listen, Sheriff—"

"*Deputy* McMillan."

"Yes, I'm up to my neck. I can be out there in three days. Isn't there someone else—?"

"Three days? Your sister's in a coma. The doctor's not sure when she'll come out of it. Having you here—"

"I understand, but I'm due at an important—"

"Important? Isn't being at her bedside important? The doctor thinks even the sound of your voice might help."

"Well, I'll speak to her."

"How? Long distance? Pardon me for asking, but what kind of a woman are you, anyway?"

In the silence that followed, Lorna gripped the phone tightly, staring at her reflection in the computer screen. Even at this late hour—with her shiny bobbed hair neatly coifed, in her high-necked blouse and gray suit with shelves of books behind—she appeared every bit the businesswoman. Her image would have fit nicely into an ad in the *Wall Street Journal*, a travesty compared to Tracy's fight for life.

"Deputy," she whispered, "I need a moment." She put him on hold.

One afternoon, twenty-five years ago in Evansville, Lorna's father, Richard, had unexpectedly returned. She hadn't seen much of her dad after the divorce. While Ann, Lorna's mother, clattered plates in the kitchen, a woman with dazzling blonde hair waited in the red sports car beyond the driveway. Her father had entered Lorna's room with a slender, freckled-faced girl squinting from behind the bulk of her father's black suit. "Lorna, Sheila and I are going to honeymoon in Italy." It seemed Richard was always off to somewhere glamorous. "This is Tracy." Dad had leaned over to push the shy six-year-old forward. "She's your sister now. I want you to be friends."

Sister?

They *had* become friends, spending summers together at Dad's place in Lake Tahoe and Christmases together in Indiana. But after their teenage years, the two drifted apart—Lorna to become a hard-charging exec, taking after her father's sophistication, and Tracy wandering off to hug trees.

The lights of the Chicago skyline blurred as Lorna's eyes brimmed with tears. Lives could change in the catch of a breath—the slip of a knife, the seat belt not worn. This phone call felt that way. Lorna sensed it. Tracy had crashed back into her life by uttering Lorna's name to the deputy. Was it possible that in the face of *that* plea, Lorna had been so blindly consumed by her career that she'd actually considered . . . ?

Dear God. She found herself disgustedly running the deputy's question through her mind: what kind of a woman was she?

6

Point Doughty

THE *TIDE RUNNER* SKIRTED THE slimy buttress of the steep cliff where January had disappeared. The rumble of the outdrive disturbed the slumber of several sea lions among the rocks. In the dim glow of the boat's running lights, a big-headed bull coughed in disgust, bellying back on a barnacle-covered boulder. Three small cows showed the whites of their eyes as they retreated sideways from the lapping breakers.

"Over there," Kellen shouted from the prow, aiming a flashlight across the waves. He had spotted a flash on the black water, where January's arm had been flailing the surface. The splashing had ceased, and now the tangle of hair and the shiny mound of January's back appeared in the swells some thirty feet from shore. "He's face down. Hurry."

Paddy gunned the throttle and guided the boat along the rocks.

Kellen had planned to use a grappling hook that he'd found lashed to the foredeck, but with a two-foot chop, a strong current, and an apparently unconscious swimmer, an on-deck rescue was now impossible.

Kellen straddled the prow, suppressing the prickle of fear that spread up his back. It had been only six months since his failed attempt to rescue Dietrich when their sailboat capsized. He gripped the bow rail, vowing that he would not let another man drown. "I don't see him." Waves had covered the lifeless form. Triangulating the distance using two landmarks on shore, Kellen marked the spot and set the flashlight down. He kicked off his deck shoes, tore off his seaman's cap, took off the life vest, unbuttoned his coat, and tugged off his shirt over his head. Tucking his cell phone and wallet into his jacket, Kellen perched on the bow. "Cut your engine, Paddy." A few more yards and he would dive in. He clutched the rail but was distracted by a whimpering sound from above.

Up on the cliff, whining dogs and their handlers peered over the edge, some of the men cradling weapons. Suddenly, a beam from a handheld flood lamp struck the boat and the surrounding water.

Paddy looked up, his face bathed in white.

"What the hell?" Kellen shouted looking up into the blinding light.

One of the hounds barked in response to Kellen's voice. A two-way radio crackled. It occurred to Kellen to identify himself as an ex-lawman, demanding to know the reasons for this harassment, but he liked neither the odds nor the angle at which he found himself.

He threw himself over the rail.

An icy sting cut to the bone as he splashed into the ocean, causing him to gasp. He got his bearings and struck out in an overhand crawl toward the place where he'd last seen January. He piked at the waist and dove headfirst into the dark water, glancing about as he swam. The floodlight panning the surface threw strangely undulating shafts of light down through the gloom.

Here and there, huge boulders jutted from the ocean floor—crustacean-covered towers with inky water uncomfortably deep between them, seventy to eighty feet at least.

Kellen ran out of oxygen.

He kicked for the surface and exploded into the night air. The *Tide Runner* bobbed on the swells twenty feet away.

Paddy had left the helm and stepped out on the foredeck. "Anything?"

"No."

A bullhorn sounded from the cliffs. "He was more off to your right."

Kellen marveled at the audacity but had no choice but to follow the suggestion.

He swam a few strokes and with another deep breath, plunged beneath the surface. The cold saltwater stung his eyes. He dove deeper, swimming a submerged breaststroke, suspended in what appeared as a jade fog. Nightmarish memories of his futile search for Dietrich haunted Kellen as a ghostly radiance created by lights on the cliff played among strands of kelp. A red jellyfish floated past his ear. The distraction caused Kellen to glance back.

Nothing there, save the sheer rock cliff face that fell away into darkness. A glittering school of fingerling fish shimmered fifteen feet below. No other movement in the gloom, and no sign of January.

Kellen's lungs began to burn. He was about to surge for the surface when a sudden flash of white caught his eye. Air bubbles spurted from his clamped lips as a looming shadow rose from the depths—the shape of a killer whale. Kellen nearly lost all his air as he recognized January's limp form humped over the animal's snout.

With a flourish of its flukes, the large whale pushed the body in Kellen's direction. The momentum left January to float upward, arms and legs hanging limply like a rag doll.

As the whale disappeared into the deep, Kellen reached out and gathered a handful of January's shoulder-length hair. With what strength he had left, Kellen kicked for the light with the young man in tow, headed toward the dark silhouette of the boat.

Kellen surfaced near the *Tide Runner*'s stern. His chest heaved as he felt the tap of Paddy's grappling hook on his shoulder. He spun and grasped the aluminum shaft while holding January's head above water.

Paddy knelt on the swim step, catching the body under both arms. Kellen rolled onto the platform, vaulting to his knees as he pulled January over the gunwale. A quick upward glance revealed that the men with guns were still watching.

Paddy bent over the body. "Christ, I think he's dead. Looks like he hit his head on the rocks."

January's lids were closed. Blood oozed from a brutal cut over his right eye. He'd lost both of his moccasins. His drenched buckskin pants, tied at the waist with several stands of rawhide, clung like extra skin to his legs.

"Let me at him." Kellen grasped the clammy jaw with one hand and held the nose closed with his other. He clamped his lips over January's mouth and blew. Kellen turned his head, pleased to feel the gentle returning puff from January's lungs. "Good. He's clear. There's no blockage." Kellen huffed another breath into the lifeless form and, turning his head again, glanced up at Paddy. "Push on his chest as he exhales."

Paddy obeyed and this time as Kellen turned his head, his cheek was splashed by the foul-smelling spurt of seawater and phlegm that gushed from January's mouth.

Kellen wiped the slime away. He overcame his nausea, realizing he would have gladly dealt with such queasiness with Dietrich had he been able to render CPR. He'd never had the chance.

Kellen breathed into January again. And again.

Kellen slid his hand from January's chin to the base of the neck, finding the carotid artery.

No pulse.

"Damn." Kellen glanced at Paddy. "Push on his heart as fast as you can between my breathing."

Paddy placed his gnarled hands over the young man's rib cage.

"Not like that," Kellen said. "You've got to pound him with the heels of your hands."

Paddy fumbled.

"Never mind. Can you do this instead?"

Paddy's eyes grew intense. "What? Blow into him?"

"Yes, in a rhythm."

"Of course."

"Then do it."

Kellen scurried around to straddle January's waist as Paddy took his place at the head, attempting to position his bearded mouth on January's.

Kellen laid the heels of his hands over January's sternum, putting weight behind every thrust as he repeatedly pressed on January's heart. "Breathe now, Paddy." More thrusts to the chest. "And again."

Kellen pushed as Paddy bent down and then looked up, his chin covered with drool. Kellen was proud of the old man, fighting through the repugnance, working to revive the kid.

As Kellen pushed several more times, Paddy rasped, "We've got to save this guy. He's got heart like nobody else."

Kellen thrust forward in a rapid cycle. He did it again. But January's famous heart refused to respond.

7

Riverside Holiday Inn
Cincinnati, Ohio

THE SMALL BLACK CELL PHONE pulsed on the nightstand as E. Trajan Morse watched Bunny Hobbs walk nude across the aquamarine carpet.

She had a particularly inviting figure, especially in those black pumps. The five-inch lift accentuated her buttocks and breasts. While the phone continued to ring its obligatory twelve times, Bunny indifferently dabbed her face with a silk handkerchief.

After all these months, she knew the phone routine . . . the successive rings ensured that the number hadn't been haphazardly called. As the pulsing continued, she retrieved her underwear from the gray armchair, strapping the black lace bra around her chest. Snapping it, she tucked her breasts into the cups, bending over just enough to let them fluff into position.

The sight of her softness bulging into place caused another stir in Trajan's groin—the Viagra was still working. He ignored the throb of another erection and reached across the bed for the receiver. Settling against the goose-down pillow, he answered, "Number please?"

As expected, there was no verbal response. The caller on the other end began entering the necessary twelve-digit code, which spelled his name on a phone pad: E T R A J A N M O R S E . . . 3 8 7 2 5 2 6 6 6 7 7 3.

Trajan's staff were the only ones who knew his phone number, but internal security within the TMC was so rigid that no one could speak to him without entering the encryption. And for good reason: officially Trajan didn't exist. If discovered, his organization, the Terrorist Monitoring Corps, would be denied by its sixteen sponsoring nations. As leader of that phantom force, Trajan was both cheered and feared by the West's most powerful countries. He'd become one of the world's most influential men.

The remaining numerical tones began sounding on the receiver as Trajan watched Bunny Hobbs kick off her heels. She slumped into the chair, lazily batting her false eyelashes as she tugged at her black nylons. Trajan's exclusive lust partner had had one Valium too many. But he didn't mind—she was a good lay, and his only option, since he couldn't risk seeking sex in bars.

Like the rest of Trajan's life, Bunny's intimacy was arranged by contract. Senator Kragen of Georgia, head of the Armed Services Committee and one of the six senators who endorsed the TMC, had referred this high-priced call girl to him. Kragen's own affair with the buxom thirty-year-old had ended, and he could vouch for Bunny's security. Trajan's needs were going to be met. During his first encounter with Bunny, Trajan made her fully aware that she'd be assassinated if she betrayed the relationship. With the enormous financial rewards, the easy access to drugs, plus the fact that she would be allowed to retire after the required two years, she seemed satisfied.

Bunny attached the garter belt tabs to the embroidered tops of her nylons as the final tones sounded on Trajan's phone. He picked up the receiver. A digital voice announced "clearance confirmed," and the incoming caller was connected.

"Trajan?" It was Calico's southern drawl.

"Who else?"

"I know, but I wanted to hear your voice before shooting my wad."

Calico was Trajan's second-in-command. Beautiful and razor sharp, she also served as counsel in his legal matters. By now she'd be lounging in a black body stocking in the TMC Learjet.

"Okay, girl. Fire when ready."

"I wanted to let you know that Shelby Spilner is here with me, resting comfortably in the aft compartment."

"Good. No hitches?"

"Well, I guess we dropped Ms. Spilner pretty hard. She never knew what hit her. Stooch isn't sure how bad she is—he clipped her in the head. While we got Shelby out, Stooch was trying to see if she was breathing, but he had to haul ass when a cop showed."

"What about the Indian kid?" Trajan sat up and studied his hairy, well-muscled body in the mirror. His bald head accentuated the intensity of his pale-blue eyes.

"Stooch and the guys are still tailing him. It was tough terrain on the cliffs, and he gave them the slip. He's in the custody of two regulars." *Regular* was anyone not in uniform.

Trajan angrily threw his striped boxer shorts across the room. "How the hell did that happen?" There had been sixteen pick ups of TMC candidates with no casualties, though some had appeared on milk cartons. Frustrated, Trajan walked to the window that overlooked the Ohio River, where taillights snaked across the bridge into Kentucky. "Does Stooch have a visual on him right now?"

"Yeah."

"Well, regulars or not, you'd better knock 'em off."

"Can do," Calico responded. "But the Indian might be dying."

"What? Where are you?"

"At the Orcas Island Airfield. Stooch is on shortwave, watching from the cliff. Right now some yokel's giving CPR to your boy in a boat."

"So he fell?"

"No. He dove and was rescued."

"Courageous. Fits his profile." The boy was as extraordinary as he'd suspected. January might well be the single key visionary to replace Irinia Malenchek—a replacement that Dr. Epstein, the TMC lab-ops chief, needed for his telepathic sessions. "Patch me through to Stooch."

"I can't. I'm fighting interference from nearby radio towers on Mount Constitution. Stooch had enough trouble reaching me on an alternate frequency."

"Ask him to update me."

Calico's voice faded into the background. "Stooch. I've got Trajan. What's up?"

Silence.

"Stooch," she repeated. "Your status please?"

More silence.

Trajan couldn't afford to lose January. Until now, the TMC effort had been moderately successful. In response to NATO's requests, the TMC was spearheaded by the United States, more specifically the Defense Department, which had gathered key counterintelligence personnel. The objective: to adopt a centralized antiterrorist policy rather than have separate efforts by various worldwide organizations. This group of agents, which Trajan commanded, formed a successful surveillance unit to combat unmanageable chaos.

With rogue states posing an increasing threat and antigovernment cults in both the United States and Europe disrupting federal activities through terror,

Dr. Epstein's experiments in psychoneurology had proved to be a credible defense. Epstein had actually succeeded in telepathic surveillance, a huge step forward when compared to the CIA experimentation that began during the Iran Hostage Crisis in the late 1970s—experimentation that garnered inconclusive results.

After September 11, 2001, during the desperation of the Bush Administration, Epstein had proven that a properly programmed, linked group of clairvoyants could funnel energy through a single super-telepath in an ERVC, an Extended Remote Viewing Chamber. While the secondary subjects opened up to a psychic cache, the primary trancer—a key psychic whose neurochemistry was altered—could accomplish the ultimate in remote viewing by mentally "seeing" targets at great distances. It wasn't until the Obama Administration realized that Internet and phone surveillance were not fully efficient to accurately track potential rogue attackers that secret funding for this renewed psychic project occurred.

The goal: track WMDs and other biological weapons. Recently, it was suspected that Chinese-manufactured anthrax suitcase bombs had been sold to an Iranian-sponsored infiltration force. Core members of this Isis/Al-Qaeda cosponsored multinational insurgency had been trained in Algeria under the French code name AVALANCHE. They were supported by sleeper agents who had resided in the United States and Canada for years. The window to track their weapons was rapidly closing.

The TMC's previous best psychic was from Europe, a woman named Irinia Malenchek. She had remotely viewed Fahad Abbas, one of AVALANCHE's key operatives, delivering what was suspected to be a prototype of an anthrax explosive to Achmed Rahid, the key contact in Baltimore. Through Irinia, Epstein had been able to psychograph Abbas, and his description was in the hands of the FBI. Still, Abbas's ability to disguise himself would make him difficult to trace. And Irinia had come undone during the experiment. Her descent into insanity was not atypical. Epstein's formula unfortunately caused intense disorientation, and since Irinia's collapse, two others had wilted away and died.

Dr. Epstein needed another visionary—tough and gifted.

Without her knowledge, Shelby Spilner had been selected through a national Internet screening through a game she voluntarily played called "Imagine." Understandably immature, Shelby showed great aptitude, though she would likely prove to be a worker bee. January, on the other hand, had remarkable qualities that fit Epstein's model. January's detection had occurred by chance during the Shelby investigation, due to their mutual friendship and psychic connection.

"Trajan." Calico was back. "Stooch says January is moving his legs. He seems to be coming around."

"Then take him."

"Our exposure is severe. We've had verbal contact with the men in the boat."

"All the more reason."

"What about the nonviolation imperative?" The TMC had pledged not to interfere with outside citizens.

"Priorities," he shot back.

"Whose?"

"Mine. And yours, remember?"

After long debate, the Defense Department had agreed that the TMC maintain its top secrecy and operate under an ethics code similar to the wartime military. That meant test subjects could, after being drafted, be held against their will. Even those who were volunteers would be released with a suicide implant in their brains they knew would remotely trigger a cerebral hemorrhage if they were to divulge involvement. Any complaints to local authorities by subjects could be stifled by participating governments. And the TMC had legal supremacy over all other national law enforcement agencies—supremacy granted through a classified statute by Supreme Courts in member nations. With mass murder by mentally unbalanced nihilists and international terrorist activity in the name of Isis on the rise with no end in sight, the TMC had to act with precision. As distasteful as it was, Epstein's test subjects were, for the greater good, considered expendable. Pentagon dissenters were reminded that in times of war, traitors had been executed—and this was a time of war. In the TMC, disloyalty by test subjects was considered treason. In other previous war times, personnel had been sacrificed without legal ramification, like the American troops who unknowingly endured radiation poisoning during atomic testing in the 1950s. It remained a perpetual question whether the TMC could successfully complete its critical mission without discovery. Time was of the essence, and Trajan was well aware of the high stakes involved—for his country and for himself. He had to protect his seat of ultimate power, which superseded even that of the NSA.

"We could track the kid and pick up him up later," Calico said. "Where would he go?"

"No."

"Then what are we doing?"

Trajan gazed across the river toward Kentucky, famous for its horses. His father had been a horse breeder in Tennessee. But his father was dead, and so were Trajan's feelings. He'd forsaken whatever family he had many years ago. Ironically, Trajan was a valued amoralist in a time when morality was under assault.

He leaned against the cold glass. "No more discussion. We need that kid. Tell Stooch. No survivors or witnesses."

8

Point Doughty

JANUARY GAGGED, COUGHED, AND DROOLED seawater. He finally gained control of his lungs, sat up on deck, and inhaled great gulps of night air. His face was twisted in discomfort as he fixed his moist eyes on Kellen. *"Chui ah,"* January said.

"What?" Kellen was amazed at the color of January's huge irises—they were the shade of kalamata olives.

"It means life giver. You pulled me out."

"How did you know it was me?"

January shrugged. "You're drenched." He nodded to Paddy. "He's not."

Kellen couldn't help but smile. He shook January's hand. "I would have never found you without the whale."

January gingerly touched the welt on his forehead. "I hit something down there. As I struggled to remain conscious, I remember sinking into the ocean and feeling the orca take me."

Paddy nodded up at the cliff. "Kellen. Thank God, they're gone."

Kellen followed his gaze. The rain had subsided. The edge of the bluff was quiet.

January pointed. "Those guys wanted my soul. There were too many this time."

"This time?" Kellen accepted a towel from Paddy, who tossed a plaid blanket to January.

January hoisted the wool around his shoulders. "They've been to my place before. Three of them almost caught me. Tonight, I realized how serious this is. I have to warn Shelby."

"Who?"

"A friend. She'll be in danger. I suspected this. That's why I've been hiding."

Paddy stepped into the cabin and hit the ignition. Over the engines rumble, January shouted to him. "Please drop me at Bartwood Lodge."

As they got underway, Kellen desperately wanted answers. "Do you know what is it they want from you?"

"It's what they are."

"What do you mean?"

January stared at the moon, which had reappeared on the rim of a cloud. "They're scavengers. They want power."

"How'd they know you'd be here tonight?"

"The same way you did."

As they reached cruising speed, Kellen studied January's face. For a young man, he possessed a rare nobility and serenity—some kind of privilege that he bore as part of his heritage. Kellen edged closer and sat next to January on a tackle box. "Tell me something—the storm and the whales. Was that your doing?"

"Doing?" January shrugged. "I have no intent. Just a fulfillment."

"I don't understand."

"Yes, you do. Or you wouldn't be dedicated to restoring the salmon."

"You know about that?"

"I do." He stared into Kellen's eyes. "The fingerling salmon you breed will return to their birthplace from thousands of miles away. Salmon would swim on dry land to reach their home. You have that same hunger—like the steel fish."

The comment stunned Kellen. What had January sensed? "You've been to my hatchery?"

"I have not. But I respect what you do."

Kellen glanced at the cliffs. "Can you tell me what happened up there?"

"You saw it with clear eyes. My sight was clouded by power."

"What is this power you talk about?"

January looked out from under heavy brows. "Do you know how life originated on this planet?"

"No. Do you?"

January smiled.

"Look. I'm asking you where that disturbance—where all that energy comes from."

"I'm the conduit, not the creator."

"But the birds, and the whales—"

"They're drawn by life's magnet. Just as it pulled you here tonight."

Kellen nodded at Paddy. "I came because of him."

January shrugged. "But you came. The reasons aren't important. Like you, I come because I'm called."

"By whom?"

"By those who wish me to see what happened long ago. To see I go blind, which is what happens on the cliff."

"You said your vision was clouded."

"Yes, but I see shadows—shadows of pain." January grunted with discomfort. "My body is torn by the rush of souls that race through my bones."

"Souls? The dead?"

"And the living." January dropped the blanket from his shoulders. He seemed troubled as he gazed past Kellen toward Sucia Island. "Out there on those beaches."

Kellen was compelled to look. "On Sucia? What's out there?"

"That's where it began. My ancestors felt agony." A tear rolled down his cheek. "They were tortured. And many centuries before, someone like me, who was touched by the universe, felt an anguish I can't comprehend." He swallowed hard. "A remarkable wretchedness reached those shores. The whales were here. I am meant to find it somehow, even if it destroys me."

January had the look of a man committed to certain martyrdom.

"Are you alone in this?"

"No. I told you." January leaned back and closed his eyes. "None of us are. We've forgotten alternate ways to communicate. In the age before memory, we had those gifts. It still remains inside us."

January breathed deeply, and a peace settled over his face. His broad forehead and high cheekbones were smoothed by composure. He had shut out the rest of the world, and Kellen decided to let him be.

Kellen watched January briefly and then noticed a flock of seagulls circling overhead on the night breeze.

In all his years as an FBI special agent, Kellen had never come across a man like January. Kellen had dealt with multiple personality disorders during years of criminal research, but what he felt from January was unique. Kellen struggled with the sensation that January seemed possessed by the essence of several individuals captured in a single body.

January seemed to embody spirits that Kellen himself had imagined as a boy visiting Orcas Island's hazy groves and placid bays. Little wonder that twenty years later, when Kellen's FBI sting operation went bad, he had sought refuge here.

He could recite by heart the cold, impersonal letter he had received. A review board had ruled that Kellen had blown his cover as an infiltrator, keying the mafia to an upcoming raid. Kellen had tried desperately to locate the person responsible—the corrupt officer within the Cleveland Police Department. But the organized crime connections were too tight. In the end, all that Kellen was left with was guilt; two fellow agents had died during a gun battle. The letter had been brief, a single paragraph that cut like a knife. Kellen was relieved of duty and sent home, much to his father's disappointment. By contrast, Kellen's brother, Kyle, had been killed during the rescue of a hostage while successfully engineering the arrest of a Miami drug lord. With Kellen's father a police officer and Kellen's brother an FBI hero, Kellen's fall from grace had been all the more devastating. He found himself wearing a cloak of shame—with every reason to shed it by escaping the city.

That's when Orcas Island had beckoned. Kellen had responded, and he had bonded with the island's forests and seas—a beauty some described as unparalleled anywhere on earth.

It certainly was tonight. The moon was now fully exposed over Buck Mountain as they cruised up the Georgia Strait. The lights of distant Bellingham twinkled in the distance. This might have been a midnight pleasure cruise, if Paddy's worried face hadn't appeared through the cabin door.

Seeing January asleep, Paddy whispered, "I've got a fix on something strange."

Kellen rose and in two steps, leaned into the cabin.

Paddy pointed to the Furuno radar scope. "Somebody just took off from the Bartwood boat ramp."

Kellen watched the screen as six green blips appeared offshore near the Bartwood Pier. The dots aligned themselves in a straight line and headed west toward the *Tide Runner*'s position.

Kellen tapped the screen. "How far?"

"A mile and a half maybe."

“Then we would see them, right?” Kellen strained his eyes through the cabin windshield. Off to the east, a series of tiny glowing orbs had rounded the bend. “What the hell are they?”

“Trouble.”

“Speed boats?”

Paddy had hoisted the binoculars, panning the dark horizon. “Too small. I don’t like it.” He hit a switch, doused the *Tide Runner*’s navigation lights, and the boat was cloaked in darkness.

The *Tide Runner* hove to, jolting January from his slumber. He vaulted to his feet and appeared at the cabin door, pulling the blanket around his shoulders. “Why are we stopping?”

“Listen,” Paddy said as they continued to drift.

Over the sound of lapping bow waves, a distant buzz echoed across the ocean.

In the glow of the radar scope, Paddy glared at January. “What could you possibly have done to piss them off like this? Are you telling us everything?”

“I have no more to say.” January frowned. He backed out of the cabin and strode toward the stern.

“Paddy, the kid feels bad enough,” Kellen said.

“He’ll feel a lot worse when we face what’s coming.” Paddy pointed over the bow. “See those lights? I’ll be goddamned if those aren’t jet skis, Kellen. These bastards haven’t given up. What the hell do we do now?”

9

President's Channel

PADDY TURNED THE BOAT AND set the *Tide Runner* at full throttle. The old hull shuddered as the outdrive kicked up a respectable wake. On the aft deck, January sat on the tackle box. Swirling wind whipped his drying hair as he held the blanket around his shoulders.

Kellen remained with Paddy in the cabin. The odometer read four thousand RPM, but for Kellen, it wasn't fast enough. "That's top speed?"

"I'm doing thirty-six knots and I'm wide open," Paddy shouted. "Not that it'll do us any good." He nodded over his shoulder at the pinpoints of light on the horizon. "Those guys'll do fifty or more."

Kellen glanced back. The jet skis were still gaining. "So where can we go?"

"We could make the Rosario Marina in twenty minutes, but they'll catch us long before that."

"So what? They can't board us while we're underway." Kellen squinted at the bobbing headlights, now only a few hundred yards off the stern. "Let them run alongside. What's the difference?"

January suddenly appeared. "I'm the difference. Without me they'll leave you alone." He dropped the blanket to the cabin floor. "Cut your speed, and I'll go over the side." He turned out the door and made a move for the rail.

Kellen was on deck in a flash. "Bullshit. You stay on board."

January turned defiantly. "When I want to go, nothing stops me." He yelled, "Slow down, Mr. O'Hearn."

Kellen grabbed January's wrist. "I didn't pull you out of the drink just to throw you back to those maniacs."

January's eyes flashed. He yanked away. "I feel your strength. But you won't hold me."

With one hand on the rail, Kellen pushed closer, nose to nose. "You go overboard and I go right after you."

January studied Kellen's face. "You've got the brow of a bear, friend. Perhaps you're more stubborn than I thought."

"Try me," Kellen whispered. He called over his shoulder, "Paddy, head closer to shore." He turned to January. "Listen. Please do this my way. At least you'll get to dry land."

Paddy shouted from the helm, "They're gaining."

January's dark eyes fixed on Kellen. "Tell me. What am I to you?"

Kellen was struck by the question. Why was he so eager to help? "You're the first shaman I ever kissed on the mouth. Is that reason enough?"

January's stern expression melted into a smile. "And you're a genuine smart-ass."

"We'll discuss my virtues some other time. Now, get inside and stay out of sight."

With a nod, January joined Paddy, who clutched the handset and dialed the VHF emergency channel. January dropped to the polished hardwood, squatting against the bench as Paddy began to plead into the microphone. "Come in, any Coast Guard unit. Mayday, Mayday. This is *Tide Runner* off Point Doughty on a southerly heading down President's Channel."

The radio crackled as a voice answered, "This is Coast Guard cutter 487. State your problem."

As Kellen peered through the door, Paddy clicked off and glanced back. "What do I say?"

"Say we're going down." The jet-ski headlights were now less than a hundred yards behind. "Anything. Just get them here."

"We're about to be rammed," Paddy barked into the radio. "In danger of sinking. *Tide Runner*, off west coast of Orcas Island, needs assistance. Come in, over."

"What's your exact position?" the radio said.

The six jet skis had now pulled within fifty yards of their stern. A bullhorn sounded in the darkness. *"Ahoy, Boston Whaler. Heave to, or we'll scuttle you."*

"Scuttle?" Kellen whispered under his breath. "Who's this asshole? Captain Hook?"

"Kellen—"

"I heard him. Keep running. Give our coordinates."

As Paddy chattered numbers into the handset, the six jet-ski riders split into two groups, coming up on either side of the *Tide Runner* in an attempt to box them in.

"Paddy, cut hard for shore," Kellen yelled. "Do it now."

Paddy responded, spinning the wheel to his left.

The *Tide Runner* leaned into a banking turn, pushing white water off its bow as the three skis on the port side were forced to jump the wake.

Kellen was delighted the maneuver had disrupted their pattern. "As they pull alongside, turn hard to starboard."

The *Tide Runner* now ran due east, skimming along a shimmering runway the reflecting moon had created—a band of gold stretching toward the shoreline.

In response to Paddy's sudden change of direction, the three skis on the right accelerated into a long arc and regained their positions, nearly abreast with engines humming.

"Cut your engines, goddamn you." The bullhorn again.

"Make your turn," Kellen shouted.

Paddy obeyed and once more the careening Boston Whaler slashed right, nearly striking two of the three jet skis. They were forced to slow down, bobbing among the waves, while the skis on the left again accelerated to close the distance.

"That works," Kellen yelled. "Now watch your portside."

On the left, the three other skis had recovered. With their engines screaming they caught up, running side by side. Against the moon's reflection, the silhouetted men aboard the portside sport craft appeared to be dressed in black wet suits—single riders on each, save the lead ski, which carried two men. The man in the front seat held a gleaming plastic bullhorn. The man behind brandished what appeared to be a bazooka under one arm—maybe a 37-millimeter grenade launcher.

Blossoms of flame suddenly spit from automatic handguns held by the other drivers.

"Holy Christ." Paddy instinctively pulled back on the throttle.

"No, damn it, Paddy." Kellen scurried toward the cabin. "They're firing into the air. It's a bluff. They don't want to kill January with a stray shot. Bank left and head for shore."

Again, Paddy cranked the wheel. With white water spraying off the bow, Paddy hit the *Tide Runner*'s throttle to straighten the boat. Tree-covered rocks were only two thousand yards away. To the south, lights from several cabins glowed on a hillside.

"Are you still there, *Tide Runner*?" the radio asked.

"Affirmative," Paddy shouted. "But not for long."

The six jet skis regrouped and now flanked the Boston Whaler. The lead skier and his passenger had again drawn into range thirty feet off the *Tide Runner*'s quarterdeck.

"Pull up or we'll sink you," the bullhorn sounded.

Paddy turned from the helm. "Kellen?"

Kellen leaned around the cabin to get a clearer view. "Cut a sharp U-turn along the beach. As close as you can."

January crouched in the cabin doorway, prepared to make his move.

"January." Kellen glanced down. "When Paddy makes his cut, dive over the side and swim for the beach."

"No problem."

In fact, there was a huge problem; Kellen began to understand that as he gauged the distances involved. The jet skis were much too fast. No matter how close to land Paddy made his turn, January's pursuers would have time to surround him before he made shore.

Kellen smacked the resin-covered rail. "No. It's not going to work."

"Last chance. Stop or die."

Kellen was on his feet and through the cabin door. "Paddy, you've got to beach this thing."

"What? That's not sand out there. That's rocks."

"I know. It'll tear her up. But we've got to give the kid a break."

"Don't make me do this. I just painted her."

"I'll help you fix the hull. Please. Take her in."

Paddy set his bearded jaw and gripped the wheel. "Oh, all right, goddamn it."

Kellen rushed back out on deck, sliding to his knees next to January. "Get ready, we're going to hit hard."

"Hit?"

"The shore. When we beach her, run like hell."

"You'll hurt the boat."

"It's okay with Paddy as long as it saves your ass."

January's dark eyes faltered. Admiration flooded his face. "I won't forget this."

Kellen wished he had time to learn more about the essence of the man. "Where do we find you?"

"I'll be among the eagles. My grandmother will know. Or Shelby."

"Who's that again?"

"Kellen," Paddy croaked. "We're there."

Kellen peeked over the rail.

The boat was two hundred yards from shore and closing fast. So were the jet skis. The rear rider on the lead ski aimed his bazooka-like-device and fired.

The *Tide Runner*'s hull shattered.

An explosion blew a large hole in the bow—causing the boat to submarine. Paddy's limp form crashed into the control panel. With a sickening tearing sound, the fiberglass prow disintegrated as the boat's stern lurched into the night sky.

Kellen was launched into the air. January went flying as if shot from a canon. As they both were catapulted over the wreckage, Kellen was strangely aware of the jet skis buzzing below. He craned his neck as he tumbled through the air, trying to maintain a view of Paddy—but then he hit. The ocean felt like cement as he landed chest first, his legs wrenching violently over his back. Air was crushed from his lungs.

Kellen bobbed to the surface, struggling to inhale, but he couldn't. He strained to look back.

The *Tide Runner*'s torn hull hissed as air escaped the forward cabin. The stern stuck straight out of the water, swaying precariously against the star-filled sky.

No sign of Paddy. The jet skis circled the wreckage. One of the riders shouted, pointing. January had surfaced thirty feet away, his black hair shiny in the jet-ski headlights.

As the skis converged on him, January dove back into the depths.

Kellen was so intent on January's escape that he didn't notice one of the jet skis approaching, accelerating straight at Kellen's head. Kellen turned in time to look up, making eye contact with the driver. The man's eyes were bright with anger under the hood of his black wet suit. Kellen saw a flash of white and felt the dull impact as the ski struck him just above the temple.

The water closed over his head, and he sank into the cold.

10

Benalmadena, Spain

ALESSANDRO VARGAS FOUND HIMSELF SMILING as he leaned back in the wrought-iron chair. From his hacienda's veranda, he could see the glistening Mediterranean. Several sailboats streaked the platinum sea—another regatta was underway beyond the marina. Along the white beach beyond the esplanade, a flock of pelicans flew lazily along the coast.

The day was bright with promise.

He took a last sip of the mimosa and set the champagne flute on the table next to the dark-brown envelope that had been sent by Giraldo Chopa, the chief archivist at the Spanish Historical Society in Madrid. Giraldo had furnished him with a transcript of a recently recovered document—an undelivered letter so faded that only ultraviolet analysis could reconstruct the ancient writing. The parchment had been found among random artifacts in some ruins on the coast of the Dominican Republic, where goods from the west had often been transferred to eastbound ships.

Alessandro's stocky personal assistant, Bernardo, had handed the package to Alessandro in the portico, where he'd been tempted to open the transcript immediately. But it had been nearly two hundred years since the letter was lost, and Alessandro reasoned that another half hour would be of no consequence. He wanted to shower and dress for the occasion. Why not have Bernardo bring the letter out into the sun after breakfast, so that it might be read on the porch?

Alessandro had taken his time showering and shaving in his large, open-air terrazzo tile bathroom. Smelling of jasmine soap and dressed in a purple shirt and cream-colored slacks, he had retrieved a newspaper he'd received yesterday from his bedroom nightstand. The newspaper had been sent by David Fraley, the curator of a small museum on Orcas Island, Washington, USA. And it, too, held pieces of a puzzle that Alessandro was determined to solve.

With paper in hand, Alessandro had seated himself at the mosaic table on the veranda. After enjoying the bountiful breakfast that Bernardo had prepared, he had glanced at an article in the paper on page one of the *Sounder*, the Orcas Island weekly. The article featured a story about the discovery of a small Native American skeleton—thought to be female—which had been unearthed during a routine excavation of a road through the heart of town. Native remains on the islands were not unusual, the article stated, but in this case an item of some rarity had also been found—a small iron-framed strongbox of Spanish origin. Its contents remained unknown, since the artifact had been turned over to archaeologists.

Alessandro hoped that the Spanish strongbox might help to solve a mystery involving an ancestor of his, Captain Roberto Ravilla, who had surveyed the Washington coastline prior to his suicide in the 1790s.

Alessandro's father, a world-renowned shipping magnate who also owned one of the casinos in Benalmadena, viewed Alessandro's passion for history with amusement, though he appreciated that his son had committed himself to reconstructing their family history.

Having cleared the dishes, Bernardo returned with a fresh pot of coffee and set it down on the table.

"Did everything taste all right, Don Vargas?" he asked in his Oxford-sounding English, which he and Alessandro spoke in all conversation at Alessandro's insistence.

"As usual. You added a touch of caliente pepper to the hollandaise, didn't you?"

With a smile his only response, Bernardo lifted the empty champagne flute and placed it on the serving cart. "Coffee?"

"After we read, perhaps?"

"We?"

"Yes, why not? We should share the news." After years of service, Alessandro considered the Basque more of a companion than a servant or secretary. "Please. Sit down."

Bernardo eyed the newspaper. "Is that something new?"

"It's promising. But first things first." Alessandro pushed the brown package across the multicolored mosaic. "I left my glasses in the bedroom. You can read it to me."

Bernardo nodded and threw a serving towel across the back of an opposite wrought-iron chair and sat down, reaching for the envelope. He gently tore the ribbing and pulled out several pieces of paper. "There appears to be a letter from Giraldo along with the transcript."

"Start there then."

Bernardo reached behind his apron into the pocket of his white shirt and donned a pair of gold-rimmed glasses. "The letter begins 'Dear Señor Vargas.'" Bernardo translated the letter from the original Spanish as he read. "'First let me thank you for your continued generosity. The Society Board wishes to express—'"

"Enough schmooze. Does he refer to the document?" Alessandro asked.

"Here at the bottom. It says, Professor Jivar confirms that the parchment recovered from the Dominican Republic is genuine."

"Because?"

Bernardo skimmed the paragraph. "Ah . . . because it bears the signature of Cerba Aquilino Lucero Martine, who was assigned to Ravilla during the San Juan Island voyage."

"Good. Now, the transcript please."

"Yes. Here it is . . . dated the twenty-seventh of June 1793." Bernardo shuffled the sheets and began to read the Spanish text. "'My Dear Francisco—'"

"Cerba Martine's brother?"

"Let me see . . . yes, according to the professor. It continues:

> I pray to almighty God that my words reach you. Our country's commitment to these islands has prompted Admiral Panjota to demand that, after Roberto Ravilla's untimely death, I maintain command of *El Trinidad* off Orcas Island, while Panjota sails the *Santiago* to rejoin the fleet off California. The recent sighting of an English ship in northern waters has convinced Panjota to assign a portion of the *Santiago*'s crew to remain here under my command.
>
> First, I assure you of my steadfast dedication to Spain, my vows to King Charles, and my continued devotion to you. I swear my continued devotion to you, dear Francisco, with a pledge each night upon the signet gold ring, which you gave to me. With this letter I entrust

to you my reputation, which may well come into question, should I not return.

I wish to report that several months ago, after Panjota sailed north, I was put in charge of a twenty-three-man shore party to venture to the interior of Orcas Island, while Captain Ravilla sailed *El Trinidad* to survey the neighboring coast.

On April 3 of this year, near a black sand beach on the north side of Orcas Island, I befriended a man of the Salish Indian tribe. He was revered by other natives as a chieftain. This extraordinary individual, who called himself Lukat, had eyes that spoke of a keen intellect. From all indications, he was a spiritual leader, if such a phrase could be applied to a savage culture.

Over time, Lukat and his sister, Imnit, took it upon themselves to become my native hosts—

"His sister?" Alessandro interrupted.

"What?" Bernardo paused.

"A woman." The description in the newspaper article had flashed in Alessandro's mind.

"Is that good?"

"Very good. Continue."

Bernardo adjusted his glasses and read on:

. . . my native hosts, whom I found to be people of exceeding kindness, and I spent many hours attempting to communicate. Imnit proved to be a surprisingly genteel woman, driven to educate me as to the riches of the forest and the seas. I took great comfort in her company.

Lukat, on the other hand, became my guide, leading me and my men as we explored neighboring villages where we were offered animal skins, hunting tools, and other trinkets.

Our first mate, Cabrillõ, an ambitious man, had shown the Indians his gold ring, flashing it in the sunshine as he made inquiry as to the possible location of similar shiny metal.

Under repeated pressure of Cabrillõ's inquiry through sign language, the Indians indicated that Lukat had something of great value in his keeping. Cabrillõ's incessant questioning resulted in the natives revealing that Lukat's prize rested across the water at a sacred place: a tiny neighboring body of land, which Panjota had named Sucia (the dirty island) due to its hidden, treacherous reefs. When Cabrillõ requested that Lukat take us there, Lukat refused. I was unable to determine the reason for his objections.

Unfortunately, when Ravilla returned, Cabrillõ circumvented my authority and convinced Captain Ravilla to pursue the natives' assertions. Hearing about the possibility of gold, Captain Ravilla wanted to be present on the journey.

To my great dismay, under Ravilla's orders, Cabrillõ took Lukat into custody, and after abusing him, convinced the poor man to lead us to the destination. I begged Captain Ravilla to clarify his motive in these methods, which struck me as cruel and inappropriate, particularly since Ravilla espoused a strong Catholic faith to the point of extreme devotion. But Ravilla had no sympathy for my views or for Lukat, whom he considered akin to an animal and undeserving of Christian charity.

When we arrived at the Sucia shore, we left Cabrillõ and the crew with the boat. Leading Lukat by a chain around his neck, Captain Ravilla ordered me to accompany him while we ventured inland for some distance until we reached a hollow. There, I kept watch outside, while Captain Ravilla and Lukat entered a small cavern.

I have difficulty describing the incidents that followed next. Ravilla had been inside the cave only a moment when I heard him scream. He emerged from the darkness shouting like a man possessed, asking God's forgiveness and charging Lukat with sorcery. He stumbled about, rubbing his eyes, asserting that he had been confronted with an abomination and was blinded by a burst of light.

I was astounded to see Captain Ravilla, after recovering his sight, turn in anger, draw his sword, and run Lukat through. When I demanded to know the reason for this senseless murder, Ravilla insisted that he had been bewitched in the cave. He began to shout like a madman, saying he would not speak of the unspeakable. The commotion brought attention to our activities, and when the other tribesmen discovered Lukat's corpse, the natives became hostile. Three of our men were killed. Although I tried to prevent it, that is when the atrocities began.

> Ravilla ordered the villages on the island to be burned to the ground. Members of our crew committed acts of intense cruelty to those Indians they captured. My shore party was forced to abandon our camp and retreat to *El Trinidad*. We anchored the ship a sufficient distance offshore to avoid being boarded.
>
> This extraordinary occurrence on Sucia Island caused me to ponder precisely what Captain Ravilla might have encountered. I was not only shocked by his reaction, I remain confused by his behavior.
>
> After the massacre, Ravilla refused to discuss the contents of the cave and withdrew from me and my fellow officers, acting strangely and walking the decks at night. Three days ago, he insisted that Lukat was still alive. According to Ravilla, he had seen Lukat on the previous night, perched in the rigging near the mainsail. Ravilla mentioned that a flock of crows had descended from the moon, entangling themselves in the ropes and manifested themselves as the Indian man's apparition. Last night I heard Ravilla ranting on deck. At dawn, the morning watch found him. Ravilla had hanged himself from the forward mast.
>
> Today, Panjota returned aboard the *Santiago* and, prior to his departure for California, insisted these events be treated with utmost delicacy. I understand his hesitancy, because in view of the slaughter that occurred, the subsequent suicide of one of the King's captains might become an embarrassment to the admiralty. Panjota has given me leave to investigate the unpleasantness. As a result, I plan to seek out the one person who might be of help. I intend to return to Sucia and make a record . . .

Bernardo looked up and shrugged. "That's where it ends. The curator makes note that the rest of the parchment had been torn away. Unfortunate. Without it, how would you . . . ?" Bernardo reacted to Alessandro's knowing smile. "In there?" he asked, glancing across the table at the newspaper that fluttered in the breeze. "You *do* have something."

"Perhaps." Alessandro reached for the article. His Oxford archaeology degree and his fascination with his family's history were about to play a hand in a two hundred-year-old mystery.

He opened the newspaper and pushed it across the table. "A few weeks ago, during a routine street upgrade on Orcas Island, the skeletal remains of a woman were found. The sheriff's department gave the bones to a local archaeologist named David Fraley. Fraley sent me this paper, so I e-mailed him, asking him to share whatever he finds during his examination."

Bernardo's dark eyes beaded in anticipation. "So what do you think it means?"

"From what you've read in Giraldo's transcript, it may be logical that . . ."

"Yes?"

"That, as Cerba says in his letter to his brother, Francisco, Cerba Martine may have indeed succeeded in seeking out 'the one person who might be of help.'"

Bernardo shrugged. "Am I missing something?"

Alessandro tapped the paper with his fingertips. "The skeletal remains of an Indian woman buried with a Spanish strongbox."

Bernardo's eyes widened. "You think *she* is the person?"

"Yes. If my guess is correct, Cerba Martine was reunited with Imnit, the sister of the shaman Lukat."

11

At Sea

THE OVERTURNED DECK OF DIETRICH'S schooner, *Mirabeaux,* vaulted over Kellen's head. He clung to the shredded stump of the sailing vessel's broken mast and struggled to keep his eyes open, hoping to spot Dietrich, who had tumbled into the depths, arms and legs flailing.

Kellen had been spared the savage undertow, though the sea tore at his clothes and threatened to take him down.

Near Westport, believing they were still a half mile from shore, Kellen and Dietrich had encountered land where it shouldn't have been. Swells of ocean had suddenly churned into ragged peaks of wind-whipped spray as huge waves sixty yards off the bow curled and broke over rocks just below the waterline. Kellen realized the *Mirabeaux* wouldn't pass unscathed.

At the helm, Kellen had steered to port in order to lay the hull over, while Dietrich tried to secure the jib. But during Dietrich's attempt to subdue the sail, Kellen realized they couldn't avoid disaster. "We'll never make it, Dietrich. Get over here," he had shouted.

It was too late.

Mirabeaux's keel struck the reef, and the impact drove the yacht into a shuddering dive.

While Dietrich scrambled aft, the incline of the listing deck caused his canvas shoes to slip. He lost his footing and bellied spread-eagle, skidding like a haul of fish across the wet planking. Dietrich's weight snapped his harness safety line, and Kellen watched helplessly as his friend slammed into the starboard rail near the pulpit. Dietrich was able to snare the stainless steel bow rail with an outstretched hand and hung there with his legs dangling over the side, screaming in panic as *Mirabeaux* bumped and scraped across the rocks.

Kellen had tried to help him. Tying off the wheel, he had scrambled forward on all fours, trying to reach his friend. But the slippery deck tilted violently and suddenly Kellen was caught in a gravity shift. To avoid falling overboard, he lunged toward the nearest reliable handhold—the main mast.

Kellen grasped the polished wood cylinder at its base.

"Hold on," Kellen had shouted, hoping that when the yacht settled he might still reach Dietrich. But that's when the schooner's death roll began. With an ugly cracking sound, the twin-masted boat keeled over. The limp mainsail crashed into the ocean, causing the main mast above Kellen's head to snap like a twig. Through the surging brine, Kellen caught a glimpse of Dietrich's flailing arms as he was sucked away by the undertow, headed for the bottom.

The ocean won its tug-of-war, and Kellen was pulled from his perch. As he was yanked aft, he was snarled in the lines of the limp sail just below the surface. He couldn't breathe. Then he'd remembered the air in his life vest. With his left hand, Kellen reached around and found the hose nipple over his right breast. He loosed the small, clear nozzle from its mountings and, tucking his head to the side, clamped his teeth around the tiny hose. It was difficult to draw through the narrow tube, but Kellen tasted plastic as the air burst into his mouth.

Inhale, he thought as he worked to untangle the lines.

That's when a voice said, "Inhale this, sir."

Kellen took a breath of night air. He coughed, stifled by the sting of an ammonia pellet under his nose. He opened his eyes.

The crashing waves of Westport had disappeared. Under a dome of stars, a young Coast Guardsman knelt at Kellen's side. In the tranquility of a forested cove, Kellen lay on the foredeck of a Coast Guard cutter. He shook his head and pushed the inhaler away, wincing as a shaft of pain struck him behind the right eye.

"He's comin' around, Captain." The sailor glanced up at the officer.

"I believe this is yours, sir." The captain bent over and handed Kellen his dripping wallet.

"Did you find the *Mirabeaux*?" Kellen asked, raising his head. "Any sign of Dietrich?"

"The *Mirabeaux*?"

"Dietrich's boat—the *Mirabeaux*. She capsized."

"Where?"

"Off Westport."

"Westport? You're nowhere near Westport, sir. You've been in an accident aboard the *Tide Runner*. Whatever you guys hit stopped the boat dead."

Kellen's gaze followed the line that extended from the cutter out into the placid inky water, where the Boston Whaler's white hull was barely visible, bobbing silently in the bay.

"She didn't go down," the captain said. "Those old Whalers are tough to sink, just like they say. Lucky for you and Mr. O'Hearn."

Kellen looked around. "Is Paddy okay?"

"He's badly hurt. Below with the medics. We have a chopper due any minute to airlift him to the medical center. His right leg was crushed, and he's lost a lot of blood. He might have bled to death if you hadn't applied that tourniquet."

Dazed, Kellen touched the throbbing goose egg near his temple. "Tourniquet? I didn't—"

"You must have. I don't know how you did it, but when we came alongside, we found both you and Mr. O'Hearn lashed high on the prow, tied with those lines." The captain pointed to a mound of wet rope on the deck. "What about your Mayday? This business about being rammed?"

Returning memories from the night: The chase with the jet skis. The flash of bazooka fire from the lead rider. The explosion.

"There were six of them. They had guns." In response to the captain's blank stare, Kellen continued. "They were trying to kill us."

He had seen January flying through the air—the sheen on the young shaman's wet hair as the riders' headlights closed in.

"January." Kellen struggled to his knees.

"What?"

"A Native American kid. You didn't find him?"

"Just you two. That was it."

"What about the jet skis? They blew a hole in our boat."

The captain shrugged. "We'll have the boat towed and check it out. I had assumed you hit a log." He nodded toward the open water. "There's plenty of night drift out there. How do you know you didn't run over a dead head?"

"I saw the flash. Heard the explosion. I was thrown clear. But one of the jet skis ran me down. That's how I got this." Kellen pointed to the bump. "The last thing I remember . . . I was drowning."

"You were under?"

"Definitely. I got hit and sank like a rock."

"Then how did you get back to the boat?"

"I don't know. What did Paddy say?"

"Not a thing. He was in agony when we found you. We pumped him full of morphine the minute we had him on board. It was obvious he couldn't have helped you."

The captain glanced up as a helicopter engine sounded beyond the surrounding hills. Dawn had crept into the eastern skies.

The young sailor helped Kellen to a kneeling position as the captain continued. "How about this January guy? Could he have pulled you out?"

"I doubt it." The cut on his temple sent another stabbing pain.

The captain tried to steady him. "Why not?"

"Because the jet skis were after *him*. They blew up the boat to capture him."

"You're calling this an abduction?"

"Yes, goddamn it. And murder, if Paddy doesn't make it." On the shoreline, a lone light shone from a cabin in the hills. "I don't see how January could have escaped. They've taken him somewhere. Unless he drowned."

The rumble of a helicopter echoed in the cove. Its lights appeared over the horizon.

The captain helped Kellen to his feet. "When that chopper lowers its cage, why not follow Mr. O'Hearn aboard? Take a ride and check yourself in at the hospital." The captain pointed to the cut on Kellen's scalp. "Have that looked at. I'm sure things will clear up for you."

Kellen stumbled slightly as he tried to regain his balance. "I guess I haven't made much sense."

"We'll see." The captain shook his hand. "If you were thrown clear like you said, you must have swum back to pull your friend onto the hull. Somehow you secured yourself and kept Mr. O'Hearn from bleeding to death with that rawhide tourniquet."

"Rawhide?" Kellen stared into the captain's eyes. "You never mentioned it was rawhide."

"Didn't I? Why? Is that important?"

Kellen almost smiled.

12

Niagara Falls
Buffalo, New York

NIAGRA'S DRIZZLE DRENCHED THE WALKWAY. Trajan brushed a hand over his bald head and felt moisture gather under his palm. He leaned against the green railing and watched millions of gallons of water spill over the fall's jagged edge as he glanced over at Undersecretary John Preston. The thunderous roar of the waterfall would prevent potential audio surveillance of conversation between the two men. Words spoken farther than six feet away were completely unintelligible.

"A torrent," Undersecretary Preston said, referring to more than the waterfall. "That's why they call themselves AVALANCHE. They mean to crush us with their weight. And they may with sheer numbers. There might be several hundred by now: American-born, Canadian, or true immigrants. All dedicated to our destruction."

"So what else is new?" Trajan turned and glanced into Preston's limpid brown eyes.

"What's new is our inability to find them. When the media divulged our surveillance on phones and the net, they found ways to go underground. It slowed them a bit, but the ultimate result could be the same."

Preston's slight build invited Trajan's momentary fantasy of tossing him over the rail into the churning water. "Terrorists never change, Preston. They're our geopolitical bogeymen. They want to kill us all in our beds."

"But now they can."

The fantasy disappeared as Trajan's gaze fell on three CIA men fanned out just out of earshot to ensure Preston's safety.

"Did you hear me? They can actually do it." Preston cupped his hand to Trajan's ear and spoke up. "Wei Ling, a Chinese double agent, divulged the whole thing during interrogation. The Chinese sold the Isis contingent of AVALANCHE a detonator small enough to atomize anthrax bacteria. It's what your Irinia Malenchek saw during her last session with Epstein—a prototype of the goddamned bomb."

"I understand."

"By now Abbas and Rahid may have distributed hundreds of miniature spray heads, each one capable of flushing anthrax over several hundred square yards. That's Chinese ingenuity."

"Borrowed from us. Thanks to your administration's soft touch on our Chinese trading partners. You're doing business with the enemy."

"Chinese policy was established during the Bush years. Yours is a naïve view of international economics."

"Is it? You're the ones with your ass in a sling, allowing China access to your technologies. And now it's coming back to bite you in the balls."

"I'm not going to debate this with you. You have a job to do."

"Okay. What's the last known destination?"

"According to Wei, the bacteria was shipped to Canada last month. Anthrax in one load—detonators in another. The detonators are small, pressurized containers like a CO_2 tube, attached to a tiny spray head. The question is, are the heads and pouches to be assembled before or after they enter this country?"

"What's your guess?"

"Each has its advantages. If the terrorists assemble in Ontario and bundle the loads in individual backpacks," Preston pointed west, "one night AVALANCHE personnel could simply stroll across the border between here and Montana. On the other hand, that increases the odds that one of them might be caught. If it were me, I'd transport the anthrax in one shipment and assemble closer to the attack date."

"Which is?"

"We just don't know. Maybe two weeks away."

"Your border security is a joke."

"I agree. But we can't station a man every fifty paces for fourteen hundred miles. They're bound to get in. After they do, they'll stash their little bombs in airport lockers, train stations, or litter bins on Madison Avenue. You realize what that means? AVALANCHE sets their timers, and hours or even days later—*bam*. It won't be like the Boston Marathon. It'll be silent and deadly. People won't be aware of the infection until thousands of fatalities occur days later."

In response to Trajan's silence, Preston pushed on. "Washington is asking me to provide assurances."

Trajan continued to stare.

"Do you hear me, Trajan? Where do we stand?"

"We're close."

"With the young fellow out west? Epstein's super psychic?"

"He's a find. Probably better than Irinia."

"Excellent."

A cloud of water vapor from the Canadian side doused Trajan's face. He brushed several droplets from his thick eyebrows. After the debacle on Orcas Island, he had been about to recon with Calico and her people in Washington State. But Preston's urgent online request had arrived, just as Trajan was about to escort Bunny Hobbs from the Cincinnati hotel room.

"Well?" Preston prompted. "When does January start?"

"We had him cornered. We lost him last night."

"You . . . you fucked it up?"

The fantasy of tossing Preston returned.

"We're still tracking him. Epstein's about to use Formula 15 on other subjects to try and key in on the guy. After all, nothing works better than a psychic tracking a psychic."

"I thought the formula was too powerful for support people. Isn't it meant exclusively for a main trancer?"

"Normally."

"What if the others blow their minds like Irinia?"

"Irinia OD'd. She blew a circuit."

"How? Isn't 15 a natural derivative?"

"Fifteen different extracts."

"Fairly common herbal origins, as I understand it."

"Some are. Though Epstein didn't get ultimate results until he laced all that with a trace of lysergic acid diethylamide."

"LSD?" Preston asked.

Trajan couldn't suppress a wry smile. "Until he stabilized the ratios, he couldn't tell if subjects were giving accurate readings or just tripping. Timothy Leary would have enjoyed the ride."

"I find your flippancy inappropriate, given the circumstances."

Had Trajan carried through with throwing the smaller man over the rail, he would likely have gone unpunished; Trajan was much too valuable to the country's future. "All right. What exactly do you and the Defense Department expect me to say?"

"Something acceptable to the committee. Something reassuring. Epstein's incompetence with the Malenchek woman suggests his methods are grossly overrated. Secretary Ashland even hinted we try and reinstate the CIA program."

At the mention of the CIA, Trajan glanced over Preston's shoulder at the nearby agents. The threat of CIA intervention was probably a bluff, a futile coercion considering that the agency's work had been largely ineffective. Yet Trajan found himself uneasily seeking justification. "Secretary Ashland forgets that Epstein's results were conclusive. You saw what we did in Baltimore."

"You call incapacitating a valuable specimen 'conclusive'?" He was referring to Irinia again. "Now you're asking me to report we've also lost this guy . . ."

"January."

"I can't tell them that. Just find him."

Preston's body would bounce twice on the concrete bulkhead before splashing into the rushing torrent. "We have another candidate—a girl named Shelby Spilner. She was January's psychic conduit."

"His lover?"

"No, just a friend. She's a kid, for Christ's sake, about to turn thirteen. Epstein thinks that once she's under the formula, she may be able to locate January."

"May?" Preston shook his head. "That doesn't cut it. I'm running out of excuses, and I know Ashland. He'll insist that the Defense Department monitors Epstein. That means an efficiency expert present at all future experiments. Are you prepared for that?"

This time Trajan smiled broadly. "I'm prepared for any damn thing you throw at me, Preston. Remember that."

13

Orcas Island

BUFFETED BY LIGHT CROSSWINDS, THE Cessna 150 dropped through the wispy clouds between Orcas Island's emerald hills.

"Got yourself a pretty day," George Brennan said, grinning beneath his aviator shades as he guided the single engine two-seater through its final approach.

Lorna nodded without reply, trying to smile as she tucked her maroon scarf into her purse. The half-hour ride from Sea-Tac Airport was almost over.

"'Course there are no bad days here," Brennan continued as they touched down. He feathered the propeller, hitting the brakes. "Not on this chunk of granite. We're in the shadow of the Olympic Mountain range. Plenty of blue skies."

From all indications, Brennan was right.

As if heralding Lorna's arrival, the sun had peeked from behind the large mound of Mount Constitution and the tall grasses near the airport's perimeter glistened.

The West Isle plane decelerated, reaching the far end of the airfield, and Brennan guided the Cessna through its final turn toward the terminal.

A bright-orange windsock snapped cheerfully on a flagpole above a small, white rectangular building that Brennan explained served as both control tower and waiting room. Near its double glass doors, a green-and-white sheriff's car waited on the tarmac, glinting in the sun.

In a few moments, Lorna was to meet Deputy McMillan, who had agreed to pick her up.

She reached into her purse, opened her compact, and brushed her dark hair. In the small mirror, a pair of bloodshot hazel eyes stared back. She quickly donned a pair of sunglasses.

She had slept little on the flight from Chicago. After rushing through the brightness of the airport, Lorna had leaned back in her first-class seat aboard the nearly empty United 757, surrounded by the odors of carpet cleaner and jet fuel. The plane had launched into a thundercloud sky at 4:55 A.M., and as raindrops streaked across the jet's windows, rows of streetlights fell away below.

Lorna felt relieved. Whatever the outcome, she was on her way. As she had departed her office, she'd informed Skip that he would have to solve his own problems: if Chad had any issue with her, she would discuss her professional destiny with him—and only him. In the meantime, she was on a personal mission that took precedence over everything. Skip Van Hollenbeck and his megalomania were left behind. Ahead lay the uncertainty of Tracy's fight for survival and the predicament of trying to recover Shelby.

Lorna hadn't seen even a picture of them since a dog-eared Christmas card arrived three years ago—with a slightly blurred snapshot of straw-haired Tracy in a tank top and shorts, holding Shelby's hand as they stood in front of the Yosemite National Park Lodge. Only nine years old and pigeon-toed, little Shelby had worn braids, sandals, and jeans. Tracy had looked frail, almost anorexic, having recently undergone a traumatic escape from her abusive husband.

Brennan hit the brakes and the shuddering aircraft settled in the yellow circle designated for arriving flights. Immediately, the waiting police car's lights flashed and the vehicle rolled forward, covering two hundred feet in only a few seconds, coming to rest near the wing.

"Welcome to paradise, Ms. Novak," Brennan said as he leaned forward to switch off the Cessna's engine.

Paradise? Not likely. Lorna struggled with the passenger door.

"That's a bit sticky. Let me help you." Brennan's leather jacket creaked as he leaned across and released the handle. He vaulted out his own door, stepping under the fuselage to maneuver a small ladder into position so Lorna could deplane.

As she stepped onto the tarmac, a burly police officer with sunglasses and a mustache stepped from the car.

"Ms. Novak, I'm Deputy McMillan." He ushered her into the front seat of a two-toned Chevy cruiser. While Brennan tossed Lorna's suitcase into the trunk, McMillan slid behind the wheel and hit a button under the dash.

Lorna was startled as a siren blared.

"Sorry," McMillan said. "But you were a bit late, and we're in a hurry. Dr. Winston wants to speak to you prior to surgery."

"Surgery? You mean Tracy?"

"No, a boating accident. Winston might be in the OR by now, but we'll just have to get you there."

"How is she?"

McMillan glanced over as he guided the car through the airport gates. "She hasn't moved."

"You said when you found her . . . she was conscious?"

"For a minute. She never got the chance to really tell me what happened. She was in bad shape, and it took all her strength to ask for you."

Lorna swallowed hard and braced herself for what lay ahead.

McMillan turned left onto the street named Horseshoe Highway, and appropriately, several hooded horses grazed in a nearby pasture. Beyond, homes and churches dotted the emerald landscape. The town of Eastsound was visible to the east.

Lorna recovered her composure. "Any news about Shelby?"

"Not yet. But the whole community's up to speed. Understandably shocked. We take care of our own up here."

Not very well, Lorna thought. "Any suspects?"

"I doubt they were locals. They used a fine-edged cutting tool to cut through a kitchen window. That's not like our troublemakers. Our break-ins are usually kicked-in doors, busted windows, that sort of thing. These were mainland people."

"You think they're still around?"

"Unlikely. We've done our best to search the ferries and, as of this morning, screen departing planes."

"This morning? What about last night?"

"We didn't monitor air traffic before dawn. But don't worry, the only plane that left last night was a Learjet registered to the government."

"So Shelby might still be on the island."

"Could be. But maybe not. If I were trying to get off Orcas without being noticed, I'd boat. Not much problem picking someone up from shore. Difficult to check. We did notify the Coast Guard, but they were pretty busy last night with that accident I mentioned. They're looking for the girl now."

Lorna felt a growing frustration. "Why not search the island itself?"

"Twenty-six miles long. Six miles wide. Lots of forest. Plenty of rugged terrain." McMillan aimed the car through an intersection. "We have only four men. And unfortunately, other duties can't be ignored."

"Then what's your plan?"

"After twenty-four hours elapse, we'll call the FBI."

"Twenty-four hours? By then, she could be miles away." Lorna hadn't intended the remark to sound quite so caustic.

"We don't have a lot of personnel, Ms. Novak, but we get the job done."

Lorna had flown across two-thirds of the United States in just over four hours, and by tomorrow Shelby could be half a world away. "After I see Tracy I'd like to talk to your boss, whoever that is."

"Sheriff Bullard will be happy to explain things," McMillan said as the car pulled into the parking lot of a rambling one-story facility. "I'll take you to the station when you're ready."

The deputy escorted Lorna up a landscaped path and through the cedar-framed doors of the Orcas Island Medical Center.

The thin, gray-haired receptionist stood and extended a hand to Lorna. "We're glad you're here safely."

"Thank you." Lorna was surprised at the familiarity. It was as if her arrival had been courteously rehearsed.

"If you need me to arrange a room for you, I'd be happy—"

"You're very kind. Perhaps, after I see Tracy."

"Of course." The receptionist pointed down the hall. "Just follow Marilyn."

A friendly African American nurse in beige scrubs nodded to McMillan and introduced herself. "Hello, Ms. Novak, I'm Marilyn. We're keeping Tracy in room 22, the last room on this wing. It's nice and quiet. Dr. Crowley is with her."

"And Dr. Winston?"

"He'll be out to meet you."

As Marilyn led them down the hallway, Lorna glanced into the partially draped rooms. In room 14, a tall blond man with a bandaged forehead stood at the bedside of a bearded patient who moaned softly. When the taller man heard the three approaching, he looked out into the hallway. "Excuse me, Marilyn, I don't like the way Paddy looks," he said, obviously concerned "Could you get the doctor?"

"We'll be right with you, Kellen," Marilyn replied. She picked up the pace until they reached the end of the hall, where an older, silver-haired man in a white smock had stepped through a door. After glancing at a chart, he looked up and smiled.

"Dr. Winston," Marilyn said as she approached him, "the patient in room 14—"

Winston replied somewhat absentmindedly, "See to him, won't you, while I chat with Ms. Novak?"

"It sounds urgent."

"Isn't everything, Marilyn? Please tend to his needs. I'll be there momentarily."

Looking flustered, Marilyn strode away.

"This has been a particularly hectic morning, I'm afraid." Dr. Winston extended a delicate hand to Lorna. "You must be exhausted."

"I'm fine," Lorna replied, accepting his handshake. "How's Tracy?"

The doctor gave McMillan a nod. "Perhaps I could speak with Ms. Novak alone."

"Of course. I'll be in the lobby."

Winston patiently watched the officer depart. "Your sister is resting peacefully," he said as he ushered Lorna toward room 22. "But before we go in, I want to explain a few things."

"Is she worse?"

"She's stable. I just thought I should warn you that her condition might change at a moment's notice. Brain injuries, particularly those that affect the memory centers, are somewhat unpredictable. Those of us who pretend to understand the mechanics of the mind are, more often than not, confounded by its complexity. I try to expect surprises, both good and bad. Right now, Tracy is in a deep sleep, brought on by a bruise in the tissues that govern vital body functions. Are you familiar with the term 'hematoma'?"

"Yes, I think so."

"Well, that's essentially what she's suffered—an extensive injury. Whoever struck her wielded quite a force." Winston reached out and took her hand. "If she is to recover, the degree of damage that will remain is the question. She's suffered a subdural hemorrhage near the cerebellum, resulting in an obvious edema to the rear at the right lobe."

"Edema?"

"Swelling. The problem is that the blood hasn't evacuated the area. That's the body's way of protecting itself. But unfortunately, if left in the cavities around the bruise too long, blood eventually calcifies and hardens. At present we are allowing time for the blood to dissipate on its own. If that doesn't happen, we'll have to surgically ease the pressure."

"Surgery? When?"

"Elective surgery, properly stated. There are inherent dangers in probing near Tracy's occipital lobes. The operation could be quite risky."

"So how do we know what to do?"

"We watch. And wait. And pray that she comes around on her own. We don't want to chance blindness for the sake of rushing a procedure. *When and if* we operate may ultimately be your call."

"Can I see her?"

"Of course." Winston smiled reassuringly. "We're keeping her room quite dark to avoid any shock to her eyes should she open them." He led her toward the door. "And I want you to talk to her. Her daughter's disappearance, as unfortunate as it is, may be one way to force Tracy into awareness. Tell her she must awaken to find Shelby. Beg her to help. Tracy has to do most of the work. She has to *want* to come back to us—if for no other reason than for her daughter's sake. Your pleading that Tracy return to you is all a part of that. Make sense?"

It made agonizing sense. The words cut deeply. In light of their separation, it was ironic that the doctor had counseled Lorna to use their potential reunion as motivation for Tracy's recovery. Lorna heaved a heavy sigh.

"Come on, now." Dr. Winston squeezed her hand. "Hang tough. Are you ready?"

Lorna wiped the moisture from her eyes and nodded.

Winston pushed the door open. From the bright hallway, Lorna could see Tracy lying in the darkened room.

A large bandage covered the entire right side of her head.

Crowley—a balding, bespectacled doctor in his forties—sat in a metal chair at the head of the bed, bathed in the glow of a tiny pin light on the headboard.

"Hello," Crowley whispered as Lorna entered. "I haven't left her side. She's breathing easily, but we're constantly concerned about her vital signs."

Lorna could see why.

Tracy's face was etched in pain—her brow furrowed in frustration, her mouth twisted in a permanent frown.

Crowley stood up and made room for Lorna.

She eased into the chair at Tracy's bedside.

Dr. Winston gave a subtle nod to Crowley, who exited quietly.

"I'm going to have to leave you two alone for a while." Dr. Winston backed toward the door. "Crowley has other patients, and I need to check on our patient in room 14. He's been in a terrible accident."

Lorna couldn't fathom a situation more grave than Tracy's.

"Take Tracy's hand, touch her. Speak to her. Let her know you've arrived to support her."

Lorna's chin quivered slightly as she looked up into the hall lights. "I'm here, Dr. Winston, for as long as it takes."

Winston nodded and retreated through the door.

Lorna and Tracy were alone for the first time in over a decade. Lorna leaned over and placed a hand on Tracy's clammy forehead. Not a flutter from Tracy's eyelashes, which rested closed. No response at all. Just the gentle wheeze of her breathing.

The delicate child that Lorna had once known had morphed into this pale, broken shell, crushed by an assailant's blow.

"Tracy, what happened to us?" Lorna asked tearfully. "And why in God's name would someone do this to *you*?"

14

Benalmadena, Spain

ALESSANDRO VARGAS STEPPED FROM THE elevator onto the third-floor landing of his hacienda. He paused outside the great mahogany double doors and gazed over the stuccoed stone banister toward the harbor.

The high-rise condominiums and commercial buildings at dockside threw long shadows across the sea of masts tucked between piers of the Puerto Marina.

The dust of the day had settled in nearby alleys, and as tiny lights began to flicker, tourists and local boaters refreshed themselves in the hotels and yachts along the promenade. The faint sound of a dance band drifted up the hill.

To the north, the lights of his father's casino twinkled brightly. English words along the marquis boasted GAMBLING - ENTERTAINMENT - CUISINE, flashing aquamarine, red, and orange, oddly garish considering the casino's Castilian castle facade.

That afternoon, for the second time, he had checked his e-mail. Nothing from America. Alessandro had refused to hover by the computer and left that task to Bernardo.

He had taken a stroll through town wearing his chinos and a loose-knit sweater, passing the casino's glass double doors. As usual, he had nodded to Robert, the shift foreman, and walked on.

Alessandro had long ago exhausted his curiosity about parlor games. Nothing quite as boring as gamblers watching a small white ball bounce into the black, red, or green slots of a roulette wheel.

"Look at them," Alessandro once said to his father, Enrico, as they walked past the pits under the casino's crystal chandeliers. "All they want is to toy their lives away."

"Then blessed are we who provide them with trinkets," was Enrico's response.

Alessandro appreciated his father's accomplishments and understood his own hypocrisy. He'd been provided a life without challenges, yet he despised the banality of the rich. And rich Alessandro was—destined to inherit his father's ranches, shipping business, and the casino.

Still, Alessandro thirsted for intellectual pursuits. He dabbled with and sometimes seriously engaged in archaeology, joining expeditions to Malta and Crete. In 1999, he had rushed to the port city of Pisa, Italy, where several Roman sailing ships from the second century BC had been unearthed. He'd been fascinated with these forty-foot-long coastal freighters that had carried wine, olive oil, and grain. This dip into naval antiquity had led him to search for stories of his ancestors.

Like an archaeologist tracking the spoor of a lost tribe, Alessandro discovered that his father's forte in shipping was well founded. The Vargas family tree was adorned with sea captains who had lived during Spain's greatest exploratory era. Having never crewed on a ship, Alessandro was nevertheless struck by the romance of men who sailed the sea—more enticing than careers of men who merely exported goods. He began to document the life of the last of that line, Captain Roberto Ravilla and Cerba Martine, the first mate whose letter described Ravilla's distress and ultimate suicide.

The most recent Martine-Ravilla clue was to be the subject of an e-mail printout that Bernardo now waved as Alessandro returned to his hacienda.

"David Fraley?" Alessandro asked.

"His reply is disappointingly brief." Bernardo handed the sheet to Alessandro. "Nothing about the strongbox."

The paper carried a simple message:

Remains found on Orcas will be claimed by the American Indian Tribal Council for proper interment after being examined by Steven Hargrove of the Seattle Archaeological Board. Fraley

"What time is it in Seattle right now?"

Bernardo stared at him blankly.

"Never mind. It must be early afternoon." Alessandro was on his way to his library. "Get Fraley on the phone . . . try the museum on Orcas Island or a home number."

Bernardo strolled to the house phone and dialed while Alessandro walked down the hall. By the time Alessandro had reached the leather-bound desk, the ivory phone with the gold handle was already pulsing on hold with the call that Bernardo had made. Alessandro picked up the receiver. "Dr. Fraley?" He spoke with the delicate accent he had acquired at Oxford.

"It is."

"This is Alessandro Vargas. I hope you don't mind that I called."

"Of course not, Mr. Vargas. But I had answered your e-mail."

"Yes, I've received your somewhat limited reply."

"I apologize if you found it brief, but there was no more to say. As I mentioned, Dr. Hargrove has taken possession of the find."

"How do I reach Hargrove?"

"In Seattle. At the University of Washington."

"Do you have his phone number?"

An awkward silence followed, and Fraley cleared his throat. "I didn't mind your curiosity at the onset, Mr. Vargas. And I even found it somewhat intriguing to communicate with you overseas . . ." Fraley wheezed as if he were struggling with asthma. "But now with Hargrove involved, I'm forced to ask what you hope to gain by this inquiry?"

"Purely personal. One of my ancestors explored your San Juan Islands. Do you remember the name Ravilla?"

"Not offhand."

"He sailed under Admiral Panjota."

"I see."

"I have reason to believe that the Spanish strongbox unearthed with the corpse proves that the Indian woman's remains were linked to Ravilla."

"How could you possibly assume that?"

"Through my research here in Spain."

Fraley coughed and recovered, forcing the words. "We believe the remains are roughly two hundred years old, which would have been around Panjota's time. But due to the complications involved, Dr. Hargrove took responsibility."

"Complications?"

"Local politics you might say. Stemming from the condition of the body.

A local Indian Council engaged in an unrelated fishing dispute chose to make these remains an example."

"I don't understand."

"The woman's skull showed extensive damage, cleaved through the frontal lobe. Since the strongbox was buried alongside, it seemed to indicate—"

"That she was murdered?"

"Yes. By white explorers." Fraley coughed again. "Though the nationality of the explorers remains in question."

"Wasn't it a *Spanish* strongbox? Do the contents indicate otherwise?"

"Actually, yes."

"Well, what then?"

"I apologize, Mr. Vargas. I really shouldn't discuss these matters without checking with Hargrove."

Angered by the evasion, Alessandro made an impulsive decision. "As a businessman who shares your interest in archaeology, Dr. Fraley, I make it a habit to contribute to institutions like yours. Or Dr. Hargrove's for that matter. I understand your position, but I've decided to visit your island and bring you a sizable donation . . . provided you allow me access to specific information. Would that suit you?"

Fraley breathed the words, "We're just a tiny museum, sir."

"You must have needs."

"Of course."

"So ten thousand dollars might prove useful?"

"I—"

"Ten when I arrive, and another ten if I'm satisfied with your cooperation. What would you say?"

"I'm afraid this is somewhat irregular."

"Exactly." Alessandro enjoyed the appeasement that had crept into Fraley's voice. "Personally, I prefer spontaneity over predictability, don't you? Would you be shocked if I said I could identify the Indian woman you unearthed?"

"What?"

"Sharing further information might be beneficial to both of us, don't you agree?"

"I suppose. But if you intend to see the remains, you don't have much time. The Indian Council is demanding the bones be interred by this Friday."

Alessandro cupped his hand over the phone and shouted downstairs.

"Bernardo, book an overnight flight to Seattle, immediately." He returned to the phone conversation. "If it's so urgent, you better tell me what was in the box."

Another long silence.

"Doctor, I've promised you ten thousand dollars."

"A parchment, very faded."

"A letter?"

"No. What appears to be a mathematical equation. And a few faded lines. Nothing meaningful. There *is* a date . . ."

"The date of the entry?"

"I suppose that's what it is—June 21—as well as a rather odd word at the bottom of the page."

"A Spanish word?"

"No. That's why we questioned its nationality. It was in English, which dates the strongbox slightly later."

"What is the word?"

"Calm."

"Calm? As in peaceful?"

"Precisely."

"Spelled C-A-L-M?"

"Yes."

Alessandro was struck by the irony—what he'd heard hadn't made him calm at all. On the contrary, he felt a flush of excitement. "That's incredible. Exactly what I'd hoped. You can expect me tomorrow."

"You can't be serious. What on earth is the significance?"

"I'll share that with you when I hand you my check."

15

Orcas Island Medical Center

IN THE STILLNESS OF THE darkened hospital room, Lorna attempted the awkward reunion with her stepsister. Shrouded by a blue cotton curtain, Lorna sat on a small leather-capped stool at the head of Tracy's bed. She leaned on the crisp white sheets, amid the aroma of starch and rubbing alcohol.

Tracy lay faceup with a clear plastic oxygen mask over her mouth and nose, her left wrist punctured by an IV. She hadn't moved, though her chest still rose and fell in an uneven rhythm.

At Dr. Winston's suggestion, Lorna had spoken to Tracy in simple phrases as if she were addressing a child who might not understand.

As time wore on, she began to converse in a more relaxed manner, assuring Tracy that she would be all right. "Come back to me," she said. "Please wake up so we can hug each other. I've missed you. I don't know where the years have gone, but we have to make up for lost time."

A trace of moisture had formed at the corner of Tracy's left eye. Perhaps she was hearing every word. Holding on to this hope, Lorna leaned in and placed her hand on Tracy's cheek.

Tracy's open mouth hung limp, sucking air from the mouthpiece.

Just under Tracy's lower lip, still visible through the plastic sheath, was a crooked, almost imperceptible scar. The injury had happened one evening when Tracy and Lorna had been playing in the deep shade of the apple orchard behind Aunt Trudie's farmhouse. Lorna's mother, Ann, had called them to dinner, and the two girls had burst into the sun, running across the pasture.

"If I beat you to the porch, you're an ugly pig," Lorna had shouted, getting a jump on Tracy, who had squealed with delight in their rush through the grass. Tracy was an agile little thing but lacked Lorna's long legs. As Lorna rounded the corner of the woodshed, Tracy was twenty feet behind, cutting through the chicken pens. She stumbled on the black hose connecting the water pump to the feed troughs and fell headlong into a roll of chicken wire. A small section under Tracy's lower lip was rent into the pattern of a small "V" after her face struck the wire's ragged edge. Ann was there in a flash and whisked Tracy away to a doctor's office for stitches.

Lorna leaned in to catch a closer look through the oxygen mask. The only evidence remaining of the childhood incident was a narrow furrow below the softness of Tracy's lip.

A soft knock interrupted Lorna's memories. A man of medium build in a gray sweatshirt peered through the crack of the door. He had a comforting expression on his unshaven face, as if he were petting a dog. Deep, dark eyes glistened from under a generous shock of brown hair.

"May I come in?" he asked.

"I think you have the wrong room."

"I don't believe so. I recognize Tracy. You must be her sister." The man stepped into the room in, revealing soiled jeans, dirty tennis shoes, and a few holes in his sweatshirt.

"Excuse me," Lorna said. He was quite obviously not a member of the medical staff. "Who are you?"

"Oh, how thoughtless of me. I'm Reverend Pelto. I've known Tracy for several months now."

"Reverend?" Lorna gave Pelto the once-over.

"I know I don't look the part. Many of us don't here on the islands. I was just over at the camp, talking to the kids. I spend a great deal of time there . . . it's quite rewarding." Pelto shuffled over to the other chair by the sink. "Do you mind?"

She did. "If you'd like."

As Pelto pulled the chair forward, the metal casters squeaked on the linoleum floor. Lorna suddenly feared the noise would wake Tracy, and then she realized how perfect that would be.

"Sorry." Pelto seemed to read her thoughts. "Though I guess we could do with a little noise in here."

Lorna smiled. "That's what they tell me."

Pelto peered at Tracy's face. "Any change?"

"No."

"A tragic thing. With Shelby. And Tracy. Yet . . ." he paused, blinking several times. "She looks at peace." Pelto nodded, as if affirming the statement for himself. "But you." Pelto fixed his dark gaze on Lorna. "Sometimes it's the one who waits who feels the most pain."

"Don't worry about me."

"Well, I can't help my concern. After what Dr. Crowley told me, I felt obligated to offer my assistance."

"Told *you*? What exactly is your capacity here?"

"I'm Tracy's pastor."

Lorna was genuinely surprised. Like Lorna, Tracy had never been a frequent churchgoer. "I don't remember her having a religious affiliation."

"She still doesn't."

"Come again?"

"It's nondenominational. The Lord's church. I hold a service under the pines at West Beach."

"So no—"

"Building? No. None needed. Brick and mortar serve little purpose. Walls keep the people out, and you can't keep the Holy Ghost in. In any case, as I said, after speaking with Crowley, I felt it best—"

"Best?" Lorna felt a twinge of panic. "Why? What exactly did Dr. Crowley tell you?"

"That her time of need is at hand. Her fate rests with the angels."

"Are you suggesting that she's . . . ?"

Pelto shifted in his chair, suddenly uncomfortable. "I only mean to put things into perspective. As with fine sculpture, to recognize the artist's work, we must look past the coldness of the stone. Naturally, I pray for Tracy's recovery, but it's best to prepare for contingencies."

"I'm sure you have the best intentions." Lorna felt the heat rising in her face. "But what were you expecting exactly? That I would welcome the idea of discussing her funeral? Is that why you're here?"

"I came to ease the burden."

"I apologize, Father Pelto—"

"Reverend, please."

"I didn't travel all this way to bury my sister, Reverend. If it becomes inevitable, so be it. But I'd rather not discuss it until she's cold." Lorna rose to her feet.

"I'm afraid you don't understand."

"Maybe so. I'm tired and upset, so please indulge me. I'm sure you mean well." Lorna walked to the door and opened it. "But for now, I'd appreciate it if you'd go back to your pine needle cathedral and leave us alone."

Somewhat off-balance, Pelto retreated. "All right, if that's how you feel." He set off toward the reception desk but then looked back. "You can always call on me."

Lorna nodded then saw the nurse passing. "Excuse me, Marilyn, is it?"

"Yes."

"Would you help with a few concerns?"

"If I can."

"Good. First, for the time being, I don't want Tracy to have visitors." It was said loud enough for the reverend to hear.

"Yes, of course."

Pelto had turned and was wandering off toward the lobby.

"And I want to know if Tracy had any personal belongings on her when she was brought in."

"All right. Anything else?"

"Yes. I need to see Dr. Crowley immediately."

16

Orcas Island

KELLEN COAXED PADDY O'HEARN'S ANCIENT VW van up the ribbon of highway known as Crow Valley Road. Not having a car of his own, Kellen had decided to retrieve Paddy's rig from the West Sound Marina while he dealt with the fallout from the last night's crime.

The brutality of the boating attack was still on Kellen's mind, though today, the beauty of the island belied pessimism. Late spring had arrived. Grassy lowlands glowed with wildflowers. Beyond, surrounding mountains were etched by groves of lush evergreens. Across the valley, several chestnut horses cavorted in a field—manes flashing auburn as they raced along the shore of a pond, scattering flocks of white geese into the cattails.

The sight should have cheered Kellen, but his mind was still back at the medical center where he'd left Paddy, pale as death when he'd come out of the anesthetic.

Coughing as he woke, Paddy had tried to sit up in bed, but Kellen had restrained him.

"What have they done to me?" Paddy asked.

Gazing out from under his bandaged forehead, Kellen had difficulty finding the words. "They . . . saved your life."

Paddy craned his neck, wincing as he tried to reach down. "My leg. What happened—?"

"Paddy." Kellen caught the searching hand, pinning it to the sheet. "It's gone. They were forced to take it."

"Mary, Mother of Jesus. All of it?"

"Pretty much."

Paddy's eyes grew wide with panic. "You mean I'm, I'm handicapped? I can't man my boat like this." He began to blink uncontrollably as the realization hit him. "What about the *Tide Runner*? What happened to her?"

"She didn't sink. They towed her in."

"But she's ruined, isn't she?" Tears began to streak Paddy's beard.

"She's badly broken up." Kellen squeezed his hand. "I'll make her right for you, I promise."

Paddy coughed again and began to have difficulty breathing.

Kellen knew the pallor of Paddy's usually ruddy cheeks was abnormal. That's when he had called to Marilyn, who was escorting a smartly dressed woman down the hall. Marilyn appeared torn between helping Paddy and attending to the woman in the tan leather jacket. But after a few moments, Marilyn reappeared.

Seeing Paddy's agitated condition, she pulled a syringe from the nearby cabinet and plunged it into Paddy's IV.

"Will that knock him out?" Kellen had asked.

"Oh, yes. He should sleep most of the day."

Kellen's investigative instincts surfaced. While Marilyn took Paddy's pulse, he leaned in and captured Paddy's ear. "Paddy, I need to jog your memory—just for a few more minutes. All right?"

"Whatever you like," Paddy said, defeated.

"January spoke of his grandmother. Do you remember?"

"Yes."

"What's the woman's name?"

"I don't know."

"Who would know? Someone in town that knew the family?"

Paddy's eyes were glazed. "Molly maybe. Molly Creed."

"Good. Thanks for that. Now, I want to report everything to the sheriff, and I need your perspective. Try to remember what happened out there last night, after the crash."

"Happened?"

"Did you see January?"

"No. I saw you," Paddy mumbled.

"Where?"

"Tied to the prow with me. You were unconscious. I woke up and my leg hurt so bad, I passed out again."

Kellen leaned down and whispered, "If I was out and you were unconscious, how did we get onto the prow?"

Kellen tried to visualize how it had been physically possible for January to rescue both of them while the jet-ski nightriders circled the wreckage. "Was it January? Do you remember him being there?"

"All I remember is . . . I used to have two good legs."

The Valium must have suddenly hit hard, mercifully numbing Paddy's mind. He whimpered for a few seconds and, turning his face to the wall, fell into a drug-induced slumber.

As Kellen manipulated the clutch pedal of Paddy's old V-dub, it occurred to him that Paddy would probably never drive the van again. Dr. Winston had removed the better part of Paddy's right leg. All that was left was a six-inch stump below the hip. Paddy driving a vehicle with a standard shift would be out of the question. Aside from driving, other simple tasks required two good legs. Paddy was right: a man without sufficient balance would have difficulty operating a small boat. And with fishing being Paddy's means of survival, his life would never be the same.

Kellen felt a rush of anger. The men responsible were out there, and the cops couldn't find them.

With his cell phone beyond repair, Kellen had used the hospital's pay phone to ring the sheriff's office. He had been sharing details of the crime with the dispatcher when he saw Deputy Frank McMillan walking toward the lobby. Kellen cut the conversation short and rushed to catch up with Frank, who took down the information. He seemed pessimistic about finding the marauders, and Kellen understood why: the details were too sketchy. Men in wet suits riding jet skis. Height, weight, color of eyes . . . unspecified. Nevertheless, McMillan promised to notify the authorities on neighboring islands in case skis on trailers were spotted.

As Kellen pulled into his home community of Beach Haven, he vowed to reconstruct last night's incident more efficiently. Rolling down the gravel-covered lane, his cabin's mossy front porch came into view. Kellen was struck by all that had occurred. A scant twelve hours ago, Paddy had stood on these front steps trying to convince Kellen to leave. In the relatively short span of time that followed, Kellen had witnessed what appeared to be a supernatural spectacle, he'd rescued January from drowning, Paddy had been maimed for life, and January had been abducted after somehow saving Kellen.

Kellen halted the van near the gnarled stump that dominated his fern-covered front yard. He killed the engine and got out. Peace. Not a sound in the forest.

The cabin's shake roof was dappled with sunlight that played through the pine tree canopy. Wild rabbits sat motionless in the long grasses near the driveway. A hundred yards beyond, thickets of raspberry and scotch broom framed the deep blue of the President's Channel. Two miles north the jet skis had given chase.

Kellen stepped onto his porch. Three delicate lime-green frogs scrambled across the cedar planking. He reached over the doorjamb to retrieve the large black spare key. As he inserted it in the keyhole, he found no resistance. The key turned much too easily.

Kellen stooped and examined the metal casing.

Scratches.

Someone had stripped the lock, breaking the tumblers within. Fearing the worst, Kellen pushed the door open and his heart sank. His favorite rocking chair lay shattered by the river rock fireplace. The sheepskin rug near the hearth had been kicked into the corner. Books from the shelves under the window seat were scattered in disarray. Papers from his teakwood rolltop desk lay on the floor.

Someone had ransacked the place.

He rushed to the window seat and reached up under the shelves. He had loosened a panel to conceal his GLOCK 9mm pistol, complete with its seventeen-shot clip. It was still there, hidden in the depression of the woodwork. He cocked the weapon and turned to survey the rest of the room. He felt violated . . . and suddenly concerned for his cat.

Kellen walked on tiptoe through the living room and peered into the kitchen. The small square door of the black potbelly stove stood ajar. Someone had opened the silverware drawer. The cleansers beneath the sink lay askew, visible through the open doors of the cabinet.

In the corner near the Dutch door, Long John's feeding bowl sat empty.

Kellen swung the top half of the door open and gazed out into the backyard near the thicket, where he hoped to catch sight of striped charcoal fur. Nothing. Just a depression in the grasses that marked Long John's favorite spot.

When Kellen first found the starving tabby in the woods behind the cabin, the cat's skittish behavior seemed to indicate it had been abused. Long John would cower at an inadvertently raised hand. Loud sounds were intolerable. Kellen had dropped a saucepan one night, and the cat had disappeared for half a day. Long John sought affection so desperately that Kellen's heart went out to the little rascal. Kellen preferred to not think about how the animal had lost an eye, but he'd named the cat Long John after Long John Silver. As he'd gained the cat's trust, he and Long John had comforted each other. Healing became their bond. Perhaps because he himself had been rejected, Kellen expressed his sympathy for all things lost and suffering by loving that mangy cat. The thought of the animal being hurt wrenched his gut.

"Long John?"

Not a sound. "God. Don't tell me . . ." He glanced into the neighboring trees. If the intruders had tried to harm the cat, they would have scared him off. He might be hundreds of yards from the house. Even farther. Unless he'd hidden inside.

With his gun at the ready, Kellen turned back through the kitchen and checked the bedroom. No sign of trespassers or the cat. "Come on, you old puss. Where are you?" Tucking the gun in his belt, he fell to his knees and peered under the four-poster bed.

As he stood, he noticed that his dresser drawers were open. His clothes were missing.

He opened the closet door.

His shirts were gone. No pants hung on the hangers save two pairs of jeans.

He hadn't just been vandalized—he'd been robbed.

AS KELLEN RACED TO THE sheriff's office, both he and the VW engine overheated. He'd broken the speed limit all the way from Beach Haven. Someone had invaded his sanctuary and perhaps harmed his cat, and he was now convinced that last night's harassment and the break-in were connected. It was unnerving to think that the jet skiers knew where he lived, while he knew virtually nothing about them. His old FBI instincts reawakened, and he began to formulate a plan—how he might scour the community for clues.

After driving a few more miles, he realized the truth. He was a civilian now. He could aid in fact-gathering, but realistically, the investigation was a job for the police. All he could do was see that they did their job.

The sheriff's blue cinderblock building came into view near the airport, and Kellen pulled into the gravel parking lot under the American flag, bringing Paddy's van to a dusty stop.

Cloaked in the smell of burning rubber, he marched toward the office ready to launch into his complaint, but after he opened the blue metal door, he froze.

The striking woman he'd seen at the medical center stood among the desks, visibly angry as she lashed out at Sheriff Bullard.

"Stop calling me 'Ms. Novak,'" she protested. "If you're going to patronize me, call me Lorna."

"All right, *Lorna*. I'll say it again. We're doing what we can."

"Not nearly enough." She gestured to McMillan who leaned against the water cooler. "The deputy's been quite accommodating, but I need *help*, not courtesy. Why the hell aren't both of you out there, right now, searching for her?"

"Our neighboring islands have been notified—"

"Understood. But I want *this* island searched."

"Ms. . . . Lorna." Bullard threw Kellen a sidelong glance. "We don't have the manpower."

"Then raise it. If you won't, I will. I'll turn this town upside down if I have to . . . post Shelby's picture on every street corner."

Shelby.

The name that January had mentioned.

Kellen stepped inside and eased the door closed.

The woman's eyes flared with conviction as she made a move toward the phone. "Give me the number, and I'll call the FBI myself."

"Who's Shelby?" Kellen edged into the room.

"Hold your water, Kellen," the sheriff said, a bit gruffly. "We called the FBI's Seattle field office. They'll be monitoring the case."

"'Monitoring?' What does that mean?" Lorna asked. "Are they showing up or not?"

Bullard hooked his thumbs into his belt. "Well, they may not, particularly if there's no evidence that Shelby was taken across state lines."

"Is that the criterion?"

Bullard shrugged. "I'm afraid so."

"They make exceptions," Kellen countered.

Lorna whirled and faced him. "I would hope so. Every second counts." Her hazel eyes, now intense and piqued with curiosity, fixed on his. “What do you know about all this?”

“Mr. Rand has no official capacity here, Ms. Novak,” Bullard piped up from the background. “He’s . . . he’s . . .”

“I’m on extended leave,” Kellen said, somewhat distracted, struck by Lorna’s captivating glance.

“Really?” she asked, stepping closer. “It so happens, I am as well.”

17

Sitnalta Security Facility
Badlands National Park, South Dakota

TRAJAN LIT A CIGARETTE AND leaned against the heavy plate-glass window, looking into the soothing blue light that washed the orientation chamber. Sounds within were cushioned, deadened by the room's padded blue velveteen walls, though Epstein's indoctrination music could be heard through the speakers. Strains of Mozart's Piano Concerto in A Major nearly masked the whimpering of the child on the examination table.

Trajan's view was partially blocked by Nurse Haupt's narrow back, but Shelby's blue jeans and black sneakers kicked nervously. Her blonde hair drooped below the crook of Dr. Epstein's arm. He appeared to have a gentle hold on the girl's shoulders.

"I'm going to roll up your sleeve now, honey," Nurse Haupt said. "That's a good girl."

Shelby Spilner's protest followed, "I don't want a shot." She sat up enough for Trajan to see her freckled face. She had attempted to cross her arms, but Epstein restrained her.

"Come on, this will make you feel happy," Epstein said.

"How long do I have to stay here?" Her thick blonde eyelashes blinked away tears.

"Just a short time," Epstein replied. "When you finish your dreaming, you'll be sent home."

"To my mom?"

"Yes."

"Mom's hurt. That man hurt her."

"The man had to keep her quiet, but she's feeling better now. She's resting."

Lies. There had been many, and there would be more. Participants in the program were told that they would be allowed to return home after their work was finished. They were promised huge sums of money. They were usually kept for a breakdown period and brainwashed and then released when their brain implants fully healed. Some were never heard from again. Those who remained were told that graduates of the program had been paid well and had become part of a government witness protection program, reindoctrinated into society. The mentally challenged, like Irinia Malenchek, were presumably taken off base for recuperation, though those left behind had no way of knowing whether *that* was a lie. They were under constant, gentle sedation . . . their food was laced with Lipithral, a mood-altering drug. TMC telepaths were kept amiable and content, until their lab sessions, when they were taken off Lipithral and given Quadrilin, a medication that promoted necessary levels of lucidity for group linkage and remote viewing.

Epstein had defended his methods to Trajan and coined a phrase that Trajan recalled frequently: "In a time of widespread insanity," the doctor had said, "there are no prisoners, just casualties."

Shelby squealed as Nurse Haupt's needle sank into her shoulder. A few more whimpers and the girl fell silent. Mozart still piped through the system.

Epstein gave Haupt some last minute instructions. In spite of their low voices, Trajan discerned that Shelby was to be prepped to receive a Formula 15 injection, a process that required shaving the nape of the neck. By tomorrow, she would be taken to the test lab to become familiarized with the Epstein's procedure. The final step would be her debut in the ERVC, the Extended Remote Viewing Chamber, where she would be assisted by other trancers.

Epstein looked back toward the one-way glass, perhaps noticing the glow of the cigarette in the darkened viewing room. With his eyes unfocused, he addressed Trajan's general location. "If you're in there, Trajan, meet me outside in the garden."

Trajan snuffed his cigarette in a sandstone ashtray and retreated to the rear of the observation booth. Exiting, he walked down the corridor past the armed guard at the east door. Trajan donned his sunglasses and stepped into the blazing heat.

A fine layer of wispy clouds had formed over the Badlands.

Mounds of colored earth—auburn, beige, even silver and black—streaked the buttes and mesas around the Sitnalta Security Facility.

Trajan entered a small recreational area landscaped with prickly pear, crushed rock, and a gushing fountain, the spot often used by the twelve medical staff members on coffee breaks.

Four hundred yards in the distance, guard towers manned by TMC agents marked the perimeter of the compound, which had been classified by the Pentagon as a missile test site.

Trajan quickly found shade near an imported Saguaro cactus as Epstein appeared, strolling out yet another metal door, from the patient ward. He joined Trajan in the shadow. "So Preston wants you to check on me?"

"No. Coming here was my idea." Accompanied by Bunny Hobbs, Trajan had had his Learjet touch down in Rapid City, eighty-five miles to the west.

"Well it's good to see you any time, though you look like hell," Epstein said, apparently amused. "Of course, you're one of the few people who takes pride in that."

An odd comment from a man whose face was ravaged by pockmarks. Epstein was one of the least attractive men of his generation. His frizzy, coal-black hair crowned his head like a scouring pad pushed off to one side. When he was out of earshot, Calico had referred to him as "Dr. Bed-head."

Trajan nodded toward the lab. "What's with Shelby? Does she have it or not?"

"Shelby's understandably immature, though her early tests show acute sensitivity. With any luck, she'll develop quickly. The moment we have a read, you'll be the first to know. Keep your people ready."

"How soon?"

"By the time you arrive in Seattle, she'll be in the tank."

"I'm not going to Seattle."

"Why?"

"Because Preston is due here as well. I have to greet him when he arrives."

"God, what is this?"

"He's threatened to become our efficiency expert. Pressure from Capitol Hill. Threats that the CIA wants to get involved."

"Doesn't he realize how ineffective the CIA programs were?"

"It might not be up to Preston anymore. There are signs the Defense Department may cave in and confiscate your psychic pool."

Epstein began to perspire freely. "Has Preston read my brief on neurobiological suspension?"

"I didn't ask."

“Have him read it. The CIA’s sessions were pseudohypnotic. This business of sinking into an alpha state and vaulting through time tunnels was fanciful nonsense. Most of their subjects were manic depressives who would hallucinate after a glass of wine.”

“I understand.”

“No, really, it’s a matter of record. Their accuracy was a joke. Remember? They placed Muammar Gaddafi six hundred miles off target. And if the CIA’s work during the Iranian hostage crisis was so effective, why no rescue?”

“Karl, I don’t need to be sold. Please calm down.”

“Nothing works like Formula 15. Look at Irinia. She placed Abbas in Baltimore, down to fifteen twenty-six, the number on the apartment building. And when you and Calico got there, you stepped into the very room where Rahid had received the anthrax. You said it yourself—the floor was covered with his cigar butts. The ashes were still warm, for Christ’s sake.”

“No argument. But Preston’s a nervous geek, and we have to perform.”

“We will. Shelby can pinpoint January. All *your* people have to do is catch him for a change.”

“Impertinence noted.”

Epstein’s gaze was now firmly riveted on the fountain. “I mean no disrespect. It’s just that all this is—”

“I’ll tell you exactly what *this* is.” Trajan pointed to the distant guard towers, feeling the surge of his ultimate power over Epstein. “It’s a playground I created for you. If I cave in to Preston, you lose it. The Estonian woman was your ace. And *you* blew it—literally, blew out her brain.”

“But she had a—”

“You’re not hearing me. This could be your last shot.”

“You mean they’re going to pull the plug?”

“Not if you put things together. When Preston arrives and sits in that observation booth, Shelby better nail her Indian soul brother.”

Epstein’s eyes darted from Trajan’s face to the guard towers. “What about this FBI guy? The one who rescued January?”

“Ex-FBI. We checked him out. Searched his house. A has-been. No official connection. Calico and Stooch are tracking him. If he gets in the way, we’ll snuff him.”

18

Eastsound
Washington

"I DON'T UNDERSTAND." LORNA KICKED the gravel. "Not a clue."

"Something will turn up." Kellen focused on the red scarf, tied loosely around her smooth neck. Lorna's creamy-white skin had flushed nearly as crimson as the fabric.

"That's not what I mean." Lorna pointed toward the sheriff's office, forty feet across the parking lot. "I mean they don't *have a clue* how this feels." Her eyes flashed emerald in the midday sun. "I'm doing nothing—*nothing*—for Tracy as she lies in that bed." Her gaze wandered off to the distant mountains, where a flock of turkey buzzards circled. "And to imagine the agony that Shelby must be—" The last word caught in her throat as she choked back tears.

Earlier she'd asked about the bandage on his forehead, and he had told her briefly about his boating accident but hadn't mentioned January's emphasis about warning Shelby. He was still trying to gauge whether he should tell her, when her desperation rekindled his own anger. "I'll help you," he said.

"What?" She pierced him with a searching glance.

He stepped closer, realizing the obligation, but still went headlong into it. "I'll do anything I can."

"But the police, they—"

"They're a decent bunch. I know those guys. But they have their procedures. I don't."

"You?"

He shrugged. "Yes. I know what it takes. I carried a badge."

"Is that what they meant in there? You're a cop?"

"Of sorts. FBI, actually." Suddenly memories from the Cleveland field office closed in—dark hallways and dark looks from associates, and air, heavy with tension. "I retired. A couple of years back."

"My God, then you could call the Seattle FBI office and explain."

"They won't care. It's not a case yet."

She jammed both hands onto her hips. "What do you mean, *yet*? Have them examine Tracy."

"This minute, every city in the country has a bludgeoned woman on a fresh police blotter, Lorna."

"And a missing child?"

"There are thousands upon thousands of missing persons every year. Law enforcement agencies are forced into a certain protocol to segregate their duties. The FBI specializes mainly in cases that affect national welfare."

"How reassuring."

"Please understand, I'm no longer official. That's a plus. I can move outside the normal circles to help you."

Her eyes brightened at the suggestion. "You'd do that?"

He was nodding, all the while digesting the consequences. Was he willing to again be responsible for someone else's survival? "I think we can help each other. Makes sense if we're both involved."

"What do you mean both? How are you mixed up in all this?"

"Well, in addition to trashing my cabin and damn near killing Paddy, I think the men who were after January may have something to do with Shelby's disappearance."

"God. What makes you say that?"

"Well, last night, just before the accident, January mentioned Shelby's name."

Lorna's brow furrowed. "Shelby and this American Indian boy—?"

"He mentioned her at the most critical time of the chase. He wanted to warn Shelby about those men."

"Why? What could Shelby and that young man possibly have in common?"

"I don't know yet. Seemed important to him. And he certainly seemed to know who was chasing him. He said they'd tried it before. My gut tells me that January's the key to Shelby's disappearance. And I believe he escaped. Otherwise he couldn't have been able to lash Paddy and me to the boat. Just how he did it, I can't say. I'll just have to ask him when we find him."

"*We*? Just how are *we* going to accomplish that?"

"January said he'd be among the eagles." Kellen looked north toward the mounds of green that stood on the horizon. "I'd start up there."

She pointed south. "There are mountains all over this island. Maybe Bullard's right about having too much territory to cover."

"Granted. But I think there's someone who can start us in the right direction. Paddy mentioned that Molly Creed saw January on a cliff near Mount Constitution. We'll track Molly down, find out where she lives."

Lorna seemed to contemplate his strategy, but then, apparently struck by an idea, she smiled. "All right. I'll go with your plan. But first, you go along with mine."

"Yours?" He hadn't considered she might devise her own. "Like what?"

She reached into her pocket and withdrew two keys dangling on a beaded chain. "These are Tracy's. I forced Dr. Crowley to give them to me. No chasing around these hills until I take a closer look at her house."

"McMillan searched the place."

"Not with an FBI man's eye. What if he missed something?"

"You actually intend to cross police tape into an investigation site?"

"I'm Tracy's relative. What do I need, a court order?"

"Could be."

"I don't have the time. Will you come or not?"

Her brazenness was catching. "All right. But do you realize what we're doing?"

"Not really. But you should. Haven't you seen your share of crime scenes?"

"Of course." Kellen flashed on Benson and Probst, his fellow agents, lying in a pool of blood in a downtown Cleveland alley. "The question is, have you?"

The remark seemed to give Lorna pause; she shook her head.

TRACY SPILNER LIVED IN THE heart of Eastsound, off Cascade Lane, some two hundred yards from the fire station. The neighborhood was unassuming, dotted with small colonial homes, some converted to art galleries and gift shops.

Tracy's robin's-egg rambler, complete with white picket fence, sat between a small duplex and a mobile home that, according to the sign, had served as a stained-glass workshop, though it was now deserted.

Tracy's gate had been draped in yellow police tape, and beyond, the front porch was crisscrossed with several large Xs.

In Paddy's sputtering VW van, Kellen circled Tracy's block while Lorna scrutinized him from the passenger seat. Her misgivings about what she might find in Tracy's home were softened by Kellen's support. In the few minutes they'd shared outside the sheriff's office, they had established themselves as partners.

As she and Kellen had driven toward town, she had described her professional background. He appeared genuinely interested—probing and measuring her responses, hearing every word—a quality she found rare in other attractive men. And he was good-looking in a rugged sort of way, with a square, athletic face that framed light blue eyes—intense but kind. His blond hair had been cropped short, cresting into a boyish widow's peak over the bandage that covered his right temple. He was broad shouldered with strong, muscled arms visible under his sweatshirt. Yet when he glanced across and gave her his reassuring smile, she felt moved by his warmth.

Kellen parked in an alley seventy-five feet from Tracy's back door and leaned over. "Hey, I've given this some thought. Maybe it's best if I go into the house first. There might be traces of, well . . ."

"Violence?"

"Yes. Someone like you might not—"

"Oh, please don't do that." He had confused her femininity for frailty.

"What?"

"I'm not 'someone like me.' I am me."

He shrugged. "Okay." He raised both hands in mock surrender. "I saw you trample the sheriff. I'm not going to get in your way." Without hesitating, he exited the car.

Lorna grabbed her purse and followed.

Kellen was walking down the alley toward Tracy's back porch when she caught up to him.

"Look, I'm sorry. I guess I'm just unloading some baggage. I don't mean to sound ungrateful."

"We've all got baggage, Lorna." He fussed with a small flashlight he had grabbed from Paddy's glove box. "Some of us have a steamer trunk full. But do you mind if we stay focused right now? You see that?" He pointed to the rear of the house, where a window had been boarded over.

"Yes. McMillan said they entered through the kitchen window."

"So there you go," he answered softly. "You want to take the lead?"

She couldn't help but smile. "No. This is still your area of expertise." She reached into her purse and then handed him the keys.

"All right. But if the unexpected happens, will you please just do what I tell you?" Kellen checked the alley in both directions and ducked under the yellow tape strung between the porch posts. He reached back. "Please hand me your scarf. No reason to leave prints."

She removed the bright silk from her neck, and he wrapped it around the door handle, turned the key in the lock, and opened the door.

He entered the kitchen, and Lorna followed.

They stepped across the light-green linoleum. She was struck by the odor of hamburger grease from a recent meal Tracy and Shelby must have cooked, judging from the dirty dishes in the sink. The walls were covered with floral wallpaper, oddly old-fashioned considering Tracy's bohemian tastes. Aside from the halo from the one unboarded kitchen window, the house seemed depressingly dark.

Kellen inched forward. "Do you know where Tracy was when McMillan found her?"

"I wasn't told."

Kellen shone the flashlight beam onto the floorboards of the hallway.

"Chalk marks ahead. I'm sorry you have to see this. There's a sizable stain."

Lorna did wince as she noted the dark residue of Tracy's blood still on the hardwood.

Kellen pushed open a neighboring door. "Looks like Tracy was attacked on her way out of this room." Several bookshelves, a rolltop desk, and a computer stand sat in the corner of what appeared to be the den. "My guess, the assailant surprised Shelby in there." Kellen pointed to the opposite bedroom. "When Tracy stepped into the hall to help, she was clubbed."

Kellen entered the den and walked toward the desk. Using the flashlight, he searched the drawers. "Usual garbage," he mumbled. "Bills, scissors, eraser . . ."

Lorna joined him and began to leaf through a wicker in-box on the desktop. "Some letters here." She opened one postmarked Boulder, Colorado. "One from her ex-husband, Bruce." She read the first paragraph in the low light. "Look at this . . . he was threatening to take Shelby in a custody battle."

"What's the date?"

"Three weeks ago. Must have upset Tracy terribly."

"Keep that. His threat makes him a suspect."

She tucked the letter into her purse. "Maybe. She left him because he was abusive."

"Violent enough to do this?"

"I don't know. Never met him."

Kellen closed the drawers and gazed over her shoulder. "What's that?" He retrieved a tan manila envelope from the pile.

He read the return address: "'National Institute for Improved Vision' with a post office box in South Dakota. Did Tracy have poor eyesight?"

"I don't remember her wearing glasses."

Kellen opened the envelope.

Lorna moved closer and read the brief sentence under the date . . . April 17.

Dear Ms. Spilner,

Your daughter, Shelby, will receive her Flex-Optics glasses in a few days. We look forward to her participation in the next phase of our Edu-net program. Our sincerest congratulations.

The letter was signed Maxine Steutchel, director of human resources.

"So Shelby did have poor vision?"

"Not unless she wore contacts. Look." Lorna gestured to the desk, where Shelby, sans spectacles, smiled brightly from a school picture. "Are glasses meaningful here?"

"Something January said. It was his reference to Shelby 'seeing' things. Keep in mind, here was a guy who had just come out of a trance in which he supposedly 'saw' things."

"You're suggesting Shelby knew something about trances?"

"That's the idea. If you'll excuse me, I'm going to make a call." Clutching the correspondence, Kellen turned and looked toward the hall, pausing to rethink his decision. "I don't think it would be advisable to use Tracy's phone."

Lorna reached into her purse and retrieved her cell phone. "Be my guest, " she said as she handed it to him.

"Thanks. It won't take long."

"Who are you calling?"

"An old friend in DC. It's just a hunch." He began to dial.

Sensing his need for privacy, Lorna wandered off.

She stepped back into the hall and headed to what was obviously Shelby's bedroom. The walls were covered with posters; some Lorna recognized—rock bands, several movie stars, things expected of a twelve-year-old girl.

The room felt lifeless, sad, and dark, like a shrine to times gone by.

On a small brown dresser sat a worn antique jewelry box, plus a stone figurine of two seals resting on a rock. A small cardboard box held picture postcards from Colorado. Next to it, a white clamshell filled with beach pebbles.

Still using her scarf, Lorna opened the dresser drawer and stared at Shelby's clothes—tank tops, underwear, several folded sweaters.

In the corner next to an unmade bed sat a battered rocking chair, and in the chair, something fuzzy.

Lorna recognized the large, somewhat frayed teddy bear that she'd sent Shelby nine Christmases ago. Something odd about that teddy in this low light; something curious about the large ribbon that adorned his neck. She walked over and felt the curled edges of the sharp objects dangling from the ribbon.

Were they bone? No. Claws. Primitive and cold.

Lorna brushed the sharp ends with her fingertips, wondering why Shelby would hang these grotesque objects around the neck.

Suddenly, Lorna sensed a movement at her back.

She whirled toward the silhouette standing in the doorway.

"Kellen, you gave me a start," she gasped. She took a deep breath and gestured to the teddy. "Look at this. Shelby hung claws from the ribbon on this bear."

"Talons," he said, absentmindedly. "Eagle talons."

"Didn't you say that the eagles and January—?"

"He probably gave them to her." Kellen sounded upset. "Listen. We've got to get out of here."

"What's wrong?"

She saw the envelope in his hand as he stepped into the room. "Marty Flowers is a research officer, an information gatherer who also works as an archivist for the FBI in DC. I've known him since the Marine Corps. I trust him."

"Yes?"

"I called him to see what his computer might cough up regarding this 'National Institute for Improved Vision.' It took him only a couple of minutes." Kellen frowned. "The Institute isn't a private firm, as I expected. It's an agency . . . an extension of the Department of Education."

"So?"

"When I asked Marty to give me a profile on the company's administrators, namely"—he held up the envelope—"Maxine Steutchel, who signed this letter, he started sounding weird. He told me to forget it."

"Forget what?"

"My inquiry. He implied that I might not *live* to hear the answer. There's a hands-off policy attached to this South Dakota institute. Officially, it doesn't exist. The organization has diplomatic immunity—an international security clearance that supersedes US authority. I've never heard of such a thing." Kellen handed her the envelope as if to distance himself from it. "If what Marty says is true, the agency could be a 'super force' unaccountable for *anything* it wants to do. That explains the boldness of the men on that cliff last night. They had no fear." Kellen looked into her eyes. "If Marty's right, and this phantom force is responsible for Shelby and January disappearing, I'm not sure where to turn."

19

The University of Washington
Seattle

"THE TRIBAL COUNCIL ISN'T THE problem. They've put the matter to rest." Dr. Hargrove swiveled his chair from the bay windows that faced Mount Rainier. "*I'm* the problem," he said coldly, turning to Alessandro. "Unlike David Fraley, I'm not inclined to be swayed by frivolous donations. Furthermore, I don't much like your tone."

Alessandro rarely swallowed his pride, but in this instance, he realized he had overplayed his hand. "I'm sorry if I offended you."

"Me? No." Hargrove straightened his bowtie and placed his hands on the lapels of his tweed suit jacket. "You've offended my profession and this institution, perhaps. If Fraley agreed to let you buy yourself in, I'm afraid I must disappoint you. I find no justification for turning over the contents of the strongbox."

Alessandro realized his error. In his haste to get to Orcas Island, he'd hurried the conversation, offering money too rashly before observing proprieties. Not wanting Bernardo to witness a humiliating retraction, he turned to his assistant. "Perhaps you should leave us for a moment."

Bernardo made a move for the door handle, but Hargrove stepped from behind his oak desk. "No need for that." He strode duckfooted across the creaking wooden floor. "I'm a very busy man, and I suggest," Hargrove opened the door, "that you both be on your way."

Bernardo sheepishly stepped into the hallway and became the object of several passing students' curiosity.

"Dr. Hargrove, if I may." Alessandro held his ground, still seated.

"Do you misunderstand? I have things to do."

"Professor, I've made a serious mistake. Please forgive me."

Hargrove placed a hand on his hip. "Very well. Apology accepted. Now, let me get back to my work."

Alessandro would have to humble himself or lose the opportunity. "My misjudgment was due to my fatigue, from flying five thousand miles overnight." Alessandro opened his arms. "I'm asking for a few more minutes to make amends."

Hargrove's thin lips clamped in irritation.

Alessandro stood. "I should have told you immediately that I've traveled here to share something with you."

"What? That your ancestors were explorers?"

Alessandro's hopes lifted. However cynical, Hargrove had reengaged. "No, something more fascinating." Alessandro pointed back to the desk. "Please."

With raised eyebrows, Hargrove gazed at Bernardo.

Alessandro waved. "It's all right, Bernardo. Come back in."

Bernardo reentered and closed the door as Hargrove traversed the room. Reaching the opposing wall, Hargrove refused to sit and leaned against the floor-to-ceiling mahogany bookshelves that framed the windows. A variety of books and pictures lined the shelves: archaeological studies, photographs of several Middle Eastern digs, translations of the Dead Sea Scrolls, and several versions of the Bible.

"All right." Hargrove crossed his arms. "I'll give you two minutes. Come to the point."

Alessandro leaned on the back of the chair. "The point, Dr. Hargrove, is a story. As an esteemed scholar, you must share my view that archaeology is most intriguing when artifacts tell a *story* about the people who left them behind."

"Go on."

"During my phone call to David Fraley, he mentioned that you've assumed the parchment in the strongbox might be English in origin."

"A logical assumption. The only legible word was English. Someone wrote 'calm' at the bottom."

Alessandro nodded to Bernardo, who opened the valise. As if offering a morsel of food to a dangerous animal, Bernardo timidly handed the Madrid transcript to Hargrove while Alessandro continued. "I assume you don't read Spanish, Professor, but kindly look at the signature at the bottom of that page."

"Cerba Aquilino Lucero Martine." Hargrove pronounced the complex name haltingly.

"C . . . A . . . L . . . M," Alessandro added.

Hargrove's white eyebrows knitted in surprise. "Dear God. They're initials." He pointed to the writing. "Who was he?"

"The man who gave that strongbox and the parchment you found inside to a woman named Imnit."

"Imnit?"

"The skeleton you've examined. Martine was there when my ancestor Roberto Ravilla entered a cave and apparently witnessed a sight that drove him to suicide."

Hargrove scratched his head, staring skeptically at the printout. "What does the rest of this say?"

"That Martine befriended Imnit, an Indian woman whom he trusted. Following a brutal purging of the Indians after the Ravilla find, Martine planned to go back to the cave to find out what the captain had seen."

"Was this the year . . ." Hargrove referred to the top of the page. "1793?"

"Yes."

"We did determine that the age of the corpse was just over two hundred years old and probably belonged to a member of the Coastal Salish tribes."

"Precisely. And now that you have Imnit's bones and the strongbox, we can make the assumption that Martine kept to the plan," Alessandro pointed, "which he described in that letter written to his brother Francisco. His initials on the strongbox parchment prove that he was able to find Imnit. I believe it also means that he *did* go back to the cave."

Hargrove returned the printout to Bernardo and fixed on Alessandro. "So it's the cave you're after?"

"Yes. What could Ravilla possibly have seen that led him to hang himself aboard his ship?"

"And this Martine fellow? Any record of what happened to him?"

"There is mention of Martine in the journal of a Captain Panjota, Martine's superior. Show him." Alessandro nodded to Bernardo, who pulled another piece of paper from the briefcase.

Because it was in Spanish, Alessandro volunteered the information. "Panjota's journal records that Martine's vessel, *El Trinidad*, was ravaged by fire and sank in the San Juans . . . no one seems to know the exact location. Panjota blamed the incident on the British, a precursor to fighting that ensued between the two nations off the Vancouver coast."

Hargrove was now visibly interested. "That's it? No further correspondence?"

"Presumably all of Martine's records went down with his ship, save one—the parchment he gave Imnit. The one she took to her grave. What do you think, Professor? Why was Imnit murdered? Did Martine bury the strongbox with her for safekeeping after some other Spanish officer killed her?"

"That's unlikely." Hargrove strolled along the far wall toward an armoire. "And that's the reason the Tribal Council settled their protest so readily."

"I don't understand."

Hargrove opened the drawer and pulled out a series of black-and-white photographs. He handed them to Alessandro. "I convinced them with these." The photos showed a skull with the jawbone set aside. The frontal lobe of a delicate head was tilted toward the camera, displaying a ragged hole. "My examination confirmed that the Indian woman's skull had been split by the rough edge of an adze . . . not a smooth Spanish blade."

"So her own people punished Imnit for her collusion with the Spanish and buried her corpse along with the box." Alessandro smiled. "I . . . don't suppose the parchment gives further clues?"

Reluctantly, Hargrove opened the top drawer of his desk. "You might as well have a look."

Alessandro had won.

Hargrove set a clear sheath on the desk pad for Alessandro to examine. Protected in clear plastic, the brown piece of paper was etched with faded ink markings. A series of numbers stretched across the bottom, and in the upper left-hand corner, a date . . . June 21. In the middle, faded lines denoting a section of coastline. A trident had been etched deeply into the right-hand margin. Next to it, a triangle with what appeared to be the stick figure of a man with arms spread at its apex. Near the bottom, above a worn edge that seemed to have been touched by fire, the initials C A L M.

"What do you make of the numbers? Do they mean anything to you?" Hargrove asked.

"I had hoped they would be coordinates," Alessandro replied, "but they don't appear to be longitude or latitude readings." The other numbers seemed to have little logic: 33, 7, 6, 45, 9, 90 and then 12.

"The date presumably denotes when the map was written?" Hargrove ventured.

"No, sir." Bernardo's first words. He stepped forward with the printout and placed it on the desk. "Martine's letter to his brother was dated the twenty-seventh, six days after the map's date."

Alessandro nodded. "Bernardo's right. The letter describes Martine's intention to find the cave. The map, drawn six days *earlier,* shows how to find it. That makes no sense." He turned to Hargrove. "Intriguing, no?"

"I suppose."

Alessandro picked up the plastic sheath. "This parchment may well be the key to finding Ravilla's cave."

Hargrove ran a hand through his white hair. "And in your wildest imagination, what do you expect to find inside?"

"If it caused one man to see ghosts and hang himself—something quite spectacular."

20

Eastsound

KELLEN WAITED FOR LORNA ON the beach. Gray clouds dotted the eastern horizon. A small flotilla of boats bobbed in the harbor, buffeted by a mild southerly breeze.

The weather had cooled a bit, much like Kellen's enthusiasm. He was troubled by what Marty Flowers had told him. Avenging wrongs was one thing—opposing a covert government tactical force that appeared to operate above the law was another.

But that was precisely what Lorna expected them to do. She had pressed him for options as they left Tracy's house. He'd confided to her that he had a few retired FBI friends who lived in western Washington—namely Stinson and Connely, contemporaries of his brother's—whom he might approach for assistance. Like Kyle, both had been risk takers. Kellen suspected they might jump at the chance for some action. Still, he was reluctant to involve anyone else for fear of endangering more lives. Kellen had already been blamed for the deaths of two agents, and the last thing he wanted was to put others in harm's way.

Lorna's lobbying continued as he accompanied her to the Outlook Inn, where she registered. He then drove her to the Orcas Island Medical Center. They checked on Paddy and Tracy. Paddy was heavily sedated, but doing all right. Tracy rested peacefully, supported by her IV feedings.

Despite a lack of visible changes in Tracy's condition, Marilyn, her nurse, announced a change in the prognosis. Tracy's blood pressure was dropping, an indication that her system was slowing down.

Seeing Lorna at her wounded sister's bedside and witnessing her tears at Tracy's frailty had moved Kellen. He had crossed the line of becoming emotionally involved. Against his better judgment, he had leaned toward Lorna in the darkened room and whispered that despite his misgivings about Marty's warning, he would do everything he could to help her find Shelby. Her eyes brimmed with appreciation.

Lorna told Kellen she would stay at the hospital most of the night. They agreed to meet at noon at the beachside park the following day.

When Kellen reached home that afternoon, nothing at his cabin had changed—it was still a shambles and his cat hadn't returned—so he straightened up the place and took a shower. Then he sank into bed.

The next morning, following a restless night, he stepped into a pair of jeans the vandals had overlooked and headed into town, where he bought a new black sweatshirt.

And then he began his inquiry into Molly Creed's whereabouts. First stop: the Orcas Island Title Office. Because Kellen had no computer at home, he first asked a clerk at the office to Google Molly Creed, but when nothing turned up, Kellen began a thorough search of county files, which also yielded nothing—Molly wasn't listed as a landowner. The clerk suggested that she might be a tenant in one of the many hillside homes that rented by the season, but after stopping at the real estate office, he confirmed that there was no rental contract in Molly's name.

Kellen was on his way out the door when he spotted Reverend Hank Pelto emerging from the post office with several packages in hand.

Kellen caught up with him just as Pelto was loading his supplies into the back of a rusty pickup truck.

"Care packages for the kids?"

Pelto turned. "Exactly. Donated volleyball equipment."

"You might request a wardrobe for yourself," Kellen said. "I see you're still wearing your 'holier than thou' sweatshirt."

"Properly stated, that's 'holier than thy' sweatshirt. Yours looks brand new."

"It is. I'm out of clothes. My place was ransacked the other night."

"You're joking. Kids, you think?"

"Bastards, I think. The same ones that smashed Paddy's boat."

Kellen and Pelto had assisted each other with several projects in the past. Pelto had been a proponent of letting Kellen put his hatchery on YMCA land.

In exchange, Kellen had volunteered to help build new log cabins at the local YMCA camp. Reasoning that the reverend knew most people in town, Kellen asked him about Molly.

"Molly's a recluse. Has no family." Pelto scratched his head. "She's also an artist. An oil painter, as I recall. I think she entered some of her work in our 'Brush with Orcas' art fair last August. If you want, I could probably find her through the community registry. It's down the street at the Chamber of Commerce."

Kellen glanced at Pelto's wristwatch. The thought of Lorna waiting for him alone on the beach made him uneasy. "I'd appreciate it. I'm supposed to meet someone at Beachside Park. Meet me there in, say, twenty minutes?"

Encouraged by Pelto's possible lead, Kellen walked the four blocks down to the water's edge. By the time he reached the shore, the weather had taken a turn for the worse—not atypical of June in the Northwest. Dark clouds trimmed in white came in from the south, and the burgeoning cold front convinced discouraged picnickers to depart. Some scurried off on foot, others loaded their baskets on bicycles and rode off. Kellen was left alone with the lapping water.

Like many of the island beaches, this narrow strand across from the Outlook Inn was strewn with rocks and little sand. Mounds of driftwood had settled high on its banks. Tucked into the heart of a small town, the bay still teemed with wildlife. In the distance, a bald eagle rode the winds. Gray seals cruised the shallows with shiny heads showing above the surface, and the sky was alive with seagulls and crows.

Like the seagulls, the husky black birds snatched mussels from barnacle-covered rocks. They carried the shellfish high into the air and dropped them onto the rocks below. If the mussel remained intact, the crows would stubbornly retrieve the mollusk, drop it again, and yet again until it shattered. Kellen found the implied tool technique fascinating, considering it was shared by different species. The seagulls certainly had a genetic instinct for cracking mussels. But crows—land-based birds—had apparently emulated the method, engaging in what might be defined as "learned behavior." From the seagulls? And learned how? It brought to mind January's apparent communication with the creatures the night before last.

As Kellen watched the seagulls and crows feast, he glanced back at the hotel. His attention was drawn to a splash of bright red in the lobby window. The triangular shape revealed itself to be the scarf worn by Lorna to keep her hair in place.

She stepped onto the latticed hotel porch and, seeing Kellen, waved. She crossed the street, looking at ease in her black jeans, tan leather jacket, and half heel boots, which accentuated her long legs.

"Hi," she said. "My, you look better. How did your search go?"

"No cat, I'm afraid."

"Oh, I'm sorry. I was actually referring to Molly."

"Of course." Kellen chuckled. "I'm still a little spaced. Nothing on Molly either. The title office was a bust, but I did find"—Kellen caught sight of Hank Pelto as he crossed Front Street a block away—"someone who can help. In fact, here he comes."

Lorna gave Pelto a nervous glance. "Oh . . . him," she said, quietly. "I'm afraid he and I didn't hit it off very well. He came barging into Tracy's room unannounced and started talking about her funeral. I wasn't ready then, and I'm not ready now."

Kellen had sensed her denial. Whenever Lorna spoke of her sister, she used terms like "when she comes to" and "after Tracy wakes up." Obviously, she'd have no part of negative thinking.

"I'm sorry," Kellen said. "I had no idea that you'd met. When I heard Pelto might have a lead on Molly, I asked him to join us. He's actually a very caring guy."

Smiling sheepishly as he approached, Pelto chose to address her first. "Now that I see you in the light of day, you're as attractive as I suspected."

Lorna accepted the awkward compliment as graciously as she could. "A bit less caustic as well, I suppose."

Pelto appeared pleased by the concession. "Your comments were understandable, considering the circumstances."

Kellen's tan face creased into a grin. "Are you going to behave yourself this time?"

"If I don't, you'll arrest me, no doubt." Pelto nodded at him. "He's an incredibly stubborn man, Ms. Novak. He still has to protect and serve—can't get it out of his system. Though now he protects wildlife . . . a savior of salmon, or hasn't he told you?"

"He hasn't."

"If you have the time, I'll show you," Kellen added. "It's something everyone should see."

"I'm looking forward to it," she said. Even in the face of his disconcerting phone call to Washington, Kellen had maintained an air of self-assurance that fascinated Lorna. He was soft spoken, yet determined.

Kellen turned to Pelto. "What about Molly?"

The reverend pointed toward the great mountain that overlooked the bay. "Up there. She lives in the raccoon highlands, a back shoulder of Mount Constitution. Very remote." Pelto produced a map from his pocket. "I drew this up. It's pretty crude. You'll have to hike the last mile or so."

Kellen gestured to Lorna's feet. "You're going to need different shoes."

"Oh, these will do."

"No, he's right," Pelto responded. "That's thick forest up there. Spongy ground." He turned to Kellen. "Have you ever met Molly?"

"No."

"Quite a character. Rumors run rampant. People say she eats wild mushrooms and runs naked through the woods."

"Come on, Hank."

"No, really. She's what some might call a naturalist. That's why she gets along with January and his grandmother. Her eccentricity falls right in line with their shamanistic nonsense."

"So do you want to come along and help us find her?" Kellen asked.

Lorna lent no encouragement, hoping that she and Kellen might have a one-on-one discussion.

"I suppose I could," Pelto said, "but I'm due at camp for the evening prayer." He made a point of fixing his gaze on Lorna. "We plan to pray for Shelby. She has friends there."

Lorna felt somewhat humbled in the knowledge that she had misjudged Pelto. "I had no idea. I appreciate it."

"Some of her friends are counselors. They're pretty upset."

Lorna had a thought. "How many counselors?"

"Fifteen in all. Ages twelve through sixteen."

"And campers?"

"On average, maybe one hundred fifty."

"Prayers would be appreciated, believe me. But how about some help? Would the campers consider searching for Shelby? I've been hoping to organize something like that. Frankly, I didn't know where to begin."

Pelto brightened. "Great idea. I'll check with the Y."

"The Y?" Lorna asked.

“The YMCA would have to approve,” the reverend explained.

Lorna’s heart sank. Red tape would probably stifle the effort.

“Now, don’t be discouraged. Have Kellen drop you by the camp in the morning, and I’ll update you on where we stand.” He nudged Kellen. “You think you know your way around the back side of Vusario Ridge?”

Kellen held the map in his fist. “Assuming your map is any good . . .”

He paused and looked down the street. A black Lincoln limousine rolled along the beachfront road.

“The first limo I’ve seen here in months,” Kellen said.

Lorna noticed how he had gently grasped her elbow, pulling her back a step as if to protect her while the stretch vehicle slowed a few feet away. He apparently associated the car with some kind of threat. Perhaps the phone call had put him on edge. He stepped forward, casually resting his right hand at his belt.

The limo came to a stop next to Pelto.

The darkened rear window lowered with a gentle hum, and an extremely handsome man with slick black hair dressed in a white silk shirt leaned out.

“Excuse me,” the stranger said in an affected English accent. His dark eyes glinted in the sun as he looked from Pelto to Kellen and finally rested on Lorna. “Do any of you know the way to the local museum?”

21

Eastsound

ALESSANDRO EASILY FOUND THE ORCAS Island Historical Museum. He had asked the limo driver to stop so he could study the dark-haired woman on the beach more closely, feigning the need for directions from her ragged-looking companions, even though the driver already knew the museum address.

The beauty of her raven hair, her full lips, and the haunting expression in her eyes stayed with him as he spotted David Fraley behind the counter of the museum with his nose buried in a book.

The gaunt curator, dressed in a pinstriped vest, nonmatching pants, and a gray shirt, looked up through his glasses and shook his head. "Sorry, gentlemen. I'm closing early. No more tours today."

Alessandro smiled at Bernardo, who stood several feet behind. The entire museum was only some eight hundred square feet, divided into four small, dimly lit rooms in what was once a log cabin, someone's private residence in the late 1800s. The walls were covered with photographs from the past—whaling vessels anchored off the Orcas shore, a lumber mill, and the Moran family mansion, which, as the photographs showed, had become the famous Rosario Resort.

Fraley gawked in amazement as Bernardo leaned forward, placing a ten-thousand-dollar check on the glass. Fraley's jaws dropped. "Mr. Vargas? You've actually done it. And so soon."

Alessandro delighted in his shocked reaction. "I would have been hours earlier if we hadn't stopped in Seattle to speak with Hargrove."

Fraley coughed several times and then finally controlled himself. "Hargrove actually saw you?"

"Yes. Early this morning. And he'll see you, too, when he arrives tomorrow."

"He's coming back?"

"I convinced him to join us."

Fraley wheezed, apparently the victim of an asthma attack.

Alessandro mused why a man with respiratory problems would work in such a dusty place. The building was filled with artifacts, photographs, maps, and articles of clothing. Fraley had more material than he had space, and Alessandro's check would go to good use.

"I thought the investigation regarding the skeleton was resolved."

"I suppose it is. But the investigation regarding the strongbox is about to begin. Hargrove is fascinated with the information I shared."

"He's not an easily swayed man."

"You would be surprised." Alessandro gestured to Bernardo. "Forgive me, you haven't met formally. This is my associate, Bernardo Costanza."

The two men shook hands. Fraley showed a noticeable limp as he edged around the glass case, filled with Indian relics: arrowheads, a shabby deer pelt, a few bits of scrimshaw. "I took a good deal of time to gather these artifacts." He gestured to the shelving. "You may wish to browse. I'm particularly interested in the Straits Salish Indians. They're a fascinating people. Rare these days. Yet, those that remain are genetically pure. It's my guess that the skeleton was Salish, incidentally. Her proportions suggest that she was of the Deneid lineage." The curator sneezed and blew his nose into a white handkerchief as he moved toward the front door. "Now . . . why did you come all this way?"

"As I explained to you, I appreciate my family tree. My ancestor Captain Ravilla committed suicide a few miles from here. I'm fascinated by the circumstances." Alessandro reached inside his jacket and pulled out a piece of paper. "This is a Xerox copy of the strongbox map that Hargrove provided . . . you recognize it, of course."

"I do." Fraley tucked away his handkerchief.

"I'm going to ask you to help me locate Ravilla's cave, the one Martine described in his letter. Hopefully, we'll see clues inside *or*," Alessandro paused for emphasis, "we may even see what Ravilla saw."

"You're looking for an object of some kind?"

"Perhaps." Alessandro pointed to the outline of the landmass on the page. "Does this look like Sucia to you?"

"It does. Those fingerlike peninsulas are distinctively characteristic. The Salish settled Sucia around 100 BC, from all indications."

"And what do you think these numbers represent?"

Fraley hobbled a few steps to a cabinet and pulled out a scrolled map. He opened the chart and placed it on the glass countertop. "As you see, Sucia's position ranges somewhere near a longitude of one hundred twenty-four and a latitude of forty-eight degrees. Consequently, none of these numbers seem to relate, unless they refer to minutes and seconds."

"That's what confuses me," Alessandro said.

"And look at this marine chart." Fraley reached into a drawer and pulled out a nautical version of Sucia. "You have another way of looking at things. These smaller numbers could denote fathoms, particularly the 7, 6 and the 9."

"Fathoms?" That had never occurred to Alessandro. "From Martine's description, Ravilla's cave was clearly on land."

"Yes, but if it's an artifact you're after," Fraley's watery eyes glinted with growing interest, "couldn't these numbers reflect the depth of the water where someone sank whatever object was found in this cave of yours?"

22

Mount Constitution

BY THE TIME KELLEN BROUGHT the VW van to a stop on the narrow logging road, the setting sun shot dusty orange beams through the fir trees that lined the ridge.

After a late lunch in town, he and Lorna had searched for shoes and then explored the mountain. During their slow exploratory drive up several one-lane dirt roads, time had drifted, and it was late in the day before they found Pelto's described site.

"Man, this is beautiful." Kellen yanked the emergency brake. "I haven't been up here before."

"I've never seen woods so incredibly lush." Having grown up in the Midwest, Lorna hadn't seen such thick overgrowth. As she stepped from the car, she felt the dampness of the air, vaporous with scents of foliage. Moss covered the ground everywhere. Bright green ferns tufted between heavily barked trunks of spruce and fir.

Chipmunks chirped in the high branches of the pines, and a redheaded woodpecker darted overhead. The gentle hoot of an owl sounded from a darkened glen.

"Lions and tigers and bears, oh my," Lorna said.

"This ain't Kansas." Kellen closed her door.

"That it isn't. More like Munchkinland."

"And no yellow brick road." Kellen pointed to a pine needle clearing. "But I'll bet that's the path to Grandma's house."

"You're mixing your movie-phors, I'm afraid."

"Speaking of afraid, let's keep in mind what Marty said on the phone yesterday." Kellen patted his stomach, raised the hem of his black sweatshirt, and revealed the butt of a gun, stuck inside his belt. He tapped the bandage on his forehead. "I don't plan to be run over again without objection. I hope you don't mind."

At lunch, Kellen had elaborated on his thoughts regarding the call—his best option, to solicit his brother Kyle's old friends who were no longer with the Bureau. Without their help, he and Lorna would truly be on their own.

Lorna pointed to the gun in his waistband. She hadn't seen a weapon like that up close, yet she felt oddly at ease, sensing Kellen's competency. "What is that? A forty-five?"

"It's a nine millimeter with a seventeen-round clip. There's one thing I want you to remember." He pointed toward the woods. "If we're surprised by someone out here, don't run. Just drop to the ground so I can get a clear shot. Do you understand?"

"I do now." The comment shook her momentarily.

"And stay right behind me," Kellen said as he moved out.

Ironic. Not that she would object, but once again, nearly three thousand miles from her office, she was taking orders from a man—a decent man from all appearances, yet she sensed her own resentment even as she quelled it.

She fell in behind Kellen, watching his broad back, as he strode ahead into the dusk. The forest grew even thicker after the clearing, and it was more difficult to see the trail as the sun hung lower on the horizon.

Lorna stumbled on a downed branch and felt a bit foolish until Kellen did the same only moments later. They chuckled about their mutual clumsiness and, kidding each other in hushed voices, they hiked on.

Some fifteen minutes later, they saw lights. A glow of several small lanterns could be seen through the trees.

Kellen immediately drew his handgun and took Lorna by the elbow as they crouched behind a thicket.

"Kerosene lamps," Kellen whispered. "No way there's power out here." Dusk had now settled on the dense woods. "We'll move in real slow. Stay on my hip." Kellen began to creep forward.

Lorna followed, amazed at the sight. Tucked among the trees were several small structures, linked together by rope bridges: the first, a tiny, circular main house with a peaked roof and a woodstove chimney; the second, a cylindrical, two-story tower with a turret; and the third, a freestanding rectangle, which resembled a matchbox laid on its side. It was as if someone had scattered building block pieces and connected them with catwalks. Everything was shake and shingle, rough or polished cedar, built on stilts to align the various elevations of the interconnected structures. Each of the strange little houses was illuminated within, by what appeared to be candlelight. A large clearing sat just beyond.

"I was wrong," Lorna said. "This *is* Grandma's house."

"And no wolves in sight yet."

"I've never seen anything like it. It's a veritable pixie palace."

In its quaint complexity, the compound would have looked perfect miniaturized under a giant toadstool.

"Think about it," Kellen said. "Somebody hauled everything up here to put this place together." He hesitated some forty feet from the front door. A series of ropes dangled from the trees—many with kerosene lanterns or birdhouses hung from the bottom. Wind chimes sounded somewhere in the distance.

"What do we do now? Knock?" Lorna whispered.

"I wouldn't. If it's Molly's house, fine. But whoever lives here certainly isn't expecting company. I'd better give a shout to warn them we're here."

"What if your jet skiers are inside?"

"I'd rather find out now than on the porch. Nothing like having a gun jammed in your face when the door opens."

"I see your point."

Kellen raised his voice. "Hello, there, anybody home?"

Lorna was startled by a voice to her right. "No need to shout there, slick."

Kellen whirled, fanning the handgun.

Lorna dropped to one knee, looking back. A wiry woman with long gray hair wearing a sundress and sandals sat in the hollow of a huge stump, peering down.

"Jesus, why didn't you say something?" Kellen asked, dropping the gun at his side. "I could have killed you."

"If it's killing you came for, a howdy from me wouldn't stop you now, would it?"

"He just means you startled us," Lorna said, rising.

"As you did me." She turned, and with her angular knees piercing her flouncy dress, she slowly climbed down the great stump, which was at least four feet in diameter. "Are you expected?" she asked, using the footholds that had been chipped into the trunk. As her feet touched the ground, the woman turned, scratching the middle of her chest. "Folks don't usually show up at Molly's house this time of day."

Kellen nodded toward the house. "Oh, so she's inside?"

"No, she's standing flat-footed right in front of you."

"Nice to meet you, Molly." Lorna stepped forward and extended a hand. "I'm Lorna. This is Kellen."

At the sound of the name, Molly's leathery face broke into a partially toothless grin. "Kellen? With a bandage on your head?" she asked in a joyous singsong. "You're Paddy's friend, are you not?"

Kellen smiled. "A good friend, I hope. Paddy's the one who suggested I come see you."

"Truly? To what end?"

"He's had an accident. Or should I say, someone tried to hurt him."

"Dear God, and did they?"

"He lost his right leg. He's resting at the hospital."

Molly's head dropped in sympathy. "Oh. Poor man." She gestured to Kellen's brow. "And you? Were you in the thick of it?"

"I was. So was January."

Molly's head reared back. "Ah, so there it is. The sense of it all."

"What do you mean?" Lorna asked. "You knew about this?"

Molly's gray eyes glinted. "Yes."

"Is he alive?" Kellen asked eagerly.

"As much as ever."

"Where is he?"

"By now, he'd be among the eagles."

"God. That's exactly what he said. The eagles. Where?"

Molly gave Kellen a stoic smile and pointed to his bandage. "I have a fine herb tincture that will make that wound heal faster." She beckoned. "Come with me."

"Wait a minute. What about January's grandmother?" Kellen asked.

"Come inside, slick. And bring the lady slick with you." Molly waddled off, humming as she went.

With a shake of his head, Kellen gestured toward the front door. He and Lorna followed Molly to the main building, a circular structure with a green shake roof.

As Lorna and Kellen climbed the knotty-pine porch and stepped inside, she was impressed by the craftsmanship. Clear cedar tongue-in-groove planking adorned the round twenty-foot room, which was furnished with a series of multicolored floor pillows scattered in a circle around a tiny woodstove. The space was warmly illuminated by several candles hung in brass holders above the windows.

"My living room," Molly declared as she held a tiny bottle that she'd retrieved on her way into the house. "My bedroom is there." She pointed to the turreted tower. "And that's my kitchen." The matchbox shape was connected to the living room by another rope bridge. "I designed the layout myself. January helped build it."

"So he's a good friend?" Kellen sat.

"There's not many who frequent these woods, but January and Marissa do."

Lorna took her place on a purple cushion. "Marissa?"

"His grandmother. She's known as Marissa Harmon in town, but she also goes by her Indian name. In the wild, she's called Naming Clouds."

"Odd name." Kellen eyed the olive drab liquid in the tiny flask Molly held.

"The ability to name clouds is a rare talent, you know."

Kellen gave Lorna a shrug.

"Something we all did as children," Lorna added, not wanting to disparage Molly's esteem. "Clouds can assume recognizable shapes on occasion."

"Oh, yes. But Marissa does it her way." Molly unscrewed the small cap off the tiny bottle. "The clouds change shapes to whatever she names them."

Kellen had begun to lean away from Molly's gnarled hands, which now poured the strange pea-soup-like liquid onto a cotton swab.

"Like her grandson, Marissa has the gift. January's parents died in a kayak accident, don't you know. Marissa renamed him January, because she felt he might be the start of something new." She reached for Kellen's face. "Let's remove that bandage."

Kellen appeared totally unconvinced. "Really, I—"

"This will heal you right up." She groped for the dressing, and Kellen flinched. "Now, hold still." Not to be dissuaded, Molly gripped Kellen's shoulder with her free hand.

Witnessing the struggle, Lorna felt she'd better intervene. "Perhaps Molly will tell us more about the eagles while she applies the lotion."

"Oh," Molly said as she removed the tape that held the gauze in place.

"That's ugly. One, two . . . why, there must be sixteen stitches." Before Kellen could object, she had dabbed the incision with her mysterious looking concoction. "You'll see." Molly smiled mischievously. "Look in the mirror in a couple of days."

"All right," Kellen said. "Thank you very much. Now where are these eagles January mentioned?"

Molly poured a bit more from the bottle. "There's several different places he might be. Only Marissa knows for sure. She's the one who took him off-island last night."

"You mean you don't know?"

"Never said I did, slick." Molly continued to dab. "This will keep that nasty cut from scarring even a little bit. You're going to be pleased."

23

The Training Room
Sitnalta
South Dakota

SHELBY STOOD ON THE OTHER side of the two-way mirror on a black mat with her blonde hair pinned above her ears.

When Shelby disrobed and Trajan saw her freckled breasts, he couldn't help being turned on. The helplessness of the child-soon-to-be-a-woman appealed to him. Sex was a form of conquest, after all, and like everything else, an embodiment of power—the reason Trajan fought to maintain his potency.

Yet, implacable as he was, the peculiarity of attaining a hard erection while standing next to the Undersecretary of Defense of the United States in an observation booth struck him as bizarre. Trajan turned aside, feigning a cough, trying to adjust his pants to alleviate the tightness.

"Get in the tank, Shelby. The water's nice and warm," Nurse Haupt's voice projected over the intercom from the other room.

The young girl pulled away. "I don't want to."

"You don't have a choice, child. This is how it's done."

"I'd rather do this in my own room with my clothes on. I don't want the doctor to see me."

"Get in the water and he won't be able to." Nurse Haupt dunked a hand. "See, it's warm and nice and blue. It'll hide you."

"No."

"I thought you liked using your imagination. You did it so well on your computer."

"That was just a game."

"Well, so is this, but it's much better. You'll see."

"I'm not playing." As Shelby turned in protest, Trajan could see the baldness at the base of her skull where the nape of her neck had been shaved. A microsiphon had been surgically inserted into her brainstem this morning. The tiny silver coupling that would feed Epstein's Formula 15 into her skull protruded just enough to reflect the gleam of the overhead halogen lights.

Shelby was understandably distraught after having been punctured like a laboratory animal. "You promised."

"Promised what?"

"That I could go home."

"And you will. After you tell us what we want. Cooperate, and we'll make sure that you see your mother. Isn't that what we said?"

"No, you said that after the operation I could—" Her objection was interrupted as Dr. Epstein entered. Shelby shrieked, crouched in the corner, and attempted to cover herself with both hands.

"Why isn't she under?"

"She's been difficult. She's embarrassed."

"Nonsense. I'm a doctor, Shelby. Haven't you ever had a physical?"

"When my mom was there," she whimpered.

In the hush of the observation booth, Preston took a pull off his cigarette and glanced over. "I never understood why the nudity was necessary."

Trajan replied without eye contact. "To eliminate physical encumbrances. Whether here, or in the actual ERVC, Epstein recommends flotation in a heavy saline solution. The weightlessness encourages a dream state and frees the libido, removing certain inhibitions."

"I suppose. But under normal circumstance, dreams aren't contingent on flotation."

"Under normal circumstances," Trajan said dryly, "dreams require sleep. The artificial state Epstein creates is accomplished through a combination of environmental and neurological stimulation. Normally, before we get to this stage of the experiment, a trancer is indoctrinated into a regimented lifestyle—a restricted diet, meditative sessions, and therapeutic hypnosis. The next step is Shelby's interaction with the other psychics in the Extended Remote Viewing Chamber. Right now, Epstein is trying to ease Shelby into her own space first." Trajan turned for emphasis. In face of the inquisition, his erection had receded. "Frankly, we had to rush all this."

"We all agree on the urgency, since you've been unable to locate January."

"Understood. But Epstein wanted me to inform you that we were forced to accelerate the process even further due to your arrival." Trajan had updated Preston on Calico's most recent report. The ex-FBI man named Kellen Rand had, from all indications, done something quite astounding. He'd visited Tracy Spilner's home, accompanied by an (as yet) unidentified woman. Though Rand's intentions were in doubt, he had Calico's full attention and was being watched closely.

Epstein stood over Shelby. "I'll leave the room so you can get in the tub. Okay?" He glared at Haupt and pointed to the IV bag. "Administer the Quadrilin. Once she's in the water, throw a smock over the tub so she feels secure."

He exited through the far door.

"Sounds like he's wearing a bit thin," Preston said.

"He's been at it sixteen hours a day." Trajan couldn't help sounding defensive. "Your presence as our 'efficiency expert' simply causes more stress."

Preston seemed mildly amused. "Me? You thought I was referring to myself? Trajan, give us more credit. I'm not qualified. The man we're bringing in is highly skilled. He's due any minute . . . incredible, considering we had to fly him in from the Ukraine."

"What?" Trajan took an almost imperceptible deep breath and asked calmly, "So who's coming?"

"Medvedev. Dimitri Medvedev. Instrumental in the former Soviet Union's psychic research program."

"Jesus Christ, Preston. They call him Rasputin. He's burned out every psychic he ever tested."

"Epstein's blown a few fuses himself. The difference is . . . Medvedev got results."

"Bullshit." Trajan reached for the wall phone. "I'm not going to allow this. I'll detain him at the gate until we get this straightened out."

"I thought you'd disagree. That's why I've arranged for my men to escort him straight to this lab."

"On whose authority?"

"The White House."

Things had come completely undone. "You've requested executive action?"

"I did. The latest news on AVALANCHE convinced the president to order a Code Red emergency. We now believe that anthrax has been shipped to several different assembly plants here in this country, and we don't have the slightest idea where they might be."

Trajan glanced into the viewing room to see if Epstein had returned.

Nurse Haupt had succeeded in getting Shelby into the water, inserting her IV, and lowering the lights.

Trajan wanted to warn Epstein about the new turn of events, but it was too late. The doctor had already joined them in the observation booth.

"I apologize for the delay," he said. "We should be underway in a few minutes."

"Epstein," Trajan said. "We have a visitor."

The doctor extended his hand. "Of course, I've met Mr. Preston."

"Not him, Karl. Preston has imported someone to monitor your experiment."

"Imported?" Epstein's face fell in dismay. "You can't simply inject someone into the privacy of my work."

"He won't disturb you. He's just an observer."

"Who? Who is it?"

Preston appeared to enjoy the suspense, answering only after stubbing his cigarette out in the ashtray on the observation window ledge. "I'm sure you know him. It's Dimitri Medvedev."

"Medvedev? That butcher? He's a CIA puppet."

"Yes. But look at the practical applications Medvedev brought to their work."

"Levitation? You consider that practical?" The doctor's crater-marked face radiated color like a harvest moon. "He has absolutely no clairvoyant history. He's a spoon bender, for God's sake. A manipulator of matchsticks."

Preston's face showed no emotion. "Frankly, doctor, that's a moot issue. Medvedev is here at the request of the Unified Russian Confederacy. The Chinese collaboration with AVALANCHE stirred concerns that Russia and its former satellites are also potential targets for anthrax terrorism." In response to Epstein's blank stare, Preston turned and, sounding bored, added, "Now, if you'll excuse me, I have to make a call."

Preston stepped into the corner, pulled his cell phone from the pocket of his three-piece suit, and engaged in conversation.

Epstein nudged Trajan. "This is disaster. What can we do?"

"Only one thing," Trajan whispered. "Take control."

"How? With these vultures hanging around?"

Trajan spoke in a regimented monotone. "Get back into your lab. Be certain things go letter-perfect. *Make* Shelby perform. I don't care if you become a ventriloquist . . . I want to hear her say she knows where January is. Do you understand me?"

"Maybe if I spoke with Medvedev?"

"They didn't bring him for tea and sympathy, Karl. He's here to condemn your ass. Now prove him wrong."

"I'll do what I can." Epstein gave Preston a rabbit-like glance and retreated toward the door.

Seconds later he had rejoined Haupt on the other side of the mirror. He began recalibrating the equipment, checking the oscilloscope, the tachistoscopic scanner, reading Shelby's initial CAT scan, gauging the formula flow, and whispering to Haupt as he went.

The nurse had succeeded in attaching the coupling at the base of Shelby's neck to the dispenser. The girl lay in the tank with her head resting on the edge, sedated by the IV mixture, apparently no longer caring that the smock, which had hidden her nudity, had been removed.

Preston finished his call and returned to the glass. "I checked. Medvedev just touched down outside the gate."

Trajan winced. The helicopter pad had been installed for *his* convenience, not for intruders.

Preston lit another cigarette and pointed toward the tank. "For Epstein's sake, I hope Shelby embarks on a productive mental voyage."

Trajan sighed, wishing he could send Preston on a trip to the morgue.

Moments later the heavy metal door to the hall opened, and a CIA agent wearing dark glasses ushered Dr. Medvedev into the room.

The doctor's bloodshot eyes, disheveled black hair, and his wrinkled dark-brown suit testified to the duration of his journey.

"Preston?" he asked in a thick accent, glancing back and forth in the low light.

"Welcome, Doctor." Preston's all too eager tone gave Trajan the sinking feeling that he was being set up. "Meet Mr. Morse, our field ops chief."

Trajan turned and shook Medvedev's strong, square hand. The midforties Ukrainian with piercing green eyes looked the formidable adversary. He was oddly robust for an intellectual, with broad shoulders and thick legs. If he weren't wearing a suit, he might have been mistaken for a lumberjack.

Medvedev's gaze shifted immediately to the two-way glass and the activity beyond. "Someone is getting a bath?"

"Dr. Epstein is creating an appropriate environment for the experiment," Trajan said.

"Is this a joke?" Medvedev chuckled. "I have been told of this technique."

"Told?" Trajan was shocked. Epstein's experiments were top secret.

Preston leaned over. "I took the liberty of sharing Epstein's brief on neurobiological suspension with the doctor in preparation for his visit."

"Interesting reading," Medvedev said. "But Epstein's ideas are *misguided*. I question the validity of using mind-altering substances." Medvedev pushed a thick finger toward Trajan's face. "Like spirit, clairvoyance is unencumbered. Connection with greater time–space continuum is not dependent on synaptic chemistry, but rather on self-imposed cerebral projection."

Trajan chose not to respond.

Medvedev had summarized the CIA's position, adapted from Dr. Carl Jung's theories of collective consciousness, that a dream-state automatically linked a trancer to a universal communications reservoir, in which impressions previously imprinted by other minds upon the physical and temporal reality might be read. Consequently, because echoes of current or past events were present, they could be perceived when a primary clairvoyant telepathically arrived at a specific destination.

Epstein had disputed that concept with his theories of "sensory intervention," in which an individual psychic willfully invaded another person's consciousness in order to remotely "view" events rather than read the neighboring environment.

Nurse Haupt signaled the beginning of the session by dimming the halogen bulbs in the experiment chamber. She flipped the switch, illuminating a black light at the base of the tank. Haupt stepped to the electronic panel to check Shelby's vital signs, while Epstein seated himself on a metal stool near Shelby's head.

Epstein's face was bathed in the now familiar blue glow of the tank lights as he began to speak in subdued tones. In a few moments, he had succeeded in submerging Shelby into a hypnotic state. He whispered to Haupt to begin the Formula 15 injection.

Medvedev and Preston moved toward the glass, gazing intently into the chamber.

A few seconds passed while Epstein continued to speak in Shelby's ear. He looked up and nodded, and in a normal voice said, "Shelby. Your thoughts about January are becoming clearer now. He is your friend. He is also lost. To help him, you must find him. The mind link you and January have is very strong. Do you recall how he visited you in dreams?"

"Yes," Shelby said weakly.

"How did he come to you?"

"Through the air. Flying."

"At night while you were asleep?"

"Yes. Later, when I was awake too. I could fly to him. We would remember all things together."

"Remember what?"

"Remember the greatness. The *all* things."

"What are the *all* things?"

"The togetherness. The feathers and the fur. The soft colors that would happen when we became other people."

"Yes. That's the fun part isn't it? You would *be* people and see what they saw?"

"Yes."

Showing his eagerness, Epstein shifted on the stool. "Well, Shelby, we want to have that fun right now. We want you to *be* January. We want you to fly to him and be with him and tell us what he sees."

Shelby suddenly lay still. The only sound in the room was the gentle gurgle of water in the tank as saline solution swirled around her limp form.

Almost an entire minute passed.

Epstein looked up at the glass again and shrugged. He focused on the girl once more. "Shelby. Where are you now? Have you found January? Are you with him?"

No response.

"Come now, Shelby. You know you can do this. Where are you?"

"I am with Nadia," Shelby said, happily.

"Who?"

"Nadia Vladichkova," she said softly.

Standing to Trajan's right, Medvedev coughed nervously. "What did she say?"

Apparently confused, Epstein had continued the interrogation. "Who is Nadia? Is January with her?"

"No. A baby is with her, right now in Kiev. Inside her tummy."

Medvedev had taken a full step back from the glass, glaring at Preston. "What do you think you're doing?"

Preston turned, confused. "Doctor, what is it?"

In the other room, Shelby continued. "Nadia's husband, Mr. Vladichkov, is a bookkeeper. He doesn't know about the baby."

"What the hell is this?" Medvedev blurted.

"It is Dr. Medvedev's baby. Hello, Dr. Medvedev."

"You filth," Medvedev shouted, advancing on Preston. "Goddamn you." He gripped Preston by the lapel. "How dare you invade my life?"

Preston had shrunk against the far wall. "Doctor, for Christ's sake. I don't know what you mean."

"Surveillance. You had me watched."

"Watched? No. Medvedev, I had nothing to do with it." Wide-eyed, Preston glanced at Trajan. "Was it you? Did you somehow—?"

"No, it wasn't me."

Epstein's shocked expression on the other side of the glass would have made Trajan laugh, if it had been his nature. Instead, Trajan simply smiled at Medvedev, who's pleading eyes darted from Epstein to Trajan to the tank and back again.

"That's right, Medvedev," Trajan said. "It's the girl. Aided by Epstein's *misguided* technique."

"But—but she—" Medvedev's eyes moved wildly about the room. "She couldn't possibly. I, myself, only recently found out."

Trajan was floored by Shelby's brilliance.

In one deft maneuver, the twelve-year-old girl had not only negated Epstein's efforts to key on January, she had scanned everyone in the booth, identified Medvedev as the greatest threat, and reduced him to a blathering fool.

24

Outlook Inn
Eastsound

FOR THE FIRST TIME SINCE her arrival, Lorna had occasion to rest. She slept well, took a shower at six o'clock, wrapped herself in an ivory beach towel, and opened the shutters of her hotel window.

The sun had risen spectacularly over Eastsound Harbor. Seagulls flew lazily up the shore. Several seals basked on the rocks, and a pair of otters with their backs shining in the morning light cavorted along the beach in the sparkling waves.

A warm easterly breeze puffed through the open window, and Lorna suddenly sensed a peace she hadn't felt before. She caught a glimpse of herself in the mirror over the dresser. The air of the islands had caressed her moist hair and created soft, curly wisps along her face . . . a natural look, compared to the sleek, sculpted style she wore for business.

Michigan Avenue seemed light-years away.

Life on Orcas seemed immune to the panic that undoubtedly pulsed through the Sears Tower at this very moment. The contrast was significant, enough to compel her decision. She picked up the phone and called Chad Hennings in Chicago. He was, of course, eager to speak with her and sounded desperately concerned about her altercation with Skip. He briefly inquired into Tracy's condition and then launched a diatribe about how she could patch things up with Waterman.

That's when she stopped him cold.

"I didn't call to talk business." She gazed past the window's fluttering drapes toward a peninsula, where blue water met the lush green shoreline of the island. "I called to inform you that I'm taking an extended leave."

A short pause, then Chad said, "Things are critical here, Lorna. I can't allow that."

"Things are always critical there. I've got a sister who's critical. I'm sorry, but I'm going to be gone for a while."

"How long?"

"I'm not sure. It could be weeks. I'll have to let you know."

"Weeks? That's not acceptable. I'm afraid I'm going to have to demand—"

"With all due respect, I no longer accept *demands*. I sympathize with your situation, but I simply need time to think things over. I'll call you with my decision."

"About what?"

"About whether I'm coming back."

Chad was understandably shocked. "Is it Van Hollenbeck? Is that why?"

"Skip's just the icing. I've frankly grown tired of eating the cake."

The Marie Antoinette analogy seemed an appropriate close, and Lorna hung up, feeling better about having made her position clear. Chad was a decent man, and she promised herself to deal with him decently, no matter what her final decision—a decision that would have to wait until Tracy's and Shelby's circumstances were resolved.

After dressing, Lorna walked to the small community hospital.

She found Tracy looking even paler than the day before.

The coma had taken its toll, and Dr. Crowley made it a point to stop by the room. "The next seventy-two hours are critical," he said, nervously fidgeting with Tracy's chart. "If we don't see marked improvement, I may have to refer you to the Virginia Mason Hospital's extended care facility in Seattle. We can't hold someone in Tracy's condition indefinitely. There are special wards for that kind of thing."

Discouraged, Lorna waited at Tracy's side until nine o'clock when, as arranged, Kellen arrived.

He looked refreshed, having removed the bandage from his forehead. The wound had indeed appeared to have rapidly healed. Noticing Lorna glance at where the bandage had been, he smiled and made reference to Molly's snake oil.

She was cheered by Kellen's good spirits. He'd just seen Paddy, who was actually sitting up and eating breakfast. Kellen was even happier that Paddy had received a hand-delivered message from Molly Creed: Marissa Harmon was to meet Kellen at a relatively secure location, his salmon hatchery, at roughly eleven o'clock that morning.

Since time allowed, Kellen suggested that he and Lorna have breakfast together at Dottie's, a small café in the heart of town.

Over coffee, they briefly reviewed their strategy. The visit to Molly's home the previous night had ended uneventfully. What had been established, however, was Molly's great respect for the "gift" both Marissa and January shared: an alleged clairvoyance. How this all related to Shelby remained unclear, except that she, too, might share the gift, explaining her friendship with January.

As anxious as Kellen was to locate January through Marissa, Lorna insisted she visit Hank Pelto at Camp Orkila to hopefully organize a search party for Shelby. Kellen suggested that they assess their priorities after their drive to Kellen's hatchery for the presumed rendezvous with January's grandmother.

On the way, responding to Lorna's curiosity, Kellen stopped at his cabin to show Lorna around. She was shocked at how tiny and primitive it was, though she voiced admiration for the serenity that he obviously cherished. She waited while Kellen once again made the rounds outside, unsuccessfully searching for his cat.

Next stop—Kellen's salmon hatchery.

The small facility was located roughly a mile from Kellen's home on the west shore of Orcas, nestled on a knoll, surrounded by marshland that Camp Orkila had owned for years.

Kellen guided the noisy VW van onto the dirt driveway. As the narrow road opened into a clearing, several ponds became visible, tucked among the tall fir trees. There was no sign of Marissa. While they waited, Kellen suggested he give Lorna a mini tour.

Still seated in the van, Lorna found the compound charming, though far less impressive than she'd expected. Aside from a cedar toolshed, the hatchery appeared to consist of three small holding ponds, a series of streams to connect them, and a fish ladder that led to the sea. A nearby spring fed fresh water into the upper pond of the system.

"Things are quiet now," Kellen said as they climbed from the van. He pointed to the fish ladder. "This October, the mature ones will be coming home." He spoke with hushed reverence, as if describing the pilgrimage of a lost tribe.

"Up that?" Lorna asked as they strolled toward the lip of the narrow channel. She couldn't picture full-grown, fifty-pound fish swimming up a ladder of ditches three feet wide by six feet long. Each gravel-filled tier of the flowing stream was roughly three feet higher than the next.

"You bet. That's how they left, and that's how they'll return. Two and a half years ago I opened that gate and off they went, over a half a million of them."

"From this small pond?"

Kellen smiled. "Of course the fish were tiny themselves. King Salmon, about three inches long. January's people call them Chinook."

"You're kidding. That small, into the open ocean?"

He nodded. "Against predators, with no maps to guide them." He gazed at the glistening bay. "When they get back, they'll be haggard. Skin decaying. Their color will have turned to a mottled gray. Ready to spawn after traveling thousands of miles."

"This is your first batch?"

"Yes. I had help getting started. A fellow who lives up-island named Jorgen showed me the process when I visited his place. He helped me set this up, my first salmon release."

"You actually created life."

"I mainly watched and learned. Mother Nature created the life. But this fall, when my seniors return, I'll be able to fertilize my eggs."

She couldn't help but smile. "I don't know if I'd admit that in public."

He grinned. "I know. Pretty wild, isn't it?"

"Since when do fish need help with fertilization? I thought it was somewhat automatic."

"It is in a natural stream, yet much more haphazard. Frankly, with the pollution and erosion today, the salmon don't reproduce very well. We simply try to ensure the result."

"We?"

"Well, Paddy was along last time. You can imagine what this means to a fisherman." He pointed to the nearest pond. "That's where we'll season the fish that succeed in coming up the ladder. You understand, this isn't murder; they're ready to spawn and die. We simply aid in the process by stripping the females of their eggs, about four thousand per fish, into that trough. Then we squirt seed from the males into those buckets." He gestured to a spawning bench holding a dozen three gallon plastic containers. "The rest is easy. We'll simply pour the buckets into the trough and stir."

"You're joking."

"Absolutely not. It's a perfectly effective way of enhancing the declining salmon stocks. Within an hour, fertilized eggs will be placed in shallow incubation trays in the stream near the upper pond. Water from the spring flows through the trays. After the babies have grown a bit, they're ready to smolt." In answer to her confused expression, he explained, "We pump sea water into the pond. The saline helps the small fish develop mature scales. That's smolting. Then they're ready to handle the salt water out there." He pointed to the bay. "A few days later, off they go."

"Down this fish ladder?"

"Exactly. That's how they know the scent of this place."

"They *smell* their way home?"

"That seems to be the consensus. Salmon have keen olfactory capabilities that lead them to the very spot where they were born." He pointed to the trees. "The mineral content of soil and the plant life give off a scent that the salmon sense. Kind of like wine . . . the way grapes carry flavors of the land on which they were grown."

Lorna gazed at the expanse of the President's Channel that led to the ocean. "In the Pacific? How could they possibly?"

"I know it sounds incredible, considering that the salmon travel to Alaska or California and back. One popular theory holds that they navigate by the earth's magnetic fields."

"That sounds a bit farfetched."

"Just a guess."

Lorna envisioned a lone salmon in the fury of the open sea, reading an internal compass. "If it's true, that's a miracle."

Kellen smiled. "I agree. Yet that's what scientists believe. My salmon will forgo a thousand other streams along the way to Orcas Island, sniffing their way to this beach, forging up this trench to their birthplace." Kellen turned and surveyed his small compound. "I get a kick thinking about that. I'm giving life to literally millions of fish, and they're giving something back—ecological benefits. Salmon carcasses provide nitrates to surrounding soils. Seals feed on salmon in the ocean. Bears and eagles wait for them in the streams. It's all part of the food chain." He spread his arms. "I play a part in that. We all need that feeling, you know? Of being connected?"

She was struck by how dynamic he looked with his short blond hair glinting in the rays of morning light. Dressed in jeans and his black sweatshirt, he appeared totally comfortable with himself. Lorna couldn't remember a man so proud of something so unselfish—a contrast to the egomaniacs to whom she'd catered in Chicago. Money and power were nothing to Kellen Rand. He gained satisfaction in what good he might do. She admired the simplicity of it. Her own life seemed complex by comparison. She remembered her desk—the reflection of herself in her dead computer screen—the perfect businesswoman, coifed, implacable, even unapproachable. She gazed down at her soiled tennis shoes on the pine needles. The berber carpet in her office seemed suddenly strangely pretentious.

"I admire you for that . . . being connected," she said. With the tip of her shoe, she nudged a tiny mushroom that had sprouted from the forest floor.

Kellen let her last words hang in the morning air.

She turned in time to catch his contented expression. "Sorry, I'm rambling."

"No, you're not. I've pondered things like that."

She stared at him, suddenly curious, fascinated that a man once so active sought a life so tranquil. And why, despite his phone call to Washington, was he willing to risk that tranquility? "Kellen, tell me. This thing with January, Shelby, and myself. Do you make a habit of helping other people?"

His brow furrowed at the question. "I have before."

"I know. But didn't you come to Orcas to retire?"

"Sure. But I didn't expect to have a boating accident either." He seemed suddenly disturbed. "There's something particularly mysterious with this January thing. You should have seen him kneeling on the deck of Paddy's boat, staring out at Sucia Island. For some reason, something about that particular chunk of land fascinated him."

"Sucia? The island with the fingerlike extensions?"

"Right. He spoke of his ancestors being tortured there."

"Is that what he visualized?"

"Apparently. He mentioned 'the rush of souls.'"

A pair of redheaded woodpeckers swooped through the trees behind Kellen. Lorna followed their flight, amazed at their agility. The two birds narrowly missed several branches, one squawking behind the other in a playful chase. They frolicked into the darkness of the forest, and as Lorna watched them disappear in the distance, she noticed several large crows sitting in a spruce tree. They seemed oddly quiet, dotting the shady boughs like dark

Christmas ornaments. Something stirred in the shrubbery below. A small doe moved through the thicket, wandering toward the beach, high-stepping fallen branches, picking a path that led past the nearly imperceptible figure of a woman, standing immobile near the trunk of a large fir.

Lorna blinked to make sure she wasn't seeing things.

She whispered, "Kellen. There's someone there."

"Behind me?" His hand moved quickly to his 9mm, concealed by the sweatshirt.

"In the trees. It might be Marissa."

"And it might not. Look away, and bend down to tie your shoe." With his back to what he could now identify as a woman, Kellen pulled the weapon from his belt, and as Lorna knelt, Kellen craned his neck to look. He dropped the weapon to his blind side. "Good morning," he shouted.

At the sound of his words, the crows chattered and lifted en masse, their large black wings flapping noisily as they flew inland.

The woman stepped forward into a shaft of light that exploded off her white hair. She wore a black-and-gray blanket over her shoulders, and she strode toward them like a cat in her moccasined feet, hardly stirring the underbrush.

As she approached, Lorna rose while Kellen asked, "Can we help you?"

"We can help one another." With her regal bearing, there was little doubt who she was.

Kellen tucked his gun away.

Marissa had put him at ease, and Lorna was drawn to her immediately. Marissa appeared calm, yet incredibly aware. Her tanned skin, stretched tightly over high cheekbones, gave the illusion of youth, though the creases around her eyes betrayed her age. Those dark eyes were fixed intently on Kellen. She stepped close, nearly under his nose. "You are the bear who will not rest."

As if greeting an old friend, Kellen smiled. "And you must be the woman who names clouds."

"It's a pleasure to meet you," Lorna said, with undisguised admiration. "You had no difficulty finding us?"

"None at all, when it is you who seek me." She turned to Kellen. "January asks for you."

"He said he'd be among the eagles. Where's that exactly?"

Marissa's gaze drifted off beyond the trees. "Up north, across the Canadian border, above the headwaters of the Skagit River. There is a hidden gorge where eagles gather this time of year. As you know, January is in danger, so he cannot come here. But he wishes you to join him."

"Is he all right? I don't understand how . . . the way he escaped that night."

"That is something I will allow January to explain. As you have seen, my grandson is an extraordinary individual. He has his own means of travel and communication. Among my people, those like January are called the tellers of stories. Perhaps he will tell you one."

25

Bartwood Lodge
The North Shore of Orcas Island

STANDING ON THE WHARF UNDER clear skies, Alessandro gazed appreciatively at the Georgia Strait—the beautiful expanse of water that had been once explored as the Northwest Passage. These briny bays were cold compared to the light-blue Mediterranean, but today they looked even more spectacular than he had imagined.

Above a sunlit fogbank to the east, Mount Baker's volcanic lava dome loomed under perennial snows. Two hundred years ago, Imnit and Lukat probably looked with awe at that mountain, undoubtedly conjuring legends of gods and spirits.

Alessandro looked back as Dr. Hargrove strode onto the Bartwood dock, dangling a set of keys in his hand. The professor had chartered a twenty-one-foot Tollycraft complete with a dinghy that now floated next to the pier. Hargrove claimed he could navigate everyone safely to Sucia Island. His white hair buffeted in the breeze as he joined Alessandro, Fraley, and Bernardo.

Hargrove pointed to the northwest. "It's my guess that *El Trinidad* sank over there, perhaps a half a mile from shore."

Dressed in his mismatched vest and pants, Fraley blew his nose into his handkerchief. "So Cerba Martine must have been aboard at the time."

"And why do you presume that?" Alessandro asked.

"His letter." Fraley folded his handkerchief. "You've shown us how Martine assumed his post as captain after Ravilla's death. We found no record of Martine's burial. He may have gone down with his ship."

Alessandro shook his head. "I don't know. Do you believe Martine could have made his final calculations while the ship was sinking?"

"Could be," Hargrove answered. "Martine's letter to his brother was dated June 27. The *Intrepid* reported the fire the night of June 30. I think we can infer that the map was aboard at the time." Hargrove pulled the protected parchment from his beige corduroy jacket. "After all, the lower portion of the map shows fire damage." He handed the plastic sheath to Alessandro and hoisted his binoculars. "I wouldn't be surprised if the hull of his warship is lying just off this side of Sucia."

Alessandro admired the professor's initiative. When Hargrove had arrived on Orcas Island last night, he appeared obsessive, visibly excited that he had discovered new clues about Martine's ship. As he dined with the others at the Outlook Inn, he had explained his findings.

From all indications, Panjota's journal was the only Spanish documentation of the *El Trinidad*'s sinking, though Panjota had been imprecise about the date. On a hunch, Hargrove inquired with the British Maritime Historical Society in Portsmouth, England, which turned up a ship's log of the *Intrepid*, an English ship that had sailed around Vancouver Island under Captain Elias Clement.

Clement's journal described how on a calm night in late June of 1793, while anchored on the western shore of the now British Columbia mainland, the *Intrepid*'s helmsman sighted distant flickering that appeared to be a burning vessel. Captain Clement's entry mentioned how he had raised anchor and sailed toward the location, arriving at dawn only to find a few charred spars in the water and a very hostile group of American Indian natives, who taunted the English seamen from shore. The location of the sinking was given as south-southeast of a landmass with many lagoon-bound islands and peninsulas, obviously the same island the Spanish had named Sucia.

Alessandro had slept on the news, but he came away unconvinced that Martine had gone down with his ship. Even now, on the dock, he tried to picture the scene 210 years ago. "I'm sorry, but the supposition that Martine died on board makes no sense. His map obviously fell into Imnit's hands, and that could only happen if Martine had abandoned his ship with the strongbox in order to deliver it to her."

Hargrove dropped the binoculars to his waist. "Suppose the Indian woman had been aboard herself? When the vessel was under attack, she could have absconded with the strongbox while Martine was preoccupied."

"No." Alessandro turned and faced Hargrove. "In Martine's letter to his brother, I sensed a regard for Imnit. He described her as 'genteel' and mentioned the 'great comfort' he found in her company. That phrasing, and the fact that she died while in possession of Martine's highly valued map, leads me to believe they were lovers."

Fraley straightened his glasses. "What? You believe he chose to leave his ship and his men in favor of a *native* companion?"

"Perhaps. Or maybe whatever Martine found in that cave drove him to shirk his duty."

Hargrove shrugged. "That's unimportant."

"A man's motivations are 'unimportant'?"

"Compared to the map? Yes." Hargrove took the plastic sheath from Alessandro and held it in the sun. "We may never know Martine's motivation. What remains are these numbers. If they're not coordinates, what does their sequence indicate?"

Fraley joined Alessandro as both men gazed over Hargrove's shoulder at the figures: 33, 7, 6, 45, 9, 90, 12.

"You think these are paces, perhaps? Distances from one point to another?" Fraley asked. "Maybe 33 instructs us to walk thirty-three steps."

"Perhaps," Hargrove said, pensively. "But if so, from what location? And what about '45' and '90'? They must be angles, some kind of geometric reckoning. Could relate to the triangle on the right of the map. It's a right triangle—a ninety-degree angle and two forty-fives."

Across the page from the triangle, a small, deeply etched trident with irregular lines lay off Sucia Island's shoreline to the east. "And what do you make of this?" Alessandro asked.

Hargrove shrugged. "Don't you think the trident simply denotes water? Ancient maps used symbols of Neptune, mermaids, etcetera, to indicate the ocean."

Alessandro looked up from the map to the green hills of Sucia. The island's inlets were tucked quite regularly between fingers of land, almost as if God had made an imprint of a giant hand on the sea. "Martine wanted this map to tell us how to find it," he said, following the topography of the small hills. "In more ways than one, it's time to test the waters."

26

The Sitnalta Facility

THE MOMENT TRAJAN ENTERED THE room, Shelby retreated to the head of her cot, pulling the pillow up to her knees. Trajan held his position just inside the door, trying to vie for her confidence. "Now don't be afraid. I won't hurt you. I just want to talk."

Shelby made no reply.

"Do you know who I am?"

Shelby nodded.

"Of course you do. Just like you knew Dr. Medvedev." Trajan eased forward to the end of the cot and gestured to the brown army blanket. "May I sit?"

In her surgical gown, Shelby inched even farther into the corner, tucking her bare feet beneath the pillow.

"What you did in the lab yesterday was amazing."

Shelby's gaze rose to the top of his bald head. Her blue eyes were wide with curiosity, but devoid of panic.

The idea had come to Trajan last night. He had explained his plan to Epstein this morning. A short window of opportunity existed, since Preston had returned to Washington and would not be back for forty-eight hours. As for Dimitri Medvedev, he had permanently postponed his participation in Shelby's experiment.

Trajan smiled his most disarming smile. "I'm very impressed, the way you saw into Medvedev's life. Outstanding how you knew about Nadia, the woman in Kiev."

At the mention of Nadia's name, Shelby's lip curled with the slightest hint of amusement. This child was a force to be reckoned with.

"You knew exactly what you were doing, didn't you? You're a clever girl. I admire that."

"Don't," Shelby said softly.

"Excuse me?"

"I don't like that."

"What? That I admire you?"

"Don't think of me like you think of Bunny."

In spite of himself, Trajan was shocked. "You know about Bunny?"

Shelby winced. "Yes. I don't like that."

"All right. I promise to try."

She glared at him from under bleached eyebrows. "I'll know."

"Of course you will." Trajan did his best to veil his growing respect. Shelby presented a challenge. He had to deal with her without knowing her full telepathic potential. Was she presently able to read him, or had she simply stored information she acquired while under Epstein's drug? Either way, she was living proof—a validation of Epstein's work. Trajan had to be careful, state his goals sincerely; otherwise, she'd see through him. "Shelby, I want to help you. But I need *your* help."

A skeptical glance. "Why?"

"Because it's important to me . . . and thousands of other people."

"You don't want Mr. Preston to take me to Washington?"

"Smart girl. That's exactly the point. I want you to be happy. And what would make you happier than anything else in the whole world?"

"To go home and see my mom. She's hurt."

"That's right. And I want to take you there. Does that surprise you?"

Shelby's pale eyelashes meshed in a squint, and Trajan wondered if she knew what was happening on Orcas Island at this very moment. Could she know that Calico had called only hours ago, reporting that the ex-FBI agent named Kellen was on the move?

"You want to find January?"

The question startled Trajan. "Uh . . . yes, of course. I need you both. Do you understand? Our country's in danger. Bad people are going to hurt us with a terrible disease. Is January . . ." Trajan had trouble finding the words, "better than you? At seeing things. The way you 'saw' Medvedev?"

"Yes. He is greater than me."

"But you two can do it together?" Trajan imagined the blending of their skills. Once united, January and Shelby might command remote viewing power beyond anything Epstein had ever achieved. If Trajan's suspicions were correct, Epstein wouldn't need other support psychics. Shelby and January would feed off each other enough to pinpoint Abbas, Rahid, and other AVALANCHE terrorists. "Do you and January see better when you *both* picture something far away?"

Her eyes brightened at the suggestion. "Yes. That's when we fly together."

"So you've been in a trance, and he somehow leads you along to see things?"

"Sometimes. Except when he sees yesterday. I can't do that."

"He sees the past." Trajan was invigorated by the implication. "Does that mean he can see *tomorrow*?"

"I don't know. He says he's learning."

"Like you learned in the lab." He pointed to her neck. "Dr. Epstein's injection helped you learn. You used your power in a new way."

"But this thing behind my head itches. I want you to take it away."

"I can't do that. I'm not a doctor. That's up to Epstein."

"Maybe Mr. Preston will take it out."

She was toying with him. Trajan tried to empty his mind of details on the chance she could read into his plan. He decided on closure and escape.

"I'll make you a deal." He inched closer. "If I put you on a plane for home, I want you to promise that you'll help me find January."

She shook her head no.

"All right. Then how about if I have Epstein remove your implant? When you and January come together, do you think you can fly without the formula?"

She seemed to ponder the question, her gaze traveling across the ceiling.

"You understand the question, Shelby? Is January going to pull you along without a problem?"

"There is no problem." She looked Trajan in the eyes with conviction and said, "January is an eagle who flies without wings."

27

The Skagit River Gorge
British Columbia, Canada

KELLEN PARKED HIS RENTED CAR in a turnout on Highway 3, just east of the Hozameen Mountains. He had obeyed Marissa's instructions to find this desolate spot, and he'd taken care not to be followed.

It took only twenty minutes to fly commercially from Orcas to Bellingham, Washington, where he chartered another flight to Hope, British Columbia. There, he had rented a vehicle and driven southeast for an hour. Once he found the crook in Highway 3 where two forks of the Skagit River collided, he doubled back on the road twice, stopping in front of a small gas station/lodge to check pursuing traffic. Aside from a logging truck, there simply wasn't any.

He saw no other hikers after leaving the road, as he picked his way through steep and rocky terrain. Great granite blocks, formed by glaciers ten thousand years ago, shouldered into the sky on either side of another white water tributary called Manson Creek. According to the map, Manson Creek fed the headwaters of the Skagit River, eventually spilling into Ross Lake some twenty-five miles south.

The country was magnificent, though rugged and cruel. Kellen worked up a good sweat as he followed spindly deer trails through sparse pine trees precipitously hung on the cliff face.

After a thirty-minute climb, he stopped and gazed into the roaring rapids below. It was just after eleven. The morning mist had lifted, and the June sun began to bake his back. He would get even more heated as he continued his climb.

As he paused, he tucked his 9mm handgun into the rear pocket of his jeans to prevent it from chafing his waist. He stripped off his black sweatshirt and tied it around his waist, just over the small fanny pack that held two sandwiches and a bottle of water. His forehead had become drenched with perspiration, and he reached up, gingerly fingering the cut.

Kellen couldn't help but smile. Maybe Molly Creed really did have something special in that sickening green potion. Kellen genuinely wished Lorna were here to see how much the wound had healed. He missed her company. But she and Kellen had decided to split efforts . . . Lorna would try to organize an island search for Shelby while Kellen tracked January.

After the breather, Kellen resumed the ascent, attacking the steeper section of the cliff, taking the mountainside in sometimes knee-high, thigh-burning strides.

According to Marissa, Kellen was to watch for a bleached patch of rock on the east face of the jagged gorge. It was across from there, she said, that January had found a cliff cave while following the eagle migration last year. It had become his occasional hideaway and a place for meditation.

Kellen understood January's penchant for isolation. Of late, Kellen had often longed for solitude. Fishing with Paddy was fine—the old man was almost a part of the sea himself, hardly a disruption. But Kellen enjoyed those moments when he'd worked his hatchery alone, fussing with the water and the dirt, surrounded only by birds and an occasional deer. And nothing could compare with the hush of his cabin, sitting on his back porch in the dappled morning sunlight while Long John rolled on the pine needles, purring and playing with the rawhide shoelaces on Kellen's boots.

Trudging along, Kellen pictured Long John's little face. The missing eye invoked sympathy for the little beggar, and he was certainly that, tugging at Kellen's cuffs when he was steeped in the odor of fresh fish upon his return from Paddy's boat.

Kellen wondered if he'd ever see his cat again. His peaceful life on Orcas had been shredded in only a matter of hours. The attack on Paddy's boat plus Lorna's crisis had flung him into retribution against an unknown enemy, reawakening protective instincts he hadn't felt since Cleveland.

What had Lorna asked? "Do you make a habit of helping other people?"

The answer was no. Since arriving on Orcas, he'd tried to avoid problems. That kind of accountability was part of the past. His sometimes blind altruism died in the alley with Benson and Probst. It was buried when his friends and family shunned him. Funny how the past could, without warning, propel Kellen into unpleasantness. As he struggled along the trail, sweating heavily, the smell of his own perspiration brought him back to those hot summer nights, the raucous laughter of men and women lounging in a dimly lit back room of Danny's Restaurant. During those late hours, when the gambling dwindled and the heavier drinkers hung out, talk around the bar got loose.

Kellen remembered faces . . . the gleam on Johnny Solupa's forehead as he'd glide around the barstools like a rotund ballerina, catering to after-hours guests. Solupa hosted the late-night club three times a week, fronting the place for Mace Calvin, the head of a statewide gambling operation, whom the FBI's Cleveland field office desperately wanted to bust.

Danny's was located in Little Italy, a few blocks off Euclid Avenue. Excellent Italian food, black leather booths. After 2:00 A.M., the doors would close, only to secretly reopen at 2:30. Exclusive patrons would be ushered through a side door to the kitchen where they would join the few privileged dinner customers who had been allowed to remain. The bar would reopen, and the gambling and seduction would commence.

Kellen had assumed the cover of a high roller from the West Coast, a power broker backed by several California oil execs who ostensibly wanted to buy the Cleveland Browns football team.

His dossier was seamless, with artificial references dating back ten years: records of fictional transactions as a racehorse broker, supposed deals with several dummy corporations, even planted traces of a prison term in the Leavenworth Penitentiary and a stint in the Marine Corps.

Under the name Frank Keeler, Kellen flaunted his wealth at the Cleveland racetrack. At the Turf Club, he eventually befriended a racing aficionado named Needles Gionelli, who had gained his nickname from plunging pins under his dissenters' fingernails. More recently, Gionelli became known for his escort service. Gionelli was the gateway to Mace Calvin, the Ohio overlord.

Kellen wore Italian suits and partied at every opportunity, often forced into proving his taste in debauchery by soliciting Gionelli's girls. Kellen even invited Gionelli to his penthouse suite at a downtown hotel. Their relationship improved rapidly when Kellen bragged about his big money connections with potential NFL team owners.

The scheme worked, and Gionelli invited Kellen to Danny's Restaurant for after hours.

After blowing seven thousand dollars, Kellen drew the attention of the management. Johnny Solupa, the thick-necked strongman who laughed too loud and too often, expressed his admiration for Kellen's style. One night, when Gionelli and Kellen were among the last at the bar, the break finally came. After a bout of backslapping from Solupa's wiseguys, Kellen was goaded into an arm-wrestling match with Solupa. Kellen won. Amid the guffaws and bottle breaking in a macho celebration, Solupa disarmingly announced that Mace Calvin wanted to meet Kellen the following night—a 2:00 A.M. rendezvous at Danny's. Calvin's agenda: how he might find favor with an NFL team's potential new owners.

The sting was set.

The FBI's Cleveland field office assigned a woman and four men, including Benson and Probst, who had tutored Kellen about the Ohio mob scene. Silberman, the supervisor of the Cleveland field office, demanded a low profile arrest. He even informed the CPD's Fifth Precinct to stand clear during the bust.

Kellen arranged to post two of the four men and the woman inside the restaurant as customers. They were to have a late dinner together and wait in the restrooms until two o'clock, when Kellen, Benson, and Probst would enter the restaurant from the alley.

The hour of closing came and a few minutes after two, Benson, Probst, and Kellen tried the side door to Danny's.

It was locked.

Out of the darkness, car tires squealed, gunshots from a passing car rang out, and Kellen dove headfirst into a dumpster.

Benson and Probst hadn't reacted as quickly. They lay in a pool of blood near the garbage cans. There were no Cleveland cops in the area as backup to track the unmarked vehicle. The agents inside the restrooms hadn't seen a thing. The mob had made its point. This was a vendetta, and Kellen was to have been killed.

The incident was classified as a drive-by shooting without motive. All gambling paraphernalia in the restaurant's back room had disappeared. With no evidence and Kellen the only bona fide witness to Calvin's alleged gaming connection, the FBI chose to drop the case.

The Bureau was embarrassed. Particularly since the Cleveland Police Department ridiculed the blown cover.

Kellen was blamed for the deaths of two agents. To wipe the slate clean, the Bureau ordered Kellen to drop out immediately. He was whisked out of town in a matter of hours.

During a subsequent hearing, FBI officials not only condemned Kellen's incompetence, they also refused to formally investigate the circumstances. Mace Calvin, they ruled, might be pursued again, but only if the investigation arose from an entirely new direction.

In retrospect, Kellen suspected that Needles Gionelli had been the leak. It was rumored that a variety of prominent Cleveland officials occasionally used Gionelli's escort service. One of them might have been a ranking officer within the Cleveland Police Department. But which one? Kellen would probably never know.

What he did know as he reached the top of the ridge was that lingering guilt from Cleveland had obliquely affected his decision to help Lorna—a redeeming act to obliterate past accusations.

He could live with that. Maybe he couldn't live without it. Lorna, Paddy, Shelby, Tracy, even Long John . . . the faces of the victims would have weighed on his conscience.

Kellen was shaken from his thoughts by movement in the sky to the north. A flock of eagles circled a distant bluff. Across the crashing river on the opposite wall of the gorge, a sliver of white feldspar creased the gray granite cliff.

January couldn't be far away.

Kellen picked up his pace, moving more easily along a relatively flat ledge. A rock face rose dramatically to his left, a drop-off to his right. He rounded a sharp turn and froze.

Several hundred feet beyond, below the spot where the eagles circled, January sat cross-legged. He was perched near the edge of the cliff beside the entrance to a small cave, dressed in deerskin britches, naked from the waist up, and in apparent meditation, his mouth forming words Kellen couldn't make out.

Kellen crept closer along the rocky ledge.

January's eyes were closed, and he held a large black crow in his lap. The bird seemed to sway to a cadence created by January's chanting.

Fascinated, Kellen watched for a few moments and resumed his approach. The roar of the rapids was deafening, and Kellen had advanced to within six feet of January before he was able to distinguish the words.

"Riu riu chiu. La guardoribera. Dios guardó el lobo de nuestra cordera." January repeated it again and again.

The crow suddenly snapped its head in Kellen's direction, noticing him for the first time.

January ceased his chanting and took a deep breath.

"Hello, Kellen," he said with his eyes still closed. He opened his hands, and the squawking crow leapt into flight.

"I'm glad to see you." Kellen meant it.

January's dark lashes rose slowly. "And I'm grateful to you, my friend. Thank you for coming."

January's chest heaved once again, and he hunched his shoulders, stretching. The jagged cut over January's right eye reminded Kellen of the spectacular dive into the sea.

"What were you doing with that bird?"

"Among other things, I was petitioning the future—through a divination of the raven."

"I see." Kellen tried to veil his skepticism. "And the language?"

"Spanish. I've had the language in my blood lately."

"And what does it mean?"

January rotated both arms over his head and twisted his torso, loosening up. "It's a sixteenth-century chant. *Riu Riu Chiu* is a bird call. And I, as a bird, am calling on *La guardoribera,* which translated means 'the guardian of the river.' *Dios guardó el lobo de nuestra cordera* means 'As God from the wolf, keeps our lamb.'" He got up on one knee. "I'm worried about Shelby. She's the lamb among wolves."

Kellen was shocked. "You knew she was missing?"

"After the boat crashed, I knew. I could sense her distress. I made the assumption that she'd been abducted by that band of rednecks."

"That's what we believe as well." Kellen shielded his eyes from the sun and watched as three eagles settled in the branches of a ragged spruce on the cliff face. "Molly Creed mentioned your 'gift.'" He fixed on January. "Can you sense where Shelby is right now?"

January squinted at the sky and then glanced at Kellen. "No. I've tried." In response to Kellen's disappointed droop of the shoulders, he added, "Look, I'm receptive, not *omnipotent.*"

"Sorry."

"Don't be. We'll make contact soon. Even though I don't know where she is, I hear her cries in my sleep."

Kellen realized how little he truly understood about this man. "Listen. I have a million questions—"

"I'm sure. But you're sweating like a horse. Let's get you out of the sun." Without another word, January rose, and with his long black hair trailing over his muscular back, he shuffled in his moccasins toward the cave.

Set back from the edge of the cliff some five yards, the cavern was the size of a small garage. Ashes from past campfires smudged the entrance. A series of strange hieroglyphics, drawn in what appeared to be white paste, covered the stone walls. Two bedrolls were spread on the dusty floor, near a set of backpacks.

January slouched against one of the backpacks, while Kellen knelt near the other.

January pointed toward a canteen, speaking up over the sound of rushing water from the rapids. "I'm afraid all I can offer is water. Want some?"

"I'll trade you for a sandwich."

"What kind?"

"Turkey."

January shook his head. "Sorry. I don't eat my brothers. But I'd appreciate the bread."

"All right." Cloaking his amusement, Kellen opened his fanny pack and handed January one of the baggies.

"Your questions?" January peeled the sandwich apart.

"Endless. I don't know where to begin."

"Start with the obvious."

"All right. This thing with you and Shelby. Why are they after you?"

"They? The jet skiers, fascists, PhDs with hypodermics? Call them what you like." January took a bite and spoke while chewing. "As the millennium broke, the collision of hope and remorse created a new generation of fools. These analytical control freaks want to put us in yokes, or test tubes, for what we possess. They call it ESP." January shook his head. "What a misnomer."

"Extrasensory perception?"

"There's absolutely nothing 'extra' about it. Everyone has it to some degree." He pointed to Kellen. "Do you acknowledge that you and I connect up here?" January tapped his forehead.

Kellen grinned and pointed to his hairline. "Matching scars."

"No." January blinked patiently. "Connected. Not like Shelby and I connect. Rather with 'compassion,' or 'synergy,' or 'friendship.' Terms that express the inexpressible. There's no adequate descriptive language for the connectivity between humans or even animals. Do you understand?"

"A relationship?"

"More than that—the voluntary invasion of another person's soul. Like love. When love is shared, it presumes upon the mental space of another individual. It doesn't require permission; it imposes itself on both parties, and often without logic. That bond can be sensed across a crowded room—a projection to which you surely relate." Kellen nodded as January continued, "What Shelby and I do is based on that same imposition, the projection of ourselves into others, and the reception of others into ourselves."

"But you said you see things."

"Sure. Once we connect, we expand into situations. We glide on the sea of energy that surrounds all of us. You're familiar with Kirlian photography?"

"Something about an aura?"

"Right. A relatively well-known phenomenon where plants and people flare light on a photographic plate when their energy emanates." January placed his hands on his chest. "When I leave this shell, this body, I travel through a flaring ocean of colors. The air is alive with rainbows. Sometimes it's also alive with pain, of course. The learning can be terribly unpleasant. Like the night we met . . . Wait." January suddenly appeared distracted. He set the sandwich on the backpack, stood, and walked to the cave entrance.

"What's wrong?" Kellen asked.

"I don't know." January nodded to the gorge. "I thought I sensed somebody out there." January listened intently, and Kellen wondered how he could hear anything over the roar of the rapids.

January shrugged and returned, squatting on the dirt. "Sometimes I can't tell what I'm feeling. In ancient times, people like me were called 'the tellers of stories.' With all the forces at work, the hard part is knowing how the story will end. You asked about the black bird—it's a link to my past. Through the crows, the past calls me." A bemused expression flooded January's face. "Someone keeps haunting my soul. I'm not sure why."

"Someone?"

"Yes. In the form of a spirit. It's strong. I sense that he was a wise man who lived on the islands a long time ago. Like me, he had a name that was not his own. His people gave it to him."

"You know the name?"

"I do. It burns in my brain. It was a word that meant 'sentry' . . . one who watches. They called him Lukat."

28

Orcas Island Medical Center

NODDING TO THE RECEPTIONIST as she walked briskly past her, Lorna barely made it through the lobby before she broke down outside. Tracy's condition had deteriorated dramatically overnight. Her blood pressure was now only ninety-five over fifty-two, and her pulse had slowed to a sleepy forty-eight beats per minute.

Dr. Crowley had called the Virginia Mason Hospital in Seattle, arranging to move Tracy to their long term ICU, but as he gently suggested, unless Tracy's condition leveled off, long-term care might not be necessary.

For the first time, Lorna truly accepted the possibility that by the time Shelby was found, she might be motherless.

The prospect brought Lorna to tears as she walked across the parking lot toward Paddy's dilapidated van. As she climbed into the driver's seat, she slammed the steering wheel with both hands, feeling helpless and angry that she hadn't reunited the family prior to the tragedy. She vowed that, if necessary, she'd give Shelby a home . . . if she could find her.

Frustrated by her lack of options, Lorna looked around inside the relic VW as if searching for answers. In his absence, Kellen insisted that Lorna drive Paddy's old beater. When she arrived at the medical center that morning, she had stopped to visit the old fisherman to thank him. Her moments with Paddy were the only bright spot of the day. As opposed to Tracy, Paddy had steadily improved. He was excited by Lorna's arrival and showed his appreciation by chattering about Kellen, how he'd pulled January from the ocean that night at the cliffs, bragging about Kellen's courage. She hadn't heard that part of the story from Kellen, of course.

Focusing back on getting underway, Lorna dried her tears and reached into her purse for the car keys. She came across several pieces of paper: envelopes she and Kellen had found in Tracy's study; the demand letter from Bruce Spilner, Tracy's ex-husband; and the correspondence from the National Institute for Improved Vision.

Tucking the demand letter back into the purse, she fixed on the "Improved Vision" envelope from South Dakota. As dissuaded as Kellen seemed from probing further, Lorna sensed that there had to be other ways of finding answers.

She glanced at her watch. It was just after eleven. She'd made arrangements to meet Hank Pelto at around noon to discuss the search. She wasn't due at Camp Orkila for an hour. She put the key in the ignition, wrenched the complaining gearshift, and maneuvered Paddy's old crate from the parking lot onto the street. At the intersection, she made her decision to take a left into town.

Driven by disappointment and the bad news about Tracy, she refused to play the victim. She desperately wanted to act, wanted to do something to help. That's why she decided on a detour and headed for Tracy's house.

Lorna parked in the same space in the alley. The small backyard appeared unchanged. Plywood still covered the shattered window, and aside from the distant sound of traffic along Eastsound's tiny waterfront, Tracy's quaint, provincial neighborhood remained eerily still. Lorna exited the vehicle, ducked under the police tape, and used Tracy's key to unlock the kitchen door.

Working her way across the linoleum, she reached the hall and sidestepped the bloodstained hardwood. She was drawn toward Tracy's den and the rolltop desk where Kellen had found the letter. A seasoned Mac G4 computer rested on the typewriter stand nearby. Lorna sat down at the desk and pulled the envelope from her purse, setting it on the writing pad. She rummaged around in the top drawer, fussing with miscellaneous articles . . . paper clips, scissors, Post-its, and more bills.

In the mess, she felt something hard: a pair of glasses. She pulled them into the dim light. The lenses seemed abnormally thick. They looked cheap, like a pair of drugstore reading glasses. Lorna switched on the green banker's desk lamp and examined the embossed imprint on the temples more closely.

Raised black lettering read: FLEX-OPTICS. The name rang a bell. She picked up the institute's envelope, opened the letter, and reread the phrase,

"Your daughter, Shelby, will receive her Flex-Optics glasses in a few days . . ."

Lorna stared at the letterhead. "National Institute for Improved Vision." There had to be more about that organization. If this was, indeed, a front for a covert operation, what were they doing writing letters to people? Lorna's gaze shifted to the computer. Even the CIA was on the Internet. Perhaps . . .

Lorna turned on the Mac and watched the screen light up. She pulled up Google and typed "National Institute for Improved Vision" in the search bar.

The URL came up easily: www.nat/inst/vis.org.

Lorna clicked on the link and watched the new page form.

The header graphic was identical to the envelope's, complete with a PO Box in South Dakota and a link to the Department of Education in Washington, DC. But there, the navigation ceased. When Lorna tried to click on the icon marked "Contact Us," the page referred her to the Department of Education. When she tried to click on "Applications," the screen flickered into a gray box that read: "access denied, site under construction."

A dead end.

Lorna continued to stare at the screen. She glanced at the letter. Her gaze rested on the phrase "her participation in the next phase of our Edu-net program." Lorna decided to search for "Edu-net."

No results.

How could Shelby have participated?

Lorna was about to again rummage around in the desk, when she realized Shelby might have used the site enough to bookmark the address. She pulled down on the menu bar and clicked "bookmarks." There, highlighted in blue, was the word "EDU-NET."

She released the mouse button and the screen opened into a colorful full-page graphic entitled "Alice in Wonderland," complete with the classic cartoons of Alice, the White Rabbit, the Mad Hatter, the March Hare, and the Queen of Hearts rushing through a rose garden.

Lorna tried to click on the graphics, but nothing happened. She noticed the illustration in the lower right-hand corner: a tubular representation of what appeared to be a telescope. Neighboring fine print read, *"Wonderland waits behind the looking glass."*

Looking glass? Was that it?

Lorna picked up the spectacles and put them on. As she glanced at the computer, the screen transformed.

The rose garden background disappeared, and on a horizon line in the distant background, Lewis Carroll's enigmatic caterpillar sat on a toadstool, exhaling puffy letters from a tiny hookah.

Lorna moved the cursor toward the letters, passing over "WHO" then "R" then "U." When she reached the question mark, she clicked and was suddenly linked to a new page with the header: "Hello, Shelby. Ready to play IMAGINE?" An instructive paragraph below asked for Shelby's password.

What would Shelby's password have been?

Perplexed, Lorna paused and stared at the screen. Then, a noise. The back of her neck rippled into goose flesh as she heard the unmistakable sound from the rear of the house: the latch on the back door had just clicked into place.

Someone had entered the kitchen.

Her mind raced. Could the police have returned to check the home? Perhaps. But what if Tracy's assailant had come back?

She tucked the glasses into her purse and rose to her feet. As quietly as she could, she stepped from behind the chair and gazed around the room. There was simply nowhere to hide.

She felt the choke of panic in her throat. The creak of a footfall on the hallway hardwood drove her off the edge. With her purse under her arm, she dashed from the room into the hall and toward the front door.

The silhouette at the other end of the darkened hallway shouted, "Who the fuck are you?"

The man gave chase, his boots rapping the floor, and Lorna covered the twenty-five feet to the small foyer in a matter of seconds. With her heart pounding, she fumbled with the front door handle. But it refused to budge, secured by a key-operated dead bolt.

It was too late.

"Who are you?" the man yelled, only steps away.

She abandoned the door and rushed into the black void of the living room. Suddenly she was in the air, having stumbled over an ottoman. She sprawled onto a musty throw rug and rolled onto her back, just as the man pounced, grabbing her wrists.

"What's going on here?" he demanded.

"Don't touch me," she screamed, trying to scramble away. She succeeded in landing a kick to his thigh, and the pain seemed to enrage him.

He shook her violently. "Tell me what you're doing here."

"This is my sister's house."

The man seemed shocked. He let go and sat back on his haunches. "You mean . . . you're Lorna?"

"Yes, goddamn it."

His voice suddenly softened into despair. "Lorna, what's happened? Where's Tracy? And Shelby?"

The familiarity came as a complete shock. "How do you know me?"

"Tracy used to talk about you."

"Dear God." Lorna's mouth dropped open. "You're not—"

"Sure, it's me. I'm her ex-husband, Bruce Spilner."

29

The Skagit River Gorge

"SO WHAT DID YOU THINK of my grandmother?" January asked, taking another bite of the bread.

"Amazing." Kellen had never met a woman as intimidating. "Looking into Marissa's eyes was like gazing into a time machine."

"She has an ancient soul. She's a storyteller too, but the least earthbound of all of us. The older she gets, the more timeless she becomes. She's begun her journey into the inner houses of the universe. But don't let her mentality fool you. She has guts." January patted the bedroll. "She spent two nights with me right here. Find me another seventy-eight-year-old that can make that climb up the mountain from Highway 3 and sleep on the ground."

"Seventy-eight? God, she looks fifteen years younger."

"And she acts it. She took the initiative to save me. I couldn't have gotten off the island without her."

"And how did she do that?"

"With her old Chevy pickup. I hid in the truck bed under a tarp. With those maniacs running around the island that night, we didn't want to attract attention on the ferry, so my grandmother chartered a barge. We drove onto a flatbed boat called the *Pentail* at Lieber Haven. You familiar with the place?"

"Not really." Kellen still hadn't explored all of Orcas Island, but he'd heard of the tiny beach resort on the southeast shore.

January stretched both arms over his head. "About four hours after I left the *Tide Runner*, my grandmother had me headed across the Georgia Strait for

Bellingham. I'm sorry Paddy was hurt. I know he's going through hell because of me."

"You saved us, man. I don't know how you did it, but I'm in your debt."

January shook his head. "No debts."

Kellen couldn't let the conversation lag another second. "You want to tell me how you pulled us out without being caught?"

A smile crept across January's face. He pointed at the scar on Kellen's forehead. "After the jet ski hit you, do you remember anything?"

"No."

"What if I said a school of dolphins kept you from drowning?"

"What?"

January smiled.

"Come on. How? The last thing I remember was jet skis all around you."

"Exactly. I was surrounded off to your flank about thirty yards. I saw one rider aim right for you. When he ran you down, I realized there was only one place for me to go. I dove ten feet under and swam in your direction."

"Could you see? It must have been dark as hell down there."

"Actually, I found you easily. The headlights on the skis lit the water pretty well. I was able to grab you and take you underwater to the *Tide Runner*. The skiers expected me to head for shore. They spent most of their time darting back and forth between the boat and the beach."

"You had to come up for air."

"No. It only took me about two minutes to reach the boat."

"Only."

"That's nothing. During meditation I've held my breath for three, maybe more."

"But how did you get me onto the prow with all that activity around?"

"I didn't. I towed you underwater to a large hole in the boat's hull and dragged you inside. Because the *Tide Runner* rested nose down, air was trapped inside the bulkhead. I kept your head in that air space and gave you CPR."

"You're kidding. What about Paddy?"

"When you could breathe, I climbed inside the boat and pulled him free. He was bleeding badly. I tied my rawhide belt around his leg and hoisted him into the hull with you. I waited while the skis circled the boat. They couldn't see us. A Coast Guard cutter made the skiers take off along the shoreline, without lights. I lashed you and Paddy to the hull before the Coast Guard saw me." January shrugged. "Then I swam for shore."

"That was quite a feat."

"Not really. I just followed my—oh God!"

Kellen reacted. "What's the matter?"

January leapt to his feet and strode to the cave entrance.

Kellen rose and drew his 9mm from his belt, joining January near the opening.

January peered outside then ducked back in. "You brought them."

"What?"

"They found us."

"They couldn't have—"

"There are three men on the ledge just south of here."

Kellen rehashed the steps he'd taken to make sure he wasn't followed. "No way. They must be hunters."

"With automatic rifles?" January stepped aside. "Take a look."

Kellen eased past and peeked around the rock.

Some 275 feet away, three men in black fatigues stood guard. From their high-tech weaponry, there was little doubt—Marty Flowers's warning about a "super force" was merited.

"I doubled back, damn it, and checked the trail," Kellen said. "I don't understand."

Fighting a sense of doom, Kellen realized that, at this range, his handgun would only deter the intruders temporarily. He turned to January. "How many ways out of here?"

"Besides the trail? Only one, and it's straight up."

"You're shitting me. That's sheer rock wall."

January pointed north. "Exactly. We could hook around the far side, beyond the cave. There's no trail. Just cliff. They would have to drop their weapons to follow."

Kellen ventured another peek. The men hadn't moved. "What's to keep them from picking us off?"

"Not a thing. Except I don't think they want to kill me."

"You're right. At a full run they won't catch up to us until we're on our way up."

January frowned. "That's it, then. Unless you want to chance a swan dive into the rapids. I'm not exactly in the mood for another one of those."

Kellen pulled his sweatshirt on, fastened the fanny pack, and cocked his handgun. "Okay. At least let me lead the way. I'll spray a few shots in their direction to keep them off-balance. Are you ready?"

January nodded.

"Let's go." Kellen bolted into the sun. As January darted behind, Kellen brought both hands high, sighting the GLOCK. He fired seven quick rounds, gratified to see the commandos cower against the cliff wall as the shots echoed in the gorge.

One of the men leveled a rifle in his direction, but Kellen whirled and, tucking his handgun into his belt, dashed after January.

In a few quick strides, he had crossed what was left of the narrow shelf at the cave entrance. The trail ended abruptly on the other side, and he was faced with the starkness of a sheer wall, which January had begun to scale.

"Climb to my right," January barked as Kellen fell in behind. He clambered, grasping for handholds, kicking pebbles and dirt from the ridges with his tennis shoes as he worked off to January's right flank.

The seventy-five-degree cliff was thankfully negotiable, though as Kellen ventured onto the face with a hundred-and-twenty-foot drop-off looming below, he suddenly felt as if he were hanging on to glass.

"Don't look back, just go," January shouted.

Kellen again hugged the cliff and began to climb. One wrong move and it was a bone-crushing slide into the rapids. Breathing hard, Kellen gained on January and parallel to each other, they climbed.

They were thirty-five feet up when the three men in black fatigues reached the cave entrance below to January's left.

"You might as well come back here," one of them shouted. The Mexican American looked combat ready, like a well-trained marine, lean and sporting a brush cut. The other two couldn't have been over twenty-five years old.

"There's nowhere to run, Mr. Rand," one of the others said. "Bring our boy down."

Kellen stopped climbing. He considered firing his gun to scatter them, but suspended against the rock, he could hardly chance reaching for the GLOCK.

"Keep moving," January whispered. "They're not going to shoot."

Perhaps January was right. Perhaps they really could escape.

"What's on top?" Kellen asked, again hoisting himself along.

"A plateau. Miles of forest beyond. We can hide there."

"Good." Kellen glanced back down at the ledge, where the leadman spoke into a two-way radio, his words muffled by the roar of the rapids.

Kellen's thighs, fatigued by the hike, began to burn. Under his black sweatshirt, perspiration poured down the small of his back.

January was a few feet ahead, near the crest of the cliff where greenery and a few sparse trees showed over the edge. He reached out and grabbed a pine's exposed roots, grasping the gnarled limb. He heaved himself upward and . . . froze.

"What's the matter?" Kellen asked, a few feet back.

January looked over his shoulder and shook his head.

Kellen fought up the last few feet and pulled abreast, only to find a dark-haired, broad-shouldered man leaning over the edge, holding what looked to be a futuristic zap gun. It appeared to be a Heckler & Koch G36 with an oversized pistol grip—undoubtedly loaded with twice the usual thirty rounds, enough firepower to take down a platoon.

"Bring January the rest of the way, Mr. Rand," the gunman said calmly. He had flat, full features, like a NFL lineman. "When you get up here, I want you both on your faces."

An African American soldier stood a few feet back, talking into a two-way radio.

Kellen nodded to January. "It's over. Do what he says."

January pulled himself the last few feet and bellied onto the grassy ground.

Kellen was right behind. He rolled onto his stomach, mindful of the bulk of his 9mm under his belt. "How the fuck did you freaks find us?"

"We're not freaks, hot shot. Just doing our duty for God and country, not unlike you at one time."

The big man stepped away, revealing a jet-black McDonnell Douglas 500E helicopter some eighty feet beyond on the plateau.

A woman with red hair, stretch jeans, black high-heeled boots, and a maroon body stocking, exited the cockpit. She was incredibly striking, with her high cheekbones and light-blue eyes. She strolled in their direction. Under one arm, she carried Kellen's cat, Long John.

She strode past the soldier. "Monk, tell Ramón and the others to take the Rover back to the main road. We'll meet them in Chilliwack." She spoke in a soft, husky southern drawl as she approached the big man. "Stooch, for God's sake, get that bastard's gun."

"You heard her." Stooch jerked his weapon into position, pointed at Kellen's forehead. "Ease the gun out, two fingers on the butt."

"So I'm a bastard?" Kellen pushed to his knees and with one hand over his head, hoisted the 9mm from his belt. He glared at the woman. "The name is Kellen." He tossed the weapon at Stooch's feet. "What are you doing with my cat?"

"Oh, we like cats." She petted Long John with her manicured fingernails.

Stooch leaned over to pick up the pistol and then turned and tossed the 9mm back to Monk, who tucked the handgun in his belt.

"We don't much like what we know about you, though," the woman continued, pursing her pink lips. "You actually are a *bastard* of sorts, aren't you? Rejected by your peers. Even your family. And you have a tendency for heroics, though not a lot of brains . . . as evidenced by your service record. Did you really think you could keep us from our business with January?"

"*Your* business?" Impressed by her apparent competence, Kellen was angered that he'd brought January to this. "I've never seen a sideshow quite like you. I didn't catch your name."

"Perhaps you'd rather catch your cat." Long John let out a complaining yowl as she hoisted him into the air, threatening to throw him into the ravine.

"No," Kellen uttered, in spite of himself.

"Ah. A soft spot for pussy. That wasn't part of your dossier. I'll keep it in mind." She petted Long John and again tucked him under her arm.

"Calico?" The black soldier waved the two-way in the air. "I have Trajan. He wants to talk to you."

"I'll take it in the cockpit." Calico began to retreat slowly toward the helicopter. "Bring them away from the edge."

The names were bizarre. Calico? Stooch? Trajan?

"You heard her," Stooch said. "Crawl." He led them along, keeping the barrel of the gun trained on their heads.

Kellen pushed forward on all fours, and January followed to his left. "I want to talk to whoever's in charge. Where are you taking us?"

Calico pivoted on the heel of her boot. "No need to concern yourself, Mr. Rand. January is the one who's going."

End of the road. They would bury Kellen in the woods. And why not? No one would find the grave. Kellen lay on his belly, making eye contact with January. "Sorry, man," he whispered.

January shook his head. "Just stay aware," he whispered back.

"Shut up. Both of you." Stooch stepped closer. "Not another word."

With furrowed brow, January sighed and closed his eyes.

Kellen's were wide open.

30

Somewhere over Montana

"I DON'T SEE THE POINT." Trajan watched the yellow plains pass some twenty-six thousand feet below the Learjet. "What's this compulsion for collecting hostages?"

"I thought we might benefit," Calico answered over the ship-to-shore band, "by finding out what he knows—who he's told."

"Is he handsome? Is that it?" Trajan understood Calico's inclination. She was frequently sexually frustrated by the restrictions of her duty.

"He's interesting."

"Bullshit. He's trouble." Trajan leaned back on the gray chaise, glancing out the Lear's porthole. "The asshole was a nuisance the minute he showed up."

"Trajan, you're not due on Orcas for a couple of hours," Calico said. "Let me just ask him a few questions."

"We're past that. We've got two days left." Trajan looked toward the rear of the plane, where Epstein had fashioned a mobile lab. In the aft cabin, Shelby Spilner's blonde hair tufted over the lip of the immersion tank. Epstein hovered nearby, managing the equipment on his own. For security reasons, Nurse Haupt had been left in South Dakota. Even Bunny Hobbs had been deported to Cincinnati so Trajan could focus fully on the task ahead. If Trajan's coup were to succeed, there would be no witnesses. Kellen Rand would certainly not be one of them. "Calico, hear me. You're going to get rid of this Kellen guy. Clear? That's an order. See you on Orcas tonight."

Trajan switched off and tucked the receiver into the cradle on the armrest.

Jack Turley, the jet's copilot, nodded to Trajan as he stepped from the cockpit. "Twelve mile visibility over Puget Sound, Mr. Morse. ETA's an hour and forty-five. We've got clearance to land."

"From the sheriff?"

"Affirmative." Jack smiled. "He offered an escort to the mayor's office. I guess they don't have too many visiting dignitaries."

Trajan smiled. "Thanks for reminding me." Trajan pulled his billfold from his suit-jacket breast pocket, opened the back flap that held his traveling credentials, and retrieved one of the cards—the FEMA ID. He slid the red, white, and blue plastic into the wallet sheath opposite his driver's license. He tucked the billfold away and eased from the plush velvet couch. Adjusting the knot on his tie, he maneuvered toward the aft cabin.

Among stacks of equipment, Epstein fussed with various monitors, checking the readouts from the printers.

As Trajan approached, Epstein knelt and unhooked the EEG bundle from the electrode pad at the base of Shelby's skull. She floated in a blue saline solution dressed only in a G-string, her nakedness glowing beneath the turquoise liquid.

Trajan leaned against the bulkhead. "How did she do?"

"Pretty well."

Trajan had expected firmer assurance.

"I'm getting readings I've never seen before." Epstein pointed to the EEG printouts. "It may be that we're pushing her too hard. The alpha pattern is steady, but she's exhibiting beta wave fluctuations in the extreme. I'm not sure what it means. She enters ERV at will, and with no strain. I had her on a simple exercise to test her. She was keyed on you for a short time and told me what you and Calico were discussing."

"All of it?"

"Snippets. She knows you have January. That seemed to irritate her, but she flashed on her mother and the EKG went crazy. Upset her badly."

"Why? What happened?"

"Apparently Tracy is losing signal, if you will. Fading quickly."

Shelby appeared to be asleep. "So why is she lying there like that?"

"I sedated her."

"Just as well. As long as you can liven her up."

Epstein pointed to the vials in the agitator. "Don't worry. I've got plenty of Quadrilin."

Trajan nodded to the second aluminum tank that sat across the aisle. "Once we set down, can you handle January and Shelby together?"

Epstein's pockmarked face creased in concentration as he studied the printouts. "Terms like 'handle' imply control." He looked down at Shelby's angelic face. "When you're dealing with the abstract energies of clairvoyance, Trajan, the paramount issue is precisely who or what is in control."

31

Orcas Island Medical Center

WHEN LORNA TOLD BRUCE SPILNER about Shelby's disappearance, his initial shock went from wide-eyed dismay to unabashed suspicion. He actually implied that Lorna and Tracy had schemed to abduct the child to prevent him from seeing her.

"Where's Tracy right now?" Spilner asked as he followed her into the alley from Tracy's house.

"That's no longer any of your concern," Lorna replied, getting into the van.

"Wait a goddamned minute," Spilner yelled, grasping the door handle.

"Let go or I call the cops now," Lorna screamed in his face.

He was so startled, he let go, and she locked the doors and started the engine. He began to rap on the window, but she hit the accelerator. In the rear-view mirror, she watched as Spilner ran into Tracy's backyard.

Lorna's first instinct was to get back to Tracy to protect her. She raced the van through town, past churches and schools. Coming to the Horse-shoe Highway, she took a right and, half a mile later, pulled into the hospital grounds. After parking the van, she bolted past the reception desk to her sister's room and found Tracy as she'd left her: bandaged, punctured by IVs, and barely breathing.

Lorna had to decide how best to insulate Tracy from her ex-husband's potential arrival. She pondered the alternatives. Since she had no idea who Tracy's lawyer was, she intended to call the courts in Boulder to locate records of the case. But that could take days. Perhaps she could get help from an attorney on Orcas? She turned, ready to search for a phone book in the lobby, but the hospital room door flew open and Spilner bolted in.

Thinking he might mean Tracy harm, Lorna blocked his path. "Keep away from her." His stunned expression soon changed her mind.

"Oh Jesus," he said, seeing Tracy in the bed. He turned to quietly close the door and removed his cap. "How did she get hurt?"

"She was attacked when they took Shelby."

Moved by his injured expression, Lorna let Spilner brush her aside as he shuffled toward the bed. He collapsed into the chair by the headboard and sat staring at Tracy's face. Finally, he rubbed his brush cut with square, calloused fingers and turned to gaze at Lorna.

"I had no idea." He blinked in confusion. "I came here because she didn't answer her phone. I thought she might have left town and taken Shelby."

Lorna was suspicious of his motives. Had Spilner attacked Tracy? Had he abducted Shelby and returned to the house to get Shelby's clothes, by chance confronting Lorna? "You're sure you don't know where Shelby is?"

"Damn it, woman. How would I know?"

"Why would you show up unannounced? Did you think you could change Tracy's mind? Take Shelby to Colorado? Was that the plan?"

"It wasn't like that. I wanted to talk." She read what appeared to be regret in his eyes. "I didn't know I would find her like this."

Lorna glanced down at his soiled denim jacket and jeans, the trucker's cap he held in his lap. As manager of a Boulder auto-wrecking yard, Spilner couldn't have fashioned written language so calculating as appeared in his note to Tracy. "You had an attorney's help with that letter didn't you?" she asked.

"I didn't want trouble," he said remorsefully, fighting back tears. "But Tracy stopped calling me. She shouldn't have done that." He reached out to take Tracy's hand.

Taken aback but moved by his childlike gesture, Lorna allowed his contact with her. Lorna knew very little about Bruce, though from Tracy's brief written account of the separation, this bastard had beaten Shelby—hurt her during alcoholic tirades and behaved abominably during the divorce.

Seeing Spilner's smudged hands on Tracy's pale skin, Lorna began to realize the grave implications. If Tracy were to die, Spilner could legitimately reclaim his only daughter. A clever lawyer would probably manage a reversal of the custody ruling, and in a matter of days, Shelby might be under Spilner's care.

Lorna strode to the other end of the small room and, creating sufficient distance, turned to face him. "You know, Bruce, I don't think you should be here."

"What do you mean?"

"Just by sitting there, without Tracy being able to . . . well, you're not considering her feelings."

He gazed down at the oxygen mask that covered Tracy's face. "From what I can see, she doesn't feel a thing."

"That's not the assumption. The doctor tells me that even in a coma she might absorb what's being said. Besides, there's the chance that she'll wake up, and I'm concerned that finding you here would be a shock. Do you understand?"

"You're asking me to go?"

"I'm afraid that would be best."

"I just came to set things straight."

"You came without permission."

"From who?"

"From her. Or her attorney. I'm unclear what rights an ex-husband has under these conditions."

Spilner looked pissed. "I'm Shelby's old man. That gives me rights."

"Maybe. But that's not for me to say. If Tracy could defend herself, I'd butt out. As her sister, I intend to protect her interests."

"Bullshit." Spilner's fists clenched around his cap. "You were no sister. Not from what I heard. You never gave a damn about her. What are you doing here anyway? I thought you were in Chicago. You after cash or something?" His gaze darted around the room. "She didn't have much, you know, working at that hardware store. And there was no money in that briefcase."

"Briefcase?" Lorna hadn't remembered anything of the kind.

"Her dad's. You gonna play dumb?"

"I don't know what you're talking about."

Spilner's eyes narrowed. "She never told you?"

"Told me what?"

"You'll never find it anyway. I'll bet she hid it."

"Bruce, I really don't care. I just prefer you leave."

In fact, she did care. If there were a briefcase that belonged to her father, she definitely wanted to see its contents. She had often speculated why, after a successful career, her father had succumbed to early retirement and fatal alcoholism.

Spilner folded his arms. "Say what you want. I'm not going anywhere."

Lorna realized that she'd need outside help. She imagined how easily Kellen would handle the situation if he were here. Unfortunately, according to Kellen's latest voice mail from Hope, British Columbia, he would be deep in the wilderness by now.

She turned toward the door, ready to find Dr. Crowley—to call Deputy McMillan if necessary. As she reached for the knob, the door opened, and Hank Pelto poked his head inside.

"Lorna. There you are."

"Reverend." She was grateful to see another face. Any face. "Please come in."

Pelto edged into the room. "When you didn't show at camp, I became concerned. Is everything all right?"

Lorna ignored the question, glancing obliquely at Spilner. "Reverend, this is Bruce Spilner, Tracy's ex-husband."

Perfunctory recognition swept Pelto's face as he leaned forward, extending a hand. "Tracy mentioned you."

Spilner smirked. "Really? And who are you?"

"Her pastor."

Spilner gave him the once-over, glaring at Pelto's shoddy sweatshirt and jeans. "Kind of a 'hippie-go-to-meeting' deal up here, is it? I forgot she got into Jesus."

Pelto smiled patiently. "Fortunately, *he* didn't forget to get into her. I'm sorry about Shelby, by the way. Lorna's probably told you that we're doing what we can."

Spilner grunted and stared at the floor.

"Are the kids willing to help?" Lorna asked.

"Yes. On the condition that the sheriff organizes the search."

"Bullard won't do that." Lorna's shoulders slumped in disappointment. "Have you asked him?"

"Not yet. I just found out. The YMCA is concerned about liability. What if one of the campers is injured during the search? The camp simply can't involve these kids without police supervision."

Lorna sighed. "I understand. I want to see Bullard now. Will you come?"

"Naturally." Pelto turned to Spilner. "Will you join us?"

"No."

Lorna shot the reverend an admonishing glance, and from his expression, she sensed that he got the message. Perhaps Pelto had been familiar with Tracy's marital problems. She added, "Mr. Spilner insists on staying here."

"Does he?" Pelto had picked up the inference. "Tell me, Mr. Spilner, how was it that you heard about Tracy's mishap? Did you come at Lorna's request?" The question came beautifully to the point.

"No. I just showed."

"I see. Well, I suppose family members should gather at these needful times."

In the subsequent awkward hush, Lorna gestured to the hall. "Reverend, may I see you outside?"

"Of course." Pelto nodded at Spilner. "Would you please excuse us?"

Spilner glared without reply, and Lorna eased from the room with Pelto in tow. The moment the door closed, she turned to plead her case, but Pelto spoke first.

"He's a bit rough around the edges."

"He stumbled into Tracy's house and scared me to death," she whispered. "He followed me here. I don't want him in her room, Hank. I'm going to call the sheriff."

"What would that accomplish?"

"I don't know. But there must be a way to keep him out of the hospital. I know Tracy wouldn't want him around."

"You can't prevent a man from grieving for his ex-wife."

"Grieving isn't his plan." Lorna dug in her purse, found the letter and thrust it into Pelto's hands. "Look. He threatened to reclaim Shelby."

Pelto read for a moment. "He obviously cares for his daughter. I'm not sure the sheriff could do anything without a restraining order."

"I'll get one."

"On what grounds? Has he physically threatened Tracy?"

"Well . . . not yet. But you see how hostile—"

"Now wait. There's enough hurt to go around. Spilner may just need a break. Did Tracy ever discuss that with you?"

"Discuss? No. She just wrote me when she left him."

"Well, she talked to me. Poured her heart out during a counseling session. It may surprise you to know that she loved the man."

"He's an alcoholic abuser." Images of Skip Van Hollenbeck popped into her head.

"But he wasn't when they met. How much do you know about him?"

"Not much." Lorna couldn't remember details, embarrassed by the lack of contact. "I think he was originally from Denver."

"And a very successful stock car driver until an accident at Daytona ended his career. Tracy had known him only six months at the time. She was pregnant with Shelby and stuck with him during a difficult recovery period. With his mind clouded by a head injury, he had few employment opportunities. The drinking followed. She used to say that he became a bigger wreck than the cars he sold at the salvage yard."

"I never knew. The years passed. I simply didn't—"

"I understand. All the more reason to act with charity."

Lorna nodded.

Pelto placed a hand on her shoulder. "I'm going to ask you to give me a chance to talk to Bruce alone for five minutes. Don't call the doctor or anyone else until I return. Will you do that?"

"All right."

Pelto disappeared into the room, leaving Lorna to stare down the hallway toward the nurse's station.

Her thoughts turned to what Pelto had said only moments ago: "Family members should gather at these needful times."

It hadn't really registered. Officially, Bruce Spilner was, until recently, her brother-in-law. He remained the father of her only niece.

How odd.

Family members were often reluctant strangers, thrust together by some peculiar marriage.

She and Tracy were precisely that. If Lorna's father hadn't married Sheila, Lorna would have never known Tracy, never neglected her, never yearned for her as she did now, never wanted to reconstruct their squandered relationship.

Perhaps her dad's neglect ultimately caused her to shun Tracy all those years. Retribution against someone who was equally a victim of a dysfunctional family? Why? Maybe Lorna's bitterness stemmed from her feelings toward her father, Richard Novak—the first man who let her down. As a child, Lorna revered him. As a teenager, she viewed him more critically. Later, she wanted to speak with him, vent her frustrations, understand what had pulled him away. But before she had the opportunity, he died.

Alone in the silent hallway, Lorna yearned for the chance to heal the old wounds. She closed her eyes and found herself praying for Tracy's life, for Shelby's safety. Immersed in her plea, she was startled when Pelto emerged from Tracy's room.

"In a few moments," he said to her, "you and I will head for Bullard's office."

"Fine," Lorna pointed to Tracy's door, "but what—?"

"Everything's fine." He smiled. "Would you like to come in?"

"Come in?"

"Yes. Bruce has something to share with you."

Lorna stepped inside and Pelto closed the door.

Spilner was still sitting in the chair. His cap was pushed back on his head, and his eyes were red as if he'd been crying.

"We've had a good talk," Pelto said softly.

Casting a look in Tracy's direction, Spilner wiped his nose. "I am going to stay," he said. "I want to help if I can. But I won't get in the way."

"Bruce will be my guest at camp for a couple of days," Pelto said. "And he asks . . . well, Bruce why don't you say it?"

Spilner heaved a sigh. "I'd like to visit Tracy every day, if it's all right."

Lorna was shocked. "I . . . I guess—"

Pelto intervened. "Bruce agrees that you, or someone else, such as myself, be present in case Tracy regains consciousness. How does that sound?"

Bruce's anxious expression actually made her pity him. "Of course. We'll make arrangements," Lorna said.

"Thank you," Spilner said. He rose, tugging at the brim of his cap, walked toward the door, pausing at Lorna's side. "And I'm sorry if I—"

Lorna could only utter, "Don't worry about it. It's been hard for all of us."

"Bruce," Pelto said, "if you'll wait in the lobby, I'll join you in a moment."

Spilner nodded and slid out the door.

Lorna was dumbfounded. "What happened? What did you say?"

Pelto smiled. "I reminded him of her love."

"Tracy's?"

"Yes. I reminded him of his daughter's love."

Lorna nodded.

"Then I reminded him of God's love."

"That was it?"

"Is there more? I simply shared the clarity of the word with him. There are some key phrases that—"

"You're telling me you converted him in five minutes?"

"No. He converted himself. The absolute truth . . . the core concepts spoken by Jesus are like molten steel. Unfortunately, that's why some turn away when the heavenly forge spews its sparks."

Lorna marveled at the pastor. "You fed him fire and brimstone?"

"On the contrary. I simply spoke the loving words of Christ. The pettiness of the human heart is crushed by that virtue. Bruce had forgotten. Many of us do."

Pelto waited, searching Lorna's eyes, as if waiting for a response. Not getting one, he glanced at the floor. "I was someone who forgot, incidentally," he said softly. "I was someone overwhelmed by the sanctimonious niceties of the social church. Ceremonial pomp dilutes the purity of the word, you know." Moisture gathered in Pelto's eyes as he now stared at her. "But something happened to me a few years ago. I began to search for the nucleic God. Not the shrouded Jehovah of the Old Testament, nor the white-bread savior of the European translations. I sought the God who burned like a flame in the books of Matthew, Mark, Luke, and John. I actually left the church, convinced that over the centuries, organized Christianity had convoluted the message until it was almost unrecognizable. All we ever needed was the word from the four Gospels." Pelto wiped his eyes and sighed. "Look at me. If I'm a man of the cloth, why do you think I dress like this?"

Lorna shrugged. "It's comfortable."

"I dress down because Jesus did. And why do you think I hold services under the skies?"

She shook her head.

"Because creation itself *is* the church. No spires, no stained glass, no statues, no ritual, no interpreters, no latter-day prophets or TV evangelists allowed." Lorna's nonplussed expression made Pelto chuckle. "There I go again." He shrugged. "Sorry. I get carried away. Needless to say, I reminded Bruce of his place in God's plan. I think he came away feeling he has a purpose here. That's what we all need. He's your partner now, Lorna, in your search for Shelby, your vigil for Tracy, perhaps even in your need for a family."

The starkness of the statement hit hard. Pelto had seen into her longing heart.

"I'd like to be your partner too, you know," he said, taking her hand. "And I've got help." He smiled. "Someday, Lorna, when the time is right, I welcome you to witness the glory of God's power under the pines."

32

Skagit River Gorge

"ON YOUR FEET." STOOCH PRODDED January's right arm with the muzzle of the automatic rifle. January lay perfectly still with his eyes closed.

In the helicopter cockpit some fifty feet away, Calico held Kellen's cat under one arm, chatting on the radio with someone named Trajan.

From his position on the ground, Kellen desperately tried to hear the conversation while conjuring a means of escape, no matter how futile.

Since Stooch was occupied with January and the man called Monk continued to gaze toward the chopper, Kellen actually considered somehow getting back to the edge of the plateau to throw himself into the ravine rather than being shot.

He would need January to create a diversion for an opening. But January had withdrawn into a trance of some kind, and his cataleptic condition couldn't be more inopportune.

Stooch tapped January on the temple with the gun barrel. "Did you hear me, Cochise? Get your wiry ass up." He cocked the rifle, but January remained still.

Calico completed her transmission and swung one long leg out the open chopper door. "Stooch, will you stop diddling around?"

"Let's go." Monk glanced at his watch.

The big man took a half step forward. "Hey, Cochise." He kicked January's arm with a combat boot.

"Don't bruise him," Calico shouted. She had placed Long John in some kind of container on the cockpit floor and hopped to the ground.

"He's fucking with me," Stooch yelled over his shoulder. "Let me hurt him a little. I'll wake him up."

"No." Calico meandered over. "We'll carry him if we have to, but I don't want him damaged. Give me the rifle."

She took the G36, showing her familiarity with the weapon as she hoisted it. "Give us a hand, Monk." She assumed a flanking position, training the gun on Kellen.

Tucking the two-way radio into a belt holster, Monk stepped over and helped Stooch roll January onto his back. Monk grabbed the young man's knees while Stooch gathered him under the arms, and together they began to stumble toward the helicopter with January slung like a wet hammock in between.

"Now you." Calico jerked the muzzle in Kellen's direction. "Take a walk."

"Walk?" Kellen rose to his knees. "What for, so you can put a cap in my ass?"

"Oooh. A pessimist. You're going to need an attitude adjustment."

Kellen got to his feet, wondering how he could disarm her. With palms out, he took a step forward. "Look, if you guys are Feds, there must be—"

"Walk not talk. Hands over your head, one step at a—" Calico glanced over her shoulder as a high-pitched squeal sounded behind her.

January's ear-piercing cries echoed across the ravine, even while he was still suspended between the two men.

"Stooch," Calico shouted over the screeching, "what are you doing to him?"

"Not a fucking thing. He's just into his weirdness."

Stooch and Monk had come to an abrupt halt.

January's face was creased with pain as he continued to scream.

"Drop him." Calico backpedaled, distancing herself from Kellen.

Stooch and Monk set January down while the howling continued.

"Knock it off, asshole." Stooch leaned over.

For the first time, January moved, spinning away from Stooch. He lifted his legs, tucking them to his chest, and rolled from side to side.

"Will you stop him?" Calico pleaded.

Monk reached for his belt, unhooking the small holster that held the two-way radio. "I'll gag the son of a bitch."

Stooch strode toward Calico, angrily reaching for the combat rifle. "You want me to stop him? I'll stop him."

"No, you can't."

"I'm not going to kill him, Calico. I'm just going to distract him."

"Epstein needs him healthy. Don't hurt his head."

"Don't worry. I'll start lower than that."

Stooch yanked the weapon away and marched back to January, who had heaved himself to his knees.

January's eyes were still closed as he knelt with arms spread, palms open to the skies, yowling through gritted teeth.

Stooch hunched his shoulders and placed the muzzle of the rifle at the arch of January's right foot. "Shut up, or I'll blow it off."

January continued to yell.

"I mean it, mother fucker. I'll pull the trigger."

"Stooch, don't." Calico took another step toward the commotion while Monk stood indecisively nearby.

In a moment of clarity, Kellen suddenly realized the nature of January's distracting display. His outburst was unmistakable—identical to his howls that night on the cliffs, which had caused—

Kellen flinched as a large shadow flitted across the grass.

Apparently also aware, Stooch had straightened up, as if in slow motion. He had barely turned his head when the first bald eagle hit him, raking its talons across the top of his head.

"Holy shit," Calico shouted.

The first bird swooped away while a second eagle landed hard, sinking its claws into the base of Stooch's neck, noisily flapping its wings while tearing at Stooch's ears and eyes with its beak.

As Stooch cried out, the lead eagle made a tight loop and aimed at a wide-eyed Monk, while yet a third swooped past Calico, who ducked away from the attack.

Reeling in pain, Stooch clutched at the eagle with his right hand, unsuccessfully trying to dislodge the predator, while the eagle continued to jab at his face.

January seemed oblivious to the commotion, kneeling at the large man's feet, but Kellen was no longer a spectator. He was on the run, having noticed the G36 rifle dangling ineffectually in Stooch's left hand.

Seeing Kellen charge, Calico screamed Monk's name and gave chase, trying to intercept. She threw a punch at Kellen's head as he ran past her, but he deflected the blow and caught her with an elbow in the temple.

Calico was knocked senseless and went down as Kellen continued running toward the others.

Stooch was still stumbling about. Monk had fallen to the ground on his back, under the attack of the first eagle. Perched on Monk's chest, the giant bird viciously flapped its wings as Monk struggled to reach Kellen's pistol, tucked in Monk's belt.

"January!"

The sound of Kellen's voice stirred January from his trance. As if awakening from a deep sleep, he lurched to his feet just as Monk succeeded in retrieving the pistol.

Monk jammed the gun into the eagle's chest and fired three shots. Blood and feathers fluffed into the air as the bird fell away.

In a flash, January was over Monk, and with a savage kick, booted the weapon from Monk's hand. The 9mm flew several feet toward the ravine, and January hurdled Monk's body to retrieve it.

"Stooch, I've got him," Monk yelled, catching January by the ankle, throwing him to the ground.

Still struggling with the first eagle, Stooch turned to level the automatic rifle in January's direction, but in that instant, Kellen was on him. Leaving his feet and tucking into a ball, Kellen threw all of his weight into the small of Stooch's back.

Kellen heard the breath rush from Stooch's lungs as he knocked the big man over.

The violent collision dislodged the eagle, but it didn't dislodge the automatic rifle as Kellen had hoped. Kellen fell onto Stooch immediately, clutching at his wrists, fighting for the gun. Kellen used all his strength to stay close, keeping his weight on Stooch's upper body, clamping the rifle to maintain control, intent on keeping the weapon's muzzle away. Stooch appeared partially blinded by the blood oozing over his forehead. He blinked, cursing Kellen as they rolled in the grass. Stooch weighed well over 250 pounds, and at 195, Kellen was losing the battle with gravity. All the while, Kellen was desperately aware of the scuffle a few feet away, as Monk and January fought for the handgun.

Monk appeared to reach the pistol first, but January toppled onto Monk's back. In their struggle, they rolled ever closer to the cliff's edge.

To Kellen's left, Calico lay on the grass, propped on one elbow, trying to clear her head.

Kellen had no time to concern himself with her—he was being body-slammed by a bull. Stooch began to use the pistol grip of the rifle as a battering ram, jacking the butt of the weapon into Kellen's stomach. His thick arms proved incredibly powerful, and with each successive blow, Kellen felt his resilience failing.

Kellen was about to lose his grip, but he had no choice but to try to hang on. He tumbled from side to side, face-to-face with Stooch, realizing that to escape Stooch's bear hug without being shot he would need to rely on his hand-to-hand combat training from years past. As he gained the proper leverage, Kellen thrust his neck forward, head-butting Stooch squarely on the nose. He did it again. And still again, not allowing his opponent time to recover. On the fourth and final blow, Kellen felt the bone and cartilage at the bridge of Stooch's nose shatter.

Stooch let out a miserable groan as blood gushed from his nostrils. He twisted in pain and, releasing his hold on the rifle, fell back and passed out.

Off toward the ledge, Kellen heard a shot.

Holding the G36, Kellen reeled, dismayed to see Monk sprawled across January. A second shot sounded, jolting the two prone bodies into immobility. Gun smoke wafted into the air, and then, with his back to Kellen, Monk rose to his knees and slouched back on his haunches.

January still lay motionless on the ground.

Kellen's heart sank, but then he spotted the 9mm in January's right palm.

Monk swiveled slowly. A wet splotch of red covered his abdomen. He stared down with a look of utter disbelief, clutched his belly with both hands, and fell backward, sprawling onto January.

January let out an agonizing cry and scrambled out from under the limp body.

With the G36 slung over his shoulder, Kellen hurried over.

January lay on his side, his face twisted in agony. "I killed him." He clutched his forehead. "God help me, Kellen, I felt him die."

"It's okay. You couldn't help it." Kellen caught the shadows of the two remaining eagles gliding toward the forest.

Sobbing, January pointed. "Don't let her get away."

Kellen whirled.

Calico was on the run. She reached the helicopter cockpit and vaulted into the pilot's seat, locking the doors on either side.

With the G36 in hand, Kellen sprinted in her direction.

The whine of the ignition sounded, the black overhead blades began to rotate, and the pitch of the MD 500E's engine rose in a steady crescendo.

Kellen took a position in clear view of the windshield and pointed the rifle at the chopper.

Calico's eyes met his.

Kellen fired several quick shots into the helicopter's undercarriage, sending bullets off the landing struts. He aimed at Calico's face, bracing the rifle with his left hand, as he gave her a thumbs-down with his right.

The chopper blades spun more rapidly as she leaned down for the controls.

In response, Kellen fired two more shots, aimed at the passenger seat. The chopper windshield blossomed two daisy-shaped holes as the seat headrest exploded into pieces.

He gave her an even more definitive thumbs-down.

She stared, nodded, reaching over to hit several switches. The pitch of the engine began to ebb and the blades decreased their rotation.

Calico leaned over to unlatch the doors with a smile on her face. With that, she slouched back in the seat and placed both hands on top of her head.

33

The Outlook Inn
Orcas Island

ALESSANDRO THANKED SADIE, THE COCKTAIL waitress, and set a five-dollar bill on her tray. She was pretty, though very young. Blonde ringlets bounced over her ears, and she wore a revealing T-shirt depicting a cartoon orca whale across her rounded breasts. Like other American women, she seemed fascinated by Alessandro's accent. She smiled flirtatiously, bowing to serve him his second martini. "So you're from Spain?" She tucked the tray under a rounded arm.

"Yes. How did you know?"

"Front desk clerk told me. That's exciting. We've never had someone from Spain stay here."

"I'm honored."

"But you don't sound Spanish—you sound English, you know what I mean?"

"I assume that's another compliment."

"I guess. How was the vermouth the first time? About right?" She had mixed the drink herself since she doubled as the bartender.

"Perfect. Thank you." He smiled.

"I use an atomizer to make them nice and dry." She pursed her lips. "Just one spritz of vermouth. Like they say, it just blows a kiss at the gin."

He raised the glass as a toast to her. "The question is: does the gin kiss back?"

She giggled. "You'll find out."

As she walked away, Alessandro ran his index finger around the top of the cocktail glass, fantasizing whether to return later to close the bar. He enjoyed the den-like atmosphere of the tiny wood-paneled cocktail lounge. In this sleepy little town, even at the cocktail hour, there were only six other people in the place. He took a sip, relishing the solitude. As was usual when they traveled, Bernardo had retired to take a bath, leaving Alessandro to his own after-hours pursuits. Bernardo's fastidious nature had been assaulted by a sweaty afternoon hike across Sucia Island, which had soiled Bernardo's clothes. He couldn't stand the mess.

In the meantime, Hargrove and Fraley were busy with their own tasks. They had returned to the Orcas Island museum to search for nautical charts. The numbers on Martine's map still proved mystifying, and Fraley suggested they scour the archives in hopes of finding clues to the numerical sequence.

The walk on Sucia hadn't yielded anything. As for caves, there were mere indentations in the rocky cliffs near the water's edge. Without clarification on the map, there was little to do but painstakingly search the shoreline, which Hargrove had discouraged. He was more interested in *El Trinidad*'s presumed sinking off the southwest shore of Sucia. With Fraley and Alessandro's assent, Hargrove had contracted three scuba divers to search the shallows tomorrow morning.

Alessandro viewed the dive as marginally important. There was no harm in it. But to Alessandro, *El Trinidad*'s exact location was inconsequential. The key artifact had already been found. Martine had transferred the strongbox from the sinking ship for the purpose of revealing the cave's location. The cave was all that mattered now.

Alessandro took another sip of his martini. He was about to pluck the olive from the glass, when he noticed the beautiful brunette he'd seen on the island enter the cocktail lounge through the swinging doors. Dressed simply yet elegantly in a white blouse, black slacks, and half heels, the striking woman from the beach strode confidently across the room and took a seat at the bar.

As she perched on one of the brass bar stools, Alessandro drank in the cut of her figure. With an eye for art, he found some women's proportions aesthetically pleasing. And this one had a particularly fashionable flair.

As her drink was served, the woman swiveled in her chair, glancing in his direction.

Alessandro caught the glint of her hazel eyes, an incidental contact that seemed to encourage her to look again . . . this time with a hint of recognition.

AS THE PERKY BLONDE BARTENDER served the daiquiri, Lorna had taken a moment to survey the room. Three couples occupied the wooden tables: a pair of ardent newlyweds, two construction men, and a middle-aged man and his wife, apparently tourists.

Lorna swiveled and glimpsed at a man in the far corner. She couldn't resist a second glance. The man with sparkling eyes and shiny black hair had, the day before, leaned out the limousine window asking for directions. He looked tan and trim in his finely tailored black blazer.

Responding to his expectant expression, she couldn't help but smile. But not wanting to appear too inquisitive, she turned and sampled her drink. The lime-flavored rum tasted good.

It had been a long, trying day. She'd been burdened by Tracy's continued deterioration, yet pleasantly surprised at Hank Pelto's support. In one afternoon, Pelto had not only assumed stewardship of Bruce Spilner, he had also helped promote the search for Shelby with the sheriff. To Lorna's surprise, Bullard had agreed. Now Pelto was to call the YMCA office in Seattle. Upon their authorization, the search could begin. The shaggy reverend had become a valuable ally, and she had admired his passion—perhaps because she had felt a similar belly-fire early in her own career. It was strange, though; now on Orcas, her career seemed so distant, even superfluous. A new, completely different world seemed to be opening for her.

"You're a stranger here, like myself?"

Lorna was shaken from her thoughts. "What?"

She turned and found the handsome man in the blazer leaning on the back of a neighboring barstool.

"I don't mean to be forward," he said with a delicate accent. "I'm new to this part of the world, and I hope you'll forgive me for wanting to make acquaintances."

"Oh, hello." His bright smile momentarily disarmed her. "I don't know many people here either."

"Was that you on the beach yesterday?"

"Yes. I remember you. In the car."

"I'm quite impressed with the beauty . . . of this place."

Lorna ignored the potentially pointed allusion. "It's very peaceful compared to—"

"The cities?" He extended his right hand. "I'm Alessandro Vargas, by the way. From Spain."

She shook his hand. "Lorna Novak. Chicago."

"I thought so. You don't have the look of an islander."

"What look is that?"

"Shall we say . . . a lesser preoccupation with appearances? Like those two gentlemen who accompanied you at the beach. Are they relatives?"

"No. Friends." Lorna suddenly found the familiarity uncomfortable. She would be seeking a way to excuse herself. "One of them is a minister."

"Really?" Alessandro digested the comment. "So you've visited before?"

"No. It's my first time. I've only been here a couple of days."

"How fortunate you make friends so easily. I haven't had time to get acquainted with local people. I'm here for professional reasons. Archaeology, actually."

He didn't seem studious enough. "In a place like this? What could possibly—"

"Archaeology has application most anywhere. Here, there's a tradition in American Indian relics, that sort of thing."

"Indian?" The word conjured images of Marissa in the shade beneath the crows.

"I'm actually in search of my family history," he said, proudly. "One of my ancestors explored these islands."

"Oh?" She was mildly interested. "How long ago?"

"Two hundred years. When the Spanish sailed these waters. He was a captain who anchored off a small island just north of Orcas called Sucia."

The name registered. Kellen made a point to mention how fascinated January had been with that specific island. "I know the place."

"Do you? Have you been there?"

"No, but I know of a man who speaks of his own ancestors on that same island."

"Really? In what regard?" Alessandro gestured to the neighboring barstool. "Do you mind if I sit?"

"No." Lorna actually didn't. Alessandro suddenly seemed quite charming, and she found herself engaged by his courtesy.

"This man, may I ask his name?"

"I only know him by his nickname. He's called January."

"Like the month? Amusing. Do you think I could speak with him?"

Lorna reminded herself to remain discreet. "He's . . . temporarily unavailable. Out of town."

Alessandro placed a hand over his heart. "Please share whatever you can. I'm in a rather frustrating search for a specific location on that island, and I welcome any and all information, believe me."

"Well, I don't know the whole story. He's a friend of a friend."

"Ah. Well, perhaps if I explain further, I can convince you to introduce me. You see, over two hundred years ago, my ancestor Captain Ravilla inexplicably committed suicide. He had seen something on Sucia that drove him to distraction. My assistant, Bernardo, believes Ravilla was burdened by guilt due to some unpleasantness with the natives. But I'm more convinced that his distress was caused by what he saw, not his regret over some torture of the Indians." Alessandro paused and gestured to her glass. "By the way, may I buy you another?"

At the word "torture," Lorna felt uneasy, filled with strange foreboding. But she was also fascinated, since Alessandro's remarks and Kellen's account of January's visions on Paddy's boat echoed a haunting déjà vu. Contemplating the improbable connection, Lorna took a final sip of her drink and turned. "You know, I will have another, thank you. But only if you wouldn't mind clarifying what you just said."

"About Ravilla?"

"Well, yes, but more specifically—what's this about *torture* of the Indians?"

34

Mount Constitution
Orcas Island

UNDER TOWERING FIR TREES AND clear late afternoon skies, Kellen led Calico and January up a steep, uneven trail on Mount Constitution. Calico had complained bitterly about being a hostage, a complete reversal from her intended plan, and she showed her disdain with repeated comments that challenged Kellen's authority.

"You know your ass is mine, Kellen," she said, stumbling up the path in her black boots. Her red hair shone amber in the setting sun as Kellen pulled her along on a tether. He had bound her wrists and fashioned a leash from a length of nylon line he found in the helicopter. She was breathing hard. "I'll have you back in custody in twenty-four hours."

"Not likely." Kellen glanced back at January who brought up the rear. "Your hospitality was short and sweet, and I had a bellyful."

"Not *my* hospitality, handsome. You weren't even invited. This wasn't your party."

"Well, I'm making it my party." Kellen adjusted the knife sheath on his belt and patted the 9mm that he again wore comfortably tucked into the belt of his jeans. "You can't kidnap people *or* cats without pissing somebody off." He could feel Long John stir in the bottom of the knapsack as he adjusted the straps, hoisting the backpack higher on his shoulders.

"You just haven't realized that you've got nowhere to run," she glared at him. "You'd be smart to turn January over to us. If you do, we'll go easy on you."

"How generous," Kellen replied. "But I actually think it's your turn to turn Shelby over to me."

"You're really fucked up about this little bitch. And I don't know who she is. How many times do I have to say it?"

Kellen had asked her repeatedly, shoving the muzzle of his handgun under her chin, as Calico flew the MD 500E helicopter west toward Chilliwack. She claimed she had no knowledge of the girl, but Kellen continued to grill her as they flew southwest over Cultus Lake Provincial Park, then south across the United States border, avoiding Bellingham air space, then west over the Georgia Strait to Orcas Island.

They had maintained an altitude under seventy-five feet to avoid radar, which had required patient flying through the low passes of the Skagit Range. After landing safely on Buck Mountain, a shoulder of taller Mount Constitution, the threesome struck out overland.

Kellen insisted they leave the chopper a significant distance from Molly's house, suspecting the machine was bristling with tracking devices. But just after the chopper had landed between the trees on a Buck Mountain vacant lot, Calico had bolted from the cockpit door. Kellen had chased her, catching her at the edge of the clearing. While they wrestled on the ground, she had bitten him on the neck. She conversely wore a bruise on her cheekbone, where he had retaliated with a short punch.

"You seem to forget," Calico said, "that we found you easily. And as long as *I* know where you are, my organization knows."

"If keeping tabs on me is so damned important, why did you try to run?"

"Escape is the duty of a POW," she responded coolly. "As an ex-marine, you should know that."

"POW? Is that what you consider yourself? Are you at war? Why would you wage war on your own citizens?"

"We don't have to justify our actions. And you don't get that either. You have no fucking idea who you're dealing with. I'm telling you—let me take January, and we'll leave you alone. We can work this out."

"I won't negotiate with someone who almost put a bullet in my brain."

"What makes you think I was going to kill you?"

"Back at the gorge? Are you kidding?"

"We never had the chance to talk."

"Talk? Like that little discussion Stooch and I had?" Kellen had mercifully left the bulky man lying on the ground, knowing that he would awaken with a hell of a headache.

"Stooch and I speak a different language," she said seductively. "I'm a lot more friendly."

He ignored her, and they climbed in silence through the lengthening shadows of the setting sun. The mountain was alive with wildlife. Occasional deer crossed the trail. Chipmunks raced through the brush with their tails whipping like miniature antennas. Here and there, a rabbit paused to stare. Overhead, the treetops buzzed with wrens, swallows, and crows.

Kellen would never look at a crow the same way again.

He occasionally glanced back at January, who had grown increasingly sullen, apparently still burdened with Monk's death. During the helicopter flight, January was near tears. He claimed that when Monk died, he had felt the stricken man's soul depart the body—a sensation that had caused him to cry out. Kellen had tried to soothe January. He'd taken Long John from the backpack that served as his makeshift carrier and placed the animal on January's lap. Stroking the cat during the flight seemed to have a tranquilizing effect on the young man, and as January recovered, Kellen was finally able to discuss their options.

Molly Creed's had always been their return destination, but now Kellen had decided to hold Calico, to interrogate her. During the hike, he began to have his doubts that she would break. Time would tell, and they were some twenty minutes away from Molly's plateau.

As they neared the summit of Mt. Constitution's western ridge, Kellen turned and noticed January lagging. January then dropped the G36 rifle to the ground and stooped over a fallen pine tree, staring at the roots.

"Hey, man," Kellen called, "what the hell are you doing?"

No response. January hung his head, leaning over with both hands on the bark.

"What's the matter? You hurt?" Kellen shouted.

"He's tripping," Calico said.

"What?"

"He's a mind rider. Probably does that on occasion. Gets sidetracked by his own head."

"Like you would know." Kellen pointed to a spruce near the trail. "Get over there. I'm going to tie you up for a minute."

Kellen took the nylon cord that cinched Calico's wrists and knotted it firmly to the trunk of the fir. "Don't get bored. I'll be back."

He left her, knowing he could see her easily from the trail. He hurried down the path toward January, who was still hunched over the log.

As Kellen approached, January was having difficulty breathing. Kellen then heard chattering and looked up. More than a dozen crows had gathered in the trees over January's head.

"What the hell's happening?" Kellen placed a hand on January's back. "Is there anything I can do? Is it Monk?"

January shook his head. "That's not it. I thought it was Sucia again . . . Lukat's spirit tugging at me. But it's something else. Strong signals from Shelby. As if she were nearby, trying to call me."

"Call you? From where?" Kellen couldn't relate to January's notion of distance. "From the next state, or the next state of mind?"

"I can't tell." Sweat beaded his face. "This is new. She's more in control than before. Not afraid. More in command of herself."

"What are you telling me? That you can find her?"

"I'm not sure." January winced. "I want you to take Calico and go on."

"I'm not leaving you."

"I need to be alone. To prepare."

"For what?"

"My grandmother will be waiting at Molly's house. Have her gather the herbs. Tell her I want to enter the mystic heat."

"Tell her yourself. It's not that far." Up the trail, Calico leaned against the tree.

"I've killed a man, Kellen. I have to purge myself before I ascend."

"Ascend? To what?"

"If I rise with grandmother's help, I think I can see Shelby. I need time alone." January handed him the G36. "Take this and go."

Reluctantly, Kellen threw the rifle strap over his shoulder and hiked back up the path. As he reached Calico, he glanced back and found that both January and the birds had disappeared.

"So it's just you and me," Calico said as Kellen untied the tether from the tree.

"Not for long. We're almost there."

"A luxury hotel?"

"Hardly." Kellen unsheathed the knife. "A nice woodshed."

"You're going to cut me?"

"Not if you behave." He laid the rifle on the ground and, keeping an eye on her, pulled his black sweatshirt over his head.

"Ooooh. Been to the weight room, have we? With a bod like that, you sure you *want* me to behave?"

Kellen pierced the lining of his sweatshirt with the knife tip and tore a three-inch strip of cloth from the bottom hem all the way around. "I'm going to blindfold you for the rest of the way." He reached up to place the material over her eyes.

"Don't. You'll smudge my eyeliner."

"You're not wearing any."

Calico struggled, placing her two bound hands in front of her face. "Don't blindfold me. Please. Can we talk?"

"We'll chat while we stroll. Discuss my favorite subject. How to find Shelby."

"Wait. There's something I've been meaning to ask you . . . really." She did her best to look sincere. "It could mean a lot. To you and the Indian kid."

He again tried to place the cloth over her eyes, but she forced her body into his, clutching his arm. He could feel the bulge of her breasts on his chest. "Kellen, goddamn it, listen."

Remembering her bite, he clenched a fist.

She flinched, but continued, "You asked about Trajan. Well, he also asked about *you*. With what you've accomplished, he's impressed. Ever consider that you might be fighting the wrong people? Think about it. You've got January. We need him. I'm number two in this operation. One word from me changes everything. Instantly. You have no idea of the rewards." She wet her lips and smiled. "It's something you and I could share, right now, starting here." She nodded toward a sunlit patch of moss under a large pine. "Over there, under that tree, if you like."

As she waited expectantly, Kellen thought about Lorna and Paddy, the despair at the hospital. He tugged his arm free and grabbed Calico's slender neck. "What you've done is kidnapped a child, bludgeoned a woman to near death, and taken a leg off my friend. You think I'd even touch you? I'm not only *fighting* the right people, I have no intention of *fucking* any of them. Now put on this blindfold, or I swear to God, I'll kill you right here."

35

The Outlook Inn,
Eastsound, Orcas Island

UNDER A HALO-GILDED MOON, KELLEN guided Marissa's old Chevy truck into the hotel's dimly lit parking lot, where he found a parking spot and killed the engine.

Dirty and tired, he sat in the vinyl front seat, scrutinizing the darkened doorways of the stores that lined the street. The glow of several souvenir stands illuminated the beachfront.

Everything looked normal, though Kellen sensed that nothing about the island would feel normal again. He had reverted to an FBI agent's edgy mindset—with a healthy awareness of his surroundings and a natural suspicion of strangers. After all, any tourist might be one of Calico's operatives, because Orcas Island would surely be canvassed by her people again. The only safe place for Lorna was at Kellen's side.

Having failed to reach Lorna by phone, he was now determined to find her and fast.

Taking one last look around, he tucked the 9mm into the front of his pants and left the truck in the parking lot, hurrying into the small hotel lobby.

A substitute clerk tended the front desk—a frizzy-haired brunette in a white blouse and gold-rimmed glasses whom Kellen had not met. She looked up, seemingly surprised at his battered condition.

"Where's Doris?" Kellen asked.

"May I help you?" She closed the registration book as if to prevent him from checking in.

"I'm looking for Ms. Novak, one of your guests."

"And you are . . . ?" Her eyes nervously came to rest at Kellen's waist.

It was too late. The missing portion of his sweatshirt, which had served as a Calico's blindfold, revealed his bare midriff and the exposed gun butt.

Kellen rested a hand over his belt buckle. "The name is Rand. Kellen Rand. I'm a friend."

"Is she expecting you?" She'd definitely seen the weapon.

"Look. Don't get the wrong idea. I'm a federal agent. Just give me her room number."

"I can't. It's against our policy."

"Then could you ring her and tell her I'm in the lobby?"

"I suppose." She grasped the black desk phone.

"Thanks. I'll be right back."

"Sir?"

"I'll check the bar in the meantime."

As she began to dial, Kellen hurried toward the rear of the main building, where he'd frequented the Outlook's walnut-paneled cocktail lounge. He blew through the swinging doors.

A few stragglers remained at the tables, sipping their drinks.

Sadie, the buxom blonde bartender, smiled as he entered. "Hey, Kellen."

"Hey, yourself. Have you seen Lorna Novak—she's a hotel guest?"

"Not sure."

"You'd know her right away. Tall, dark. Pretty. Sometimes wears a red scarf."

She seemed suddenly put off by the mention of a rival. "Oh. Yes. She's with Mr. Vargas."

"Who?" No one could be trusted. "Who's Vargas?"

"Spanish guy. Check the dining room. They were there a couple of hours ago."

Kellen hurried down the hall.

Remembering the desk clerk's reaction, he paused behind a large potted plant and removed the GLOCK from his belt. Wanting to keep the gun hidden but handy, he placed it under his sweatshirt into his left armpit, tucking his elbow to keep the 9mm pinned against his ribs. He rushed toward the foyer and passed a befuddled middle-aged hostess. Surveying the tables, Kellen spotted Lorna at the rear of the dining room with a smooth-looking man in a dark jacket and open blue silk shirt. Kellen recognized the slicked black hair.

As Kellen approached, the stranger from the limousine looked up, surprised.

Lorna turned toward the source of Alessandro's gaze. "Kellen, my God." She scooted back in her chair. "What happened?"

"We need to talk."

Her eyes widened with concern. "Did you find January?"

"I . . ." Kellen wasn't about to openly share information. "I don't have data on Shelby. I just need—"

"Are you okay? You look—"

"Beat up. I know. I apologize. Please come with me."

She rose. "Of course. Oh, this is Alessandro Vargas. We've had an interesting—"

"Alex . . ." Kellen dismissed him with a nod, placing a hand on Lorna's elbow. "Please."

"Perhaps I can be of assistance," the foreigner said. "From what Lorna has told me—"

"Look. I don't mean to be rude, but I don't have time right now."

"Yes . . ." Lorna took a half step and gave the Spaniard an apologetic smile. "You'll have to excuse us. I'll explain things to Kellen and we'll be back."

"No, we won't."

"What?"

"We can't. Let's talk outside."

As Kellen pivoted and walked toward the door, he was disappointed to overhear Lorna waffling. Before making her exit, she asked Vargas to stay, saying she would return to say good-bye.

Kellen sidestepped the hostess's critical glare and entered the foyer, where he was surprised by Deputy McMillan. The desk clerk had called the sheriff, not Lorna's room.

The deputy seemed almost relieved. "Kellen . . . it's you. Goddamn it, what are you doing in here like that?"

"Like what?"

"Look at you." McMillan looked to his waist. "Are you carrying?"

"I've got a permit, and you know it."

"That doesn't mean you can scare the bejesus out of people. Give me the gun. You can pick it up later. You'll make the night clerk a lot more comfortable."

EAGER TO HEAR WHAT KELLEN had discovered, Lorna apologized to Alessandro one last time and hurried to the foyer, only to find Kellen handing his gun to Deputy McMillan.

"What's the problem here?"

"Nothing serious, Ms. Novak. We're just going to confiscate this weapon for a time." He tucked the gun into his belt.

"Why are you doing this to me?" Kellen asked.

"Don't get peeved. We can't have people flashing guns around town. You're free to stay, but the gun is outta here." Tipping his hat to Lorna, McMillan walked toward the bar.

Lorna tried to force a smile from Kellen. "Hey. I'm glad to see you, you know. What the hell happened?"

"I found January."

"You did?"

Kellen pointed to the dining room. "But I didn't want to—"

"Where is he?"

Kellen lowered his voice so the hostess couldn't hear. "Hiding at Molly's."

"Did he know anything about Shelby?"

"Only that she's missing. Marissa is prepping January for some kind of séance session. The 'mystic heat,' they call it. Imperative you be there, he says. Better bring your luggage and stay. We're all in danger."

"From whom?"

"I barely got away, Lorna. They followed me and damn near killed me."

"Is this your covert ops bunch?"

"No doubt at all—Marty Flowers was right."

"Catch up with McMillan and tell him."

Kellen shook his head. "We've been through this. It won't do any good. They're above the law."

"But they're not shy." Lorna had been anxious to share the news. "I found them on the Internet."

"You did? Well, good. I suppose that serves as evidence if we need it. But right now, we've got to buy time. These people are well trained and persistent. Poor January had to shoot one of them. We escaped in their helicopter and took a hostage. I've got her hog-tied in Molly's woodshed."

"Her? A woman?"

"A bitch." He tugged at his sweatshirt collar, gesturing to the welt. "She bit me."

"Did she?" Lorna succumbed to the erotic suggestion. "And where did you bite her?"

"Oh, stop it. I punched her out."

"Was it really necessary to bring her?"

"She flew the chopper. And yes, I intend to interrogate her." Kellen began to edge toward the lobby. "Let's go."

"Wait. Will you do me a favor?"

"Tell me in the truck."

"No. Take one minute and talk to Alessandro."

"Who? You mean that guy? Hell, no."

"I promised."

"What could possibly—?"

"It's January. And that island out there. Sucia. It might be important."

"Shit." Kellen squinted in disgust.

"Now, how do you know this doesn't mean something important?"

Kellen sighed. "All right. Five minutes. But when I say—"

"If you want to leave, we will."

"Good. And don't you tell Picasso where we're going."

Lorna led Kellen back to the dining room, amused by the pout on his smudged face. One of the things she found endearing about him was the combination of boyish charm and irascible will. Compared to a smooth Alessandro, Kellen was vulnerable, yet powerful and delightfully rough around the edges.

Alessandro seemed ambivalent about Kellen's return, but he stood politely as Kellen pulled up a chair and Lorna resumed her seat. Lorna watched as the two men became acquainted.

Alessandro graciously offered Kellen a glass of wine, but Kellen declined, mentioning the shortness of time. At Lorna's suggestion, Alessandro gave a brief account of himself. Kellen listened tolerantly as he summarized his Spanish ancestry and his natural curiosity about Captain Ravilla and the mystery surrounding a specific site on Sucia Island that the captain had found.

"Kellen, tell him what January said about Sucia," Lorna prompted.

"I thought you already did." Kellen glanced at the wall clock over the mantle.

"Yes. But tell him the specifics."

"Well, he . . . talked about pain. That he was drawn to the place. He spoke of feelings he'd had . . . the rush of souls. He mentioned that his ancestors were tortured on the beaches."

"Did he tell you how long ago?" Alessandro asked.

"Something about centuries before."

"Centuries? Two hundred years, perhaps?"

"I don't know."

"Well, Lorna tells me that his grandmother refers to January as a storyteller." Alessandro gave Lorna an apologetic shrug. "Perhaps that's precisely what he's doing . . . just telling stories. One could also assume the young man's fantasies are inspired by something he studied in a history book."

"Could be." Kellen restlessly shifted his weight in the chair. "But I sensed he was feeling things that confused him, not things he'd read."

Alessandro nodded. "Is he by chance a member of the Salish tribe?"

"I believe he mentioned that."

"My associate, Dr. Fraley, has established that the Salish settled Sucia Island."

"And?"

"The connection may be significant."

Kellen clasped his hands conclusively and glanced at Lorna. "Well, that's it then. Good luck in your search." He rose. "Sorry I couldn't be of more help."

Alessandro folded his napkin. "I still would enjoy discussing things with this January."

Lorna interjected, "We might arrange that upon his return."

"Good." Alessandro stood. "In the meantime, if either of you speaks with him, ask him if he remembers specifics. Places. Names. Anything."

"Names?" Kellen pushed his chair back under the table. "He did say that a name kept bothering him."

Alessandro had reached for the dinner check and the pen. He paused. "Really? What name would that be?"

"It was a strange one. He said something about crows and . . . what was it? Luke? Luke something. I'd never heard—"

"Dear God. Could it have been *Lukat*?" Alessandro had dropped the pen.

Kellen actually smiled. "Yeah. That was it. How did you know?"

Alessandro's olive complexion blanched as he stared into space. "The crows in the rigging."

"Alessandro?" Lorna was concerned by his expression. "You feeling all right?"

"Me? Oh, yes." Alessandro glanced at Kellen. "How on earth would you know about the crows?"

Kellen shrugged. "Crows seem to hang around January a lot. When he's meditating."

"Lukat." Alessandro gazed out the window into the darkness. "Did he mention anything about a cave?"

"A cave? No."

"What's so extraordinary about the name?" Lorna asked.

"Nothing as extraordinary as this January fellow might be." Alessandro frowned pensively. "Lukat died on Sucia Island in 1793. There are only four other people alive familiar with that name. One is a curator in Madrid. The second is my assistant. The last two are my associates."

Alessandro glanced from Lorna to Kellen, trying to formulate a plan. He desperately wanted to include January in the expedition. Barring that, he wanted Kellen's help.

"Do you realize," Alessandro said, studying Kellen's bruised face, "that tonight, from out of nowhere, you uttered a name that has probably been unspoken for two centuries? That's no coincidence. This January's talent may well become a focal point of my research. His clairvoyance may deal with matters he himself doesn't understand."

"Possibly. We'll have to discuss this again sometime." Kellen tugged at Lorna's elbow.

"Can we stay in touch?" Alessandro pleaded. "This might be terribly important."

"To you, maybe. We've got more pressing issues." Kellen nodded toward the dining room door. "Go grab your stuff, Lorna. I'll wait in the lobby."

To Alessandro's disappointment, she extended a hand. "It was interesting talking with you. Thanks for dinner. I enjoyed it."

"You're really leaving?"

"She really is," Kellen said.

"When will I see you?" Alessandro had become fascinated with the beautiful woman.

"Yes, when?" Lorna glanced at Kellen.

"A day or two," he said. "We'll give you a call." He began to lead Lorna from the room.

"Mr. Rand." Alessandro quickly signed the check and hurried to catch up, arriving in the dimly lit hotel lobby just as Lorna ascended the staircase to go collect her belongings. "Lorna mentioned that you recently had a boating accident?"

"Did she?"

"My father and I love ships. I understand the attraction of venturing onto the water."

"Practical, when you live on an island."

"Of course."

Kellen turned and edged farther toward the lobby's front window and stood gazing out past the curtain.

Alessandro eased forward to rejoin him, trying to capture his interest with perhaps a more familiar tone. "Kellen, I don't mean to intrude. I sense that you're preoccupied, but I need some closure here. I'm willing to pay for the information."

Without turning, Kellen replied. "You're right. I am preoccupied."

"Did you hear what I said? I mean *real* money here."

Kellen pushed the curtain even farther aside and stared into the street. "Now there, why did you have to mention money? I was 'preoccupied,' but now I don't give a shit."

"January utters a name from my past, and you don't intend to help me with that?"

Kellen glanced over his shoulder. With the flicker of the flaming hearth in his eyes, he turned and leaned in, lowering his voice. "In the dining room I listened to your personal history, Mr. Vargas. Now, I'd like to give you a snapshot of my own. I came to this island to get away from limousines, fancy clothes, and guys like you, who think they can buy their way through life. Now why don't we call it a night?"

Kellen's cool hostility gave Alessandro pause. Like Professor Hargrove, Kellen had no apparent interest in financial matters. Alessandro was again on the verge of missing an opportunity.

He made the decision to reach into his blazer, but Kellen reacted by clutching Alessandro by the wrist. "Right there is just fine."

Shocked, Alessandro could only croak, "It's just my wallet."

"I don't give a damn about your money."

"You don't understand. I want to show you my map."

"Oh. Now it's a treasure hunt."

"Please allow me." Alessandro tried to reach for his wallet, but Kellen slid his hand inside Alessandro's lapel and retrieved the billfold. He glanced at it momentarily and pushed it into Alessandro's chest.

Alessandro quickly opened the flap, pulling his copy from within. "The original version of this chart is safe. But I keep a Xerox with me." He unfolded the document and handed the page to Kellen. "Look."

Kellen shoved it away. "What's the point?"

"While you wait for Lorna. Please."

Kellen shook his head in resignation and examined the paper in the glow of the fire.

Alessandro pointed. “That’s the outline of Sucia. This was drawn two hundred years ago. Do you think January could make observations about the coast . . . or perhaps about these other pictures: the trident or the triangle?”

“What about these bow-and-beam bearings?”

Alessandro startled. “What?”

“The numbers.”

Alessandro’s mouth dropped. “You mean you understand them?”

“Someone reckoned a specific position on shore while they navigated. I thought your father was a seafaring man?”

“We weren’t sailors. We owned the company.”

“Most ocean-going seaman would know this calculation.”

“You’re joking. Please explain.”

Kellen pointed. “The telltale numbers are the 45 and 90 degrees entered with the 6 and the 9. That means that at 6 minutes into a course, someone took a 45-degree bearing off the bow. Nine minutes later, a 90-degree bearing off the beam, probably on some object on shore. The first number ’33’ should really read 033, indicating the heading of north 33 degrees. The second number ‘7’ indicates the speed.”

“My God. And that’s it?” Alessandro was floored at the ease with which Kellen had solved the riddle.

“It’s a technique used to mark reef hazards at sea. Or when someone’s in a hurry to make notations with no other map references available.”

Alessandro was genuinely excited. “You mean I could derive a specific point on shore by reenacting this maneuver?”

“Not quite. What’s missing is the point of origin, where the course was initiated. You’d have to know that.”

“If you knew where the course ended, could you do the same?”

Kellen’s brow furrowed in concentration. “I think so, by calculating it in reverse. But a course doesn’t end, Mr. Vargas. It may alter, or reverse, but it doesn’t stop dead in the middle of the ocean.”

Alessandro broke into a smile. Hargrove was right all along. “It does in one particular instance.”

“Like what?”

“When the ship sinks.”

36

Mount Constitution

AS LORNA WATCHED THE LARGE campfire send a crazed nebula of embers into the starry sky, she felt like one of those tiny specks of ash. Her life, having been launched into the unknown, would land where it might. Her career, once so important, paled compared to matters at hand. She hadn't spoken with her office in days, and she had no desire to do so. For now, she was content just being a guest at Molly's pixie palace.

Molly, in her orange sundress; Lorna, in her jeans and tennis shoes; and Kellen, still wearing his battered sweatshirt, hunched near the fire. Even Long John had joined them as they gathered on the logs and chunks of driftwood near Molly's barn, where their elongated shadows danced on the worn planking. To the south, the three geometric shapes of Molly's multistructured home hulked in silhouette. Beyond, the crumpled contour of Molly's shabby woodshed stood out against the moon.

Inside, Calico remained captive. Shortly after her arrival, Lorna insisted on being present while Kellen interrogated the government agent. During the questioning, Calico took an intense dislike to Lorna, directing much of her hostility toward her. Kellen had responded sternly, even threatening to harm her. But Calico appeared not only undaunted by his threats, she seemed to actually enjoy the prospect.

"Where's Shelby now?" Kellen had shouted, gripping Calico firmly. "Who's Trajan?"

With piercing eyes, Calico glared at Lorna while under the weight of

Kellen's forearm. "You're both dead, you know that?"

"Then we have nothing to lose." Lorna leaned against a post.

"Nothing but your virginity."

Kellen shook her. "Answer me. Where are you keeping Shelby?"

Calico ignored him. "Lorna. Where were *you* this afternoon? Doing your nails?" Kellen clamped down on her neck. "Your boyfriend and I were alone in the woods," Calico croaked. "He's hung like a moose."

Kellen had her in a choke hold.

Calico strained to look up. "I could have saved you, Kellen. Now you and your Barbie doll are toast. Count on it."

At that moment, Marissa had appeared at the shed door dressed in a robe, announcing that January was ready.

Marissa guided January, bleary-eyed and speechless, to the fireside. While Lorna and Kellen took their places, Marissa helped January sit cross-legged on a grass mat. Marissa took her place next to Lorna and cautioned everyone to speak quietly, though no one was to address her grandson directly, since his immersion into his trance had already begun.

According to Marissa, January had chewed a potent mixture of herbs and mushrooms that Marissa had gathered that afternoon. He'd fallen asleep on the pine needles in a nearby glen.

Lorna hadn't seen the young man prior to his emergence from the thicket, and she was struck by his physique. Lanky and yet broad in the chest, January cut an impressive figure, naked from the waist up, his long black hair tufted over his shoulders.

After settling on the mat, January heaved several sighs and raised his hands toward the warmth.

"He is to assume power over the fire," Marissa whispered.

Swaying back and forth, January began to hum in a monotone.

Kellen leaned over. "This isn't how he was at Point Doughty. He seems much more controlled." In his lap, Long John stared at January.

"It's hypnotic," Lorna said.

As if responding to January's wavering rhythms, the fire's sparks swirled a steady updraft into the darkness. Perspiration gleamed on January's brow.

"I've seen this before," Molly said softly to Kellen's right. "It throws me every time."

January's drone faded. The sinew along the base of his neck stood out.

Striations etched his shoulders, while his abdominal muscles rippled with every breath.

Beyond the fire against the dark towering pines, a shimmer caught Lorna's eye. Small reflecting splashes of light glimmered in the hollows, reminiscent of the tinsel-like iridescence thrown by aspen leaves caught in the autumn sun.

"Look." Lorna pointed. "Are those fireflies?"

Marissa responded calmly. "No, dear. What you see are eyes reflecting the flames."

"What? Bats?"

"Owls."

"There must be dozens." Lorna cupped her hands around her eyes. In the evergreen boughs, tiny feathered faces became visible.

"They offer the capacity to see in the night," Marissa said. "January seeks help for his vision. He is about to tell the story."

January had craned his neck in birdlike fashion and jettisoned his right arm upward, his fingers jutted like storm-torn branches. *"Mortiada."* The word burst from his throat. *"Umni artand prospo lumbrik."*

"What's that?" Kellen whispered.

"He says, 'The innocent one is imprisoned in the belly of the blackbird.' He speaks of Shelby in an ancient tongue," Marissa added. "The language all people spoke at the dawn of time."

January's raised right hand wracked like a gnarled root. His face twisted in discomfort as he spat the words. *"Krandis numliriko apena. Chui ah te lepritu."*

"What?"

"The bird does not fly. The life giver can pluck the child away."

"Who's the 'life giver'?" Lorna asked.

Kellen smiled. "That's what he called me when I pulled him from the ocean."

January's arm collapsed to his side. He began to moan.

Marissa leaned toward him. *"Kana?"*

"Ushmon parta bradia," January whimpered.

"Shelby is crying."

"Tis noma en sirk."

"They have punctured her neck. It hurts."

Lorna felt sick. "Can he tell us where she is?"

Marissa touched his arm. *"Ka ha?"*

January's head turned. *"Oha Trajan. Akurdo insulai."*

"She is near," Marissa said. "With a man called Trajan. Somewhere in the islands."

"In the islands?" Lorna asked. "What about this black bird?"

January's head slumped forward.

Marissa gazed off into the trees. The flapping of hidden wings faded into the forest. She shook her head. "The story has ended. He is spent. I can't ask him."

"We'll wait until he wakes," Lorna said.

"He won't recall his own words."

"It could be a helicopter. Calico's was black," Kellen said.

Lorna asked, "You think that's what he means?"

"Maybe. But why keep Shelby in a chopper? Really confined," Kellen said.

"Another kind of plane then. Maybe they'd planned to fly her off-island but simply haven't."

"Why abduct her and leave her stuffed in a crowded fuselage? It must be a larger plane, but bigger aircraft don't land around here."

Lorna flashed on the deputy's comments when she'd first arrived. "The day after Shelby disappeared, McMillan mentioned that an Orcas flight the night before was recorded as a *government* plane—a Learjet."

"A Lear." Kellen's eyes caught the fire's glow. "Jet skis. Helicopters. A Learjet? Sure. Why not. But where? There must be six airports in the islands that can handle that sized jet."

"Did you hear what he said about Shelby crying? We've got to do something."

"I understand, Lorna. But this Trajan guy has a heavily armed force. We need help."

Marissa moved to January's side and began to salve his face with ointment. She glanced across the flames. "January has some young friends in the Lummi tribe."

"Thanks, but we need firepower." Kellen handed Long John to Molly Creed. "Lorna, how much money can you raise?"

"By when?"

"Tonight. Now."

"I've got some funds. I could call my bank—"

"I'm going to need at least forty by morning."

"Thousand?"

"Make that fifty. Can you do that? Where's your cell phone?"

"In my bag."

"She left that in the house," Molly said and pointed toward the structure.

Kellen was on his feet striding toward the porch.

"What do you have in mind?" Lorna asked.

Kellen stopped and looked over his shoulder. "Remember my brother's buddies in Seattle? Connely and Stinson? They're retired. Both wild asses in their day. They might itch for another shot at some excitement."

"But I thought—"

"Right. I didn't want to get others involved . . ."

37

Next Morning
Orcas Island Museum

HARGROVE BURST THROUGH THE MUSEUM door. "I think they found it, Vargas. It must be *El Trinidad.*"

"Are you sure?" Alessandro felt more excitement than he'd anticipated.

"Well yes, by default, it must be her."

"Isn't that incredible, Alessandro?" Bernardo stepped briskly from behind the counter where he had been toying with scrimshaw Indian relics. "Where is she?"

"The divers located her four hundred yards offshore. Most of the wood has turned to sludge. No outline of a hull to identify." The professor's khaki shirt was still spotted with water. "But look at this spike." Hargrove thrust a nine-inch, partially decomposed metal peg forward. "It's a deck bolt, no question." He pointed to the fat end. "This square-cut forging places this spike in the late eighteenth century. I called the data bank at the university and ran a check. The bolt is most likely from a ship of the Carlotta line, built at Valencia. The *El Trinidad* was just such a ship."

Alessandro smiled. "You were right all along."

David Fraley shuffled from the back room, his eyes squinting from the brightness coming through the open door. "Does that mean we can estimate Martine's course?"

"It does." Alessandro reached for one of the nautical charts that were scrolled on the shelf. He opened it and laid it on a glass case full of scraping tools as the others gathered around.

Alessandro set Martine's map next to the marine diagram. "The map shows 33, 7, 6, 45, 9, 90, 12. Where would you estimate the divers sighted her?" He glanced at Hargrove.

"Here." The professor's finger stabbed the marine chart at a spot west of Sucia Island's Danger Reef. On Martine's map, the hand-drawn trident rested at a comparable location.

"The trident wasn't a symbol for water at all," Fraley said. "It indicates the shipwreck."

"Regardless of where Martine's course began, it appears he sailed north thirty-three degrees and anchored. And if the trident shows us where the *El Trinidad* sank, we would navigate in reverse toward the opposite direction at a speed of seven knots." Alessandro set a straight edge on the chart. "The number *12* is paramount, because, according to Kellen Rand, it represents the twelve minutes elapsed between Martine's last ninety-degree beam reading of the cave and the time he anchored. If we make our first ninety-degree sighting on the landmass at twelve minutes and repeat that nine minutes later at a forty-five degree angle, the two tangents should meet at the cave's location on shore."

The four men stared at one another.

It was difficult to believe the solution had been found.

"What are we waiting for?" Hargrove sputtered. "My boat's still at the Bartwood Pier."

Alessandro felt invigorated. "What else do we need? A compass?"

"We have that on board," Hargrove answered. "What we do need is a pelorus. We can borrow one from the marina."

Alessandro had only a vague recollection of the rare instrument. "A sighting device, isn't it?"

"A flat card with two sighting vanes to be exact. Invaluable in this case. Binoculars would also be advisable."

"I have binoculars in the car," Bernardo volunteered.

Fraley raised a hand. "I'll bring my charts."

Alessandro smiled. "Good. This is the beginning."

Fifteen minutes later, they arrived at the Bartwood dock. Rain showers had blanketed the interior of Orcas Island, hanging near the mountains, while a mile offshore, Sucia Island gleamed in the sun.

Near the barnacle-covered pier, two of Hargrove's divers packed their equipment into a small truck. The third diver—a bearded man in a black wetsuit—

leaned against a dock piling, having a smoke. As Hargrove's party approached, he exhaled a puff. "Back so soon?"

"My associates insisted," Hargrove said as the others strolled onto the gray planking toward the twenty-one-foot Tollycraft.

The diver smiled. "If you'd like, we'll be back at dawn tomorrow to begin salvage."

"Fine. I'll meet you then." Hargrove had contracted the dive team for 5 percent of the haul, provided what was found brought a profit. The other 95 percent was to be divided equally between the professor, Alessandro, and Fraley. Since *El Trinidad* was a military vessel, there was little hope of finding significant stores. But there was always the chance of antiques or coins, and the potential for booty held the divers' fee to a reasonable fifteen hundred a day.

Hargrove took the helm of the Tollycraft and started the engine. The others settled in the stern. In a few minutes, they were underway.

Nineteen minutes later, after traveling through a light chop off Sucia's eastern shore, the Tolly approached the red buoy the divers had left. Hargrove cut the engines and maneuvered adjacent to the buffeting flag.

While Fraley remained aft, Alessandro and Bernardo stepped into the small cuddy cabin, joining Hargrove at the helm.

"So the opposite heading to Martine's 33 degrees north would be 327 degrees south?" Alessandro asked, checking the floating compass on the console.

"Correct." Hargrove adjusted the tiller. "I'll set the speed at seven knots."

"I'll note the time." Alessandro checked his watch. It was seventeen minutes past ten. "We should travel for twelve minutes before marking the first angle."

"Right." Clutching his briefcase, Hargrove stepped aside. "Perhaps Bernardo could steer while I help with the calculations."

"My pleasure." Bernardo grasped the chrome wheel.

Alessandro led Hargrove out on deck.

Fraley, who had been viewing the shore with binoculars, surrendered them to Alessandro, while the professor retrieved the pelorus from his briefcase. The small instrument consisted of two vertical sighting vanes that rotated over a compass-rose imprint on a flat card. The professor secured the card to the deck rail with tape.

On their new course, the Tollycraft began to pass Sucia's four fingerlike islands and peninsulas, which protruded toward the east. Sucia, like a right hand laid flat on the ocean surface, held waterways between its digit-like land extensions. Between the thumb and index finger lay Echo Bay with the index finger being North and South Finger Islands; between index and middle finger lay a tributary of Echo Bay; between the middle finger and ring finger lay tiny Snoring Bay with the ring finger being Wiggins Head; and between the ring finger and a little fingerlike peninsula lay Fossil Bay. Alessandro had forgotten how slow seven knots could be and how long twelve minutes could take. But eventually, the second hand on his Rolex ticked into place.

Alessandro tapped Hargrove on the shoulder while he was sighting the vanes on the pelorus. Hargrove marked a section of the island. He pointed. "That's ninety degrees—near those large boulders."

Fraley referred to his chart. "That's Johnson's Point."

Alessandro hoisted the binoculars and peered toward the tree-lined hill, the "middle finger" of Sucia—a promontory between Echo Bay and Snoring Bay. "We didn't walk those rocks, by the way."

Hargrove turned. "We chose not too, if you'll remember, due to the uneven footing. But don't get ahead of yourself. We have another reading to take."

"Very well." Alessandro panned the area with the glasses. "I don't see any caves."

Fraley sneezed and pulled his handkerchief from his pocket. "I better go inside. Once we establish the tangents, are we really going in?"

Hargrove nodded. "Of course. Is there a problem?"

Fraley pointed toward the gold vegetation. "That Scotch broom is going to kill me."

"Let's hope your suffering will be worthwhile." Alessandro smiled. He panned the binoculars, inspecting the shoreline. Several seals sunbathed on the rocks. A large flock of birds appeared inland over Sucia, settling somewhere in the trees.

Moments later, Alessandro's Rolex reached its mark. "There," he said.

In response, Hargrove sighted the pelorus. The professor frowned. "It appears to be the same hill as the one indicated on Johnson's Point." He squinted at the vanes once more. "The tangents intersect at the summit."

Alessandro knelt on deck. "You're sure the first angle was right?"

"Bernardo," Hargrove shouted. "Pull the throttle back into neutral."

The boat slowed, and Bernardo appeared. "Did you find it?"

"Yes," Alessandro said. "We've proudly discovered a hill. I hadn't expected that." Alessandro handed Bernardo the binoculars. "The tangents meet at that outcropping."

A single column of rock jutted to the sky above a tree-barren abutment.

Bernardo raised the binoculars. "And what did you expect?"

"A depression. A cave. Something. From Martine's description, it sounded as if . . ." Alessandro asked Bernardo, "Where's that transcript?"

"Right here." Bernardo set the binoculars down. He rummaged in his valise and handed Alessandro the Madrid translation.

As the breeze buffeted the papers, Alessandro leafed through until he found the passage. "Here it is." He translated as he read aloud: "'Captain Ravilla ordered me to accompany him while we ventured inland for some distance until we reached a hollow. There, I kept watch outside, while Captain Ravilla and Lukat entered a small cavern.' Does that sound like a hilltop to you?"

"'For some distance,'" Hargrove quoted. "Your cave might be on the other side of that rise."

"Perhaps. But then the tangents are incorrect."

"Forgive me," Bernardo said, "but may I see the Xerox? I believe Martine has told us what to do." Alessandro shrugged and pulled the folded paper from his safari vest. Bernardo opened it and showed the others. "You see, this triangle is not a triangle at all." He pointed to the three-sided drawing that included the stick figure at its apex. "The triangle is that hill. And this manlike figure indicates that, for whatever purpose, Martine wants us to stand at the top."

38

A Private Airfield
Orcas Island

WELL-CAMOUFLAGED BY DENSE UNDERBRUSH, Kellen, January, Jake Connely, and Bob Stinson knelt in their fatigues near a barbed wire fence that lined the lone runway. Ninety feet away, on the steaming asphalt, the wings of a black Learjet dripped rain from a passing summer shower. The sun occasionally peeked through the drizzle-laden clouds over Mount Woollard, splashing rainbows into the glens below. In the heavy air, the tiny airfield was dead quiet, except for the sound of water trickling through the pine needle boughs over Kellen's head.

"You sure this is the one?" Stinson whispered, shifting the weight of the 12-gauge street-sweeper shotgun that lay across his lap.

"It's the only jet in the islands," Kellen said. "At least that's the latest report."

Last night, Kellen had awakened Marty Flowers in Washington, DC, with a request that was nebulous enough to not involve Marty directly. It took a half hour before Kellen could convince Marty to drive to his office and do Kellen the favor. Kellen needed to locate an aircraft in the San Juan Islands, and through the Bureau's computer banks, Marty was to access daily satellite-imaging data from Vandenberg Air Force Base.

Skycast, an ecological research bird launched in early 2000, had passed over the northwestern United States, studying global warming impact on coastal plain vegetation. Using Skycast's infrared photographs that were less than five hours old, Marty had been able to create computer-enhanced enlargements of eight small island airports. The pictures revealed only one nonpropeller aircraft—a Learjet on this private airfield, nearly hidden among the trees.

"But are we sure it's the right plane?" Stinson's surly gaze rested on Kellen. Of the two, Stinson had given Kellen cause to regret his decision to include them. He asked too many questions and appeared the least sympathetic.

Kellen brushed a pine branch aside and gave January an inquisitive shrug.

"I . . . yes. This is the plane," January said softly.

"Because you can *feel* it?" Stinson asked.

"Yes," Kellen interjected.

"And without a Ouija board?"

"Look, Bob—"

"Kellen," Connely cut in, "a few questions are okay, don't you think? You've got to admit, this is a bit off the edge."

"All right." Kellen pointed at January. "But I'm not going to keep justifying his abilities when you've both been paid in advance."

Stinson wiped moisture from his graying temples. "Let me tell you something. If Kyle hadn't been your brother, you couldn't have paid me to ride this merry-go-round."

"Bob," Connely said. "Give Kellen time to call his play."

During the phone negotiations with his brother's old academy buddies, Kellen had appealed to their sense of adventure, and eventually, Lorna's generous offer took hold. Both men agreed to act as Kellen's backup for twenty-five thousand dollars apiece—not bad for one day's work. They had driven north from Seattle at the crack of dawn and, through Marissa's contacts at the Lieber Haven Resort, were conveyed to the island aboard the barge *Pentail* in order to avoid unnecessary exposure on the ferry.

While Lorna and the other women guarded Calico at Molly's mountain hideaway, Kellen and the men changed into fatigues at a gas station. Then he chauffeured his team through the orchards of Crow Valley in Marissa's old pickup. Arriving at the secluded acreage, they approached on a dirt road that bordered the runway at the far end of the field. The airstrip, which had been cut through thick groves of alder and fir, was said to be owned by Mac Steen, a shareholder in Microsoft. The retired executive lived in Bellevue and occasionally flew to the islands, where he toyed with his restored aircraft.

Kellen looked from one man's face to the other. Stinson had just turned fifty-one, Connely fifty—the age Kyle would have been, had he lived. They had all attended the FBI Academy in Quantico, Virginia, and later served together. Connely had been there when Kyle was killed.

Kyle's memory cut a wide swath even now. Kellen would again be judged by his fabled older brother's standards. "You think Shelby's in the plane?"

January shook his head. "I only have echoes."

"What does that mean?" Stinson asked.

"She might be asleep. I'm not sure."

Stinson grimaced and slapped the stock of the shotgun.

In response, Kellen gave him a critical frown. "He's perceptive, not infallible."

"How do we know they're not in the shed?" Stinson pointed to an outbuilding that apparently doubled as a communications shack. Several antennae sprouted from its aluminum roof. "I could just walk up and knock."

"No. You're backup. I'll be the point on this." Kellen wasn't going to put either of the men in additional jeopardy. "The objective is surprise with no casualties. I want to catch them off guard and retrieve the girl. That's all."

"They don't know me from Adam," Stinson insisted. "I could just stroll up without the gun and check things out."

Kellen unstrapped the G36 that he'd slung over his shoulder. "If they're in the jet, you'll be caught in the cross fire."

"How about if I work my way behind the hangar?" Connely took a stick and began to draw in the dirt. The doorless structure sat nearby, housing a twin-engine Beechcraft 18 and an immaculately restored P-51 fighter. He nodded toward Kellen. "If you stay here and I'm over there, Stinson can make his move toward the shack, and we'll have them in a three way."

Kellen felt decidedly uncomfortable about splitting the team. "Why not stay together and flush them out?"

"How? The jet's buttoned up. If they spot us, all they have to do is taxi to escape." Connely gestured to the ammo bag that held the grenades. "Short of blowing up the plane, we couldn't stop them from taking off."

"You're right." Kellen nodded to the olive drab duffel. "Pass me a Colt." Connely rummaged in the bag and handed Kellen the CAR-15 rifle.

Kellen hoisted the gun to his shoulder. Through the viewfinder, he surveyed the tail ailerons, up to the top of the fuselage, and down along the belly of the jet until his gaze came to rest on the landing gear. "They can't escape if they're crippled."

"What?" Stinson asked.

"I'll put a few rounds in the tires," Kellen said.

"You think that will bring them out?" Connely asked.

"If you were inside and things suddenly tilted, wouldn't you step outside to see why?" Pulling wire cutters from his jacket, Kellen nodded to Stinson. "If you stay in the trees and work your way around to the rear of the shack, you have a clear shot at the Lear's forward hatch. Or, if anyone inside that shed tries to come out, you have them with the Street Sweeper." The 12 gauge with its circular magazine was, in effect, a machine gun that fired shotgun rounds. Kellen scooted forward and began to cut the barbed wire. "I'll blow the tires from here and approach in their dead spot directly behind the tail. By the time they lower their air stairs, I'll be under the belly of the plane. Anyone who exits will be looking down my barrel. And Connely," Kellen reached over and handed him the G36 rifle, "from your position near the hangar, you can blanket the area."

Stinson nodded toward January. "What about Oz the Magnificent?"

"I want him right here in the underbrush. Out of sight. I don't want to risk his capture again."

"Sounds okay to me." Connely checked the oversized magazine on the G36.

"Okay," Stinson agreed. He turned to January. "Don't mind me, kid. I'd like to catch your act sometime."

January's dark eyes rose. "You'll never see me again."

Connely paused as he stuffed grenades in his pockets. "What's he mean by that?"

Kellen wondered too. "What are you saying?"

January refused to reply. He got to his feet, crab-legged over to a large spruce, and sat.

Kellen joined him at the base of the tree. "What's this crap about not seeing you again? Are you heading back to the Skagit?"

"No. My mind is fragmented. I sense Shelby, but I'm being called away." January stared off into the morning mist that drifted lazily between the trees.

"Away? Where? I don't like the look in your eyes."

"What do you see in my eyes?" January fixed his gaze on Kellen. "Windows of the soul? Or portals to my past? The man called Lukat is with me, even now." January nodded up into the broad-needled boughs of the California spruce.

Kellen followed his gaze into the upper branches and was amazed to see them adorned with at least a dozen crows, staring down with their beady eyes.

"Holy shit."

"They wait," January said. "For the truth."

"Kellen," Connely whispered from the rear. "Are we doing this or not?"

Kellen glanced over his shoulder. Both men were loaded and ready. "Yeah, take your positions." Kellen pointed a finger in January's face. "You stay here. I don't want you to move."

January nodded, and Kellen sidled back toward the barbed wire fence.

Crouching, Stinson and Connely moved off to the left flank and disappeared into the trees.

Moments later, Kellen saw Stinson wave from behind the shack. Connely's camouflage cap appeared around the rear corner of the hangar.

Kellen cocked the CAR-15 and hoisted the rifle to his shoulder. He took a deep breath, exhaled, and, sighting the black rubber through the viewfinder, squeezed the trigger and fired five quick muffled shots.

Both tires squealed and collapsed. The Learjet lurched and then settled.

Kellen was running before the hiss of the air subsided. With the rifle held at his waist, he scrambled to a kneeling position under the still wobbling belly of the jet. The outer hatch lock clicked, and the hydraulics began to whine above. The stairway descended, dropping toward the runway.

A lone pair of shiny black shoes stepped onto the asphalt.

Kellen made his move, darting forward.

An unarmed man dressed in a dark-blue pilot's uniform rounded the air stair railing, gawking under the fuselage. Kellen was in his face instantly, pointing the rifle at his nose. "Keep your mouth shut and get on your knees."

"Who the fuck—?"

"I said shut up."

The man obeyed and knelt. Kellen's quick glance toward the shack showed no movement. Stinson was still poised off to the side with the Street Sweeper held high in his left hand. Stinson's split-fingered hand signal to his eyes with the right followed by a thumbs-down indicated that he saw no one else.

Kellen nodded upward. "Is the girl inside?"

"What girl?"

"Shelby."

"Look guy, I don't know who—"

Across the tarmac, the shack door swung open. A man in full-length coveralls with a wrench in hand stared wide-eyed in the direction of the plane. Before Stinson could detain him, he darted back inside.

Kellen pointed. "Who's that?"

"George somebody. A mechanic."

"Where's Shelby? Trajan? The others?"

"I don't know what you're talking about. This is a government aircraft. I'm the pilot."

"I know exactly what this is. Turn around." Kellen got down and spun the man, placing the rifle muzzle under his right ear. Staying low and using the pilot as a shield, Kellen prodded him toward the air stairs. "Give me your name."

"Turley. Jack Turley."

"Who else is aboard?"

"Wilson, my navigator."

"Get him out here, now."

Turley shrugged and shouted, "Hey, Dan. Step outside, will you?"

From inside the cabin, the muffled response.

"I said come out here a minute."

Connely advanced cautiously from the direction of the hangar. Stinson had eased forward, peering around the corner of the shed, keeping an eye on the door.

A blond man in white shirtsleeves and epaulets appeared on the stairs.

Kellen dragged Turley out from under the plane. He pointed the CAR at the navigator. "Down here, hands high."

"What the hell?" Dan Wilson stepped gingerly down the stairway.

Connely had now reached the nose of the plane and inched forward along the belly of the fuselage.

Kellen turned to Connely as he approached. "Cover these assholes."

"Pleasure."

Stinson had tapped on the shack door with the muzzle of the Street Sweeper and growled something about blowing the door off, forcing the mechanic to emerge.

Kellen carefully ascended the air stairs and, rifle held high, peered inside. From his position at the hatch, he could see left to the cockpit and right through the cabin. The interior of the plane was lavishly appointed with gray velvet seating, computer bays and television monitoring, plus what appeared to be chaise sleepers.

Kellen inched into the aft cabin, checking the berths.

Several oscilloscopes and what looked like heart monitoring equipment were secured in a storage bin. Odd cargo. Two oval aluminum tubs occupied the rearmost portion of the compartment, along with canisters of what might have been oxygen. Some liquid remained in one of the silver tanks . . . a residue of blue spotted the drain. Kellen touched the rim of the tank and found a length of blonde hair. Shelby's? Kellen tucked the hair into his pocket and moved forward.

The galley and the cockpit were vacant. No one else aboard.

Kellen was checking the flight manifest to see if a flight plan might clarify the plane's origin when he heard Connely shout from outside.

"Kellen, get your ass out here."

Kellen rushed to the hatch and, as he stepped down the stairs, saw Stinson holding a handset he'd apparently ripped from the shack wall.

"This bastard radioed for help," Stinson said.

Kellen heard the sirens.

Off to the north, where they had left Marissa's pickup truck parked on the dirt road, two flashing green-and-white sheriff's cars had broken through the underbrush and now raced down the runway.

"Lower the guns, guys," Kellen said as the cars screeched to a halt.

Sheriff Bullard, flanked by Deputy McMillan and a third patrolman, exited their cars, drawing their guns, using the car doors as shields.

"Drop your weapons," Bullard shouted. The weapons clattered to the asphalt. When he was close enough to recognize Kellen, Bullard's face flushed with anger. "Goddamn it, what are you doing here?"

"We haven't done anything illegal, Sheriff. I thought that Shelby—"

"Shelby what? Is she here?"

"No, but—"

"So why are you threatening these men?"

The mechanic had stepped away, glaring back at Stinson. "That man shot the tires out from under that jet, Sheriff."

"Hold on, George," Bullard cautioned. "We'll get to all that."

"There's a connection," Kellen objected, "between this jet and—"

"*This* jet radioed the Orcas Airport and our office this morning requesting permission to land. The Federal Emergency Management Agency is making routine rounds of the outlying county's earthquake preparedness," Bullard said.

"Earthquake preparedness? Bullshit. Check the plane. It looks like a high-tech doctor's office in there."

"Kellen, you're way off base. I personally escorted the FEMA administrator to the mayor's office two hours ago."

"What?"

"And who are these soldiers of fortune?" He nodded to Connely and Stinson. "Let me see some ID."

The men surrendered their billfolds.

After examining their licenses, Bullard shook his head. "Ex-FBI? God. I should have known." He returned their wallets and turned to George. "Any other damage to the property?"

"None that I can see," George said.

Bullard glared at Turley and Wilson. "Either of you hurt?"

Turley shrugged. "Just surprised, that's all."

"Well, so am I." Bullard turned to Kellen. "You want to explain this?"

Kellen glanced from Turley to Wilson. "I just did."

"You don't mind if Deputy McMillan escorts Mr. Connely and Mr. Stinson to the ferry, do you? Gentlemen, stay off the island for a while."

Stinson and Connely leaned over to pick up the rifles.

"Oh, and leave the weapons."

Connely glanced back over his shoulder. "Sorry, Kellen."

Bullard turned back to Kellen. "You can pick up the guns along with your nine millimeter in a day or two, after I ask whether the Feds plan to file damage claims."

39

Sucia Island

ALESSANDRO'S FRUSTRATION MOUNTED AS HE realized that the crown of the hill they had just climbed was not porous at all but rather a solid granite base covered by grass and moss. Shading his eyes, he squinted against the sun, surveying the peninsula. "There are no caves here."

"And no caves in sight." Hargrove peered through the binoculars, scouring the lowlands to the west. The placid waters of Echo Bay lay two hundred meters to the right, the narrow inlet of Snoring Bay a slightly lesser distance to the left.

With his valise in hand, Bernardo lingered at the base of the rock column they had spotted from the boat. The column was a tapered shaft of boulder that rose some twenty-five feet in the air.

Fraley, whose asthma had grown worse when they came ashore, chose not to join the fifteen-minute climb and remained with the dinghy.

Hargrove lowered the binoculars and shook his head. "I just realized our problem. It's the trees. If we were meant to view some kind of cavern from up here, how could we do it with this much greenery? We can't see the ground."

"And two hundred years ago, the vegetation must have been entirely different," Alessandro added. "There's new growth, and trees that were standing then may be down now. We may have to comb every square meter of the area." He glanced back at Bernardo, who had wandered to the opposite side of the stone pillar and now reappeared, clambering over the rough stone in his oxford shoes.

Bernardo removed some papers from the valise and placed it on the rock. He carefully sat on the leather case to prevent soiling his pleated pants. Alessandro marveled at the man's stamina. During the steep ascent, while Alessandro and Hargrove perspired freely, Bernardo never removed his jacket. Leafing through the transcript, he appeared dry and comfortable.

"What are you doing?" Alessandro shouted.

"I'm reading Martine's letter," Bernardo called. "To compare it to his map."

"Why? The pelorus tangents were irrefutable."

At Alessandro's insistence, they had repeated the entire maneuver on the boat, starting at the *El Trinidad*'s sunken location, again assuming the 327-degree course heading, rechecking the bearings before finally going on shore.

"We must trust Martine."

"So?"

"And he gave us this hill to climb."

"Agreed. What of it?"

Bernardo tapped the paper on his knee. "The rest of the answer must also be in here. Maybe we should be reexamining his writings instead of casting about."

Alessandro had come to appreciate the quiet wisdom that occasionally emerged from this polite, proper man who had become his friend.

"Hargrove." Alessandro tapped the professor on the shoulder. "Let's join him. He may have something."

Hargrove grunted and followed Alessandro to the mound, where both men knelt on the yellow grass beside Bernardo.

"What do you think of this?" Bernardo pointed to the top of the Xerox.

"The date?" Alessandro shrugged. "June 21."

Bernardo cocked his head. "The first time we dealt with the date, it bothered you. Do you recall?"

Alessandro did recall. He had used the incongruity as a ploy to entice Hargrove. "Yes, it crossed my mind before," Alessandro said, "but without result."

"Well here we are, again in June, over two centuries later," Bernardo added. "Today is the fifth, which makes the twenty-first sixteen days away."

"And that's the solstice!" Hargrove said, suddenly animated. "Which might mean something. Perhaps Martine drew his map on—"

"No," Alessandro said, "we all agreed on that. The letter to Martine's brother is dated June 27. He had obviously *not* been to the cave prior to that date. That's why he mentions his *intent* to return. That places his map after the twenty-seventh. It means Martine consulted with Imnit and then went back to the cave. That's why she had the strongbox and the map."

"Then why date the map June 21?" Hargrove asked. "To mislead us?"

Alessandro turned and surveyed the horizon. To the south of Sucia, Orcas Island and other islands, Matia and Patos, dotted the nearby ocean. Under scattered clouds to the east on the mainland, Mount Baker loomed majestically, witness to Lukat's mystery two centuries ago. "Yes, why use an erroneous date to distinguish a location? Unless . . ." Alessandro was suddenly struck by the notion. "Of course. The Indians."

Bernardo looked up from the map. "What?"

"The Indians didn't use calendars. They knew nothing of *our* sense of time."

"So?" Hargrove asked.

"What they did know," Alessandro indicated the mountain, "was the passage of the sun as it reached its northernmost sunrise point on the horizon, there over Mount Baker."

"Yes," Hargrove said expectantly.

"So the cave was oriented in honor of that event," Alessandro said. "It was dug, Hargrove. Artificial. Not a natural opening at all."

"I'm still not following you."

"Lukat was a wise man. A shaman, prophet, a medicine man, whatever you wish to call him. He was the guardian of the cave and its contents. The cave had some spiritual significance to the Indians, don't you see? Not because they found it, but because of what they put in it. And the cave was placed, or aligned, with respect to the solstice. And that's why . . ." Alessandro's eyes came to rest on the spire of rock at the summit of the hill. "There." He strode to the two-story-high column of stone and placed his hands on it. "It's this."

"It's what?" Hargrove asked.

"This immobile finger of stone . . . the reason Martine noted the top of the hill on his map. This natural, immutable marker would mark the passage of—"

Hargrove rose. "The sun," he said in awe.

"Yes." Alessandro smiled. "The sun."

Bernardo had also risen. "Why? How does that column of rock—?"

"Look, Bernardo." Alessandro pointed at Mount Baker. "In the summer, the sun rises in the northeast over that mountain, throwing its long rays of light onto this stone." He jabbed a finger at the boulder. "And this spire of rock creates an equally long shadow, which," Alessandro turned and strode to the edge of the rise, "must fall to the southwest. Not here on this peninsula, but rather across the water onto the next." He pointed across the narrow inlet of Snoring Bay, which at that point was a mere fifty yards wide. "There. Onto that opposing hillside."

They all studied the opposing slope that rose from the water's edge. It, too, was covered with trees.

"But where?" Hargrove asked. "I see no caves."

"Why would you? Upon discovery by Ravilla, the contents of the cave led to the torture of the natives. Since it was dug by the Indians, it follows that they would hide it again to avoid further trouble. Tomorrow morning, we'll return at dawn, and our rock column's shadow should fall somewhere on that hill. I think we can successfully estimate how much farther the shadow might travel on the solstice. And once we find that location, gentlemen, we dig."

40

Mount Constitution

IN THE DISTANCE, THUNDERHEADS PILED over Mount Baker, threatening a summer storm. The air had grown heavy in the twilight. Moisture from the valleys had been lifted by the last heat of the day and now collected in dark gray clouds that hung over the forest.

Kellen guided Marissa's pickup over the dirt road that traversed the back side of Vusario Ridge—the same trail that he and Lorna had taken to search for Molly's house.

Kellen brought the truck to a stop as the vehicle's headlights rested on the same patch of crushed weeds where Kellen had earlier parked Paddy's van. He killed the engine and glanced over at January who, having discarded his fatigues, now huddled shirtless on the front seat with his buckskin-covered knees drawn to his chest.

Kellen's own frustration over the Learjet fiasco was aggravated by January's open despondency. "All right." Kellen yanked on the emergency brake. "You want to tell me what's going on?"

January stared through the windshield.

"Look, we blew it. You know it, and I know it."

January's blinked fretfully.

"Are you pissed off? Hey, I was angry too, but there is no shame in trying."

January uttered his reply, without turning. "The shame is my brain. It's on overload. I can't key on Shelby."

"Why? The mushrooms?"

"No. The herbs are just to help. They block triviality so I can concentrate." He faced Kellen and tapped his own forehead. "It's all up here. I should be able to control it. It's a matter of will." January let his moccasined feet slip to the floor. "I have the power. But lately, only part of me is here today. And the other part—"

"What? This Lukat thing?"

"Yes. It takes over. Just like when it drove me to the cliffs." January slapped the vinyl seat. "And it's tearing my head off."

Kellen shrugged. "How can I help?"

"No one can help. I'm the one who feels the dead. I'm a sentinel from the past. I may even be from the past." January's eyes were anxious, searching. "You know how crazy that sounds? There's not much written about shamanism and schizophrenia. But there should be. I studied mental health when I first realized what was happening to me. And after what I experienced, I can recite the dictionary term for you verbatim. 'Schizophrenia: delusions, hallucinations, varying degrees of emotional or intellectual disturbance.' Then there's my favorite phrase: 'psychotic disorders characterized by withdrawal from reality.' Reality?" He turned to Kellen. "Whose reality are they referring to? I'm living in a world without barriers, man. I find myself crossing time, space, and language. How would you like to wake up one morning and find yourself half a planet away from your own bed?" He looked away. "That's what started happening to me at Stanford. It has to stop, Kellen. If it doesn't, I won't be able to control it. You can tell those anal-retentive researchers for me, I never claimed to be something I'm not." He looked at Kellen. "I am what I am. They've crucified people for less."

Kellen grasped him by the shoulder. "I'm not going to let them get to you."

"Really? What makes you think you can stop them?"

"I'll find a way. We'll go to Molly's and talk about it." Kellen opened the door and stepped out. "Paddy told me you had heart like nobody else. I believe that." Kellen tried to smile. "Let's get through this."

January nodded and jumped out.

Kellen started down the trail with January falling in behind. The silent, dusky woods seemed to close in as they began to hike. The stillness was broken by the sound of an occasional twig snapping under their feet as they moved along. There was no wind and no rain—only the ghostly forms of occasional animals among the pines.

After a mile or so, Kellen noticed the lantern lights on Molly's property. The friendly aroma of wood smoke drifted through the alder groves. "Looks like they've lit another fire in that fire pit," he commented. "Maybe they're cooking out."

Molly's unmistakable silhouette appeared by the crackling flames. Dressed in one of her flouncy gowns, she tended the embers with a long stick.

Kellen was gratified to see Long John frolicking in the nearby grass. He could see Lorna watching the cat as she sat on one of the stumps near the fire. Clearly, Lorna had been taking good care of him.

Kellen had called her cell phone and spoken with her in the afternoon, reporting the unfortunate encounter with Bullard. She had taken the news badly, expressing a growing impatience.

"Hey, guys," Kellen called out as he and January approached the fire. Both women looked up at the sound of the greeting "We're back." Kellen said, grinning.

Lorna seemed strangely sullen, unsmiling. She didn't rise to greet him. Molly looked away. It was then that Kellen noticed the tethers. Lorna was tied at the feet with a line that led back to the barn. Molly was similarly restrained, her right ankle shackled to one of the stumps.

"Hello, sunshine," a voice said to Kellen's right. It was Calico, stepping from the shadows, holding the other end of the line that bound Lorna.

"I'm sorry, Kellen," Lorna moaned.

Kellen instinctively reached for a gun that wasn't there. His GLOCK was at the sheriff's office.

January had turned as if to run, but he seemed to change his mind.

"That's a very good boy," Calico said. "Don't you even move."

Aware that he could use the cell phone in his back pocket to call for help, Kellen glanced around before pulling it out, noticing shapes of several men in the trees.

"Didn't I tell you we'd get you, Kellen?" Calico nodded to a large silhouette holding a customized G36. The shadow stepped forward, emerging into the halo of the fire. It was Stooch. His forehead was gashed by the eagle attack; his nose was heavily taped, giving him the look of a professional wrestler. "I've thought about you, Kellen—with every fucking breath, believe me," Stooch grunted. "And breathing's not easy. You broke my nose, asshole. Now it's payback."

"Not quite yet." A bald man in a dark suit with bright blue eyes stepped from the barn door and walked in their direction. "First, there's business to do."

The clatter of metal gear sounded in the trees as three other commandos stepped forward. Two carried MP5 machine pistols, while the third held an Israeli TAR 21 pointed at Kellen's chest. Kellen recognized the third man from the Skagit Gorge—the man with the brush cut, Ramon.

"I'm Trajan," the bald man said.

"I've heard of you."

Trajan stepped closer. "And not too happy about it, I see. You mind emptying your pockets?"

Kellen handed him the car keys and his cell phone. "So where's Shelby?"

"Oh, she's safe." Trajan nodded toward Molly's compound as he thrust Kellen's things into his blazer pocket. "She's over in that strange little round house with Dr. Epstein. We'll keep you safe too, January," Trajan added. "I want you to know that."

January glared without reply.

"How did you find this place?" Kellen made eye contact with Lorna to see if she was all right.

"You're surprised?" Trajan asked. "You shouldn't be. Like the Learjet today—we're always a step ahead. And you know why . . . because our people wear an electronic mesh in their clothes." He fingered his lapel. "My suit is made of the stuff. So is Calico's. Our clothing acts as a homing device to track where our people are." Trajan nodded to Kellen's jeans. "We sewed a similar liner into the belt of your jeans. That's how we followed you to the Skagit canyon."

"When you ransacked my cabin?"

"It was my chance to go through your shorts," Calico crooned from the rear.

"Knock it off, Calico." Trajan glared at her. "Call Briggs. Have him bring the chopper." Gesturing to Kellen, Trajan turned to Stooch. "Keep that muzzle on his back." Then turning toward Ramon, he demanded, "Bring the women."

Kellen peered through the twilight. Glancing Lorna's way, he again established eye contact with her and mouthed Marissa's name.

Lorna responded with a subtle shake of the head and a shrug, flitting her eyes toward the forest, indicating that Marissa had wandered off.

While Calico was speaking into a short-wave radio, Stooch and two of the commandos closed ranks behind Kellen and January, prodding them toward Molly's geometric home.

Ramon used his combat knife to loosen Lorna's ropes. He cut the shackle from Molly's leg and escorted the women as they trailed the others.

"You're being detained," Trajan said, slightly ahead of Kellen, "because our operation requires utmost secrecy."

"You're breaking the law," Kellen said.

"You think so? Walk with us, January. I want you to hear this." Trajan waited until one of the commandos nudged January forward so he strode abreast of Kellen. "Mr. Rand, it was *you* who impeded the welfare of the United States by delaying January's conscription. He was meant to help detect an incursion of terrorists who, even now, are trying to destroy our country. We have two days to locate several different assembly sites that hold enough anthrax to kill millions. My organization was designed to aid other law enforcement agencies. You should understand that, since you're a former FBI agent. Our goal, simply stated, is to deter terror."

"What about *your* terror?" Lorna and her guard had caught up to Trajan. "You kidnap people without giving a damn."

"That's an unfortunate requirement, Ms. Novak." Trajan threw a casual look over his shoulder. "Dr. Epstein's technique demands absolute commitment of our subjects and the forfeit of their 'normal' lifestyle. You see, we're in a deadly conflict. Sacrifice is required by other special forces of our military. And this is similar. Shelby was simply an unexpected underaged talent."

"Rationalize it any way you want. You're a cold-blooded mercenary," Kellen said as they arrived at Molly's porch.

"Am I?" Trajan rested his arm on the pine banister, standing in the halo of the house lanterns. "We're endorsed by NATO, my friend." Trajan looked around at Stooch and the others, who had settled in a circle, keeping Kellen and January at gunpoint. "What you see isn't the entirety of the American contingent. Internationally, there are several hundred of us. In the war against chaos, we're the strike force—the last line of defense. We're the heroes. What do you think that makes you?"

Trajan paused as a frail twelve-year-old girl in braids stepped from Molly's front door. She was escorted by a frizzy-haired man in white coveralls.

Lorna turned to face the door. "Oh my God. It's Shelby."

The hint of a smile crossed Shelby's lips. "Aunt Lorna?"

"Yes, sweetheart." Lorna started toward the porch stairs, but Ramon restrained her.

"Leave her alone," Shelby protested, gazing from Lorna to Molly, to January, and then to Trajan. "You promised that I could see my mother."

"I'm working on that," Trajan said. "Epstein, take Shelby and join Calico."

Kellen's gaze drifted toward Calico, who held a bright flashlight as she moved into a clearing that measured some seventy yards square and sat directly in front of the house.

Epstein complied, grasping the struggling girl by the shoulders, dragging her down the steps toward the grass. A small gauze pad was taped to the nape of Shelby's neck.

"Why can't I be with her?" Lorna asked, angrily.

Waiting until Shelby was out of earshot, Trajan whispered. "Frankly, what's the use?"

"What?" Lorna asked. "What are you going to do?"

Trajan shrugged. "Isn't it obvious? You know more than you should, Ms. Novak. I wanted to let you live. But I'm afraid that's no longer an option."

The rumble of a helicopter echoed over the mountain. Distant lights gilded the treetops. Some 120 feet away, waving her flashlight, Calico spoke into her radio. The chopper, an MD 500, came into view.

Realizing how little time they had, Kellen looked around, desperately seeking salvation. Stooch and his men seemed attentive to Kellen's every move. Their machine pistols were pointed at his back.

Trajan stepped forward, watching Calico guide the landing. Lights washed the bordering trees as the chopper descended. In the passing glow, Kellen caught what appeared to be the shadow of a woman among the alders. He blinked. The area was again cloaked in darkness. Had he seen Marissa?

The helicopter settled to the ground with its blades still spinning. In the illuminated cockpit, the pilot named Briggs brought the engine down to an idle.

Trajan smiled as he turned. "Mr. Rand, Ms. Novak . . . this is good-bye. Molly, thanks for your most peculiar hospitality. Stooch, they're all yours." He beckoned to Ramon. "Bring January."

Realizing that he would probably be buried somewhere in the forest by these killers, Kellen watched for the opportunity to disarm someone. Dying in a fight appealed to him a great deal more than dying through mass execution, and he vowed to save Lorna if he could. He glanced back at Stooch, who carried the G36. If some diversion would occur, Kellen would launch himself backward and grasp the weapon. He prayed silently for a break—any kind of opening.

Trajan was halfway to the helicopter when he realized that his hostage was not in tow. "Well, Ramon?" Trajan asked. "What's the hang-up?"

"Move it, dipshit." Ramon had been prodding January with the TAR 21 but to no avail. January didn't flinch, and Ramon inched around the young man to see his face. "Son of a bitch. Trajan, the motherfucker's asleep standing up."

"What?" Trajan asked, retreating toward them.

January's eyes were indeed closed.

As Trajan retraced his steps, Kellen heard the trees rustle. For the first time today, wind moved through the forest.

Ramon unsheathed his combat knife, pressing the tip of it under January's chin. "Come on, bright boy, or I'll put a dimple in your neck."

"Don't do that, you idiot." Trajan brushed Ramon aside. "He's not asleep. He's in a damned trance." He turned and shouted, "Epstein, get over here."

"At least he's not screaming this time," Stooch said, warily glancing up at the leaves in the trees overhead that continued to move. "We could just pick him up."

"Don't touch him." Trajan replied. "I want him handled properly. Epstein, come here, for Christ's sake."

"You want me to leave the girl?"

"Calico, watch Shelby," Trajan barked.

Calico's flashlight bobbed across the clearing and settled near the trees, where it illuminated the ground near Shelby's feet some sixty feet away.

"Come on, come on," Trajan yelled.

As Epstein plodded toward the porch, the sound of a rising wind grew louder in the forest. The lanterns on the ropes swayed. Small pine branches, bits of leaves, and grass began to flash through the beams of the chopper's landing lights. A fresh gust from the west tousled Epstein's hair as he approached. After examining January's face, Epstein turned to Trajan. "We've got to distract him somehow. I think he's doing this." Epstein gestured to the swaying trees.

"You're kidding? The weather?"

As if in response, lightning flashed over the mountain, illuminating Trajan's face.

"Yes," Epstein nodded. "I've heard of trancers being able to move air. I'm going to have to snap him out of it. Don't worry, it won't hurt him." Epstein reared back and, to Kellen's amazement, slapped January across the cheek. "I'm ordering you. Stop this," he shouted. He slapped him again.

After the second blow, January's body jerked and his lids flew open. His eyes flooded with awe. "Avalanche," he shouted.

Trajan whirled. "What did he say?"

Sheet lightning illuminated the clearing, followed by several volleys of thunder. As the last rumble subsided, Calico's voice could barely be heard over the whine of the chopper. "Trajan. Damn it, come here. Now!"

Trajan pointed at January. "Epstein, watch him." He bolted in Calico's direction. By the time Trajan reached her, Calico had stepped back, shining the flashlight on Shelby, who had fallen to her knees.

Calico's muffled voice exclaimed. "Hey! It's not January. It's her!"

"Oh God," Lorna said. "Kellen, look."

In the glow of Calico's flashlight, Shelby's face had twisted into a grotesque grimace. Her mouth had opened in a silent scream.

"Epstein, do you see her?" Trajan pointed. "What is this?"

Ignoring Trajan, Epstein grasped January's shoulder, completely awed by January's display. "Did you hear what this man said?" Epstein shouted with an astounded expression on his face. "He just called out Rahid's name."

"I need you here, goddamn it," Trajan yelled.

Epstein let go of January and rushed to Trajan, who was now beside himself. "Make her stop. Whatever it takes, make her—"

His last words were lost as a searing bolt of lightning struck the alder grove on the west side of the clearing. Trajan and Epstein turned, shocked as another fork crashed to the south, igniting the leaves.

"Holy shit." Stooch gawked at the aircraft. "That was close."

A third bolt lashed through a stand of fir to the north, splintering a large pine in half.

In the cockpit, apparently aware of impending danger, Briggs frantically hit his switches, having chosen to lift off, revving his motor as the four overhead blades spun.

It was too late.

The canopy of clouds above the mountain illuminated with yet another flash, and a fourth jagged shaft of lightning severed the air and struck the helicopter dead center.

The MD 500 shuddered and then exploded, throwing fire and debris everywhere. A wall of hot air and shrapnel blew the windows out of Molly's house and knocked January down.

Stooch and his other three commandos cowered under the concussion, their eyes squinting from the impact.

The moment Kellen had prayed for had arrived. He launched himself at

Stooch, throwing an elbow at his bandaged nose that resulted in a gratifying crunch. Bellowing in agony, Stooch collapsed to his knees, and Kellen clamped down on the G36, wrenching the rifle away. He whirled toward Ramon, who was closest, and fired off several quick rounds.

Ramon's face exploded into a sea of blood. He toppled to the ground.

The air came alive with flashes as the other two commandos returned fire.

Confused, Molly stumbled toward Kellen. She took three shots in the back and fell in front of Kellen.

Ducking low to the ground, Kellen shouted "Lorna! Get under the porch!" as he fired the G36 over Molly's crumpled form.

Lorna scampered toward Molly's house as Kellen hit the first commando high in the ribs and the second in the shoulder, bowling him over. Kellen glanced back to make sure Lorna was secured, and as he turned again, he saw Stooch roll to one side, grabbing the first fallen commando's MP5.

Within a second, the machine pistol was pointed at Kellen's face. Stooch began to pull the trigger.

From nowhere, January was in midair. He landed across the big man's chest, diverting his shots, which scattered wildly, splintering the porch.

Kellen was unable to shoot as the firing continued, afraid he would hit January. But January quickly lost his hold on Stooch's neck and rolled off his chest, dropping to his feet directly into the path of the weapon.

Kellen watched helplessly as January took a burst of flesh-ripping rounds in the gut. January screamed, clawing at the MP5 as he fell to the ground.

Kellen swung the G36 high, clamping the trigger, and fired a stream of bullets into Stooch's chest. With a look of disbelief, Stooch dropped the MP5 and keeled over.

As the last of Kellen's gunfire echoed through the clearing, only the crackling sound of flaming trees remained.

"January's hit," Kellen yelled to Lorna, clambering to his feet.

Lorna ignored him and instead rushed toward the clearing, where Shelby lay slumped among smoldering clumps of grass. Calico's mangled body lay a few feet away; Trajan's mutilated form not far beyond. White chunks of what must have been Epstein were scattered about.

Hesitating a split second to see that Molly was beyond help, Kellen knelt at January's side. He was breathing, but his naked belly was laid open by multiple close-range shots.

"Lorna," Kellen shouted.

Lorna had gathered Shelby and guided her back to the porch.

"He's alive," Kellen called. "Look inside and see if Molly's got bandages—"

"No." January moaned, reaching to grasp Kellen's wrist. His eyes were glazed with pain. "It's over."

Kellen looked over at Lorna. "Don't listen to him, we'll put some pressure on the wounds and—"

"He has only moments."

Kellen looked back toward the direction of the voice. "What?"

Cloaked in a beige blanket, Marissa had appeared near the railing of the porch. "He has only moments. Do not waste them." Expressionless, save the moisture in her eyes, she approached and, stepping around January, knelt at his head.

January swallowed hard. He coughed and spit blood. Then he spoke, whispering words Kellen couldn't understand.

Marissa leaned down, with her ear at January's mouth.

"He speaks of the vision," she said. "Things that he saw."

"What vision?"

"In the turmoil, we were linked. He, the child, and myself over there." She pointed to the trees. "He had achieved the clarity, until Shelby chose vengeance . . ."

January's bloody hand grasped Marissa by the hair, and she again bent down.

As January continued to speak, Lorna stepped up and placed a comforting hand on Kellen's shoulder. Her other arm was around Shelby, whose smudged face was streaked with tears.

Moments passed as Marissa listened closely to January's whispers. She glanced at Kellen. "January says that through the man they call Rahid, he saw anthrax in the warehouses of two cities in the western plains."

January's eyes blinked more slowly. His breathing became more labored.

"The name on the trucks is West-Haul." Marissa said. "He could not see beyond Denver and Fargo. There are others."

"God." Kellen winced. "If that's what they wanted to know, he didn't have to die for that."

January again tugged at Marissa, and she listened once more. Her tears dripped from her cheeks onto January's face, blending with his blood. "January says that with his power, the pages of the book were turned. The stories fell like leaves. He wishes you to finish one of the stories tomorrow when you go to the cave."

"The cave?"

"Sucia," Marissa sighed. "He says he is part of that story."

January again tugged, and Marissa bent down.

"Artok hu chui ah?" she asked.

January replied and Marissa looked up, fixing on Kellen. "And to the life giver, a returned peace. January wants Kellen to remember a name. The name is Cavendish."

Kellen looked at Lorna, who shrugged.

Marissa gently removed January's hand from her hair, placing it in her lap, and then sat up.

January inhaled a halting breath. He lifted his face to the sky. *"Enuk shta . . . tormada,"* he whispered. With a face filled with wonder, he gazed at the heavens and slowly, the life in his eyes began to dwindle. As his hopeful expression faded, his head slumped back and his hand fell from Marissa's lap. Marissa placed the palm of her right hand over January's forehead.

Shelby gasped and began to cry.

Kellen's eyes brimmed as he gazed into the trees. "I never imagined someone like him could exist." He reached down, searching for Lorna's hand. "And now that we found him, he's gone."

While Shelby stared longingly at January's now calm face, Lorna stood and embraced Kellen. Then she turned to Marissa. "I'm so glad you were here so he could speak to you, Marissa. What was that last thing he said?"

Kellen was amazed to find the old woman smiling as she looked into each of their faces, her eyes soft with a strange satisfaction. "January spoke in ancient words. In English, they mean, 'Remember me . . . it is not the end of my story.'"

41

Dawn, the Following Morning
Near Sucia Island

LORNA CLUTCHED THE CHROME RAILING. She lifted her chin, allowing the salt spray from the bow wave to gently douse her face. Emotionally drained, almost feverish with fatigue, she was understandably exhausted after only four hours of fitful sleep.

At 4:30 A.M., her hair still wet from a frantic shower, she had jumped into a pair of blue cargo pants and a T-shirt. Racing through the vacant lobby, she took several croissants and a thermos of coffee from the Outlook Inn kitchen, which she shared with Kellen and Marissa in Marissa's pickup as they drove through a stubborn mist that hung over gray pastures.

Kellen had chartered a twenty-eight-foot SeaSport from the West Sound Marina. Ian Latham, the skipper, was to pick them up at 5:00 A.M. But when they reached the Bartwood Pier, there was no sign of the boat, and the time to meet Alessandro on Sucia Island was approaching.

When Ian arrived he explained that the SeaSport had had engine trouble, and he was forced to choose an older and slower Glasspar boat, which had made him an hour late.

By the time Kellen, Marissa, and Lorna were loaded into the aging thirty-foot fiberglass hull, the sun had already risen.

When they were underway, Lorna closed her eyes and let the muscles in her neck relax. Her head bobbed with the rhythm of the Glasspar plowing through the bumpy waves. The astonishing impressions of the night before would be with her forever—Molly's death, Lorna's reunion with Shelby, and January's farewell to Marissa. Four commandos had been killed in the gunfight. Epstein's body parts were strewn in the weeds. Calico had been beheaded and Trajan had been mangled by one of the helicopter's unhinged rotor blades when the engine exploded. Shelby had escaped injury because she'd been lying low when the shrapnel struck the victims of her rage.

In the gloom that followed the fury—while Marissa held January, mourning her grandson—Lorna and Shelby sat with Kellen, speaking softly on the porch steps in the glow of Molly's lanterns. Shelby told them of Epstein's mysterious laboratory in the high desert and the implant in the back of her neck, which Epstein had finally removed at Trajan's insistence.

Lorna had consoled Shelby with frequent hugs, particularly when Shelby asked about her mother. Lorna found herself using the expression Pelto had used—that Tracy's fate rested with the angels. And Lorna promised to take Shelby to the Orcas Island Medical Center as soon as possible.

As Lorna held Shelby in her arms, Kellen excused himself to cover the bodies with Molly's bedding and to search the area. He had a number of concerns about the crash site. Trajan was carrying Lorna's cell phone at the time of the explosion; Kellen found it shattered on the ground. Calico's shortwave was still intact, but Kellen refused to use it for fear of being traced.

Since Molly had no phone, they were without communication.

"In one way, that's exactly what we want," Kellen had said, returning to scoop Long John off the porch, caressing his uneven little head. "The last thing we need right now is cops rousting us with questions." He joined them on the steps and pointed to the dead commandos.

"I just blew those guys away, even though it was self-defense. Remember whom we're dealing with. I'd probably face jail during an inquiry."

"They were going to kill us," Lorna objected.

"That's right. But as Trajan said, in the war he was fighting, we were the enemy."

"Who would side with amoral animals?"

"Well, whether you like it or not, they were acting on higher authority. And I don't know if I'm comfortable with that in a federal courtroom. I'm sure Shelby wants no part of what they'd planned for her. It's ironic that, in the end, January did have the answers they wanted." Kellen's eyes softened as he glanced down at the young man's face. "He died because of those answers, and somehow we have to deliver the message. The anthrax obviously has to be stopped. But how do we do that without jeopardizing ourselves? Or Shelby?"

Marissa listened silently, seated on the ground with January's head still in her lap.

"Is there anyone else we can contact?" Lorna asked. "Someone in the government?"

Shelby nodded. "A man named Preston. With the DOD."

"Department of Defense?" Kellen said. "Wow. This could be tougher than I thought."

Lorna dabbed Shelby's face, wiping away the grime. "Was he someone in the lab?"

"For a short time. I sensed that Trajan was afraid when Preston was there."

"Why afraid?" Lorna asked.

"I think he was Trajan's boss."

Holding Long John under one arm, Kellen squatted and reached for Shelby's hand. "Did Preston know where you lived? Could he find you again?"

"I don't think so . . . maybe. I think Trajan kept it a secret."

"But you're not sure."

"No."

Kellen leaned back on the porch steps, gazing out over the helicopter's smoldering wreckage. Deep in thought, he petted Long John and then placed the cat on the stairs and leaned forward. "We're lucky everything happened on the back side of the mountain, away from town. The smoke isn't visible at night, and fortunately, this fire isn't going anywhere. I think I can clean things up. I'll bury the remains and burn the clothes so Trajan's people can't find the graves. But we have to make a pact. Do you all understand that? We have to erase any trace that we were here. What time is it?"

Lorna strained to see in the lantern light. "About nine forty-five."

"We've got plenty of tools in Molly's shed. I'll be done by midnight." He nodded humbly. "Marissa, we can lay January to rest wherever you like. We'll have to tell Paddy to keep his mouth shut. And since Molly had no relatives—"

"What are you saying?" Lorna had been shocked at the inference. "Pretend it never happened?"

"Pretend nothing." Kellen shook his head. "Just a plain, old-fashioned cover-up. I know it sounds callous. But consider our alternatives. Forget about my problems defending murder charges. Do you want Shelby to be victimized again? Hounded by the press? Snarled in a government investigation about how the helicopter crashed?"

Lorna nodded and turned to Shelby. "Do you understand what Kellen said? If someone asks about this, you simply don't answer."

Shelby nodded.

"And we want you to try hard to remember everything you heard during the experiments," Lorna added. "We have to find a way to notify the government."

"That means getting word to Preston about the anthrax without exposing ourselves," Kellen said.

Marissa spoke up. "Have you forgotten January's wish—that you go to the cave?"

"Of course not," Lorna said. "We intend to honor that. It was obviously something that he . . ." She paused, struck by an inspiration. She had suddenly made a connection. "Alessandro," she said with some amazement. "I think he can help us."

"What? Why the hell would you want—"

"We could make a deal, Kellen," Lorna said. "He doesn't know about Molly's place, Trajan, Shelby, or any of it. All we have to do is use Alessandro to convey the news to Preston—a telegram, a quick anonymous phone call. He could arrange it somehow from Spain. Untraceable enough for you?"

Kellen's eyes brightened. "You think he'd do that?"

"For me, I think he would."

"What exactly are you willing to offer him in return?"

Lorna appreciated the hint of jealousy. "Marissa," she answered simply.

"Marissa?"

Lorna turned to her. "Alessandro wanted January involved in the search on Sucia. Since he also seeks some kind of cave, there may actually be a meaningful link to January." Lorna paused. She suddenly felt awkward, negotiating favors with Marissa on the heels of January's death.

Marissa must have picked up on Lorna's sudden hesitancy. "Don't be uncomfortable," she said reassuringly. Her dark eyes gleamed in the lantern light. "I agree with what Kellen says. And I will go. Not because you ask it . . . but because January's spirit will be there."

The Glasspar boat bounced as it hit a trough and Lorna opened her eyes, bringing her thoughts back to the present.

Marissa was staring at her, cloaked in a beautiful charcoal blanket embroidered with silver eagles.

At the helm, the skipper chatted with Kellen, who looked refreshed in yet another black sweatshirt and a fresh pair of jeans. He had torn Trajan's traceable lining from his other pair and burned it. While Kellen remained at Molly's with Marissa last night, Lorna had driven Shelby to town, stopping at a phone booth to call Hank Pelto. Lorna decided that for the next twenty-four hours, the best place for Shelby would be at her mother's side until Lorna returned to the hospital after the Sucia outing. On the phone, without great detail, Lorna simply told Hank that Kellen had found Shelby in the woods. She asked the reverend's support during what would undoubtedly be a painful vigil until Tracy's passing.

Lorna realized that Bruce Spilner would inevitably come into the picture, and she asked that Hank supervise Bruce and Shelby in her absence. Hank graciously offered to meet her at the medical center, and he volunteered to have Shelby stay at camp with her friends. When Lorna returned to the van, she told Shelby that Bruce had arrived in Eastsound. To Lorna's surprise, Shelby seemed somewhat uplifted at the prospect of seeing her father. Lorna sensed that Shelby welcomed any family support during this sad time.

And it was sad.

When they arrived at the hospital, upon seeing Tracy, Shelby had come undone. She and Lorna wept together at Tracy's bedside. Dr. Crowley captured Lorna in the hall and asked to speak to her alone. In his office, he expressed his regret. Lorna should prepare for the worst: Tracy had crossed the point of no return, and it was now simply a question of when.

Lorna had considered staying at the hospital, finding some other means to have Kellen deal with the work ahead. But as she visited Paddy's room to tell him of Kellen's request for secrecy, Lorna found herself overcome by her feelings for Kellen. He had risked his life, sacrificed his peace of mind to help her. If Alessandro were to become the device to inform Washington about the anthrax, she would have to be the one to seal the deal.

It was just after eleven when Lorna left for the Outlook Inn to see Alessandro.

She found him in his room, dressed in a bathrobe and about to retire. Using Alessandro's continued interest in her to engage him, Lorna explained that January had wanted to be present at Sucia, but that regrettably, in hermit-like fashion, he had unexpectedly disappeared. Since both his grandmother and January were synergistic in their beliefs, Lorna thought it might be helpful if Marissa came instead. Alessandro jumped at the opportunity, as she expected he would. Lorna had smiled and asked that in exchange, Alessandro do her a favor. Could he have a trusted confidant in Spain forward an anonymous message to a man named Preston in Washington, DC? Alessandro appeared naturally suspicious, but Lorna stated how terribly important the message was to her personally. She claimed it was a way to solve a problem that had arisen with a disgruntled client. She assured Alessandro of its propriety, but he insisted that before agreeing, he must know the content of the message. She had fortunately given some thought to its composition. The message was to read: "Check West-Haul Trucking warehouses in Fargo, Denver, etc., for avalanche gear."

Alessandro evidently found the terminology innocent enough and promised to have one of his father's trusted employees at his Benalmadena casino send a fax immediately. Lorna asked that she might stay to witness the call. He agreed, and while she waited, Alessandro phoned Spain, where it was already morning. She heard him order an American casino worker named Robert to research the needed number, go to a local fax service, and send the message anonymously. Satisfied, Lorna thanked Alessandro profusely and then went to her room. She collapsed into bed, only to awaken to the surrealism of this morning's boat ride to Sucia, which had now nearly ended.

Lorna looked around. Ian Latham had pulled the Glasspar into a narrow, placid waterway called Snoring Bay. Steep hillsides rose on either side of the tiny inlet as the boat headed toward a pebble-covered beach.

As they motored slowly among the seals and seagulls, Lorna spotted Alessandro's party, high above the breakwater on the southern side, where the shadow of the preceding peninsula cut a jagged line along the rocks and trees. The whine of a drill and a generator motor echoed across the small bay. Alessandro had mentioned that they would have plenty of digging equipment.

"Looks like they're hard at it," Kellen said as he joined Lorna on the bow. He gave her a once-over. "Are you okay?"

"Exhausted."

"Understandably. But holding up?"

"Anxious to get back to the hospital. Shelby being alone right now bothers me. She's got Bruce and Hank of course, but without you near her for protection, I'm a bit concerned."

"Don't be. I anticipated that. She's in excellent hands."

"What?"

"Realizing that there is a chance Shelby might still be in danger, I called Connely last night. He'll be watching her while we're on Sucia."

"How did you manage that?"

"It didn't take much. He felt like he hadn't earned his money, actually wanted to help. No one will even know he's there. Not even Spilner."

Lorna marveled at Kellen's ingenuity. "Thank you so much. I feel much better about that."

"I did too." Kellen gazed back at Marissa, who still sat in the stern of the boat. "I knew we both had to be here this morning. As tribute to his memory, if nothing else."

"A promise is a promise."

"Speaking of which, you're absolutely sure about Alessandro—"

"I was there, remember? Heard every word."

"All right. But there's no way back if—"

"Kellen, I did what I could. As your friend the reverend would put it, sometimes we just have to live by faith."

Kellen smiled. "You're right. That's exactly what he'd say."

Ian launched the dinghy and helped Marissa aboard. Lorna took a seat alongside Kellen, and in less than two minutes they stepped onto the beach. Leaving Ian with the boat, they plodded through underbrush and salal, at times waiting for Marissa, as they negotiated the challenging climb.

As they reached the dig site, the sound of drilling had been replaced by raised voices.

Alessandro appeared to be engaged in a heated discussion.

Two other men stood aside while Alessandro and a white-haired man argued about numbers of some kind.

As Lorna, Kellen, and Marissa approached, the Spaniard waved his hand in disgust. "We're back to abstractions again. Ten feet, twenty feet, forty feet. Higher. Lower. Suddenly we have over a hundred square meters to cover."

"But we can determine the variance," the white-haired man said. "We may need a survey crew, but it can be done."

"Engineers?" Alessandro countered. "You're going to call in engineers to solve an astronomical problem?" Looking fashionable in taupe designer jeans and a safari vest, Alessandro turned and finally acknowledged Lorna. "Good morning. We've already begun, as you see . . . with questionable results." He pointed to the generator and the rock drill that was still stuck in the ground and turned to Kellen. "I want to again thank you for your maritime expertise, which seems to have guided us successfully." Alessandro extended a hand to Marissa. "I appreciate your willingness to join us."

"It is where I am meant to be." Marissa took his hand with a gracious bend of the wrist.

"In any case," Alessandro gestured up the hillside, "please meet my assistant Bernardo Costanza." The portly, conservatively dressed man carrying a briefcase nodded. "And this is David Fraley of the Orcas Museum." Fraley had just blown his nose and gave an embarrassed wave. "And this is Dr. Hargrove of the University of Washington. I have informed them why you all deserve to be here."

They shook hands all around, and then Lorna asked Alessandro, "Are you having trouble?"

"Well, perhaps you'll have some ideas." Alessandro pointed across to the top of the opposing body of land one hundred yards across the inlet. "That rock outcropping at the summit of Johnson's Point was to throw its shadow upon this hillside at sunrise—a sign of where to dig. But as you see, at the location indicated, we hit solid rock under the topsoil. Not once, but several times."

Three other holes were visible near the drill, plus some picks, several shovels, and flashlights. A Geiger counter and another unidentified silver container sat upon a canvas.

"Dr. Hargrove pointed out the potential errors," Alessandro added. "Doctor . . . ?"

Hargrove wore a tool belt holding several chisels over his khaki shorts. He rubbed his unshaven face. "We gauged the location on a shadow thrown by a summer solstice sunrise. What hadn't occurred to any of us until our failure was our inability to determine whether the site is based on the tip of the shadow or the base. The shadow of that twenty-five-foot pillar thrown onto this hillside at sunrise is a full seventy feet long and nearly thirty feet wide. Secondly, since we're estimating its lateral location based on a solstice over two weeks away, we have the additional variability of some twenty to thirty feet from side to side. Probing an area thirty-by-seventy is not what we had hoped."

Alessandro dabbed perspiration from his tanned forehead. "The fact is, these variations cannot be accurately determined without proper equipment."

Lorna pointed to the canvas. "What's that next to the Geiger counter?"

"Oh." Hargrove stepped in. "You're looking at a rather marvelous piece of machinery I was able to borrow from the Quaternary Research Center at the University of Washington. This version is brand new, only just available: a Portable Field Particle Accelerator. PFPA for short."

"Sounds nuclear."

"Well, it is. And extremely expensive. It measures the rate at which carbon atoms change into nitrogen atoms. You've probably heard of carbon dating. This is simply a quicker means of determining carbon 14 deterioration. It's a bit less reliable than lab work, but it gives capable readings within ten percent of actual age in a matter of minutes."

"But equipment isn't what we need right now," Alessandro said. "We either need more manpower to dig up a large portion of this hillside or brain power to determine whether two weeks from now the shadow will rest farther east, and how far."

Lorna sensed that someone was missing. Marissa. A quick look around showed the elderly woman had wandered to the crest of the hill. She stood silently and dropped her blanket to the ground. She looked west and extended her arms.

"What is she doing?" Alessandro asked softly.

"I think we're about to understand the reason she's here," Kellen said. "Look there, on the horizon."

Lorna followed his gaze. What seemed to be a small black cloud had appeared over Sucia, a quarter of a mile away. Everyone was curious as they climbed the hill, proceeding until they were only a dozen feet from Marissa.

As Kellen surveyed the landscape, he began to smile broadly. "You know what that is?"

"Birds," Alessandro said.

"Crows, to be precise," Kellen said.

"They're coming this way." Lorna was awed at the sight. "Dear God, there must be hundreds of them. Kellen, what is this?"

"The first night I saw January, Paddy called me a doubting Thomas. I'm a merchant of miracles now. Nothing surprises me." He glanced over at Marissa, whose closed eyes had begun to moisten.

Lorna and the others watched as the flock drew near. The black birds flew overhead, crying out in a raspy staccato, circling repeatedly, and finally swooping over Marissa and alighting in a large madrona tree some thirty feet away.

"We've got company," Kellen said.

Lorna turned and found Marissa chanting something under her breath.

Alessandro had stepped closer to Kellen. "Are you suggesting that this is an omen of some kind?"

"Damn right I am. Look." Kellen pointed to the madrona, where at least forty of the crows had fluttered to the ground and now paraded about like sentries at a gate near the base of the tree, pecking at the earth. "What do expect them to do, dig the hole for you?"

Alessandro's dark eyes sparkled with renewed excitement. "Bernardo, Fraley, help me." Alessandro led the men back down the hill to the canvas, and setting the heavy equipment aside, they bundled the shovels and flashlights. Ascending once more to the summit, Hargrove and Bernardo were in the lead, scattering the crows near the tree as Fraley limped along behind. They unwrapped the gear under the tree branches, and Kellen chose a shovel and began to dig.

Alessandro rolled up his sleeves and joined him shoulder to shoulder. They hacked away, while Hargrove used a pickax to loosen the dirt.

"No rocks so far." Kellen grunted as he worked down to two feet.

Lorna turned to check Marissa, who had opened her eyes and now stood watching the activity, having once again gathered the blanket about her.

Lorna felt drawn to her and wandered in her direction. "The crows?" she asked. "Is this what you expected?"

Marissa's face glowed with vitality. "The shaman is a reflection of a greater power. We are not the miracle, but the messengers."

"Messengers of what?"

"We share in the wonder of life that surrounds us daily. It is not we who are great, but life itself. The flight of a hummingbird is as grand as the explosion of a star. And no less amazing are your thoughts, which have no limits at all. The last time you dreamt something that you thought was real, what did it tell you? What did it say to you when you awoke? It should have reminded you that all things are possible. For you, Lorna, it is a lesson learned by an open heart. To some people, the miraculous appears to be everyday. To others, every day is a miracle. Which person are you?"

Alessandro exclaimed, "Damn it. More rocks."

The clank of metal sounded as Kellen jabbed his shovel into the now-sizable hole. "Wait. This time, you're going to love the rocks. They've been stacked in here."

"Blocking a passage, perhaps?" Hargrove asked.

"That's my guess." Kellen fell to his knees, straining to lift a two-foot chunk of granite. "Here, form a line."

As the men began to remove the stones, Lorna took Marissa's hand. "I don't have much experience with miracles. But I'm willing to learn."

"Then go." Marissa gave her a nudge, sensing her eagerness to rejoin the others.

"Thank you for who you are," Lorna said. She strode across the underbrush toward the madrona, which the crows had now abandoned.

As Kellen budged another stone, Hargrove exclaimed, "We've broken through."

Alessandro barked, "Bernardo, some lights."

His assistant scampered to the canvas and returned with flashlights.

Alessandro knelt, shooting a beam through the opening. "This is it. I see a wall back there."

Hargrove squatted next to Kellen. "How far?"

"Twelve feet or so. It seems to make a turn." Kellen strained with another boulder. "Let's get the rest of these."

One by one the remaining stones came away.

Alessandro turned, as if capturing the moment. "Well?"

"Take the lead," Hargrove said.

Alessandro stepped through, and Hargrove and Bernardo followed.

Kellen helped Lorna into the depression, ushering her inside as Fraley brought up the rear.

Lorna found herself in a chamber some fifteen feet square at the bottom. The walls were braced with large gray trunks of wood, peaked at the ceiling.

"See how this is constructed, Hargrove." The dankness seemed to muffle Alessandro's voice. "Like a pyramid to hold the earth above." He touched one of the logs. "Look at this. They're petrified."

Hargrove patted one of the trunks. "You're right. Stronger that way, though there's not a great deal of weight up there. That peak couldn't be more than six to eight feet below the surface."

"Look at the artwork." In the mustiness of the chamber, Alessandro's light panned the pale timbers. A row of childlike pictures of birds, deer, and bear had been carved at eye level. "How old do you think, Fraley?"

Fraley sneezed. "These are new to me. I could only guess."

"Then guess. Two hundred years, perhaps?" Alessandro suggested.

"Perhaps . . ."

Kellen had moved ahead. "Check this out." Alessandro joined him. "There's a second chamber ahead."

Fraley limped along, followed by Bernardo and Hargrove.

As the others crept forward, Kellen waited for Lorna and pointed to the timbers in what appeared to be a passage connecting the two rooms.

In this corridor, the animal carvings had been replaced by the unmistakable likenesses of killer whales. "They're orcas, Lorna. Remember? January mentioned the whales in his vision."

The place was eerie. Lorna felt as though the past itself was watching. They had entered a sanctuary from another time.

Alessandro's voice rang through the corridor. "Hargrove, where are you?"

"Coming." Hargrove stumbled past Bernardo and Fraley and joined Alessandro in the next chamber.

Lorna and Kellen pushed in from the rear as Alessandro's flashlight shone on what appeared to be an alcove. Against the back wall, a solid block of wood, six feet wide by three feet high, sat on the ground. On top, a large mound of dried animal skins had been piled nearly to the ceiling.

Hargrove frowned. "Looks like a shrine."

"What's that on the floor?" Kellen asked.

Lorna panned her light down and gasped as her beam revealed a skeleton. Alessandro knelt. In the halo formed by the flashlights, the skeleton lay head-first toward the altar. Its right arm extended as if reaching for it. The flesh had long ago fallen away, but remnants of a pale blouse and what appeared to be a red jacket partially covered the torso.

The glint of metal caught Lorna's eye. "Alessandro, check the right hand."

Alessandro leaned down and gently lifted the cadaver's wrist. "It's a ring." Alessandro gingerly eased the jewelry from the decomposed finger. "And it's emblazoned with initials." He focused his light. "Four letters entwined. F M and . . ." Alessandro's mouth dropped. "C M."

Bernardo edged forward. "Cerba Martine's ring." Tucking his flashlight under one arm, Bernardo dug in the valise and produced several papers. "I remember it being mentioned in his letter to his brother. Yes, here it is. 'I swear my continued devotion to you, dear Francisco, with a pledge each night upon the signet gold ring, which you gave to me.' C M and F M, Señor. Cerba and Francisco Martine."

Alessandro shook his head. "Why is he lying here?"

Hargrove shrugged. "As you speculated, he returned to the cave."

"And?" Alessandro turned. "What happened?"

"Apparently he died."

"How? Murdered?"

Hargrove nodded. "Presumably, by the Indians. Just as Imnit was. She died with the Spanish strongbox on Orcas Island, and he was killed here. You yourself said the two lovers were punished."

Alessandro shone his light on the skeleton. "I see no hole in his skull. No evidence of an adze blow."

"Perhaps he was stabbed to death." Fraley used a fresh handkerchief to again blow his nose.

Alessandro panned the clothing. "Difficult to tell. But let's assume he was killed. From Martine's own account, Lukat, the wise man, considered this cave sacred. Why would the Indians leave a corpse to disgrace their holy place?"

"Maybe they locked him in." Kellen stepped into the light. "When they sealed the entrance."

Alessandro assented. "That makes sense to me."

"I don't think so," said Hargrove. "I think they sealed the cave not knowing he was inside."

"Really? Without a word from him? Allowing himself to be entombed?" Alessandro questioned.

"Why come back at all?" Lorna asked.

"Indeed." Alessandro shone his flashlight around the dusty chamber. "What was so extraordinary about this place? And what shocked Captain Ravilla enough that he would run his sword through Lukat?" Alessandro focused his beam on the altar. "Surely not this pile of skins."

Kellen stepped forward and touched the mound. "Maybe there's something underneath."

The rank heap didn't invite handling.

Alessandro looked back. "Bernardo, could you perhaps . . . ?"

"Me? Ah, as you wish." Bernardo carefully shed his suit jacket, and in his white shirt and suspenders, strained to reach the top of the stack and began removing the tattered pelts.

Hargrove nudged Fraley. "Lend a hand, will you?"

Wincing, Fraley retreated. "The dust, sir. I don't think I should."

"Here." Kellen handed his flashlight to Lorna and stepped in. "Let me get them, Bernardo. I'll hand them to you."

Kellen began to remove the top deerskins, handing them down, while

Bernardo stacked them on the floor next to Martine's bones.

Lorna shone the light over Kellen's shoulder, and as the dusty pile came away, she began to see something white. A creamy-colored object had been exposed.

Lorna craned her neck. "There's . . . something."

Hargrove gawked over her shoulder. "Feldspar, perhaps?"

Fraley stood on tiptoe. "No, scrimshaw. Whalebone."

Kellen was now able to remove several skins with each handful.

As the layers fell away, the pale object revealed itself to be not a chunk at all, but the top of a vertical pole. Kellen hoisted another load, and the vertical piece joined a horizontal bar. Yet another layer, and Lorna noticed the shape of what appeared to be a human head and shoulders.

"What *is* that?"

Alessandro strained to see. "How strange." Losing his patience, he tucked his flashlight into the waist of his designer jeans and rushed to the pile, tugging at the dusty skins, pulling them away in lumps.

Fraley sneezed and covered his nose with his handkerchief.

As the last of the skins fell limply at his feet, Alessandro stood transfixed.

A shudder of incredulity rose up Lorna's back.

Hargrove stumbled sideways and braced himself on Kellen's shoulder. "That's impossible."

"No, it's not. It's sitting right there," Kellen said softly.

In momentary silence, everyone stared at the fully revealed artifact: the pale likeness of a man suspended on a cross. The four-foot-high carving had been crudely chiseled, with blocky hands and feet on a body tattooed with intricate totem-like etchings. The blunt facial features were indistinct, save the eyes, which were awkwardly large for the face and outlined in black—a style common to northwest Indian art.

Hargrove turned to Alessandro with a scowl. "What is this? Some kind of joke?"

"Excuse me?"

"You invited me to this farce?"

"I had no idea—"

"Of course you did. You tricked me into being present at this unveiling." Hargrove snarled his words. "What did you want? My accreditation?"

Alessandro reacted with equal fire. "You think I forged this thing?"

"What other explanation could there be for this travesty?"

"That it's legitimate," Fraley said quietly.

"I beg your pardon?" Hargrove redirected his attack. "What's gotten into you?"

"Look at the size and the striation." The weathered artifact had yellowed, its surface cracked by intermittent moisture and drying over time. "That's carved from the rib bone of a whale."

"And?"

"Reminiscent of other early work of the Salish tribes."

"How early?"

"I . . ." He sniffled. "Hard to say. It's unique."

"So, you give it credence?"

"I give it a chance."

"All right, Fraley, if you say so." Reluctantly resigned to his colleague's assessment, Hargrove shook his head. "Perhaps the thing is genuine. But I must tell you, Vargas, I'm more prone to believe you're the victim of an elaborate hoax."

"I don't feel victimized. I think it's two hundred years old." Alessandro touched the object. "Let's test it. Let's prove me wrong. Shave a small sample from its base and put it through the PFPA." Alessandro looked over his shoulder. "Bernardo, could you assist Fraley in bringing the equipment inside?"

"Fine." Hargrove shrugged. "And suppose you're right. What if it is two hundred years old, what does it prove? It simply means your Lukat and his cronies had prior interaction with Europeans who wore a crucifix."

Alessandro cocked his head. "I was intrigued by your reaction when you first saw it. What did you feel?"

Hargrove had removed a small chisel from his belt. "I . . . I was . . ."

"Angry? Revolted? That's how you acted."

"I suppose. I'm a Presbyterian after all. I'm used to representations of Jesus that—"

"Are white man's art."

"Not that, really." Hargrove pointed at the statue. "Just something less animalistic."

"That must have been Ravilla's response. He abhorred it. Found it demonic, perhaps."

"I can see where it might be disconcerting," Lorna said.

Bernardo returned, carrying the canvas. He dumped its contents on the cave floor. "I still have to get the Geiger counter," he said, excusing himself and passing Fraley, who entered the chamber holding the Portable Field Particle Accelerator in both hands.

"Fraley, bring the generator to the cave entrance and fire it up." Hargrove pulled a long electric cord from the back of the PFPA box. "I'll let you know when we have power."

Not wanting to miss anything, Lorna shouted after Fraley, "Invite Marissa to join us."

Lorna and Kellen looked on as Hargrove leaned on the altar using a small battery-powered saw to nip notches in the backside of the artifact. He chipped away with his hammer and chisel and removed a piece of bone the size of a nickel.

Bernardo brought the Geiger counter, and after the generator sounded outside, Fraley was back. "Ready when you are."

Lorna turned. "Marissa?"

"No sign of her. She must have returned to the boat."

Hargrove slid a panel on the device, revealing a series of illuminated dials and meters. He opened a small trap door on the opposite end of machine and placed the bone sample into what appeared to be a leaded chamber and touched a button. The PFPA emitted a soft humming. "This will only take a few minutes," Hargrove said.

Lorna eased over to Alessandro. "What do you think?"

"Well, I'm obviously completely dumbfounded. I had expected to find some golden idol, evidence of a native cult. What I now believe is that Ravilla was so taken aback by finding a symbol of his faith in this primitive place that he thought Lukat had tried to mock his Christianity. That's why he killed him. Obviously, a savage carving of Christ produces a variety of responses. Look at Hargrove. He was upset. Still, I believe that Ravilla was influenced by his own unbalanced state of mind after murdering Lukat. That's why Ravilla took his own life."

"Okay, regardless of Ravilla's issues," Kellen stepped in, "a carving this large would take months, wouldn't it? Would this Lukat guy fabricate something this elaborate just to impress Spanish explorers?"

Alessandro shrugged. "We would have to study their culture to speculate—" He paused, interrupted by a clicking sound. "What's that all about?"

While Bernardo looked on with interest, Fraley had stooped over the skeleton with the Geiger counter. He looked up, embarrassed. "I was just checking the area, when I got a reading here. Very mild though, fifteen rads."

Hargrove left the PFPA. "It must be the ground. Let me see." Hargrove knelt at Fraley's side and yanked the sensor from his hand. He dangled the lead wire and touched the sensor to the earth near the cadaver. Nothing. Then he placed it in direct contact with the skeleton's femur. The clicking resumed.

"It's hot," Kellen said.

"Not very," Hargrove responded. "Fifteen rads is hardly a blip on the screen. Nine rads isn't uncommon for a plain old environmental reading anywhere on the planet."

Alessandro had joined them. "But it's more than the average."

"True." Hargrove handed the counter back to Fraley and stood. "We can have it checked at the campus lab if you wish."

"I think that would be worthwhile," Bernardo interjected. "Señor, you remember Martine's account of the flash that Ravilla saw?"

"Yes, I do," Alessandro replied.

"How's that?" Hargrove asked.

"Probably nothing of any immediate consequence. Ravilla apparently experienced some kind of light emission." Alessandro shook off the comment. "I don't know much about radiation. What kind would this be anyway?"

"We won't know until we check."

"But I've heard about half-life," Alessandro said. "Does that imply the readings would have been much higher in the past?"

"Not necessarily," Hargrove grumbled. He turned and strolled back toward the PFPA. "It depends on what kind of particles we're reading. Some types of radiation have almost eternal half-lives, which means . . ." He stared at the control panel. "Dear God."

"What is it?"

Hargrove appeared shaken. "Now I'm going to insist we take the artifact to the campus along with the bones. Test them both under strict laboratory conditions."

"Of course," Alessandro said. "But why?"

Hargrove's pale eyes rose to the primitive cross that hung above the altar. "The radiocarbon readings in this machine indicate that this piece of whalebone is, give or take ten percent . . . two thousand years old."

42

Two Hours Later

THE *GLASSPAR,* WITH IAN LATHAM at the helm, plowed across a placid sea under sunny skies. On the foredeck, Kellen lay on his back with his eyes closed. He'd finally worn down after last night's meager two hours of rest.

Lorna was too restless to sleep. Seated at Kellen's side, she toyed with Ian's binoculars, panning the horizon, watching the coastline and spotting some of the homes that were tucked into the forests.

Hargrove's Tollycraft followed in their wake. Through the field glasses she could clearly see Hargrove at the helm. Alessandro, Fraley, and Bernardo had gathered in the stern around the tightly wrapped brown canvas that held their find along with small bone samples from Martine's remains.

The Tollycraft breached the *Glasspar*'s wake and began to bear westward, headed down President's Channel toward West Sound, where a seaplane was to fly Hargrove to Seattle. The professor had asked several technicians at the Quaternary Research Center to stand by for analysis of the whalebone.

Lorna waved at Alessandro.

The Spaniard waved back.

The *Glasspar* veered away, and Lorna lifted the binoculars back at Sucia. A few fishing boats trolled near the shore. Lorna panned the beaches, wishing she could spot Marissa. The old woman had asked to be left on the island for the day, explaining it was her way of mourning her grandson. Kellen had extended the courtesy. Since he had chartered the boat for twenty-four hours, Ian was to return at sunset and pick her up.

Earlier, while Alessandro and the others packed the mysterious artifact, Lorna had wandered to the beach at Snoring Bay, curious and concerned about Marissa. She found her seated on the rocks, staring at the waves.

"Marissa, there you are," Lorna had said. "Didn't you want to see what they found in the cave?"

Marissa had acknowledged her with a soft smile. "My eyes are old. What they see no longer matters."

"But they found a large crucifix. A totem carved from a whalebone."

"Who did they say was hung upon it?"

"Well, no one said . . ."

"They didn't name the man?"

"No, they didn't. Some might argue that it was Jesus, but that's just so much conjecture."

Marissa stared at her. "January would have wanted them to name the man."

"Excuse me?"

"If he had been alive to see it, he would have wanted that." The old woman rocked back on her haunches and arose. "Where is Kellen? I have a favor to ask."

No more was said, and when they located Kellen, Marissa had made her request to stay.

Lorna trained the field glasses over the bow, checking their destination—Bartwood. She'd be at the hospital in fifteen minutes. Colorful umbrellas spotted the deck of the Bartwood Lodge restaurant. A police car with its lights flashing sat in the parking lot just beyond the dock.

A police car?

She dropped the glasses and shook Kellen. "Kellen, ask Ian to stop."

"What?"

"Tell him we want to go to West Sound instead."

"Why?" She pointed and handed him the binoculars.

Kellen sat up and peered at the lodge. "Holy shit. They found the bodies."

"How could they?"

"I don't know."

Ian opened the sliding window and pointed to his radio receiver. "Kellen, there's someone who wants to talk to you on ship-to-shore."

"Who?" Kellen asked.

"He's in that police car over there."

"Here it comes, Lorna." Kellen winced and got to his feet. "We have a lot of explaining to do."

"What do we tell them?"

"Let's see what they want. Don't volunteer anything, and call your lawyer." Kellen guided her across the deck and along the narrow catwalk into the cuddy cabin. Ian waited at the helm, holding the receiver.

Kellen took it. "This is Kellen. Over."

The voice answered over the speaker. "McMillan here, Kellen. Are you coming in? Over."

"If that's what you want," Kellen said hesitantly. "What seems to be the problem? Over."

"I was going to wait 'til you got here, but there's someone with me who can't stand it. I'll put him on." Kellen gave Lorna a quizzical look as the speaker rustled.

A joyful voice chimed, "Are you just trolling out there, or did you catch anything? Over."

"Paddy? Is that you?" Kellen broke into a broad grin. "What are you doing out of the hospital?"

"They released me this morning. I'm a crutch-wielding terror. You should see me hobble down the halls. But that's not why I'm here. Is that lovely Novak woman with you? And can she hear my voice? Over."

"Yes, over."

"Lorna Doone, you'll be happy to know that your sister, Tracy, is awake and asking for you."

Lorna clutched Kellen's arm. "Dear God." She blinked back the tears as Paddy continued, "Your niece, Shelby, and Mr. Spilner are with her right now. The good deputy came to give you an escort back to the hospital, and I couldn't resist the ride. Over."

Lorna was unable to speak. She had resigned herself fully to Tracy's death. She could only nod, grin, and wipe her cheeks.

Kellen gave Lorna a hug and smiled. "Paddy, if she could talk, she would tell you how happy she is."

"No, let me . . ." Lorna reached for the microphone and fought through the lump in her throat. "Paddy. You don't know what this means. Thank you so much. Would you ask McMillan to please call the hospital? Have them tell Tracy that I'm on my way."

43

Eastsound

WITH ITS LIGHTS FLASHING, MCMILLAN'S patrol car propelled Lorna toward the medical center, while Kellen and Paddy shared a jovial reunion in the backseat.

As the car raced through the farmland, Paddy chirped about the fishing he and Kellen would do.

Lorna fidgeted with the beige windbreaker on her lap. Though she had taken the time to thank Deputy McMillan for his courtesy, she remained silent otherwise, her mind already six miles ahead, already with Tracy. Lorna hungered for Tracy's first words, her first smile.

The ride to the hospital took less than eight minutes, and after the car pulled into the parking lot, Lorna tucked the jacket under her arm and excused herself.

Kellen smiled and encouraged her to go ahead while he helped Paddy with his crutches.

Lorna rushed past the reception desk, down the wing to Tracy's room. As she reached the door—

"Lorna." She was startled by Dr. Crowley, who intercepted her in the hallway. She turned.

"A word with you," he said softly, approaching in his white smock. "We're just as excited as you are about Tracy, but until we have sufficient time to thoroughly test her, I'm asking that she not be overstimulated."

"What?"

"We're going to give her a CAT scan early tomorrow morning, which will tell us exactly where she stands. For now, I want you to enjoy her, but try to keep the excitement level to a minimum. She's still weak and requires careful handling."

"You mean she's not out of danger?"

"The fact that she's awake doesn't guarantee there's no residual damage inside. Don't get me wrong. I think it's marvelous that you say hello. But Mr. Spilner and Shelby have been with her for a while now, and though it may be difficult, I'm going to ask that everyone leave in a few minutes to give Tracy recuperative rest."

"But—"

"I know it sounds odd to give somebody time to sleep after being in a coma for so long, but that's exactly what she needs. Okay? Go in and enjoy, but for tonight, keep it brief."

As Paddy and Kellen appeared around the corner, Dr. Crowley smiled but wagged a cautioning finger at Paddy. "Pipe down. This place is for soft-spoken sick people, not wild men like you."

Paddy's cheeks bunched in a feigned wince. "Forgive me, your eminence."

Lorna nodded to Kellen. "I'll go in alone. Doctor's orders."

Crowley shrugged. "Sorry, guys. You can wait out here."

Lorna cracked the door open and peeked in. Bruce Spilner stood at the foot of the bed. Shelby sat in the metal chair with her hair down, which hid the patch of gauze at the base of her neck.

Lorna nodded to Bruce as she eased into the room.

Shelby turned, "Aunt Lorna."

Tracy's matted head rolled to the side. Crow's-feet creased her pale face as she recognized Lorna, and she bit her lower lip. "Oh God, it's you," she said.

Lorna's tears gushed as she dropped the windbreaker to the floor, kneeling to take Tracy's hand.

"I remember you being here," Tracy whispered, "heard you speak as if far away. I thought it was a dream." She looked up at Shelby. "But then they told me."

"I didn't think we would ever—" Lorna choked as she remembered her plans for Tracy's funeral, "be with you like this."

With a deep sigh, Tracy nodded. She still looked terribly feeble, and it was obviously tiring for her to speak.

Lorna sat and stared at her, not wanting to force the conversation. Years of separation had culminated in this bittersweet moment. Tracy heaved another deep breath, and Lorna now realized what Doctor Crowley meant. Tracy's body had paid an enormous price for having been debilitated.

"Your open eyes are the most beautiful thing I've ever seen," Lorna finally said, smiling. "There's so much to talk about."

"Yes." Tracy swallowed with effort.

"But there's time," Lorna continued. "I promise. We'll have plenty of time together."

A knock at the door, and Kellen poked his head inside, smiling at everyone. "Lorna, I'm sorry. Dr. Crowley . . ."

Lorna looked back at Kellen. "Yes. And he's right. We should go."

Tracy made eye contact with Kellen. "Who's that?" she asked Lorna.

"A very good friend. I'll tell you tomorrow."

Holding a new IV bag, Marilyn, the nurse, pushed past Kellen. "All right, the vitamin train is about to leave the station. All visitors must disembark."

Even as Marilyn stepped to the IV stand, exchanging the bags with her pudgy hands, Lorna seemed unable to leave Tracy's bedside. Shelby gave her mother a kiss on the forehead and began to exit with her father, but Lorna seemed locked in position.

Dr. Crowley waited patiently in the hall as Shelby lingered at the door.

Kellen introduced himself to Bruce Spilner, who shook his hand warmly. "Shelby told me how you helped. Thanks for all that."

Kellen nodded, wondering how much Shelby had told her father, hoping that Spilner would maintain silence for the sake of his daughter's future.

"Everyone outside please," Crowley said.

Noting the doctor's urging, Paddy had quietly slipped off.

"Lorna," Kellen coaxed, leaning through the doorway as Spilner and Shelby exited. "It's time."

"Tomorrow," Lorna said.

Tracy nodded, and Lorna began to retreat reluctantly, finally joining the others outside.

"Daddy and I are going to have dinner at the camp," Shelby announced proudly. "Do you want to come?"

Lorna glanced down at her smudged T-shirt and gave Kellen a sidelong glance. "Connely?"

"Just talked to him. Still with us until tomorrow morning."

Seeming relieved, Lorna sighed. "You know, I'm really tired. I could use a bath." She knelt down and gave Shelby a kiss. "I'll see you both here tomorrow after breakfast."

Shelby happily took her father's hand, and Spilner led her down the hall while Lorna gazed longingly after.

"You could still join them," Kellen said.

"What? Oh . . . no. I'm exhausted. And a bit restless."

Kellen understood the feeling. There had been so much activity over the last forty-eight hours, it was difficult to imagine just sitting still.

"You think Bruce will be okay?" Lorna asked. "With Shelby, I mean?"

"After I saw what Shelby is capable of last night, yes. And with Connely still on board, you're fine for the night."

"Where was he—?"

Kellen smiled. "In the lobby while you were with Tracy. Reading a magazine in the corner." He wondered how well she would fare all alone at the Outlook Inn, where Alessandro was due back later tonight. "Disappointed?" He nodded to Tracy's door.

"A little. So much wasted time . . . not enough talk."

"Why don't you talk to me?"

Lorna gave him a quizzical glance. "Aren't you tired?"

"I'm exhausted. But I could use some company. And I can't see you back at the hotel, alone, waiting for morning. Why don't you let me buy you dinner? McMillan can drop us back at the inn. We can pick up Paddy's van, drop him off at home, and you can decide what you want to do."

Lorna had decided.

Two hours later, she sat in the window seat of Kellen's cabin, toying with Long John's fuzzy ears. Sipping a glass of Chardonnay, she watched Kellen as he prepped the logs in the fireplace. The chaos of the last days had finally ebbed, and she'd been able to relax with Kellen over dinner and review all that had happened. She had gazed into his kind, unassuming eyes, finally fathoming who he was. His incredible heroics were offset by his salmon hatchery, his charming affection for his cat, the warmth he showed Paddy, and his steadfast loyalty to her. He had acted the hero, but his sincerity was more than an act. As she took stock of him, a growing desire to be with him emerged.

"Each of us is going to have to disappear for a while," Kellen said as he crumpled newspaper and stuck it in the fireplace. "At least until we know it's safe." He looked over his shoulder. "Shelby most of all. Do you think Tracy can manage that?"

"She has to," Lorna replied, stroking Long John's back.

"I don't mind leaving," Kellen said, placing the kindling and several shafts of cedar on top. "I haven't been off the island in two years."

"Where will you go?"

"Somewhere in the country. I'm just not into city life anymore."

"I understand." She had no desire to return to her penthouse.

Kellen put a match to the paper and stared at the flames.

After chauffeuring Paddy home, they had eaten at the West Sound Deli. Over some wine, Kellen voiced his concern about Alessandro's wire reaching Preston in Washington. Lorna reminded him that, though it seemed like an eternity, less than twenty-four hours had passed since the wire had been sent. The fate of the country still hung in the balance. Though it felt admittedly quixotic to have thrown that message to the winds, Lorna pointed out that what they had decided at Molly's was still true—they had no other way to react to the emergency without burdening themselves forever with complications . . . and worse yet, criminal prosecution.

Kellen's sense of duty bothered him. After the third glass of wine, he explained why. He told Lorna how his otherwise brilliant career had been destroyed, and he admitted that she was the first person with whom he'd shared the details.

Lorna focused intently as he told his story about Cleveland, and she was suddenly gripped by the desire to hold him. He had been so strong through their mutual adversity, yet the same boyishness that had earlier attracted her to him now made her want to comfort him. She had never before completely given herself to a man. The men who had become her lovers had to win her over. Yet here with Kellen, for the first time, she was overpowered with the idea of winning him instead.

Kellen finished his tale by saying he had resigned himself to the past. He then broke off the conversation with the suggestion that he take her home. She had surprised him with the recommendation that after a nightcap, they go for a walk on the beach near his cabin.

With the drink now in hand and the walk yet to come, she resumed the conversation. "Nice fire."

"I learned to build them here on the island," he said, staring into the flames. "Just down the road at Camp Orkila."

"Where exactly will you go? When you leave, I mean, to get lost for a while?"

He knelt at the hearth on his sheepskin rug, stoking the flames with his back to her. "There were a couple of places my dad took us fishing when I was a kid." She was taken with her need for him and quietly set the cat aside as he continued, "I just remember yellow land, big rolling blue skies, and cattails by a pond."

Lorna quietly slipped off her T-shirt and gently unhooked the clasp of her seamless bra.

Kellen stabbed at the wood with a poker. "And they've got mountains. Have you ever heard of a place called Whitefish, Mon . . . tana?" He had turned.

She smiled, raising the glass in a toast.

He returned the smile, his eyes falling to her naked breasts as he shook his head. "I've had a couple of shocks in the last two days, but not like this one." He reached for his wine and rose to one knee.

"No." She leaned forward. "Let me come to you."

His brow knit in amusement. "Anything you say. I can't believe your skin. You're just beautiful."

She stood, and he followed her with his eyes as she stepped over Long John. She approached, knelt on the rug, and threw her arms around his neck. "Kellen Rand. One thing I've learned about you is that you're cool under fire." She leaned in and whispered in his ear, "But don't you think it's time we heat things up a bit?"

44

The Next Day
Eastsound

SEATED IN THE METAL CHAIR at Tracy's bedside, Lorna couldn't stop staring at her sister. "You look a lot better with your eyes wide open."

Tracy had made huge strides in the last twenty-four hours, but she was still pale and weakened by her ordeal. The sponge bath she'd received had not improved her matted hair, and she was still supported by IV feedings since her stomach had shrunk.

Bruce and Shelby were off to clean up Tracy's house and pack Shelby's things to prepare for their trip to Colorado, leaving Lorna and Tracy alone in the hospital room.

Tracy smiled and reached for Lorna's hand. "I still can't believe you're actually here. I haven't gotten used to that yet. When I woke up yesterday and saw Bruce with Shelby, I thought I was dreaming. But then, when you arrived, it was as if I had gone to heaven."

"No more talk about dying, please. We're way past that. Dr. Crowley showed me your CAT scan. There's no sign of the hematoma at all. He says you're a milestone of medicine. He's never seen anything like it."

"I'm just so grateful that . . ." Tracy choked up. "God's given me another chance."

"I know."

"In every way, I mean. Have you talked to Bruce?"

"Not alone. Not since we first met."

"But do you see how different he is?"

Lorna had to admit—the stubble-faced curmudgeon who had thrown her to the floor in Tracy's living room bore no resemblance to the doting Bruce Spilner who now catered to Tracy's every need. "Shelby seems to be getting along with him, I'll say that."

"Do you know, Lorna, I'm so happy about recovering, that I'm worried about my judgment. I've actually started believing in Bruce again. Yesterday, before you arrived, he put his head right here," she patted the starched sheet near her hip, "and he cried. He couldn't stop crying, and I wept right along with him. When it was over, he jumped way ahead of himself and talked about us having a chance together." Tracy's moist eyes panned the ceiling. "I've got to be awfully careful, but I actually think we might do it. It would be best for Shelby."

Lorna squeezed her hand. "You'll find your way, no matter where that takes you. Even if it isn't here on Orcas. Until we're sure that Shelby's free from harassment, you may have to stay away. You used to like Colorado, didn't you?"

"I still do. I look forward to seeing Fort Collins. I've never been there."

"Then it's a good place to sit this thing out."

Tracy adjusted her head on her pillow. "What about you? Chicago? Your career?"

"I think we're going to disappear for a while."

"We?"

Lorna couldn't help but smile. "Kellen and myself. He's worried about our exposure here. We're going to spend a month in Montana. Seems like another good place to lose yourself. It should be beautiful this time of the year."

"You're quitting your job?"

"If things work out, we'll probably move back here in the fall."

"Kellen and you? When did all this happen?"

"It's been happening all along. But last night, after we left you, I was going to go back to the Outlook Inn, and I couldn't bear to be alone. Kellen sensed that and invited me to dinner. Somehow we wound up at his cabin." Lorna grinned. "And it was great. Now I know what it's like to make love on a sheepskin rug." She laughed. "His cat played with my hair the whole time."

Tracy chuckled. "God, listen to you. The media queen becomes a wood nymph."

She laughed again, and Lorna loved seeing her so happy. She took Tracy's hand in both of her own. "We'll see more of each other. It's what families do, you know?"

"Yes." Tracy sighed. "There is a tomorrow, not just a yesterday. I wonder what Dad would say if he saw us now. What a strange man he was. I think he learned how to love too late, after you and I were already long gone. Money and good times were all that mattered to him. I learned a lot when I read that . . . did I tell you there's a briefcase full of his things?"

"Bruce mentioned that."

"Well, Bruce used to think it had value. It's nothing but business papers. But when my mom passed away in Canada, I inherited Dad's stuff. Weird letters, some of them. The people he did business with weren't exactly—"

The door flew open and Hank Pelto entered, holding a huge bouquet of flowers. "Hello, you two." He gave Lorna a peck on the cheek and Tracy a gentle embrace. "I hope I'm not interrupting."

Seeing his beaming face, Lorna couldn't object. "Of course not. Glad to see you."

Pelto placed the arrangement on the small dresser. "Both of you look marvelous." He pointed out the open window. "It's a glorious day out there. And I can tell you the town is absolutely abuzz about the whalebone crucifix. It's the biggest news since they raised ferry taxes."

"News? Who's spreading it?"

"Your Spanish friend. He's proved himself to be a publicity hound. He held a mini-press conference at the Outlook this morning. It was beautiful. Bernardo, his butler or whatever, acted as his press secretary. The local paper is having a field day with him. What a character. I like him, actually." Pelto was bubbling with energy. "He's done more for me in the last two days than I could have done in a year."

"How?"

"I held a service at camp last night, Lorna. An inspired place called Chapel Rock. The place was packed. Being Wednesday night and no other churches in action, I hit the mother lode."

"You're saying because the cross was found?"

"Absolutely. Seeking the Lord. It's refreshing, I can tell you. And Tracy, you're a big part of it. Rumor has it that your miraculous recovery was directly tied to the find. You know what? I agree." Pelto was absolutely giddy. "Oh, incidentally, Kellen's on his way over."

Lorna was floored by his exuberance. "What are you on, Hank?"

"On?" Pelto beamed. "I'm on fire. But I promised I wouldn't say any more, so I won't. Kellen wants Fraley to tell you in his own words."

"Fraley?"

"Well, it all happened when Marissa dropped by the museum to deliver some things to Fraley since she's leaving town and—"

"She is?"

"Well, much like you all."

"How did you know about that?" Lorna asked.

"Kellen confided in me, as did Marissa. She wanted Fraley to have some old pieces she's had since childhood—Indian things for his collection. What he doesn't want, I get to keep for the camp. We have our own little Indian lodge. Anyway, when Kellen arrived to pick up Marissa, Fraley shared some news. Kellen sent me ahead, but he insisted Fraley join us. They'll be here any minute." Pelto hustled back to the door. "I'd like to wait, but I've got to hit the restroom."

Lorna laughed. "Well don't let us keep you."

"Okay. But don't start without me."

Lorna was suddenly saddened. "Strange. I hadn't thought about Marissa having to leave. The impact of this thing . . ."

Tracy reached out. "And to think I missed most of it."

"You were at the heart of it. Obviously you knew about Shelby's talents long before anyone else."

"I did. It was like living with Edgar Cayce. She kept answering my questions before I asked them. Passing tests in school without cracking a book. It was scary."

"And now? What are you going to do with her?"

"Make her lunches. Take her shopping. Everything possible to ensure she's just a happy teenager."

"You think you can ignore her talent?"

"That will be her choice."

"She'll have a hard time forgetting what happened."

"Maybe. But I believe Shelby can learn, adjust accordingly, and live a normal life. I'm going to try hard to give her the happy home she deserves. It wasn't until the divorce that she began to travel outside herself, you know. As if searching—"

"Hey." Kellen stuck his head inside the door.

Lorna turned. "Well, there you are . . ."

"Sorry for interrupting, but I've got some people who want to say hello. Has Pelto been here yet?"

Lorna pointed to the flowers. "Yes."

"Then you won't be as surprised, but nevertheless . . ." He stepped aside and ushered Marissa into the room.

Lorna came to her feet and gave her a hug and then introduced her to Tracy. David Fraley eased in and shook Tracy's hand. Pelto arrived again, making his second entrance by doing a small jig. "I didn't say anything, nothing at all."

Kellen gave him a smack on the shoulder. "Good." He turned and closed the door.

Seated once more, Lorna took Tracy's hand. "Well, we're ready . . ."

Tracy smiled. "What is it?"

Kellen gave Lorna a sidelong grin. "I'm glad to see everyone in such a good mood. It's been a hell of a week." He glanced back at the door. "I don't know why I closed that. Everyone's going to hear about this in a few hours anyway. But, Lorna, I wanted you to know that as a member of Alessandro's expedition, you were a part of something truly monumental." He glanced sideways at Fraley, who nodded and smiled.

Lorna was bursting with anticipation. "What, for God's sake?"

"Well . . ." Fraley, dressed in his usual unmatched pants and vest, stepped forward. "This morning, I received a call from Dr. Hargrove. He had some rather startling news."

"The carbon dating results?"

"Not yet. The lab won't have conclusive figures for several weeks. What Hargrove mentioned was a follow-up phone call he received from the Archaeological Institute of America. He had notified them of our find on Sucia, of course." Fraley cleared his throat, and Lorna noticed that he hadn't blown his nose once. "The NAS informed him that a rather unlikely coincidence occurred. During the last forty-eight hours, three other crucifix artifacts of prehistoric origin have been located. One in Africa, one in Mongolia, and another in Australia."

Lorna's mouth dropped. "Like ours?"

"No. Each with its own distinct cultural character, in keeping with the primitive tribes that ostensibly made them. Other archaeologists—American, English, and Chinese—had been engaged in similar digs, working independently, each knowing nothing of the others. Hargrove tells me that, as in our case, the preliminary dating of each of these sculptures is universal. Each carved roughly two thousand years ago."

Lorna looked around the room. Marissa wore a soft, knowing glow. And Pelto looked like the proverbial kid in a candy store.

Lorna tried to absorb the news. "What do you think it means?"

Fraley shrugged. "Well, in our case, it's historically correct. I found records indicating that the Salish Indians settled Sucia Island just prior to the year AD 1. Kellen, Marissa, and I talked about that development for a while before we came over. That's why we were late." Fraley almost chuckled, as if embarrassed. "It was quite a discussion with—" he nodded to Kellen, "a nonpracticing Christian," pointed to himself, "an agnostic," and gestured to Marissa, "and someone whose beliefs I can't define."

Marissa smiled at the remark.

Fraley continued, "But it was Marissa's perspective that I find most refreshing."

As if on cue, Marissa glanced at Lorna and unfolded her hands. "When January had visions, he was not certain of what had taken him. He only knew that, like a sick child with a stomachache, he had to bring forth the ailing thing inside him." She used her fingers like a delicate brush, painting the air as she illustrated her points. "It is my belief that my grandson was heir to a legacy of the spirit, as we all are. In his case, he had a mission to tell about what his people suffered on the island two hundred years ago and what his forefathers had carved eighteen centuries before. It is my feeling that Lukat and January were of one mind. And depending on what you believe, perhaps even of one seed in eternity's garden." Marissa paused to look at each person in the room. "There is much hope in the idea that Christ's death in Jerusalem two thousand years ago sent a mind wave around the planet that was felt by primitive people. The shaman, like Lukat and January in other cultures, received the vision, perhaps without understanding it. And yet, based on what they saw, these wise men honored the experience by carving totems like the one you found." She looked from one face to the other and folded her hands once more and took a step back. "That is what I have to say."

Hank Pelto heaved a deep sigh. "Marissa beautifully expressed what I feel, though in a different way. The find proved to me that Christianity was meant for even the most primitive people, not just for some elitist European tradition. We all know the damage resulting from that. Our faith still suffers from divisive policies. But here, with the dawn of a new millennium, the find reminds us of the universal nature of God. It cries out against denominational prejudice. How can we not take joy in that?" Obviously moved by his own feelings, Pelto paused and looked around the room.

In the hush that remained, everyone seemed to digest the thoughts that had been shared.

Lorna gazed up at Kellen, and he winked. Then the room came alive with discussion as Fraley, Marissa, and Pelto began to exchange further views.

Kellen kept staring at Lorna and, finding the right moment, he eased out the door, gesturing for her to join him.

Lorna gave Tracy a pat and excused herself, finding Kellen in the hall.

"I thought we might get a breath of fresh air," he said. "There's something I want to show you."

"All right."

Kellen seemed particularly pleased with himself.

She gave him a playful jab in the ribs as they strolled down the corridor. "What's gotten into you?"

"There's something at work here. I don't know how, but people just seem different today."

"Different?"

"Well, Pelto's obviously a basket case. But Marissa seems more alive. And did you notice Fraley? He wasn't limping this morning. They all seem vital and inspired. I really enjoyed listening to them." He looked over and smiled. "But not as much as I enjoyed last night."

She took his arm. "Enjoyed? Kellen, I loved it. By the fire with you and Long John? I could do that *every* night."

His voice fell into a whisper. "You know, that's what I had in mind." They had rounded the corner to the lobby. "We're going to have a lot of fires, Lorna. Enough warmth to make up for all the coldness we've ever felt. Everything's all right. The world is a better place this morning in so many ways. See what I mean?" He stopped near the seating area and pointed to a copy of *USA Today* that lay open on the coffee table.

"Kellen." Lorna gasped and picked up the paper.

In fat black letters, the headline read: TERRORIST THREAT NARROWLY AVERTED; the subhead: FBI ARRESTS 51 IN OVERNIGHT RAIDS.

Lorna read the opening sentences:

> In an unprecedented nationwide sweep, Federal Bureau of Investigation agents foiled a plot to terrorize American cities with biological weapons. Among those arrested were Fahad Abbas and Achmed Rahid of the Syrian Liberation Front, an organization operating in the United States and Canada under the code name AVALANCHE.

Lorna smiled. "Alessandro's fax."

"*Your* fax. None of his would have been possible without you. It sounds like they found all of it."

Lorna tucked the paper under her arm. "I'm going to keep this. What an event."

"Wasn't it?" Kellen led her toward the lobby doors. "Couples have stories about how they met at a high school prom or a cocktail party . . . you and I fell in love during a potential anthrax attack."

Lorna laughed as she stepped outside into the sunlight. The flowerbeds of the Orcas Island Medical Center grounds were lush with summer blossoms. The air was redolent with heather and lilac. Off on the horizon, the ocean gleamed.

"One other rather interesting footnote," Kellen said with a furrowed brow as they paused by a rose bush. "Before January died, he said something that kept haunting me about giving me my life back. You remember?"

"Vaguely. Things were pretty traumatic."

"I thought he was referring to how we saved each other. My rescue in the water, and . . ." Kellen swallowed hard, "his taking those bullets for me at Molly's. But he mentioned a name that night. Cavendish. Do you remember that?"

"That's right."

"I thought about that. Enough to make a few calls this morning. Turns out Cavendish was a name from the past—a police lieutenant who still works in Cleveland's Fifth Precinct."

Lorna drew a blank. "So how does that affect you?"

"Well . . ." Kellen glanced wistfully at a bank of clouds that had formed in the east. "We may never fully understand how incredible January was." He grabbed Lorna by the shoulders and looked into her eyes. "Now that I've found you, I don't ever want to go back to the past. But January gave me the avenue to do just that. In his dying breath, he passed me the name of the informant who tipped off the Cleveland raid that ruined my reputation."

"He actually did that?"

"I'm sure of it."

"Kellen . . . you could clear your name."

"With what's happened, I'm not going to try. As you know, I can't afford to get back in the spotlight. Besides, my life is ahead of me."

"That's how I feel. The past no longer matters. As incredible as the find may be, what means more to me is that I found so many other things. This place, my family, and you. Even myself."

"Well then," Kellen smiled. "Do you suppose we can both settle down for a while?" He took her in his arms and kissed her deeply.

In the distance, Mount Constitution towered.

Above the summit, a remarkable number of unmistakable silhouettes etched the azure sky.

Lorna pulled away. "Look, Kellen. Isn't that just above the ridge where—?"

"Yeah." Kellen squinted. "Bald eagles. Near Molly's place. I've never seen that many together."

"There must be dozens of them." Lorna felt a glow, watching the great birds soar in the sun. "When January left you that first time, he told you he would be among the eagles. Remember?" She laid her head on Kellen's shoulder.

"Yes." Kellen smiled. "And I *know* that's where he is . . . he's up there with them."

A READER'S GUIDE

QUESTIONS AND TOPICS FOR DISCUSSION

1. Orcas Island in the state of Washington becomes the catalyst that geographically bonds all the influential characters in *The Find*. Examining the plot, and particularly considering the characters' introductions, you will find that these characters often form triangulations of influence upon one another. For example, in Kellen's case, the first triangulation consists of 1) Paddy, January, and Kellen. Then you have 2) Lorna, Chad, and Skip in the radio industry, and 3) Lorna, Tracy, and Shelby as family. There are ten in total; perhaps you can think of additional combinations.

2. As a man and woman who are drawn together by the end of the story, Kellen and Lorna arrive at common synergies. Considering their diverse backgrounds before they meet, what elements in their personal and family lives are similar? How are their value systems different? How does the "Orcas Island experience" level that playing field?

3. Discuss the cultural clash between eighteenth-century Spain and the Native Americans who lived on Orcas Island. How does that story element mirror the cultural clash between the values of January and Marissa vs. Trajan's black ops.

4. There is an obvious connection between two shaman: Lukat, the shaman who lived in the late 1700s, and January, the shaman who embodies Lukat's spirit. In your opinion, was January's death necessary to bring closure to the brutality that was endured by his ancestors two

centuries before? Why or why not? If so, how did January's passing bring deeper significance to Captain Ravilla's demented views?

5. You may have noted obvious parallels between January and the crucifix in the cave—Fraley and Alessandro consider the crucifix "a find," and Trajan refers to January as "a find." How is that connection meaningful? Is it made more meaningful because January prophetically mentions to Kellen that he must "ascend"? What biblical comparison clarifies January's symbolic similarity to the crucifix?

6. Based on Marissa's summation in Tracy's hospital room of the find's discovery, do you believe Marissa intuitively understood the connection between January and the discovery in the cave? Is that why she asks Lorna if the man on the cross had been given a name?

7. While psychic remote viewing is commonly dismissed as fantasy, it is a fact that both Russia and the United States experimented with that form of ESP for years. A comprehensive history of various clairvoyant tests conducted in different countries in the late twentieth century is well documented in reliable online and print sources. While remote viewing is now classified as "pseudoscience," *The Find* used that psychic experimentation as the foundation for speculation that clairvoyants could accomplish visualizing distant events through chemical augmentation—i.e., Formula 15, which Dr. Epstein develops in the story. Considering that the CIA did psychic experimentation for some sixteen years, as mentioned in the foreword of this book, it begs the question why the exercise took so long to disprove. If you are interesting in exploring the topic further, there are forty-six books listed on Goodreads on the subject.

8. January represents the ability to psychically connect with humans as well as animals. Do you believe there is a mental connection between animals and humans? Why or why not? When you hear of porpoises rescuing human swimmers as sea, does it make January's rescue by an orca whale more believable? Can you recall other similar animal/ human interactions?

9. A growing body of science is dedicated to animal intelligence. Besides the dramatic whale rescue and eagle attack, do you remember the small observation Kellen makes on an Orcas Island beach—where crows learned how to open clam shells by watching seagulls drop the clams on rocks? That's a fact too; I observed it personally on Orcas and chose to add it to the story. Is there anything in your pet's history, or in the history of a friend or family member's pet, that validates the idea that animals are smarter than most of us believe? Explain.

10. *The Find* is actually three different plot lines that weave together to reveal several different story goals. Can you specify those story goals? Perhaps you can specify those story goals and name the specific moment(s) that those story goals are met.

AUTHOR'S COMMENT

I'm sure each of you has, at one time or another, been in a place where your spirit was lifted or where you felt in touch with the world and with yourself. It may have been a moment on a vacation, or if you're fortunate, somewhere you could enjoy for a longer time. Orcas Island was a place like that for me.

I went to camp there as a boy, revisited it as a young adult, and came to live there for twelve years later in my life. As esoteric as it may sound, that particular body of land—with its calm coves, rich forests, and quaint towns—had some magic to it for those who could appreciate the mystique; no wonder it is a destination for artists of all kinds.

It may seem odd to the reader that I chose this island's idyllic environment as the setting for a plot that includes elements of brutality, but it was precisely the juxtapositioning of that violence against the pastoral peace that Kellen Rand so desperately wanted from Orcas that gave the story an inherent undertone of tension. It was also that contrast between possible tranquility and the pressures of business life that prompted Lorna Novak to reexamine her values.

As for the chemistry between story elements: Kellen and Lorna represent the interlopers, thrust into the texture of the island environment, whereas January and Marissa are as much a part of the land as the animals, which they demonstrate by having the animals be a part of them.

Against nature's neutrality, I enjoyed portraying the clash of cultures, both past and present, and the contrast of pantheistic and Christian views that arise from the story.

Finally, as I'm sure you sensed, the true protagonist of *The Find* is January, who forsook a high-profile college education to return to nature as a reflection of the lifestyle clash experienced by the other characters.

January's swan dive from the cliffs, with his arms spread wide, is the emblematic act of the martyr, driven by forces beyond himself that eventually lead to his true martyrdom in the act of dying for his friend. In taking that role, January is also "in the flesh" what the find in the cave iconically represents as the universality of faith, a faith that Hank Pelto, the reverend, would acknowledge as having no walls or restrictions.

For all its symbology, though I hope you found the thematic elements in the book intriguing, I hope even more that you enjoyed reading the novel as much as it was my privilege to share it with you.

Until next time, all the best,
Rainer Rey